Raves for J. K. Beck's Shadow Keepers series

WHEN BLOOD CALLS

"J. K. Beck builds a dark, compelling world in *When Blood Calls,* the first in a paranormal trilogy. . . . Sexy, thrilling and teeming with weird creatures and unexpected alliances, this story will have readers eager for the next installment."
    —*BookPage,* "Romance of the Month"

"A page-turner! Riveting, dangerous, and not to be missed!"
    —#1 *New York Times* bestselling author
    Sherrilyn Kenyon

"J. K. Beck expertly blends pulse-pounding romantic suspense with an evocative and original paranormal world. The result is a red-hot page-turner."
    —*New York Times* bestselling author Kresley Cole

"A compelling blend of dark paranormal romance and gritty urban fantasy."
    —*New York Times* bestselling author Lara Adrian

"From the very first page, you'll be enveloped in the story of *When Blood Calls* and the rest of the world will disappear. Beck has created compelling characters, a story rich with paranormal creatures you can empathize with and a plot that will make readers ask, 'What would I do if it were me?' Once you start the book, don't plan on moving until you've finished the story."
    —*RT Book Reviews*

WHEN PLEASURE RULES

WHEN WICKED CRAVES

"Beck can always be counted on for a fantastic paranormal tale. This third addition to the immensely popular and enjoyable Shadow Keepers series may be the best yet. Tight, action-packed suspense combined with one seriously imaginative plot will have readers whipping through page after page of gripping suspense and sizzling passion. A wonderful world readers will want to visit time and time again."
—*RT Book Reviews*

"The passion, twists and turns in *When Wicked Craves* will keep you entranced from the first page until the last."
—*Joyfully Reviewed*

"Lovable characters, great action, scary monsters and super-hot scenes, what more could you ask for?"
—*Night Owl Romance*

WHEN DARKNESS HUNGERS

WHEN DARKNESS HUNGERS

J. K. Beck

BANTAM BOOKS
NEW YORK

A Bantam Books Mass Market Original

Copyright © 2012 by Julie Kenner

Published in the United States by Bantam Books, an imprint of The Random House Publishing Group, a division of Random House, Inc., New York.

BANTAM BOOKS and the rooster colophon are registered trademarks of Random House, Inc.

ISBN: 978-0-345-52565-9
eISBN: 978-0-345-52566-6

Cover illustration: Craig White

Printed in the United States of America

www.bantamdell.com

9 8 7 6 5 4 3 2 1

Bantam Books mass market edition: June 2012

For Shauna, editor extraordinaire

WHEN DARKNESS HUNGERS

CHAPTER ONE

The two vampires moved with steady purpose, the low fog curling around their ankles as if the oily darkness of the moonless night were caressing them. And why wouldn't it? Hadn't Sergius often embraced the darkness, drawing it close like a lover, letting it wrap around him, smothering him even as it soothed him with its warm familiarity?

And yet he yearned to be free of it—unbound from the pinch of the dark. That was why he'd come tonight, because he'd heard rumors about this witch. About her extraordinary powers. How she could heal. How she could make people whole.

People, perhaps. But what about vampires?

Her gifts might not extend to his kind. More than that, she might refuse to help him. He shoved the possibility aside, burying it beneath a blanket of false optimism. No matter how poor the odds, he had to try. The burning inside him had become so violent—so *raw*— that he had no other options. Because if he couldn't ratchet back the darkness, it would certainly consume him. And once that happened, Sergius would be gone forever, lost inside an inky black void filled with only the scent and taste of blood.

"There," Derrick said, grabbing Serge's arm and tugging him to a halt. He tilted his head back, his nostrils flaring. "Can you smell it?"

Sergius glanced sideways at his companion, noting the harsh gleam in his eyes and the hardness of his jaw. He forced his thoughts aside, afraid that Derrick might somehow discern his true purpose merely by glancing at his face. With a sigh, he closed his eyes and let the night wash over him. The magnolia trees were in full bloom, and the cloying perfume of their blossoms battled with the more woody cologne of the cypress and pine trees that dotted this stretch of land upriver from the Vieux Carré. He caught the scent of the Mississippi River, the coolness of the water coupled with the fetid tang of decay. And beneath it all, the pungent, heady smell of death.

"War," Derrick said. "It's as if the stars have aligned for our pleasure, bringing death and chaos along with the approaching Union fleet." He sighed. "I haven't dined so blissfully well since the British blundered into the colonies. Although, no. We feasted well in 1812. Do you recall?"

"How could I not?" Serge replied, the memory bringing a fresh wave of decadent hunger. They'd spilled much blood those nights. Had practically bathed in the sweet, metallic liquid. At the time, Sergius's daemon had roared in ecstasy, powerful enough to battle down Serge's petty protests and hesitations. Strong enough to take over until Serge lost himself in the warm, glorious wonder of fresh blood, only to claw his way back to the surface days later, heavy with self-loathing and furious with his inability to suppress the daemon as so many of his kind had managed to do.

The daemon lived in all vampires—a bone-deep malevolence that emerged from the human soul when the change was brought on. But some vampires were able to successfully fight it, to regularly battle it back down until their human will took precedence. Serge did not count himself among that fortunate group. His daemon ran high and wild. Pushing. Craving. Battling Serge's will with such persistence over the centuries that he inevitably succumbed, sliding into a bloodlust that caressed him as sweetly as madness.

How he envied those of his kind who had learned to either tame that vileness, or at least conjure the strength to suppress it. He longed for the mental clarity that accompanied being in charge of his own body and mind.

He'd been fighting his daemon for almost two millennia now, and its power still humbled him. Even now, his daemon was rising at the mere thought of blood.

Beside him, Derrick threw his head back and laughed, undoubtedly anticipating the glory of the kill. He shared none of Serge's hesitations and experienced none of Serge's guilt. They had traveled together on and off for years, and Serge knew that it was almost time for them to part ways. Being with Derrick only stoked the hunger that burned deep within him. Tonight, though, Serge had his own purpose for joining Derrick. *The witch*. But that was not a purpose he intended to share. He knew only too well that Derrick would neither understand nor approve. Like Serge, the younger vampire had a daemon that clung close to the surface. Unlike Serge, Derrick was more than happy to fan the flames of its appetite.

"How far?" Serge asked.

"Just down that lane." Derrick thrust his hand out toward the left, indicating an overgrown dirt road. There was no moon, but with his preternatural vision, Serge could clearly see the once white plantation house, now gray and in disrepair. And not because of the war thrumming around them and threatening to subsume this genteel property, but because of neglect, pure and simple. The occupants of Dumont House had priorities other than the upkeep of their family's homestead. The Dumonts were vampire hunters.

"They may not all have gone on the hunt," Serge said. According to Derrick's sources, the Dumont men had ridden earlier, intent on their goal of attacking a vampire nest hidden within the tombs of the St. Louis Cemetery that bordered the Vieux Carré.

"I hope they didn't," Derrick said. "Nothing would please me more than to drain them dry and leave them to rot in the cotton fields. Nothing, that is, except doing the same to their women."

An unwelcome trill of pleasure shot up Serge's spine, brought on by the inescapable truth of Derrick's words. There was pleasure in pain. Pleasure in the release of blood. In letting the daemon rage free and surrendering to the power of its foul appetite. Pleasure, yes. But torment, too.

"You're quiet tonight," Derrick said.

"I'm savoring the feed." The lie came smoothly to his lips, and he knew that Derrick would not doubt him.

Derrick laughed, low and hearty. "Ah, my friend. So am I. Look—one of the slaves making rounds." Across the clearing, a dark figure moved. An elderly male carried a single candle, the flame protected by a bowl of glass. He walked swiftly, his head turning to and fro, and Serge couldn't help but wonder if the slave had sensed their presence. But surely not. The inky night was impenetrable to human eyes. Undoubtedly he feared for the safety of the menfolk in the city, and was ill at ease with his obligation to protect the women in the big house.

Beside him, Derrick stood as still as a statue. "You hesitate?" Serge asked. "That old man would have made a tasty appetizer."

"Let him live and suffer from the knowledge that he had no way to protect the females." He turned to Serge, eyes dancing with mirth. "Besides, I prefer the flavor of blood that's not quite as aged. Come on."

They strode boldly to the house, then rapped hard at the heavy front door. At first, there was no sound from within; then Serge heard the light tread of footsteps. A woman. He imagined her in a loose gown, breasts full and unbound by a corset, her lithe limbs naked beneath the thin material. Immediately, his body tightened and the daemon twisted within, ready to take and taste. And oh, by the gods, wasn't that so very tempting . . .

The footsteps stopped on the other side of the door, and for a moment there was only the tremulous sound of a woman's breath. Then the stern clearing of her throat, as if she was bolstering her courage. "It's late. Who's there?"

"We come to warn your men," Derrick said, thickening his accent. "The Yankees approach, and they mean to occupy this property. Is your husband home?"

"Who are you? I don't recognize your voice."

"The brothers Wilcox, ma'am," he lied smoothly. "We've ridden hard from Metairie Ridge to warn your pa. Please, this plantation can't fall. Not with its proximity to the river, the train, and the main road. Let me speak to your menfolk."

Serge caught the scent of her hesitation. The rumors of the Union's impending arrival were as thick as the famous New Orleans fog, so Derrick's story was wickedly credible. More than that, he'd used the Wilcox name, referencing the two brothers who were known to be well-placed Confederate supporters. A risky proposition if the woman knew the men personally, but brilliant if she believed.

"Please, ma'am," Serge said. He saw Derrick shift forward, as if losing patience. With one solid blow, Derrick could break down the door, and that was a result Serge didn't want. The noise would draw the rest of the house's occupants, and he needed to face his quarry alone. "We must speak to your father. Open the door and call him down. We realize the impropriety of the hour, but war ignores all social graces."

For a moment, he feared that the woman would brush off his plea. But then he heard the *thunk* of the lock turning. A moment later the door swung inward, revealing a young woman of about twenty. Derrick and Serge bowed deep, removing their hats in a broad, gallant motion.

"My husband is gone this night," the woman said. Behind her, a burly black man stood, his expression fierce. Clearly, he was there to make sure no harm came to the mistress of the house.

"Your father, then."

"Dead these many years. Please, tell me what news, and I can inform my husband upon his return, or Sampson can ride to him now if it is urgent."

"Oh, it's most urgent," Derrick said, hooking an arm around the woman's waist and moving so fast to Sampson's side that he surprised even Serge. In mere seconds the man was on the ground, his neck snapped neatly in two. For a moment the room was completely silent, as if time hadn't yet caught up with the horror. Then the dam broke and the woman's scream filled the night, only to be cut off a second later when Derrick sank his fangs into her pretty, pretty neck.

He drank deep, then pulled away, his mouth bloody as he looked at Serge and shifted the woman as if in invitation. "Care for a nibble, my friend?"

By the gods, yes . . .

The scent of her blood enveloped him and her soft moans teased his daemon, urging it to come out. To play and to feast. He could practically taste the coppery warmth of her blood flowing over his lips, could feel the softness of her skin beneath his fingers and the feather-light beat of her fluttering, fading pulse at his lips. The pleasures of blood rivaled even the pleasures of the flesh, and right then the daemon wanted both. Wanted to get lost in the hedonism of sweetly spilled blood.

No.

No, goddammit, no.

His body tightened as he dredged up the remnants of his own will to force the daemon back down. *He* was in charge. Serge. Not the daemon. Not here, goddammit. Not now, when he'd come so far and with such an urgent mission. "Only a nibble?" Serge said in reply, forcing amusement into his voice. "I'm looking for a feast. Not a wench with the honeyed taste of fear already drained from her."

Derrick chuckled. "The first bite is indeed the sweetest, though the struggle that follows adds spice." He gave the woman a shake and she writhed in his arms, the pungent scent of her fear reaching out to Serge and making his hunger rise. He took a step toward her, then halted.

"Enjoy," he said. "I crave the hunt as much as the kill." He didn't wait for Derrick to answer, afraid that if he stayed he would succumb. Instead he turned and moved swiftly away from the woman's moans and the seductive scent of her pain.

The kitchen was only a few yards from the big house, and he found the witch there. She stood behind a large wooden cutting block, a hatchet that had undoubtedly beheaded many chickens lodged in the wood in front of her. A single candle illuminated the room, and the flickering orange reflected in the woman's dark eyes. In her hand, she held a stake, and the absence of any scent of fear told Serge that she knew how to use it.

"You are a fool to come here, vampire," she said.

"Help me, and you will survive the night."

A single brow arched, making her beautiful face even more exquisite. Her *café au lait* skin glowed in the candlelight, her striking cheekbones and aquiline jaw giving her the appearance of the lady of the manor rather than a slave. "You're a cocky beast. I assure you, I'll survive. You will not be so lucky." She twisted her hand, just enough to bring the stake into the light, making the wood glow warm.

For an instant the lure of sweet oblivion washed over him, and Serge lost himself in the temptation to draw her wrath and accept the stake. To allow death, that most elusive of companions, to finally take him. He couldn't do it, though. There was no fear—he'd lost himself too many times to the unknown darkness that was the daemon to ever fear the relative calm of death. But there was stubbornness. And, yes, there was the passion of his will. The small pleasures of the flesh and of the earth. He had once craved immortality with all his soul—so much so that he had compromised that very soul. He had made himself what he was, and he would remedy that error. Somehow, someway, he would make himself whole. And then, once he had lived life without the pain and horror of the daemon's madness, perhaps he would welcome death. But that day had not yet arrived.

"I can make him stop. The vampire I came with. He's in the main house right now, and I doubt that your mistresses will survive the night without my intervention."

Her thin smile was as cold as any he'd ever seen. "You're a fool if you think they matter to me. I'm nothing but chattel to them."

"And your own life? Do you value it so little? You put on a pretty show of bravery, but you know what I am. You know what I can do. And I'm not alone. Are you truly so foolish as to believe that whatever claim you have over the dark arts will protect you from one who has lived within that darkness for centuries? That you can protect your child? Your lover?"

He watched her face carefully as he spoke, noted the way her eyes flattened and the line of her mouth thinned. She meant to give nothing away, and yet she'd failed. His words had hit the mark, and he knew that the information for which he'd paid such a steep price had been true. Evangeline truly was the daughter of voodoo queen Marie Laveau. She had taken a lover—a Dumont house slave named Tomas. Most important of all, she had a child, a five-year-old girl who lived on the Dumont estate and was the product of a liaison between Evangeline and Carlton Dumont, the master of the house.

Serge didn't want to kill the child, but if that was what it took to get what he came for, then the little girl would die. Not because he would will it so, but because the daemon was pushing too hard. He could feel its cold edges pressing against his mind, against his will. Sharp, like a knife-edge, and so very demanding. He'd come here to turn that knife back on the daemon itself, to lock it deep inside and give him that control. She could give him his life. And by doing so, she would save her own.

But if Evangeline refused him, he knew that he couldn't hold it in. The daemon would explode . . . and no one near him would be safe.

"Tomas is not here," she said with an arrogant lift of her chin. "Nor is my sweet Lorena."

He could smell the lie upon her. "Do you doubt that I would do it?" he snarled, taking a step toward her. He needed her scared. Needed her willing to do what he asked. "Do you doubt that I would leave your child drained upon this very floor? That I would sink my teeth into your lover's neck?"

Her jaw tightened. "Why should I help the likes of you? A vile creature that kills for gain and pleasure?"

A surge of anger rushed up within him, and he wanted to attack. To lash out and cut the insult out of her. But he battled it down, forcing the daemon into submission, drawing on what little strength he had in order to keep his fingers clenched tight around the fraying strands of his control. "I do not wish to be that creature."

She snorted. "Liar."

He took a step toward her, and her eyes went wide with victory. As if she knew that he was weak and undeserving.

"Do not condemn me to remain this way." The words felt ripped from his throat, and he clutched the side of the butcher block, his nails cutting gouges into the hard wood.

"Condemn you? You're already condemned. Killer," she spat. "Destroyer."

His fingers sought the blade that was sunk deeply into the block. They curled around the handle, and he pulled it free. She didn't flinch, but her eyes never left him.

"A killer I am," he admitted. "But so are you. Do you think I have not heard the stories? That all the people in Jefferson Parish are ignorant of your methods and those of your mother? You draw blood for power. You kill to satisfy your own whims and plans. You may not have fangs, Evangeline, but you do have claws, and you are not so different from me."

"Persuasion is an art, vampire. And one in which you lack skill. You should woo me, not insult me."

"With false niceties? We both know what we are. But beyond that, I know what I want to be."

"I am not interested in your desires." But he could see in her eyes that she was lying. He'd piqued her curiosity, and he pushed forward, taking advantage of that small victory.

"Hear me now, witch," he said, then hurled the hatchet across the room. It sailed past her ear, then landed with a *thunk* in the wall, the blade buried to the hilt. "I want the daemon cut out of me. I want it gone."

Her expression never changed, but he thought he saw respect in her eyes. "That is not possible. Even for one of my skill, I cannot remove that which is a part of you."

"Yet you *are* skilled—if the rumors are true, you're even more skilled than your mother." He glanced at her face and saw that the flattery was working. "Surely you could do something." He took another step forward.

"There is blood on my hands, Evangeline. Blood that I did not wish to shed. I will take responsibility for my own actions, but these deaths are not mine to claim, and yet they haunt me. They torment me."

"And you wish me to believe that even with the daemon locked up deep inside, you would not kill? The hunger would not drive you to drink of the vein? My master has killed many vampires, sir. I know well that not all of those kills were made when the daemon was high. Some of your kind simply enjoy the hunt and feed on the pain."

She was right, of course. Derrick was just such a vampire.

"How do I know that you do not count yourself among them?"

"You don't," he said simply. "But I don't know, either. I crave the chance to find out."

"And if you also crave the blood?"

"I will," he said, because to lie to this woman would get him nowhere. "What matters is whether I can control it."

She remained still, her eyes piercing him, and he knew that he had surprised her. The question was, had he intrigued her, too? He waited with the kind of patience he'd not displayed for many a year. But for this moment, he would humble himself. He needed her help, his self-respect be damned.

"There is no guarantee. And you must trust me fully. There may be pain. There will most surely be blood. And if you attack—if I fear for my life—I will not hesitate to stake you."

"Can you do it tonight?"

"Keep your word, and it will be done."

Derrick. He turned to go. To find and stop his friend from killing the humans in the big house.

"Tomas," she said. "Find him first. Protect him."

"And your daughter?"

"She is my worry, not yours."

He nodded, then continued toward the door, but he hadn't gone two steps when it burst open wide. Derrick stood there, his linen shirt stained red. He held a man in his arms, the scent of death already clinging to him. With aplomb, he tossed the body onto the floor of the kitchen, then turned a grinning visage to Serge. "So. You found her."

Serge felt his body turn cold. "Her?"

"The Dumonts have themselves a witch." He took a step forward, his foot landing on the man's ribs. The sick crunch of breaking bone filled the cookhouse, matched only by the wounded, keening wail of Evangeline herself.

"Tomas!" she cried, then turned to snarl at Serge. "Never! Never will I—"

But she didn't get the words out. He couldn't let Derrick know that he'd asked the witch for help. He had to quiet her, and he rushed forward, knocking her to the ground. He had no intention of hurting her. No plan to permanently silence her. But fear and fury were driving him forward. Fear that he'd lost his chance for a cure. Fury that Derrick had interrupted. And, of course, there was the hunger. And she was warm in his arms, her own fear tugging at the daemon. Teasing it. Taunting it. Until it overcame all strength and burst out in a blood-red rage.

The daemon took over, and in a hungered frenzy he

sank his teeth into the witch's neck and drank deep, drawing in her fear, her anger, her wretched power.

The part of him that remained Sergius faded deep inside, curling up with self-loathing. But the last thing he saw before the daemon subsumed him was the stern silhouette of the four Dumont men, their crossbows aimed at Derrick and himself.

And the last thing he thought was that if nothing else, the sharp sting of death would finally rip him free of the daemon.

CHAPTER TWO

Present Day

It was well past midnight on a moonless night, and still there were no stars visible over Hollywood. The lights were too bright, the area too vibrant. It thrummed with a kind of painful energy, as if it were trying too damn hard to be hip. To overcome the seedy reputation spawned by years of pimps and hookers and back-alley drug deals. The lights brightened up the place, and the Disney theater and revamped shopping areas gave it a new gloss. But scratch that sparkling surface, and the grime still showed.

Serge knew all about dark underbellies, and as he crouched on the roof of the Kodak Theatre, his eyes trained on the narrow alley between the buildings, he felt right at home.

Below him, two vampires moved leisurely in the dark. Their strides were long, their manner unconcerned. And why not? As far as they knew, they were the baddest asses out that night. But of course, they didn't know who was watching them. Didn't know that the most bad-ass of all creatures was up on the rooftop watching their every move, planning his attack. Planning his feed.

Idly, Serge wondered what they'd think if they knew that he was on the roof. He was legend now, the stuff of gossip and rumor. And the two vampires in the alley— Mitre and Colin—had undoubtedly heard the stories.

They would know that the daemon had been strong in Serge. That it had repeatedly vanquished him, sucking him under until all he could do was succumb . . . and then emerge to swim in a pool of self-loathing.

He'd tried once to have that part of him suppressed, cut out, destroyed. He hadn't cared how. Had cared so little, in fact, that he'd begged a witch to do the deed for him. But that adventure hadn't gone as planned, and he'd been lucky to escape with his life.

The vampires on the street, however, would know nothing about his escapades in New Orleans. The stories they would've heard would be much more recent. Tales of how he'd been cursed. Transformed into a mindless creature that had lashed out wildly, destroying at the discretion of the vile human who controlled the curse.

He'd been a machine, a goddamn lapdog, and he'd hated it. Hated knowing someone else was pulling his strings. That neither his body nor his mind was his own.

And then the human who'd created the curse had been killed, and with his death the torment had been lifted.

Serge had been an assassin's tool. And then, suddenly, he wasn't.

He was back to being Sergius. Or so it appeared. But it wasn't true. The Serge he'd once been had fallen away, like a snake shedding its skin. Now, after almost two thousand years, he no longer knew who he was. More to the point, he no longer knew *what* he was. Because though he once again looked like Serge and felt like Serge, a new type of wretchedness lived within him, warring with his daemon for supremacy. Turning Serge into a creature he didn't know and didn't fully understand. A beast with a new kind of hunger, darker and more demanding. Less controllable. Far more terrifying. And he was completely alone.

When he'd been under the curse, he'd had the ability to draw out victims' life force. To leave them weak on the ground as he transformed into whatever creature they were—jinn, paradaemon, vampire. He'd assumed that this power would disappear along with the curse.

He'd assumed wrong.

In the days after the master's death, he'd wandered through France and Italy, shunning the company of friends, of other shadowers, of humans. He'd walked and he'd slept and he'd fought a growing hunger that he didn't understand. As a vampire, he'd craved blood. Needed it. Became weak without it. When his daemon was high, he'd take that blood however he could get it, the more violent the better. But when he'd managed to wrangle the daemon into submission, he'd still needed the blood—both physically and emotionally. He lost himself in it, in the sweetness it offered, in the rush it gave him. He kept the daemon satisfied by feeding that need—by taking the blood from willing humans, violently, painfully. He'd push them to their limits, especially the females. Would watch the need on their faces, then revel in satisfaction when the pain hit.

And then he'd drink deep and glory in the knowledge that—except for those few occasions when he'd lost his tight grip on control—this debasement kept the evil locked deep inside him.

But this new hunger . . .

It wasn't bloodlust so much as *life* lust. He craved and he took and he killed.

He hadn't known it about himself until the first time the hunger had overpowered him. He'd gone in search of a faunt, a human willing to sell blood to a vampire. The hunger felt different, but he'd hoped that taking the blood would satiate him.

He never made it that far.

With little warning, the hunger had reached a tipping point, transforming his body into something harsh and unfamiliar, his skin reptilian, his mind gone, nothing remaining but the need to feed.

And he had.

Though Serge now remembered none of it, he'd awakened beside the body of a desiccated werewolf—and he'd felt the power of the wolf surging through his veins.

That was when he understood what had happened. The curse may have been lifted, but a beast was left behind. The beast was hungry, and when Serge refused to fill that hunger, it would take matters into its own hands.

After that, Serge learned more about what he was and how he needed to feed. He drained life force, killing his victims and becoming that which he had drained.

It was a reality he despised, but there was no escaping it: To live, Serge had to kill.

And that was when he made his decision—he would feed off the rogue vampires, the killers, those who were a plague upon the human world. He would remain a vampire, and in that small way he would retain some bit of the Serge he knew as well as some tiny amount of control.

Now he stood on the rooftop looking down at the vampires who would provide his next feed. The hunger wasn't yet overwhelming, but Serge had learned the hard way that it was safer to remain sated so that he could pick his victims. Otherwise, the beast might burst forth and suck dry an innocent. And so he methodically watched the vampire community, keeping tabs on those vamps that had turned rogue. Because he'd spent so much time living off the grid, slinking through sewers and alleys, basements and drainpipes, he saw things that other vampires missed. Witnessed actions that other vamps were certain took place in total privacy.

If the hunger wasn't rising, he made a note of the rogues. Their scent. Their characteristics. Their names if possible.

Then, when the first niggles of hunger started, he could seek out one of his personalized, pre-approved meals.

Tonight that meal was named Mitre. He hadn't known about the companion, Colin, but if he turned out to be rogue, then Serge would add him to the meal plan as well.

Now, though, he wanted them to separate. Attack Mitre in front of Colin, and Colin would have to die, too, because leaving witnesses was unacceptable. And so he watched and listened. Eventually, they'd part ways. And because the beast's low rumble hadn't yet worked up to a growl, Serge still had time to be careful.

The two vampires rounded a corner, moving into the alley behind the Hard Rock Cafe. Serge waited until he was certain they wouldn't see him, then leaped across the alley to the restaurant's roof. It was lower than the theater's, and he could more clearly hear the vampires' conversation. It flowed over him like white noise, mundane talk about females, sports, the monotony of being a young vampire in Los Angeles, and their hero worship of some of the older, more worldly vamps.

"I'm really gonna meet him?" Colin said, and the tone of awe in his voice caught Serge's attention.

"Shit, yeah. He's looking forward to it. Been working with me since he came down from Chicago. Not happy, either. I talked to him a little last night, and he's pissed we haven't recruited more. Done more damage to the fucking PEC," he said, referring to the Preternatural Enforcement Coalition, the organization that investigated, prosecuted, and adjudicated crimes committed by shadowers. "And, of course, the fucking humans."

"Not happy? Maybe with some of the others, but not me. I've taken out half a dozen on my own."

A slow curl of anger rose up in Serge. They were talking about humans, of course, and Colin was boasting about his kills. Serge had suspected that the rogue population in Los Angeles was organized. Now it looked like he had confirmation. But who was pulling the strings?

"Yeah, he thinks you're doing all right. But still, six is hardly a dent," Mitre said. "And it's sure as hell not enough to keep the PEC hopping. He wants them chasing their tails, the useless bastards."

"Useless is right. Doing all that shit—making all those laws—and most of them are there to protect the humans."

"They're our goddamn food supply, and the city is our hunting ground. The PEC, the Covenant, the whole damn thing just shifts the natural order of things." Mitre frowned and shook his head, his demeanor much like a politico arguing to a TV camera. "It isn't right."

"Shit no."

"Hey, hold up." Mitre tilted his head up, and Serge stepped back, melding into the shadows. "Smell that?"

Colin's nostrils flared as he sniffed the air. Then a slow grin spread across his face. "Human. And close. What do you think? One block?"

"About that. Come on."

Serge caught the scent, too, and hurried to keep pace. Any humans hanging out in an alley at three in the morning were probably up to no good, but that didn't mean they deserved to be a vampire's meal.

He caught sight of the human the same time that Mitre did. The vampire stopped, then held out a warning hand to Colin. Below Serge, the vampires stood in the shadow of a building. Beyond that was an open trash bin filled with cardboard and rotting food. The metal was rusty, and the ground near the bin was so covered with cockroaches it seemed to move. A squat, muscular male leaned against the bin, hand extended as he exchanged a small plastic package for several bills presented to him by an emaciated female with corn-husk hair and clothes too short and too tight to be either modest or sexy.

"That's all ya got?" the girl asked.

"Come back tomorrow, bitch. Now blow. I got other business to do."

She went, her steps uneven, her demeanor meek. The male smirked, then pulled out a wad of bills and started riffling through them. Satisfied, he shoved them back in his pocket and started to walk away. A second later he stopped, blocked by the two vampires who'd moved into his path with exceptional speed.

Here we go. As Colin yanked the male toward him, Serge crouched, ready to spring to the ground. Ready to save the human and feed the beast.

He didn't get the chance. A heartbeat later Colin turned to dust, a small pile on the ground topped with a wooden arrow.

"Holy fuck!" The drug dealer's words echoed Serge's sentiments exactly, and he scoured the shadows, looking for the shooter.

"Are you an idiot?" A female voice burst from the darkness. "*Run.*"

The male didn't hesitate. He took off down the alley, leaving the shooter to contend with Mitre, whose initial expression of surprise had contorted into one of pure, furious hatred.

"Goddamn little bitch."

The woman had shifted position, bringing her into the dim ambient light, and for the first time in centuries, Serge felt knocked over by the sight of a woman. She was tall and curvy, and managed to look both feminine and tough in black jeans, a black mock turtleneck, and a battered black leather jacket. She had a square face with a strong jaw and a wide, beautiful mouth. She moved with power and confidence, but there was something about her that seemed vulnerable, making him want to reach out and touch her. It was, he finally realized, the gleam in her eyes. A lonely, pained light that seemed to cry out, as if she was on a desperate quest, and was suffering under the weight of the knowledge that it might never end.

None of that, however, lessened the impact of the woman as a warrior. She held a crossbow in her hands, and it was aimed right at Mitre. "I'd tell you to run, too," she said, "but I'm not interested in a chase. All I want is to see you turn to dust."

"Bitch," he said, spitting the word as he lunged forward. Serge tensed, ready to jump into the fray, but the woman had it under control. She released an arrow, causing Mitre to howl in pain even as he slammed into her. He rolled over, and Serge could see that the arrow had landed square in his chest—but not in his heart. In seconds Mitre was back on his feet—ready to kill the woman and use her blood to heal.

Well, shit.

Except once again, the female impressed him.

As Mitre turned toward her, she tossed the crossbow aside and pulled out a stake. Almost simultaneously she scrambled to her feet and rushed the vampire. Serge didn't expect it any more than Mitre did, and the vamp lashed out clumsily, protecting his heart and catching her hard across the jaw. She stumbled, but kept on coming. Mitre reacted instinctively, kicking out hard and fast. His foot slammed into her gut, and she fell backward. He leaped on her, but she was ready, and with a flick of her wrist she shot another stake out of her jacket sleeve, using some sort of concealed spring-loaded device. Once again it missed his heart, but even so Serge wanted to applaud. Whoever this girl was, she knew her stuff. Knew especially that the first rule of vampire hunting was to stay alive.

"Keep on coming, vampire," she said. "I know I will."

For a second Mitre seemed to think about it. Then he turned and raced down the alleyway. Serge rose, intending to race after him. Despite the pleasure he'd taken from the impromptu performance, he hadn't forgotten that he'd come out tonight to feed.

A small sound of pain held him in place, though, and when he looked back, he saw that the woman had stumbled trying to get to her feet. She held a hand to her head, and he realized that she'd hit it hard on the pavement when Mitre had knocked her down. She'd put on a good show for Mitre, but if he hadn't decided to run, he'd have surely destroyed her. That she'd managed to pull off such a blatant bluff impressed Serge all the more. He stayed still, watching her, afraid that her injuries were serious. One minute. Two. And then finally she squared her shoulders, gathered her things, and marched unsteadily in the opposite direction that Mitre had fled.

Serge sprinted silently along the rooftops, keeping her in sight until he saw her pause by a Ducati motorcycle. She winced as she slipped on a helmet, then straddled the thing and fired up the engine. A moment later she was gone, and Serge was left with an odd sense of loss.

Ridiculous, of course. That sense of loss had to be because of Mitre, not the woman. *Mitre*. The goddamn rogue was not only still out there, but wounded, too. That meant he needed to heal. That meant he needed blood.

And that meant he needed to kill.

Shit. While Serge had been fretting about the woman, he'd let a killer slip away.

The thoughts were still swirling in his head when he backtracked to the scene, leaping down to the alley floor so that he could catch Mitre's scent. With luck, he'd find the bastard on the next block. With even more luck, he'd find him before he killed a human.

Luck, however, wasn't cooperating. He tracked the vampire easily enough, but the trail ended abruptly in a parking lot. He doubted that Mitre would have used his dwindling strength to transform into mist. Which meant that the rogue had made his escape the old-fashioned way—he'd left in a car.

Goddamn modern world. It was a hell of a lot easier to track a few centuries ago. And now someone was going to die because Serge had been too damn slow— and too damn distracted by a woman.

CHAPTER THREE

Derrick Gregorck stood on the balcony of his penthouse apartment, a finger of single-malt Scotch swirling in the fine crystal he held in his hand. Below, traffic moved at a crawl along Wilshire Boulevard. Cars, not buggies or horses.

It still amazed him.

He lifted the glass to his lips and tossed back the drink—at least Scotch hadn't changed over the last 150 years. The world, though . . . that had changed dramatically, and it pissed him off that he'd missed seeing these wonders unfold.

That bitch of a sorceress . . . Those fucking Dumont men . . .

It had primarily been the males, of course. But if Derrick hadn't drained Tomas and then gone in search of the witch he wouldn't have been in the cookhouse when the men returned. Bad luck all around. Worse luck that they'd entombed him rather than staking him through the heart. They'd captured him with nets woven from thin strands of hematite, a metal that sapped a vampire's strength. Then they'd pierced him through with metal stakes. The heart. The gut. He'd bled and bled and bled until he was nothing but a dried-out shell withering on a cold stone floor.

But still he'd been alive. Alive and as helpless as an infant, unable to move. Lost inside his own thoughts, a perverse miasma of images and emotions. He'd been too weak even to order his mind, and he'd floated in a dream state for days, weeks, years. Had anyone found him, they would have seen what appeared to be a mummified corpse. But of course he wasn't found. Those Dumont bastards had planned their revenge well, and he'd been well hidden in their private cemetery, tucked away in a secret room beneath the family tomb.

Derrick still didn't know what had finally initiated his return to consciousness. Insects, maybe, finding a home in his mouth. Dying and rotting and attracting rats. Perhaps the creatures had fought. Fought, and then bled.

It was the blood that was key, of course. Somehow, a few drops of blood had entered his mouth. And then a few more, and then more still. At first, those drops brought only torment, for the amount was insufficient to infuse his body with life. They merely made him more aware of his hellish condition.

That was when the months ticked by at a painfully slow pace. No longer was his consciousness swirling with no conception of time. Instead, he felt the turning of the earth. Saw the shift of light in the dim seams of the ceiling above him. The light was odd, and he realized later why—it was streaming in through the stained-glass window of the family crypt beneath which he was trapped. Just as well. Had he been bathed in a full sunbeam, he would have truly met his end. Most days, he wished for exactly that.

Slowly, though, his strength grew. Worms and leeches and all manner of disgusting creatures nested within him, and though their bodies gave him no relief, when there was blood it added to his strength. After a time, he was able to move his jaw and his tongue, and that victory allowed him to snap down upon the creatures. He could kill, and he could feed. And because their rotting carcasses remained in his mouth, more scavengers would come to meet their demise, and nourish him in the process.

Over a century passed with Derrick trapped inside his own head, his daemon roaring and unable to hunt. His mind spun, full of fury, madness kept at bay by the simple act of plotting revenge. Even that happy thought was ultimately defeated. By the time Derrick had regained his senses and could move his weakened body enough to slide out into the world, the Dumont men were long dead, entombed above the very crypt where Derrick had suffered his long imprisonment.

He'd made his way to the house, setting out at dusk and arriving only an hour before dawn, so slow was his progress. Once there, he slit the throat of the first person he found, and drank his fill of fresh, flowing human blood. *Ah, the glory. The power.*

Not even close to sated, he drank again from the next human to pass through the back door. Only then did he look around and note the changes to the world. Strange enclosed buggies that moved under their own power. Lights that burned without gas or wood. He marveled at these things—but even such wonders could not keep him from his goal. Stronger now, he accosted the next person he encountered—a female who arrived in one of the metal carriages. She quivered in his arms, said that she was only the maid and didn't know where the family kept its money. He assured her it wasn't money he was after, and asked the name of those who lived in the house. Her reply—"Dumont, sir"—sent great shivers of joy through him. His tormentors may have already passed from life, but Derrick could still feast upon their heirs.

Once he learned that the family was asleep upstairs, he feasted upon the maid. Not because he was still weak, but because he'd wanted to quash her humanity. Humans had tormented him, and now humans would pay. Starting with the Dumonts, of course, but he had no intention of stopping there. They thought they'd beaten him? Trapped him and bound him? Perhaps for a time, but they were nothing but food for the worms now, whereas he had been resurrected, much like their God. Hell, he *was* a god, and it was by his hand that they would live or die.

He'd crawled from that wretched tomb almost fifteen months ago, and had spent the last year meting out his own justice against the humans, rallying other vampires to rise up against them, too. What was the point of being a god if you allowed the baser creatures to bind your nature? Why did the PEC punish those vampires who acted in accordance with their natural urges and fed off humans? His race was becoming weak, and it disgusted him. And he had made it his mission to bring as many of his kind as possible around to his way of thinking—in the process thinning out the humans, even while growing stronger on a diet of their rich, delicious blood.

Tonight, he'd invited two of his most impressive protégés to join him in his penthouse at dawn. They were young vampires, still able to go outside during the day, and he intended that they would talk throughout the daylight hours, then hunt together once the sun dipped below the horizon. He enjoyed conversing with young vampires, who were able to give him insight into the changed world much faster than his own observations could manage. Of late, though, these tête-à-têtes served an additional purpose—they helped him gauge the level of fear within the community.

In Chicago, where he'd settled for a few months before coming to Los Angeles, the vampire population had been deservedly arrogant. Derrick had gathered them around him, shared his views, and christened those who agreed as members of his League, just as he had in the other cities he'd stopped in during his trek from New Orleans. They'd hunted, they'd killed. They'd known their proper place, and their actions had shown it.

Here, though, something heavy hung in the air. A hint of fear. A tidbit of trepidation. The League was still supreme, and Derrick was rightfully proud of the influence he'd had on the local population, but there was no denying the truth. Some of their number were disappearing. Staked, Derrick believed, so that nothing was left but ash.

That was bad enough. What was worse was the fate of the unluckier ones, a fate that Derrick couldn't even think about without shuddering in revulsion and being bombarded with memories of his time in that despicable tomb. Four of his best men had been found desiccated. Shriveled and dried out like Derrick himself had been. Yet these vampires had been beyond reviving. Blood had no effect on them whatsoever. Derrick's spies within the PEC had told him as much. They were dead and gone—and no one understood why. Had they been infected with some unknown agent? Attacked with an unheard-of weapon?

It was a mystery Derrick intended to solve. Unfortunately, though, he didn't even have an inkling where to start, and while the young vampires he'd recruited were as eager as he was to learn the truth, he had yet to encounter one who felt like an equal rather than a student.

How he longed for a worthy partner. So much so that one of the main reasons he'd come to Los Angeles was the rumor that Sergius was here. He missed the company of his old friend. More than that, he missed Serge's ruthlessness and the dark vision they'd both shared. Serge was an equal, an ally. And he would be an asset to the League.

When Derrick had first crawled from the tomb, he'd assumed that Serge had suffered a similar fate. Either that, or the witch had staked him. Then he began to hear rumors that Sergius was alive. Alive, and wild. A thing possessed, literally. Strange, disjointed stories. Some said that Serge had been cursed. Others, that his daemon had finally gotten the better of him. All agreed that he'd killed. And not just anyone—Alliance representatives. The very shadowers Derrick had fast come to despise. The very ones who kowtowed to humans, protecting the insignificant creatures through the Covenant and treaties and an unspoken acknowledgment that the plight of the shadowers was to fade into the background while humans infected the world.

As soon as he heard a whisper that Sergius had been sighted in Los Angeles, his decision was made for him. He'd come to reconnect with his friend. So far, he had yet to find him.

A sharp rap at his door pulled Derrick from his thoughts. He drew out his pocket watch—a souvenir of the last Dumont man he'd killed—and frowned. Mitre and Colin were late, and Derrick had no patience for tardiness. He moved to the door in long, liquid strides, then opened it smoothly, letting no sign of his irritation show. He knew how to handle men, and how to dole out recriminations. But what he saw when he opened the door surprised him. Not Mitre or Colin, but Jonathan, looking as frazzled as Derrick had ever seen him.

"What's happened?" he demanded, stepping aside to let Jonathan stumble past him.

"Colin's gone—staked—and Mitre's a fucking mess. He called me. I was at the Z Bar, and I went to him. Told him I'd help him hunt, but he was out of his head. Said he'd get his own damn blood and then he'd kill the bitch if it took him a lifetime to find her."

The words spilled out, but Derrick understood. Some female had staked Colin and injured Mitre, who was now on the hunt, searching out healing blood.

"Mitre said she was good. Trained. I gotta think maybe she's the one who's been—"

"Giving us all the problems," Derrick finished for him. "Yes, I'm inclined to agree." He turned away from Jonathan for long enough to school his expression into one of calm control. It wouldn't do for one of his men to see how deeply the news had cut him. When he turned back, he knew that the younger vampire would see nothing but a veneer of determined strength. "Mitre will be in touch once he feeds. And then we'll have him take us back to the place where the woman attacked him. We'll find her scent. We'll track her. And then I will personally make sure that she understands why it was a very bad decision to go meddling in the affairs of vampires."

CHAPTER FOUR

Alexis winced as Leena pressed an ice pack against the knot on the back of her head. "Thanks," she said, then reached up to hold the pack in place. "I appreciate you being here, but you should have gone home. You look wiped."

"Bet I don't look as bad as you do. Besides, I wanted to wait and see how it went. I'm glad I did. You got hurt because of me."

Alexis had been inspecting an abrasion that ran down the side of her thumb and over her wrist, but now she looked up into Leena's face and saw the guilt and regret in her friend's eyes. "That is such bullshit. You don't have a thing to be sorry about."

"How many vamps have you staked since I told you the truth? You've been training like a . . . well, like an I-don't-know-what, and you've nailed almost a dozen now. And *this* one you miss? Not once but three times?"

"Thanks so much for reminding me."

"I shouldn't have told you. It messed up your concentration. Got under your skin."

"Conversation over," Alexis said, because Leena was right. But no way was she going to admit it.

"Want to talk about it?"

"I just . . ." She trailed off, glancing at the diamond-shaped scar on her wrist as she tried to gather her thoughts. "What if I don't get the chance again?"

"You will. That's why you came to LA. To find the vamp who killed your sister. And you're not even certain that the one who got away was the guy. Maybe you did dust him."

Alexis shrugged. Leena was right, of course, but until she knew for sure, the thought was cold comfort. They'd known only that the vampire who'd killed Tori was in that alley. They didn't know which one he was.

"You'll get him," Leena said firmly. "*We'll* get him." She gave Alexis a stern, motherly glance, ironic since she was the younger of the two. After a second she reached for her cane and stood. "Coffee or ibuprofen or both?"

"I'll get it."

"Sit. Keep the ice on that knot. I'll bring you coffee first, and if that doesn't work we'll shift over to the hard stuff."

"Bourbon?"

Leena snorted. "Whatever works." She limped off toward the kitchen, and Alexis realized that she was smiling despite the pain in her head and her frustration at having missed the second vampire. And why not? She had an important mission and a damn good friend by her side.

Hard to believe that so much had changed so fast. She'd once been hopelessly naïve. Now she wasn't.

She could remember with absolute clarity the day it had all started. She'd been a young FBI agent, ridiculously proud at having been handpicked for a newly formed national task force with only one year out of Quantico under her belt. She'd been assigned to the New York office, where the task force was based. It had been created to investigate a series of violent deaths that had crisscrossed the country, the nature of the fatalities suggesting that the deaths were related, possibly by interstate cult activity.

The murders were showing up in clusters all over the States, but the highest percentages were in dense urban areas, which made sense if the FBI's gang- and/or cult-related theory was accurate. Somewhere, though, there was a ground zero. There had to be a leader who was organizing all of this. Some David Koresh–type nutjob with a Dracula complex who was telling his followers to go out and suck the blood from his victims—yes, *suck*— and to do it from the neck.

It was sick. It would be one thing if all these folks did was drink blood from a butcher store and wear black and file their teeth to points. Weird, perhaps, and certainly not Alexis's thing. But harmless enough. That's not what they were doing, though, and they'd crossed a line. A very dark, very scary line.

Unfortunately, whoever these people were, they weren't stupid. They were operating under the radar and doing a good job of it, too.

The case had been occupying her time 24/7, but when her college roommate flew into town to audition for a soap opera, Alexis took a rare day off. They'd been out shopping—playing a game where they picked the tourists out from the locals—when Antonio Gutierrez had called. He was the SAC—Special Agent in Charge—and he'd offered no niceties about interrupting her day off. "Get your ass down to the First Precinct," he'd said. "Ask for Detective Lanahan." He'd clicked off, and Alexis had turned to Brianna.

"Let me guess. You've got to go."

"The exciting life of an FBI agent." She spoke ironically, but the truth was that she loved it. The job. The excitement. It was what she'd worked toward since she'd turned twelve. That was the year her sixteen-year-old sister Tori had gone missing, and even though her parents and the police had told Alexis that Tori had run away, Alexis refused to believe that her sister would leave. Not Tori. Sure, life was shit at the Martin house, but Tori had always been the one who stuck up for Alexis. Who comforted her when their dad went off on one of his tears. Who'd dried Alexis's eyes when their mom had thrown out all of Alexis's favorite books because she'd caught Alexis reading under the covers with a flashlight, and rules were rules were rules.

No, Tori wouldn't leave Alexis. Not on purpose. She'd been taken—Alexis was certain. And for years she'd fantasized about joining the FBI and tracking down the son-of-a-bitch who'd abducted her sister. After her parents died six years ago in a Colorado plane crash, Alexis had discovered Tori's diary in a box in their attic, and she'd been forced to acknowledge that maybe her sister *had* run away. It had been a hard reality to swallow, but not as hard as the horrible truth that the diary had revealed—a pattern of physical and verbal abuse from both parents, with the worst being the way their father would creep into Tori's bed at night.

The words had been practically etched onto the page, Tori's pencil pushing so hard that it sometimes ripped the paper. The scrawled, rambling sentences were accompanied by strange splotches—dried tears, Alexis assumed—along with awkward, violent sketches that were enough to make Alexis nauseated. Remembering, Alexis shivered. She'd been boxing up her parents' personal effects when she'd found the diary, and the uncomfortable emptiness that accompanied the loss of her parents had morphed into anger when she learned what they'd done to drive the older girl away. If Alexis could have taken some of that abuse onto her own shoulders, she would have, but she hadn't even been aware it was going on, even though Tori's diary made clear that it had been a pattern since she was in first grade. She'd run because she couldn't take it anymore, but she'd stayed as long as she could to protect her little sister. Knowing that, Alexis loved her even more. But to her shame, she still hated her for leaving.

She knew she was an emotional mess where her family was concerned, but she'd channeled her roiling emotions into her work. Even once she'd realized that Tori had left of her own accord, Alexis's desire to join the FBI hadn't faded. By then, the thought of being an agent—of honoring that badge and helping victims of unspeakable crimes—had invaded her soul, become a part of her. She'd clung to the dream, shifting it around only slightly for Tori's benefit. Alexis was no longer looking for her abductor; now she was looking for Tori herself. She wanted to throw her arms around her sister and tell her that their parents were dead. That Tori could come back. That she could be a big sister again.

It was a fantasy that Alexis clung to with determined tenacity. So far, she'd done everything a civilian could do to search for her sister, and a few things only an FBI agent could manage. One of these days she was going to ask official permission to use FBI resources to track Tori down. She had to, because Tori was all the family she had. Considering what she now knew about her parents, Tori was all the family she'd *ever* had.

Until then, though . . .

Well, until then, the FBI was her life. And if Gutierrez

wanted her on her day off, then she'd been more than ready to go.

What she hadn't understood was why she was going to the police department. By then, the task force had been in place long enough that the cops knew to call the FBI and the forensics team from the get-go. It had to be a cold case. An unsolved crime filed away that the local cops had dug out to pass off to the task force. A pain in the ass for the cops, maybe, but for the task force it could be gold.

She'd arrived at Lanahan's office eager to see the file, and he hadn't disappointed. After the briefest of introductions, he'd passed her a thick sheaf of papers fastened with a binder clip. "Only a few months old," he'd said. "So tepid, not cold. But the detective assigned didn't realize he should call you folks in."

"Didn't realize!" Alexis said, but Lanahan only shrugged.

"There were wounds on the neck, but those weren't the only injuries. Sure, he should have realized, but what can I say? He fucked up. And he's moved on—Kansas, Nebraska, one of those corn-fed states. Soon as I got the file, I called you folks."

She skimmed the initial detective's notes from the scene. "Unidentified female?" she asked, glancing up at Lanahan. "She's a Jane Doe?"

"It's all there," he said. "We didn't get anything back with prints. Girl looked to be a recovering junkie—but there wasn't any physical evidence of drug abuse. She did have some old puncture wounds on her neck and some scar tissue on her wrists. Could be drug-related, but the coroner thinks no."

"Self-mutilation."

Lanahan shrugged. "Who knows. Our guy canvassed the streets, but he didn't come up with anybody who knew the female."

"She was found in the subway system?" Alexis asked. The answer was on the report, but she wanted to hear what this detective had to say. As she waited, she flipped pages, looking for the crime scene photos.

"Not far from the Battery Park station," he confirmed. "In a pile of debris in one of the homeless squats."

Alexis frowned, hating the thought of some poor girl, probably a runaway, holed up in one of the areas carved out within urban subways where the homeless would park their carts, warm their hands over Sterno cans, and trade needles and bottles of Jack. At her lowest, she wondered if that was where Tori had ended up, but always immediately banished the thought.

"I can take you there if you like," Lanahan offered.

"That would be great," Alexis said as she flipped another page. She knew she wouldn't find a clue, but just being close to the scene and seeing what the victim saw could help. "Maybe we could go—"

She stopped talking, her eyes riveted on the morgue photo in front of her.

"Agent Martin?"

She could hear the concern in Lanahan's voice. She didn't care. She couldn't look away from the page.

Because despite the bright fuchsia hair and emaciated cheeks, Alexis knew that face. *Tori.*

Her stomach cramped, and she had to force her hands not to shake. Her sister had been murdered. Violently. Brutally. And by the very killer that Alexis was looking for.

Time slowed to a crawl, and it seemed to take forever

for her to lift her head to meet the detective's eyes. "I'm going to catch him," she said slowly and carefully, in a voice that didn't sound like her own. "I'm going to catch all of them. And I'm not going to stop until they're all behind bars."

She wouldn't stop until she'd avenged her sister.

At the time, though, she hadn't understood what that meant or just how deep into the world of nightmares she'd have to sink in order to make good her promise.

♦

Images of Tori's ripped neck and emaciated body had tormented Alexis for days. She worked the case constantly. She didn't sleep, barely ate, and the other members of the task force started to tiptoe around her, afraid of setting off a burst of temper coupled by a steel-bladed tongue. After she'd yelled at one of the interns for not pulling a fingerprint record fast enough, Gutierrez called her into his office and told her to sit her ass down.

"I'd rather stand."

"Consider it an order, Agent."

She sat, but on the edge of her seat. There was no relaxing for Alexis anymore. Nothing but the hard push to get it done, and the damnable frustration that came with knowing she was failing at that one simple task. Failing the task force. And most of all, failing Tori.

"There are other victims in this case, Agent. Other leads to follow that might track back to your sister's killer. But you're too close, Alexis. You need to back off. Focus on another file, another victim. Either that or resign from the task force altogether. Or take a leave of absence," he amended, apparently seeing the glint of steel in her eyes.

"You're burning yourself out, and that's not doing anyone any good, least of all Tori."

"She's my sister," she said, pouring herself into the words. "I can't just walk away."

"I'm not asking you to. I'm just saying that it's time to come at this from a different angle. She's one of ours now, the FBI's. The task force. They're all good agents, Alex. Solid. You know that. Back off a little. Clear your head. And then you can come back to it fresh."

"Sir, I understand what you're saying, but I don't think—"

"Or you could consider a transfer." For a moment the words hung in the air. "You could go to Los Angeles."

At his words, her entire body went stiff.

"The task force is up and running there, too."

"I don't want to go back to LA." She'd grown up there, but it had never been home. Not after Tori had left, anyway. Now it was just a place on a map. Her childhood friends had all moved away, and even Brianna lived in New York now, having gotten the part in the soap. And while Alexis liked Edgar Garvey, the LAPD's liaison with the task force, whom she'd met when he'd done a week of training with the FBI, he was undeniably odd with his strange beliefs and wild conspiracy theories.

Most of all, though, she couldn't move that far away from Tori.

"If LA's out of the question, then there's always Dallas or Chicago."

Dear God, they were determined to get her out of there. Had she really screwed it up that bad?

Of course she had. Hell, she knew she had. The question now was how to fix it.

Play it smart, Alex. Screw up, and you're screwing Tori.

She tilted her head down, focusing on her hands, fingers twisted together in her lap. "You're right about my lack of focus. I owe you—I owe the Bureau—an apology."

"You don't," he said. "There's not an agent here who wouldn't be equally preoccupied under similar circumstances. But I need you on your game."

"I'm not interested in a transfer, sir. I realize it's a lot to ask, but could we take that off the table?"

He regarded her evenly for a moment, then nodded. "Take a few days, get your head straight, and come back refreshed."

She'd promised to do just that. Of course, she'd been lying. On her days off, she spent her time doing the same thing she'd done when she'd been active: prowling the streets, searching the subways, talking to the homeless, the vagrants, the lost souls with vacant eyes and hopeless faces. Had Tori been one of them? Alexis was certain that she had, and that reality cut deep into her soul. Because despite the undercurrent of anger and worry that had surged through her ever since Tori's disappearance, she'd always held on to hope. Hope that Tori had managed to get away. To make a real life for herself. But if this was where she'd ended up—this dark place where cruel eyes watched you and hope was something that moldered in the shadows—then what had been the point? Why had Tori left home—left *her*—if she was only going someplace worse? If she was simply stepping out into the world to meet a new kind of monster, one that wouldn't just hurt and belittle her, but would actually kill her?

"Dammit, Alexis, *stop it.*" She pressed her fingertips to her temples and looked away from a filthy homeless woman with missing teeth who was staring at her with pity. She didn't want the woman's pity—didn't need it. She was there to do a job, and it was better for everybody—herself, Tori, the task force, and all the other victims—if she could get her act together and get her head back in the game.

With renewed determination, she turned back and forced herself to look hard at the homeless woman. When she did, she could see that despite the years of dirt that had settled in her deep facial wrinkles, the woman's eyes were still sharp. This was her domain, this small corner of a subterranean world, and she watched silently as what passed for living went on in front of her.

Alexis knelt, bringing her to eye level with the woman. "I'd like to ask you a question. Is that okay?"

Gums smacked, causing strands of spittle to sparkle in the dim light like perverse gems. "Sounds to me like you already asked."

"Fair enough. I've got another."

The woman blinked. Stared. Waiting. Alexis had the impression that was what she did the most. Waited. She pulled out the picture of Tori. The crime scene photo, because the one in her wallet showed a healthy, vibrant girl. Not a strung-out, fuchsia-haired junkie. "This girl. Do you know her?"

"Dead," the woman said. "If you're looking for her, you're not gonna find her." That wide grin. Those strands of spit. "Not unless you're planning to follow her to hell."

"How do you know she's dead?"

"Got eyes, don't I?"

Alexis's heart pounded against her rib cage, so hard that she feared she'd crack a rib. "You saw her? You saw her killer?"

"Saw the cops find her." The woman raised one bony finger and pointed. "Dump spot. Under some newspapers. Not that she was reading. The dead don't read."

"No," Alexis said, choking out the words. "They don't. But you read. You pay attention. You listen and watch. Can you tell me what you saw? What you learned?"

"Saw nothing. Heard nothing. Just that she was dead. That the girl was dead." She shrugged. "Not the only one."

"What do you mean?"

"People die, don't they?"

They did, Alexis thought. People died, and people like her were left behind, either to mourn them or to stand up for them. Where Tori was concerned, Alexis was trying to do both. "Are you saying there were other bodies?"

"Down here? Always will be. This is where the monsters live." Those sharp eyes narrowed, becoming almost lost in the creases of the woman's face. "That's what you're looking for. A monster."

"Damn straight. Can you help me?"

"Not me. The girl. Maybe. If you ask nice. Sugar and spice, not snails and tails."

The sharp eyes were starting to dull; whatever dementia had brought this woman down into the subways was setting back in. "Wait," Alexis said, clutching the woman's wrist, then squeezing until the old lady looked her in the eye. "Who's the girl? Where can I find her?"

"Can't," the woman said. "She finds you. In here." She tapped her temple. "That's where she lives. Squeezes inside and looks around. Looks inside your head for the monsters. Now, go on with you. Bedtime now. Gotta tuck in Mr. Padgett." She slipped her hand in her pocket and Alexis saw the pocket move. A rat's pointed nose and beady black eyes emerged, staring her down and daring her to stay.

She thought about taking Mr. Padgett up on that dare, but she'd gotten as much out of the woman as she was going to get. The old lady was fading fast, cooing to her rat and swaying softly like a mother with an infant.

Alexis got the hell out of the subway, her mind on the girl. A girl who got into people's heads. A girl who found monsters. That was a girl Alexis wanted to meet. But how the hell was she supposed to find her?

CHAPTER FIVE

In the end, she didn't find the girl. The girl found her.

For two days, she'd continued to canvas the subway tunnels near Battery Park. She still asked about Tori, but now she was also asking about the mysterious girl. She'd wanted to pull more information from the old woman—she'd gone so far as to bring a sandwich from a nearby deli—but the woman and her rat were gone, lost to the tunnels like so many others.

It happened at dusk on the second day. Alexis was tired. Dirty. And getting damn discouraged, too. She'd just about decided that Gutierrez was right—she needed to go home and get her head out of this. Watch mindless television. Drink wine. And try to find some semblance of a center, because her life was spiraling down into obsession. She knew that—could feel the tug of the drain spinning her round and round. But dammit, she wasn't quite ready to give up.

For the night, though . . .

She'd been pushing so hard, she could feel the exhaustion in her bones. For just one night, she'd go home. Take a bath, drink some wine. Then hit it hard again in the morning.

She dragged herself up the steps, letting the flow of Friday-night revelers push her along, like flotsam in a never-ending stream. As she reached street level, she saw a woman step away from a railing. She'd been leaning there, long blond hair fluttering in the evening breeze, the yellow lamplight giving her a fairy-princess glow. Alexis slowed, remembering. She'd seen that same woman when she'd descended the steps two hours before. She'd noticed the dress—a fifties-style sundress with a cinched waist, the kind of retro outfit that was all the rage lately. The dress was white with tiny pink dots, and the girl had paired it with pink flats, making her look both sophisticated and innocent, the kind of look that Alexis liked, but never tried because she was afraid it would make her too Marilyn Monroe, and that didn't fit her image of a badass FBI agent.

This time it wasn't the dress that interested Alexis; it was the girl. Why the hell was she still there two hours later? More important, why was she now walking toward Alexis, her gait uneven as she favored one leg?

"I think maybe you're looking for me," the girl said. "I'm Leena." She stuck out her hand to shake, but Alexis only frowned.

"You?" She'd been searching for a girl, yes. But she'd expected someone older. Rougher around the edges. The kind of girl who prowled sewers and would be noticed by the vagrants who lived down in the dark. But Leena? She probably wasn't more than twenty-two, and looked like she could be part of a sorority group touring New York for the day.

The girl laughed. The kind of genuine laugh that Alexis and Brianna often shared when they went out for drinks and gossip. "Not what you were expecting?"

Alexis bristled, then forced herself to relax. The girl was right—she *wasn't* what Alexis had been expecting. But what had that been? Some mysterious, shadowy figure? Some dark girl with hollow eyes who'd tell her the secrets of the sewers and lead her straight to her sister's killer? All things considered, the girl in the dress was a pleasant surprise. Assuming, that is, that she could help at all.

"What makes you think I'm looking for you?"

"I watch. I pay attention. And Marion told me you were looking for me."

Marion. The old lady. Alexis hadn't even asked for her name, more proof that Tori's murder had thrown her off her game. Any other victim and she'd never have let a witness go without getting a full ID. And yet with Marion, she'd chatted the old lady up and then moved on. Maybe Gutierrez was right; maybe she needed to get the hell out of New York. Except she wouldn't. She couldn't. Not until she had a lead on the bastard who'd killed her sister.

She focused on Leena. "So why was I looking for you?"

Leena didn't laugh, but her mouth curved up in amusement. "Because I know things." She shrugged. "I don't always tell what I know, and I don't always get it clear in my head. But I'm legit. Hell, call the NYPD if you don't believe me."

"You're a psychic." *Shit.* Like Alexis needed that kind of bullshit.

"And you're a skeptic. That's okay. Give me your hand." She stuck hers out again, then left it hanging in the air. She raised her brows, waiting for Alexis to take it. Fine. Whatever. She took Leena's hand. She wasn't sure what she expected—Sparks? A tingle in the air? A booming voice from the heavens? None of that, but there was something about Leena's face. As Alexis watched, the girl seemed to lose color, then a moment later she yanked her hand away and wiped her palm hard on the material of her dress.

"I'm sorry," Leena said. She sounded breathless, like she'd just run sprints. "Your sister. Oh, God, your sister."

Alexis was already falling before she realized that her knees had buckled. She grabbed for the railing, but found that Leena had a hold of her arm. "How? How did you know?" She hadn't told anyone she was looking for her sister. Just that she was with the FBI. That she was working a case.

"I'm so sorry. I shouldn't have blurted it out like that." She licked her lips. "Marion was right to tell you about me. I can help. Or, at least, I'd like to try. Can we talk?"

Alexis, who'd never believed in bullshit supernatural stuff, nodded immediately. "There's a deli," she said, nodding across the street.

"My shop isn't far from here. But we need to go somewhere else first." She paused, lips pressed together as she studied Alexis's face.

"What?" Alexis demanded, suddenly afraid that Leena had changed her mind. But she couldn't have. Alexis wouldn't let her. This was the first lead she'd had—if you could even call it a lead. But it was a door. An opening. Something. It was all she had, and she wasn't about to let it go. "What's wrong?"

"You need to meet someone. Someone who knew your sister. I—will you trust me? Will you let me take you there? Meet him first, and then afterward you can ask me whatever questions you want?"

It was a ridiculous way to proceed, and everything in her agency training told her she should very firmly tell

Leena that this wasn't a damn scavenger hunt, and that Alexis wanted to know what was going on right then. But all she did was nod. She had to know, and if that meant taking a risk and following some girl who maybe, *maybe,* could get into people's heads, then she was damn well taking it.

"I see stuff," Leena explained as she casually pulled a folded walking stick from her purse and extended it. She used it as they moved back down the stairs into the subway station. "I touch someone and sometimes nothing happens, but sometimes I see. And right now I see that you don't believe me."

"Your psychic powers are truly astounding," Alexis said with a laugh. "I'm sorry. But since I'm with you, it's obvious that I must believe a little." Possibly the girl was a grifter. Possibly Marion had seen a resemblance between Tori and Alexis and she'd been sucked into a huge con. That was what her rational part said. But her rational part was overwhelmed by the part that wanted to believe she'd found an ally and an asset.

"Don't worry. You're not hurting my feelings. I get that I'm a freak, believe me. But after you meet John-O and after you see my shop . . . well, then you can tell me if you're still hesitating. Okay?"

Leena smiled, and Alexis caught herself smiling back. "Okay."

They took the subway to Times Square and emerged blinking into the light. "He works in the back of one of the souvenir shops," Leena said.

"Your vision showed you that?"

"My vision showed him with Tori," she said, her sister's name catching Alexis's attention. She was certain she hadn't mentioned it to Leena. "He and I've crossed paths before," Leena continued. From her expression, the crossing had been a less-than-pleasant experience.

"Who is he?"

"A son-of-a-bitch." She skirted easily around two tourists taking up the entire sidewalk as they gawked at the chaos that was Times Square. "Here." She pulled open the door of a shop with so many knickknacks and so much neon in the window, Alexis couldn't even locate the name of the place.

"Leena, Leena, Bo-Beena!" A man who had to be as wide as he was tall spread his arms behind the counter and grinned, showing a row of brilliantly white teeth framed within a fiery red beard and mustache. "And you brought a friend! Tourist? Looking for T-shirts? Snow globes?"

"John-O," Leena said, and Alexis watched the man's effusive expression shut down.

"John-O? But he's not—"

"Don't bullshit me, Leroy. I need to talk to him. She needs to talk to him," Leena added. She looked harder now, and Alexis had to admit she was impressed. Even in the girlie outfit, Leena had serious chops, and Alexis relaxed a little, letting a tiny bit of hope ease its way inside her. Maybe, just maybe . . .

"Aw, hell, Leena. Didn't you hear? John-O's dead. Found him in Central Park just a few days ago. Throat ripped out. Hell of a thing. Ironic, you know?"

As far as Alexis could tell, there wasn't a damn thing ironic about it, except for the fact that she'd heard about the guy. He'd hit the task force's radar right as Gutierrez was pushing Alexis out the door. She turned to Leena. "John-O is Johnny Osgood Fitzhugh?"

"One and the same. You know him?"

"You want to tell me why you've been dragging me all over town to meet a pimp?" *No. I don't want to know why. Don't want to know that about Tori.* And yet she had to hear. Had to soak it all in, process it, and try to make it right in her head somehow.

"Hey," Leroy said, holding his hands up as high as if this were a stickup. "He didn't do none of that shit in my place."

"Not interested, Leroy. That's not why we're here." Leena cocked her head toward Alexis. "Dead end. Come on."

"So my sister was turning tricks." She'd intended the words to come out as a question, but based on the cold, knotty sensation in her stomach, she already knew the answer.

"Yeah," Leena said. "But there's more. I wanted you to meet John-O first, get a sense of what I'm about to show you. But, well . . . oh, hell. Let's head back to my place."

Leena's place turned out to be a tiny storefront in SoHo with a simple paper sign that said PSYCHIC. Although Alexis had asked her new tour guide to give her some hint of what this was all about, Leena refused to say anything until they'd arrived.

"We're here now," Alexis said, closing the door behind her and breathing in the scent of herbs and spices. "Tell me." Her patience had worn completely thin, and if Leena dodged the question once more, Alexis was going to whip out her badge and drag the girl in for questioning. She'd gone along with the charade for Tori's sake, but enough was enough. "No more mystery bullshit. Tell me what you know."

"Lock the door," Leena said. "You're not going to

want to hear this, and I'm not going to want to be inter-rupted."

Alexis did, then followed Leena through a cleverly concealed door hidden by the wall paneling. It opened into an office. Like the front, the scent of the office area was cloying. Lavender and anise, rosemary and carda-mom, all mixed with other scents that Alexis didn't rec-ognize. In addition to shelf after shelf of dried herbs and spices, hundreds of crystals covered tabletops and shelves. Some even filled baskets that sat on the floor. The lighting was dim, made that way by a scarf tossed over a bare bulb. A little too new-agey for Alexis's taste, not to mention claustrophobic.

The chairs were uncomfortable, with straight backs and lumpy upholstery. They were done in red velvet that had become threadbare over the years. Leena sat in one, then scooted it around until it was right in front of the other. Alexis took the hint and sat. "Well?"

"I could be wrong—I'm usually not, but I only got a glimpse."

"A glimpse of what?"

"John-O is—*was*—not your average pimp. I'm sorry," she added in a rush. "I'm not saying that your sister was selling herself. Well, maybe I am, but not in the way you think."

Alexis realized she was gripping the seat of the chair so hard that her fingernails were digging into the wood. She told herself to relax. To think of this as just another case. Yes, it hurt thinking of Tori that way, but what the hell did she know of Tori's life? Considering the child-hood she'd had, would it really be that unusual if Tori had gone out into the world and sold her body? God knew it was a skill set she'd acquired the hard way.

"Are you okay?" Leena was looking at her with inescapable compassion in her eyes.

"Not really," Alexis admitted, realizing as she spoke that those weren't words she'd say to just anyone. She liked this woman. More than that, she trusted her to tell her the truth about her sister, and to make hearing that truth as painless as possible. "But don't stop. I need to know."

"You're an FBI agent," Leena began. "No, don't look at me like that. You didn't tell me, but I saw that, too. I didn't mean to pry, but I can't help it. This stuff comes into my head, and then it's stuck there."

"So I'm an agent." Alexis couldn't help but stiffen as she sat there, feeling exposed and vulnerable.

"I'm just saying that you must know about weird shit."

She thought about the marks on Tori's neck. On the necks of all the other victims. "Yeah, you could say that."

"Drug rings, white slavery, pedophile kidnappers. All sorts of fucked-up people, right?"

"How was John-O fucked up?"

"He serviced the vampire community." She paused as if waiting for Alexis to respond.

She didn't have long to wait. "What do you mean by 'serviced'?" She leaned forward in her chair, eager for what Leena had to say. Neck wounds were the one common thread among the task force victims. The idea of real vampires was ridiculous, of course, but a cult that had gotten a little too into the whole Dracula/*Twilight* thing? Finding folks who fit that profile had become one of the FBI's priorities.

"You believe in vampires?"

"I believe that some people do. And that some of them might kill for it. It's all about the blood, right?" She knew damn well that even some folks she considered educated believed that vampires and ghouls and things that went bump in the night were actually real. Edgar, for one. Even though he'd spent years with the LAPD dealing with very human bad guys, he still believed that bloodsucking vamps walked the earth. Hell, even Brianna had been too freaked out by the possibility of bringing forth demons to go to a Ouija Board party in college. Ridiculous superstitions and runaway imaginations as far as Alexis was concerned. She knew damn well that monsters existed. But they were still people, the only inhuman thing about them the way they thought and acted. She ought to know; she'd grown up with two of them.

"The blood is what they crave," Leena said, nodding sagely. "And John-O got it for them."

"He pimped them out." Alexis felt bile rise in her throat as she imagined her sister selling herself. Not for sex—or not *just* for sex. But for blood. "Dear God. Somebody actually paid my sister to suck her blood?"

"I'm so sorry."

Alexis didn't realize that she'd risen and was pacing until she had to turn to get her bearings in order to look at Leena. "How do you know all of this?"

Leena looked at her hard. "You're not the only one who's lost someone you love."

"No," Alexis said. "I'm sorry. Of course I'm not."

"You want to find your sister's killer. How far are you willing to go?"

"As far as I have to."

"And when you find him? What then?"

Alexis hesitated. The proper answer was that she'd arrest him. That she'd dump him into the system and see him behind bars.

She said none of that. Instead, she told Leena the truth. "I'll kill him."

"Damn straight," Leena said. "But how?"

"A bullet. Fired in self-defense, of course. At least that's what I'll say when I get called to the carpet for discharging my weapon and killing a suspect." *What am I doing?* Her tongue was far too loose. Even charged up as she was about the possibility of getting help from this woman, Alexis wasn't a reckless person. Yet she'd just blurted out the kind of thing that could cost her her job, not to mention her freedom if she was prosecuted for murder.

Around her, blue smoke twined through the room. "The air," she said, suddenly realizing. "Oh, shit. What have you put in the air?"

"I'm sorry. Please don't be mad."

"Too late for that."

"I had to know for certain."

"Know what?" She was tense, primed to get the hell out of there and leave Leena in the dust. Except she didn't want to go. Whether it was the drugged air or her belief that Leena could help her, Alexis didn't know. She might regret it, but she was staying.

"Whether you could handle the truth." She grabbed her cane and pushed herself up, then took a couple of steps toward the back of the room. "Follow me."

She led her into a secret hall, hidden by dusty shelves covered with herbs and old, rotting books. The scent of decay almost overpowered Alexis, and she blinked, trying to force her eyes to adjust to the darkness. Her hand went to her hip, where her gun was still holstered beneath her jacket. She heard Leena laugh. "You won't need that. It wouldn't help anyway."

"Where are we going?"

"Through my building. To see one of them."

"Your building? This whole place belongs to you?"

Leena turned and offered Alexis a sunny smile. "I only invite the public into the storefront. You know, for readings and things. But this building has been in my family since the late 1800s. I actually live on the top floor. But we're not going there. We're going down. Into the basement." That said, she opened another door and started down, holding onto the handrail tightly as she limped down the stairs.

Alexis followed, her mind and muscles on hyperalert. She believed that Leena meant her no harm, but she was trained not to be stupid. And she'd never been one to trust easily.

They reached the bottom of the stairs, then moved down a dark hall barely illuminated by widely spaced yellow bulbs. Finally, they reached a steel vault door, the shiny metal looking out of place against the ancient brick-and-mortar walls. The door was sealed with an intricate locking mechanism. Alexis watched, curious, as Leena operated the lock and opened the door.

Alexis gasped. The room was much brighter, lit by candles tucked into depressions in the stone. And there, at the back of the room, was a shirtless man chained to the wall by his ankles and his wrists.

"Dear God," she whispered, reaching for her gun. "Shit, Leena, what have you done?"

"He's not a man," Leena said, not the least bit perturbed by Alexis's reaction. "And neither was the monster who killed your sister. It was a vampire."

"Have your sick fun on someone else's time," she said, pulling her weapon. "Now unchain him, and then put your hands against the wall."

"Shit, Alexis. Do you have to be so goddamn pedantic?"

"*Excuse* me?" The gun felt heavy in her hand, and she realized that whatever drug had been in the air in the other room was still affecting her.

"Watch. Just watch." And with a speed that defied Leena's limp, she lunged forward and shoved a wooden stake into the trapped man's stomach.

He roared, then flailed against the chain, some pitiful, trapped beast.

But Alexis didn't feel sorry for him. Not anymore. Because she got a look at his mouth. At his fangs. And then, just when she was about to tell Leena to back off so that she could have a second to think, Leena plunged the stake in a second time—this time into its heart. And the creature in front of them immediately dissolved into a pile of dust.

"Told you," Leena said. "And now that you know, nothing's ever going to be the same."

CHAPTER SIX

"Alexis? Hey. Wake up, girl."

Alexis peeled her eyes open and tried to focus on Leena, who was carefully depositing a cup of coffee on the table in front of her. "Sorry," Leena said. "That bump on your head makes me nervous. I'm not sure if I should let you sleep."

"I'm fine," Alexis said. She'd slid sideways into the chair, and now she righted herself, shaking out her arms to ward off the urge to sleep. "But you really have to tell me the truth. Is he still alive?"

"I swear, I just don't know."

Alexis bit back a frustrated groan. "There were two vampires in the alley," she said. "I know that one of them was the one who killed my sister—you're the one who told me. So how can you not know if the killer is the one I dusted?"

Leena reached across the table and took her hand. "Alexis. You know why. I've already told you how all this works. Or doesn't work, as the case may be. It's mysticism, not science. Nothing's exact."

"But you have the map. You saw. Can't you do it again? Can't you see if he's still out there?" She looked at her friend's face, at the pale skin, almost paper-thin from exhaustion, and immediately felt like a total shit. "I'm sorry. I shouldn't have asked. I know I shouldn't press. I mean, you told me how much it drains you, but I'm just—"

"Eager?"

"That doesn't even begin to describe it." Dear God, this was why she'd come back to Los Angeles: so that she could find and kill the vampire who'd killed Tori. And now she was so close, she could almost touch the truth. Except somehow it kept escaping her.

No matter what else happened, she was eternally grateful to Leena for revealing that horrible truth about Tori's death. But that wasn't the only thing for which she owed Leena. Because it turned out that Leena Dumont was descended from a family of vampire hunters who'd made their home in New Orleans. Leena herself was descended from a plantation owner and a slave named Evangeline, who just happened to be the daughter of voodoo queen Marie Laveau. Which pretty much explained how Leena came by the woo-woo, magical stuff: Her family tree was filled with psychics and witches and voodoo and all sorts of mystical whatnots.

After Alexis had gotten her head around that rather freakish reality, she'd asked Leena if she could use her psychic whatever-you-call-it to locate Tori's killer. Leena had hesitated at first, then agreed to try, but told Alexis not to get her hopes up.

It had been strange to watch Leena pull together an odd variety of herbs and roots, then boil them in a cauldron like something out of *Macbeth*. They'd sat there in the smoke-filled room, both of them holding a photograph of Tori onto which Alexis had smeared her own blood—the blood she shared with her sister.

Alexis hadn't really expected anything—the whole situation was just too damn weird. But after a few moments, Leena's head had shot backward, her eyes had opened wide, and she'd let out a long, strange moan. A moment later she'd fallen over, clutching her head and crying for Alexis to please, please, please turn out all the lights.

Alexis had hurried to comply, then knelt by Leena's side, not sure if she should touch her or call a doctor or bring her a handful of ibuprofen.

It had passed quickly—according to Leena, the migraines never went away that fast—and when she was herself again, she said that she'd seen a place. The Hollywood sign. The Capitol Records building. The Hollywood Bowl.

Tori's killer was in Los Angeles—where exactly, Leena couldn't say. But it was a start. And Alexis had known it was time to come home.

It had been an unusual beginning for a friendship, but a solid one, and after that the two had formed a plan. Alexis had taken Gutierrez's advice and quit the FBI, and Leena packed up her things and made the trek across the country, too. "My building's not going anywhere," Leena had said. "And no offense, but you're a total noob. Try to do this completely on your own and you'll get yourself killed before you even have time to go shopping at the Beverly Center. Besides, a psychic opening up a shop in California? How can I go wrong?"

Alexis had argued, but only for form. As selfish as it might be, she longed to have a friend with her who understood what she was facing.

Her parents' Brentwood house had been sitting empty for the last year—Alexis had been considering selling it after the tenants had moved out. Now she moved back in, grateful for the extent of her parents' wealth. Since their death, she'd rarely touched her inheritance, choosing to live off her FBI salary rather than what she considered blood money. But upon her return, she spent like Lindsay Lohan on a shopping spree, writing checks left and right to various electronic and hunting/sport supply companies. Let Mom and Dad finance her vendetta against the vampires and her search for Tori's killer. It was the least they could do considering they'd meted out their own brand of torture.

She turned the massive wine cellar into a combination workout studio and mission control center. The room had been kept locked while the house was rented, since her parents' wine collection was still there and worth a fortune. But when she'd moved back, Alexis had brought in a representative from Sotheby's to take the more expensive and rarer bottles away for auction, keeping only a few for herself tucked away in one corner. Everything else in the room was given a full overhaul.

Now the cellar was a technological masterpiece, a command and weapons center that rivaled anything she'd had access to while at the FBI.

Leena had turned down the offer to be her roommate, saying that she was used to living on her own. And even Alexis's argument that the house was so big, both of them might as well be living alone, hadn't swayed her. At first, Alexis had been disappointed. She didn't want to return alone to a house filled with the ghosts of her memories, but once she was settled, she realized it wasn't as bad as she'd anticipated. There was something healing about being in complete control of a place where she'd once had to tread softly or else risk getting whipped. Or worse.

Still, she had to admit it was nice that Leena was there

now. Her head was throbbing, and if she'd come back to an empty house she would have just sat on the couch and licked her wounds. Now she could sit on the couch and gripe to her friend.

"I'm so sorry," Leena said, dropping into the chair opposite her. "First it takes me forever to figure out a way to pinpoint the sorry SOB, and then it turns out I didn't even really manage to do that."

"Don't you dare apologize," Alexis said, realizing she was being a complete shit by complaining. "You've been amazing. I know how much I owe you."

"Including for that bump on the head," Leena said with a frown. "I'm the one who sent you to Hollywood Boulevard."

"You're the one who changed my life. Everything I know about this evil we're fighting—it's because of you."

A smile curled the other woman's lip. "Just don't get yourself killed and we'll call it even."

"Deal," she said, then winced as she adjusted the ice pack.

Leena winced too, in sympathy. "I should have the strength to look again tomorrow. It's not soon enough, I know, but . . ."

"It's perfect," Alexis said firmly. She was lying, of course. She wanted Leena to look now, but that desire came from a selfish place, and she didn't want her friend exhausted or suffering through more migraines.

At the same time, she knew that she couldn't do this alone. They'd become a team, she and the psychic— more accurately a witch, she supposed, but somehow calling her friend a witch just rubbed Alexis the wrong way.

After Leena had dusted the vampire in New York,

Alexis had been more than a little freaked out. Now, of course, it seemed absurd how blown away she'd been by the realization that not only did vampires exist, but Leena'd had one chained up in her basement. Alexis should have seen the signs—hell, the whole task force should have. But that kind of stuff belonged in the world of dreams and nightmares, not in New York or Los Angeles or Anywhere, USA.

Might not belong, but it was there anyway, and once she got over the shock Alexis had been determined to fight them. Fight them all—but find the one who'd killed Tori.

She'd told Leena the whole story. About her childhood and her big sister and her emotionally distant parents who, as it turned out, hadn't been quite so distant with Tori. She'd shared her anger at her parents and her hurt that Tori hadn't been able to suck it up and stay for her benefit. And her guilt for feeling that way, because goddamn her selfish heart, she didn't really wish that Tori would have just gritted her teeth while her father grunted and sweated and pushed himself into her. Did she?

She'd confessed it all, and Leena had said all the right things, and told her that of course Alexis hadn't really wanted Tori to suffer, but that didn't mean she didn't wish she was still there, beside her. Leena's own mother had been abusive, it turned out, and while she'd gotten the limp fighting vampires, Leena was pretty sure the migraines had started when her mother had beaten her so hard she'd hit her head against the hearth. "I felt different after that," Leena had said. "And then the headaches started. I didn't care, though, because my mother died that night. A heart attack, the doctors said, but I didn't believe it. She didn't have a heart. Not a real one, anyway. Sometimes she was the best mother you could want, but it would turn on a dime. She'd sort of fade into herself, and then she'd be someone else entirely. Someone vile and mean, and I hated her."

They'd bonded over their past, and now, together in Los Angeles, they were facing the future together.

CHAPTER SEVEN

Edgar Garvey stamped his feet and shook the rain off his coat as he pushed through the doors of the Beverly Hills Police Department. Before he'd moved to LA twenty-five years ago, he'd been assured that it never rained in Southern California. That would teach him to listen to pop music. He'd thought the city would be dry like his hometown of Phoenix. Hadn't LA been plunked down in a desert just like the sprawling Arizona metropolis?

"It's a doozy out there," Gus said. The white-haired old man worked the reception desk. With its art deco architecture and Beverly Hills location, the station got equal parts cops, criminals, and tourists wandering through the front door. Gus pointed them all in the right direction. "Supposed to clear off within the hour, though."

"Just hung around long enough to ruin my shoes," Edgar said. He'd pulled the night shift, and had spent the day at home, listening to the rain patter on his roof. It had cleared up briefly around dinnertime, then started up again right as he was grabbing his keys to head out the door.

He snatched the paper off Gus's desk and perused the headlines, not in any hurry to get to his desk. When he'd worked Van Nuys, he'd been respected, at least for most of his stint in the field. But here, Edgar knew damn well that the other detectives talked behind his back, silently counting down until his retirement came through in six months.

"So how come you aren't out there?"

Edgar folded the paper back, his finger marking the page with *For Better or For Worse*. He got one hell of a kick out of that comic strip. "Thought we already established that. The weather's a bitch."

Gus laughed. "Thought we established that it's gonna clear up. Nah, I'm talking about the body they found over in Franklin Canyon. Aren't you working with the FBI on that task force?"

Edgar put the paper down, comics forgotten. "What body?"

"All I know is a couple stumbled across a girl with neck injuries. Sanders didn't tag you?" he asked, referring to Lieutenant Elijah Sanders.

"Musta been an oversight," Edgar said, already moving away from the desk and pulling out his phone. *Shit, shit, shit.* He tapped out a text just before he stepped onto the elevator and lost the signal. *We may have one. Stand by.*

When the elevator opened on the third floor, Edgar was stewing. He didn't even notice the heads that turned in his direction, then immediately turned away, uninterested. These men weren't his friends, his buddies. They weren't watching his back. When he'd first transferred over, that fact had rubbed him raw. He'd been newly married. A flatfoot suddenly hooked up with a Beverly Hills beauty, and a sitcom star to boot. Nobody had understood what she'd seen in a schlub like him, but Gilli had shared his beliefs—his certainty that there was

something else out there. The press had called her eccentric. His fellow cops had called him a crackpot.

After the wreck, they'd shut up. Not because they
thought he was any less of a freak, but because it seemed
untoward to rib a man after his wife drove her convert-
ible over a cliff. By then, Edgar didn't give a fuck what
they called him. Make fun of him, don't make fun of
him. None of it would bring Gilli back.

Today, six-plus years after her death, he still didn't
give a shit. He knew the score—knew what was really
going on. More than that, he had a job to do and a new
partner to help.

And he wasn't keen on Sanders mucking up the works.

The door to Lieutenant Sanders's office was shut tight,
and the cheap vinyl blinds that allowed the detective privacy from his squad were down and closed. That usually meant that the lieutenant was in a ripe fury, and
when the LT was pissed, it was best to stay out of his
way. Not happening. Not today.

Edgar strode right up to his door, ignoring the stares
of the other men. Especially ignoring the under-the-
breath comments that were just a little too loud. *"Guess
he thinks that tinfoil hat can protect him from Sanders,
too."* *"Maybe he's made a deal and Sanders is going to
bite it at the next full moon."*

Shit.

Yeah, he was trying to ignore it. But it pissed him off.
Couldn't help it. And when he burst through Sanders's
door, it was Edgar who was in the ripe fury. Sanders
was simply kicked back, feet up, barking orders into the
phone.

Two long strides, and Edgar was at his desk. One firm
motion, and he'd disconnected his call.

"What the fuck?" Sanders yelled. "Goddammit, Garvey, you just hung up on the mayor."

"Am I, or am I not, the liaison between this office and the FBI's task force?" He said it calmly, without raising his voice. Inside, though, he was cursing a blue streak.

"You burst into my office and then have the gall to ask me if I remember your fucking job? How can I forget it with you waving the fed card every time it suits you?"

Edgar ignored the dig. The rivalry between the feds and the local cops was legendary. And that meant that Edgar was now a traitor to his kind. Considering his kind hadn't ever really wanted him, Edgar was okay with that. "A dead female in Franklin Canyon. Fatal wound to the neck. I talked to Gus on the way up, Sanders, and he knew enough to know that's got task force written all over it. So why the hell didn't you call me?"

He knew he was getting worked up, but this was important. For years he'd been labeled a crackpot, but now he finally knew that he'd been right all along. There really were monsters out there in the world, and tinfoil hats weren't going to keep them away. Ignorant detectives like Sanders weren't going to, either. "Well?" he demanded. "Or did a federal task force simply slip your memory?"

In front of him, Sanders's face was cycling through a series of expressions, the changes so fast and furious it was almost comic.

"I have never," he sputtered, "*never* kept you or the FBI away from a case. But Penny Martinez has nothing to do with the task force investigation," he said, referring to the victim by name.

"That isn't a call you're authorized to make."

"And I didn't. The feds did. Maybe you need to stay in better touch with your team, Garvey."

"You're saying the FBI said that the Penny Martinez case has no relevancy to the task force investigation?" Edgar pressed. "That's insane."

"Not the FBI," he said. "Homeland Security."

Edgar took an involuntary step back, startled. "Homeland?"

"They're all feds to me," Sanders was saying, unaware of the effect of his words. "Different injury. Different details." His brow furrowed, as if he was trying to remember something. Edgar's heart pounded against his rib cage. He wondered if Sanders could hear it.

After a second, Sanders shook his head. "Anyway, they were very clear. All my officers were sent packing. And a high-ranking agent spoke to me personally. Apparently, this is a matter of national security. What the fuck is wrong with you?" His diatribe ended with narrowed eyes and intense scrutiny. Edgar felt his face heat. He tugged at his collar, trying to catch his breath.

"Indigestion." *Suck it up, Garvey. This isn't new; it's just confirmation.* He squared his shoulders, trying to gather himself, then pointed a finger at Sanders. "If I find out you're screwing with me—"

"Yeah, take your best shot," his lieutenant said. "Shit, Garvey. You're out of here in six months. Can't you just try not to ruffle any feathers until then?"

Oh, hell, he wished he could just sit back, especially now that the truth was squeezing the air out of his lungs. Gilli had always believed that they'd worked their way into the government. The dark things. The evil ones. That they'd climbed all the way up to the White House.

That they were well positioned for a coup. Edgar hadn't gone that far. It was too hard to believe. Too terrifying.

But he believed it now, even though he hoped to hell he was mistaken.

He didn't think he was, though. And he feared that his beautiful, supposedly eccentric bride had been right on the money.

Vampires existed. They'd eased their way into the human world. They were poised for an attack.

And if what Sanders said was true, they were neck-deep in Homeland Security.

CHAPTER EIGHT

Edgar slid the car to a stop, shifted to park, and kept his hands tight on the steering wheel.

"Say it if you have to," Alexis said. She knew what he was going to say. That she shouldn't have come. Hell, if she was in his position, she'd probably say the same thing.

"You shouldn't have come. What? Why are you smiling?"

"No reason." She grabbed the handle and pushed open her door. "Come on. Near the duck pond, right?"

He gave a miserable nod, then cut the engine, killing the headlights. After a moment he got out of the car and met her by the hood, his footsteps making a squelching sound as he moved over the soaked grass.

"There," she said, pointing to an area about five hundred yards away that glowed with eerie illumination. "Homeland's forensics team must've set up lights."

"You should let me handle this on my own."

"Not a chance," she said. "You said the time of first assault was estimated to be sometime early this morning, right? Well, that would have been not long after that vamp I wounded got away. And you know as well as I do that he was looking for a meal. I'm thinking he found one in Penny Martinez." She kept her voice detached and professional, but inside she was twisted in knots. "And if what you heard from the responding officer is true, he found her, fed off her, and kept her alive for hours. Time of death was just a few hours ago, just around nightfall, right?" She shuddered. The vamp must've had a tarp or something to keep him out of the sun during the long hours of torture. Somehow the fact that he tormented the poor girl in broad daylight made the heinous act even more vile.

"He might not be the killer. And even if he is, it's not your fault."

Like hell. She shrugged off his words. "My fault or not, I'm working the scene." She picked up her pace.

He was breathing hard when he caught up to her. "What if someone at the scene knows you?"

"I was FBI, not Homeland. And you said yourself it's not a task force matter. Who would I know?"

He didn't answer, but he looked so unhappy that she stopped walking.

"Come on, Edgar, no one will know who I am." He made a snorting noise. "Fine. If someone figures it out, then we'll say that *you* didn't know the truth, either. As far as you know, I'm FBI all the way, and I've just pulled a huge scam on you."

"Sometimes I wish that was true. I'm just not sure I'm—"

"What?"

"I'm not sure I'm comfortable with the whole thing. You pretending to be something you're not."

She let his words slide off her. She'd made peace with her decision to leave the FBI. She had a mission, after all, and pretending to believe that a cult was bleeding victims dry wasn't helping that purpose. It was a waste of time, and she didn't miss it. The only downside was the fact that an FBI badge did open certain doors. But the interesting thing was that you really only needed the badge and the attitude. She already had the 'tude. And fortunately, she'd had plenty of money to acquire a new badge once her official one had been turned over to headquarters.

"Are you 'comfortable' with what's going on, then?" she asked. "With what killed Penny Martinez? People are dying, Edgar, and there aren't enough of us fighting. We need whatever advantage we can snag. This isn't a random crime we're talking about. It's evil. Pure and simple."

"You think I don't know that?"

"I think you're scared," she said.

"Damn right I am." He hunched his shoulders and trudged on. She followed, silent. What could she say to that?

After a moment, he slowed his pace, then waited for her to step in beside him. "So. Did you kill him?"

Alexis recognized the words as a peace offering. He was asking her if Leena had gotten her mojo on again and looked at her magical mystery map. The one that could pinpoint Tori's killer.

"She tried. Spent the whole day sleeping then came over with all her stuff right before you called me. But she was too spent. She couldn't see a thing." Alexis tried to keep the disappointment out of her voice, but it was hard. She'd found satisfaction in hunting vampires, whether they had anything to do with Tori or not. They were vile, destructive, murderous creatures, and the more she could take out the better. But that didn't change her soul-deep obsession with finding her sister's killer. She wanted him dead. And then she wanted to dance in his dust and spit on his memory.

"It's still amazing," Edgar said, gently touching her

sleeve. "She actually managed to come up with a spell that lets you see if the son-of-a-bitch is still kicking."

"I know," Alexis agreed. "Believe me, I don't mean to sound disappointed or ungrateful. I just wish—"

"That she could control it at will? That kind of stuff's gotta be exhausting. It's amazing to me that she can do it at all."

"Definitely mind-blowing."

"And even if she'd been all primed and energized, there was no guarantee that she'd see the spark, right? Doesn't it only fire up if Tori's killer is actually on the hunt?"

Alexis nodded. "Ironic, huh? I can see that he's out there, but unless I manage to move fast, he'll kill some other victim before I can avenge Tori."

It had taken Leena months to figure out how to create the map, and even now it wasn't perfect. As Edgar had said, it only displayed the killer's location when he was actually on the hunt. To Alexis's mind, that was a major downside, as evidenced by what happened last night. Two vampires, and no idea which one was her bad guy. Not that she was complaining—she was patient as hell. More than that, she was willing to do whatever was necessary to find Tori's killer. She'd proven that much when Leena had told her she'd need her help to make the map functional.

"My help?" Alexis had asked. "You mean you need my blood again?"

"I need more than that. I need a promise."

"A promise?"

"All magic has a price, especially magic that's tied to vengeance. You want to find a killer, so the price is death."

Alexis's heart had skipped a beat. "I don't understand."

"You have to promise to kill the vampire if you find him."

"Well, yeah. That's the point."

"And if you don't, then you have to promise to die in his place."

"Like suicide?"

"You make a blood promise," Leena had explained. "You break the promise, the magic takes your life. Are you willing to do that?"

"I already told you." She hadn't hesitated, even for a second. "I find him, and that vampire is dust." She held out her arm. "Do whatever you need."

Leena had taken the blood she'd needed from Alexis's wrist, and now she absently rubbed the small, diamond-shaped scar.

"You *will* catch him," Edgar said. He didn't know how the map worked, or what Alexis had done to fuel it. "What you're doing—devoting your life to hunting these things—it's amazing. And it's not like you're going to be openly rewarded. No one's going to throw you a parade. You'll be lucky if they don't call you crazy. Trust me, I know about the crazy part. But I also know that you're fighting the good fight."

"Thanks." She shot him a smile. "Knowing you're here to hold my hand through the rough spots made the move a lot easier."

"I got your back, kid."

"I know," she said, and she meant it. Leena was her friend, her adviser, her most valuable resource. But Edgar had become her rock.

"Thin crowd," Edgar said as they crested a small hill.

Alexis frowned; Edgar was right. Usually murder scenes drew the lookey-loos. "The bad weather, maybe.

And we're a bit off the beaten path." Still, with police band radios being all the rage, the remote location of a crime usually didn't keep the crowds away.

She easily made her way to the yellow tape with Edgar at her side. Once there, she focused on the drama playing out in front of her. It was a murder mystery, and right away she could identify the key players, although she had to admit that they were playing their roles in an unfamiliar way.

The man she thought was the medical examiner, for example, did nothing other than press his hand to the victim's forehead. No inspection of the body. No thermometer to detect the core temperature. Just that single touch.

It was weird.

She eased left, following the tape until her line of sight shifted and she got a view of the vic. Penny Martinez. Female, twenty-eight years old, just like she'd heard. And right there in plain sight, Alexis could see the vicious neck wound.

"Like hell this case doesn't fit the task force parameters," Edgar said.

"Damn sure fits ours," Alexis agreed. She took hold of the crime scene tape, lifted it, and slid under, ignoring Edgar's muttered curse as he followed. As she'd expected, one of the uniformed officers scurried over to them. She flashed her counterfeit badge, forestalling his prattle. "FBI. This crime scene is part of an ongoing investigation."

"I'm sorry, ma'am, but—"

"It's okay, Officer." Another man approached, Hollywood-handsome in a suit that was only slightly rumpled. He extended his hand; when she ignored it, he offered it to Edgar. "Severin Tucker," he said. "Home-land Security."

"Detective Edgar Garvey, and I think we've got a little problem here. This case is part of a joint task force between the FBI and local law enforcement."

"This case is outside the FBI's jurisdiction."

"I'm afraid that we're going to have to agree to dis-agree on that," Alexis said. She marched past him toward the body. "You want to tell your man there to get his hands off my vic. You people never heard of preserving the scene?"

Tucker didn't say anything. She saw him glance at an-other man—this one taller, with broad shoulders and dark hair and a scar marring his right cheek. The man nodded, and Tucker seemed to relax. "He's one of our forensics experts," he said, nodding at the man fondling the body. "I assure you, we're doing everything possible for the victim."

Like hell, she thought, though she didn't say it. She just frowned and kept on walking, certain that any sec-ond someone was going to take her by the elbow and lead her forcibly away.

Fortunately, there wasn't any trouble. She reached the body, glanced down, and got a closer look at the violent puncture on the female's neck. The supposed forensics expert was still crouched over the body, his hands on the victim, and despite the fact that Alexis was both cu-rious about what he was doing and irritated that he was manhandling a victim's body, right then she had her own problems.

She glanced around, checking to see how much atten-tion they were paying to her. But Edgar—bless him—had Tucker wrapped up in deep conversation, and the rest of the officers were giving her a wide berth. With luck, she'd have a few minutes to maneuver.

Slowly, easily, she dropped into a squat, hoping she presented the appearance of a woman who wanted a closer look at the body. She pressed a hand to the ground as if balancing herself. What she was really doing was digging her fingers into the ground to collect the dirt she needed for Leena.

The witch's first project when they'd arrived in Los Angeles was to find vampires for Alexis to hunt. "Can't you just look into a crystal ball and find them?" Alexis had asked. "Then we'll go to the cemetery or the spooky mansion and dust them during the daylight?"

Leena had responded with a massive eye roll. "First, *we* has to be *you*." She tapped her leg and shrugged. "I wish I could be in the field, but I'd be dead within a minute. Second, vampires aren't equipped with OnStar. I can't just flip a switch and have their locations show up on Google Earth. It's more complicated than that."

So while Alexis had focused on training and getting into the best shape of her life, Leena had hooked up with some of her sources in the psychic-witch-new-age fringe. It had taken a few weeks, but eventually Leena had found a way. "Everything has an aura, right?"

Alexis shrugged. Until recently, something so very woo-woo would have prompted her to roll her eyes. Now she was willing to believe.

"So all we need to do is track the vamp's aura."

"How?"

"By accessing some of the vamp's energy."

"Again I ask: How?"

"I've been thinking about that," Leena said. "It's not the perfect solution, but the simple fact is that a vamp is going to leave aural residue on and around his victim."

Alexis's stomach twisted. "So you're saying I can hunt them after the fact."

"Like I said, not the perfect solution."

"No, it's not." She drew a deep breath. "But it's better than nothing. At least I can start by going after the vamps we know have murdered humans. Hunt them, kill them, take them out of the equation."

The dirt held that auric residue, and once Alexis had a handful, she stood up and casually dropped it into her pocket.

Time to get out of here.

She turned to find Edgar and realized he wasn't where she'd anticipated. Frowning, she glanced over the scene, but stopped when she saw a man in the distance. He was standing by himself in a copse of trees, well past the crime scene. His face was half in the shadows cast by the bright lights that Homeland had set up. It was an attractive face, with classic lines highlighted by a hint of stubble, as if he couldn't be bothered to shave. But it wasn't his looks that caught her attention—it was his eyes. She couldn't make out the color, not from such a distance, but she had the impression that when she saw them up close she'd learn that they were slate gray, as hard and unyielding as a rock.

She stared—and realized that she'd stopped breathing because seeing him was like looking in a mirror. Her own emotions reflected right back at her. Frustration. Hate. Regret.

And a burning need to get revenge against the worthless subhuman who'd done this to an innocent girl.

CHAPTER NINE

Her.

Serge looked across the field into the eyes of the woman from the alley, and everything he was feeling—rage, hunger, regret—was reflected right back at him. She'd come for the same reason that he had—because a rogue vampire had escaped, wounded and hungry and looking to feed.

She blamed herself just as Serge did, and the anger and frustration clung to her body like perfume. He breathed it in, welcoming its power and taking selfish comfort in the feeling that, for this singular moment in time, he wasn't alone. Because right then they both sought the same thing: Mitre's head on a goddamn platter.

And it *was* Mitre who'd snuffed the life from poor Penny Martinez. Serge had caught the scent the moment he'd arrived. Slightly putrid with an undercurrent of copper, like blood left to rot in a drain. It twisted on the wind, kicked up by the shoes of the PEC agents who were stomping all over the scene. Faint because of the rain, not even strong enough for a vampire to catch. But Serge was more than that now. His senses were keener. His body more finely tuned.

The woman had wounded Mitre, and he'd raced away searching for food. And because Serge had been too damn slow, a girl now lay unseeing on the cold, hard ground, surrounded by agents of the PEC, all trying to find a clue to her killer.

Damn it, damn it, god-fucking-*dammit*.

A slow, dangerous anger bubbled up inside him, and he clenched his fists, his nails cutting so hard into his own palms he drew blood. He needed to leave—to track Mitre's scent before he decided to attack another human. But once again the woman had stalled his departure, and though she had turned her attention to the body, Serge couldn't rip his away from her.

He stepped back into the shadows cast by the copse of trees and watched as she knelt by PEC agent Ryan Doyle. Only a few humans knew of the PEC's existence, and in the United States, it was neatly hidden within Homeland Security.

Serge knew that Doyle hadn't been randomly assigned to the case; he'd been called in because of his unique skills as a percipient daemon. As Serge watched from a distance, the agent pressed his hands to the girl's forehead, trying to pull out the last images she'd seen before dying. The last bursts of emotion.

Trying to see her killer.

The body was cold, though, and Serge wondered if Doyle would find anything. Time was the strongest enemy. It taunted everything it touched. Even the immortals, who should be able to wield time like a weapon, staggered beneath the weight of eternity.

Serge scowled, irritated by his self-pitying thoughts. If time was punishing him, it was only because he deserved it.

Behind Doyle, Luke paced. Lucius Dragos, the newly appointed vampiric liaison to the Alliance. The new governor of the Los Angeles territory. A man who had reluctantly assumed the mantle of power. A man who had once been Sergius's closest friend. Now, as far as Serge knew, Luke believed him to be dead. It was better that way. Though Luke's daemon lived close to the surface, he had finally learned control, unlike Serge who repeatedly succumbed. Now he had the beast to contend with, too. Luke hardly needed that weight added to the incredible burden of responsibility recently heaped upon him. No, Serge walked a new path, and he had to walk it alone.

Within the crime scene tape, Tucker approached the woman. As he did, Serge tensed. He knew what was coming, and he hated the thought that the agent was going to play with this woman's mind, erasing her thoughts and changing her memories. He knew it had to be done, but it seemed criminal to alter the will of a woman who'd proven to be so very strong.

There was, however, nothing Serge could do about it. Not unless he wanted to reveal himself to the group. And that was definitely not on tonight's agenda.

As Serge watched, Tucker and the woman walked back toward the small group of humans that had gathered behind the crime scene tape, joined as they went by a short man in a rumpled suit jacket. When Serge had first arrived, the crowd of humans had been massive. But Tucker and a couple of the vamps on the PEC staff had moved among the crowd, giving the humans the most massive of mind fucks and making them suddenly realize that there wasn't anything to see, and that they had at least a dozen other places they'd rather be and a handful of other things they'd rather be doing.

Now Tucker once again pulled his mumbo jumbo, this time including the woman and the rumpled man along with the few reporters and new onlookers who'd come by to see what the lights and action were all about. A few moments later the crowd, including the woman, dispersed. Serge swallowed the raw bitterness that rose in his throat, the knowledge that the woman had lost that rage and purpose sitting in Serge's gut like a heavy stone.

But he could go now. Somehow the fact that she'd left the scene released him as well.

He started to move away, then saw Doyle take his hands off the body and stand, a bit unsteadily. Serge hesitated, interested to see if the paradaemon had pulled any images from Penny Martinez's last moments alive.

"Agent?" That was from Luke, who'd moved to Doyle's side and was watching him closely.

Tucker took Doyle's arm. "Give the man some breathing room. He has to get his own head back."

Serge stood perfectly still, focusing on their words, his curiosity keeping him rooted to the spot.

"She was surprised," Doyle said, his voice strong, but singsong. Like someone under hypnosis. "And then she was afraid. It grew, that fear—it filled her." He closed his eyes, shook his head. "I pulled out too fast. Her emotions—they're still clinging to me." He shuddered. "Her thoughts were a jumble." His words were coming fast now. "*Shouldn't have come through the park. Was daylight, so it's gotta be safe. Shouldn't have come alone. Should have brought a Taser. Pepper spray. Run! Run!*"

"What about images?" Luke asked, his voice deliberately soothing. "Did you see the one who did this?"

In the trees, Serge leaned in, as if that would make the answer come faster.

"Had to go deeper." Doyle's voice was weak now, as

if he'd used up everything inside him. "Into the black. Had to go all the way inside."

"Dammit, Luke," Tucker said. "He hasn't fed in days. Let me take him to Orlando's and we can do this back at the office."

Orlando's was a soul-trading bar, and Doyle was a paradaemon who fed off human souls. His gift, Serge knew, drained him, leaving him a shell if he didn't feed. Luke knew that, too, but he only shook his head, silently denying Tucker's request. "Come on, Doyle. What did you see?"

Tucker's face hardened and he tightened his grip on his partner. But he didn't protest again.

Doyle drew in a deep breath. "Vampire," he said, which wasn't exactly the most astounding of revelations. "He was injured. There was pain all over his face. But even so, this wasn't just about the feed. He drew it out for hours. Tormented her. Lorded the kill over her, but didn't end it until the fear had quickened in her veins."

"His daemon," Tucker said.

A muscle in Doyle's cheek twitched. "No. I could see it on his face. It wasn't the daemon," Doyle said, his voice filled with loathing. "He just got off on it."

"But you saw him," Luke pressed.

"Yeah. Considering how much time they spent together, our Penny got a good look at him. A pointed chin. Heavy brows. Pale green eyes. I got him," he said, tapping his temple. He shot a hard look at Luke. "Now we just have to find him."

Serge felt his jaw tighten and he sniffed the air, searching for a particular scent. Doyle might have identified the killer, but Serge intended to find him first.

CHAPTER TEN

"Well, that was a waste of time," Edgar said as they slid back into his car, his words making Alexis sigh and shake her head even as she sent a text message to Leena: *Got the dirt. On my way home.*

"Not a waste," she said. "Penny Martinez was killed by a vampire."

He turned the key, firing the ignition as he managed a derisive snorting noise. "You know I love you, Alexis, but this was a nothing crime scene. Not related to the task force. Not related to vampires. I think you've hit that point where you see what you want to see."

"We really need to work on your conditioning," Alexis said.

"Hey, I passed the physical." He patted his belly, which was starting to get a little round. "Kicked my ass, but I passed."

"Not that kind of conditioning. This kind." She tapped her forehead. "It took me three solid months of training with Leena to be able to withstand their mind tricks—and she told me it took her almost two years."

"What the hell are you talking about?"

"They pulled a whammy on you. The vamps. Those agents. All those dudes who were supposedly working for Homeland Security." Possibly they really were working for Homeland. Hadn't Edgar once told her that his wife had believed that vampires had infiltrated all levels of the government? God, what an idea.

"A whammy?"

"Listen," she said, and pulled out her iPhone. She'd turned on the recorder as soon as they'd arrived at the scene, and now she scrolled backward until she reached the banter between her and Edgar as they'd walked toward the site. "Hang on." She fast-forwarded a bit, found the conversation she was looking for, and unplugged her headphone so that Edgar could hear, too.

"*Agent? Detective Garvey?*" It was Tucker's voice. Alexis kept her eyes on Edgar and saw the flicker of confusion cross his face.

"When did you record this?"

"Just keep listening."

"*I have something I need to say to the onlookers. I think you might be interested. Care to join me?*"

"*Sure.*" That was Alexis.

A few seconds of silence, then, "*Folks, we're going to have to ask you to leave now. Obviously there's nothing going on here, as you can all plainly see. Nothing to remember, nothing to think about. You came because you heard about a crime scene, but it turned out to be nothing even remotely interesting. So dull, in fact, that you're going to delete any photographs or videos you might have taken, or expose the film if you're using a traditional camera. Head on out now. Thanks so much.*"

The speaker emitted a staticky shuffling noise as the crowd moved away. Beside her, Edgar said, "What—"

"Just wait. There's a little bit more."

"*That was meant for the two of you as well, of course,*" Tucker said.

"*For us?*" Edgar asked.

"*There's nothing of interest to either the FBI or the LAPD. This case isn't within your jurisdiction. The position of the body hides the other injuries, but there's more than just a neck wound. This is related to a terrorist threat we've been following, and of course we appreciate your discretion.*"

"*Discretion,*" Edgar said. "*Of course.*"

"*You understand, too, Agent—?*"

"*I do. Yes. Discretion is clearly key.*"

"*I'm glad we understand each other. Obviously I can't go into the details, but you need to walk away. Just forget. But be confident that you're not walking away from one of your victims. She's not yours, and we'll do everything we can to catch her killer.*"

They'd reached her house, and Edgar pulled haphazardly into her driveway, almost slamming into Leena's car, which was parked in front of the closed garage door. "I don't remember," he said, turning off the engine and killing the headlights. "Obviously we had the conversation, but I don't remember a word of it." He looked at Alexis, and there was both fear and confusion in his eyes.

"It'll be fine," she promised. "But let's get inside where we can talk. Besides, I want to get Leena started on this," she added, with a pat to her pocket. A nonsensical gesture from Edgar's perspective, since Alexis could tell by looking at him that he didn't remember her taking the dirt.

He followed her toward the house, and the door flew open as they approached. "Was it the one that got away?" Leena asked. "Do you know?"

"No way to tell." Alexis grimaced, then looked hopefully at her friend. "Did you try again? Too see if Tori's killer is still out there?"

"I tried. Got nothing. Either I'm too tired, you actually killed the bastard, or he's not on the hunt right now."

"Wait," Edgar said as he followed Alexis past Leena and into the house. "Back up a second. You're not bullshitting me with that recording?"

"You're surprised? Come on, Edgar, isn't that part of all the movies? How vampires can control a human's thoughts?"

Leena shot a glance between the two of them. "What happened?"

"Some vamp agent put the whammy on Edgar. Me, too. Or at least he thinks he did."

Leena focused her attention on the detective. "Guess I'm going to have to teach you how to block, too."

"So you're saying that Penny Martinez really was killed by a vampire?"

"Oh, yeah," Alexis said. "We just don't know which one." She reached into her pocket and pulled out a handful of dirt, then deposited it in a small glass bowl that sat on her coffee table. "But at least we can track it."

Beside her, Edgar pressed his fingertips to his temple. "Shit. Shit, shit, *shit*."

Alexis caught Leena's eye, but she only shrugged. No help there. She took Edgar's arm and eased him toward the couch. "This doesn't change anything. You knew they were vile. You knew they were clever."

"Why didn't you tell me before that they could do that?"

"I didn't think about it. I guess I figured you already knew. I'm the one who was late to the party, remember? You and Leena have known about vamps for ages."

Edgar made a *hmmph* sound. "Didn't know about this. Shit."

"Don't feel bad," she said. "That's the way it works, you know? But we're fighting back. You're still with me, right?"

He took a deep breath and rolled his shoulders, then cracked his neck. "Yeah, kid. I've got your back."

Alexis shifted her attention to Leena. "Are you up for a tracking spell, or did trying to find Tori's killer wipe you out?"

"I can do it."

"You sure?" Now that they'd moved to the better light of the living room, Alexis could see how pale Leena looked and how bloodshot her eyes were. "Another headache?"

"Threatening," Leena said. "But it hasn't burst out yet."

"Maybe you shouldn't track him," Alexis said, hating the fact that even as she spoke she was hoping Leena would disagree. She didn't want her friend to suffer another migraine, but at the same time she was itching to go back on the hunt. She no longer cared if the vamp that killed Penny Martinez was the same one she let get away. He was on her radar now. He was *hers,* and she was going to take him down.

"She can track him even if he's not hunting?" Edgar asked.

"Right. So long as we have the dirt. It's like a mystical thread. A bit of his aura is with us, and then we follow the thread to where the vampire himself is."

"Not a bad explanation," Leena agreed. "And because there's a physical—or metaphysical—connection, it doesn't sap my strength."

"Let's get to it," Alexis said. "Penny may have just been an appetizer."

Nodding, Leena took the bowl with the dirt to the kitchen, where she'd stored jars and bottles of the various herbs and other ingredients she used for her spells. As Alexis and Edgar sat on stools at the granite-topped kitchen island, Leena went to work mixing the dirt with various ingredients and muttering a series of words that, as she'd explained, were chosen to pull out and harness the powers of the earth.

Finally, she closed her eyes and with arms extended held the dirt out in her hands. She'd formed it into a small ball, and now it glowed with a slightly silver tint. After a moment, the glow faded. Leena opened her eyes and handed the ball to Alexis. "Can you tell where he is?"

Alexis shifted the ball in her hand so that she could better examine its smooth surface in the light. The crust on the dirt felt like aluminum foil, with dark spidery lines crisscrossed like veins. The only imperfection was a red pinpoint dot. "At the beach," Alexis said, looking up at Leena. The dark lines formed a map, and the red dot showed the vampire's location. Unfortunately, the map on the ball didn't have street names, just thick and thin lines representing streets, highways, the coast, and other landmarks. "Pass me the map book and let's see if we can't narrow it down."

Leena opened the junk drawer on her side of the island, pulled out the thick Thomas Guide of the area, then flipped pages until she found a map with the same curvature of coastline that showed on the ball. Alexis peered over her shoulder. "Venice Beach," she said, then slid off the bar stool.

Edgar frowned. "That's it? How the hell are you supposed to find him? Venice is small, but it's not that small."

"Alexis will hold on to the ball. When she's getting close, it will begin to warm. And be careful," Leena added. "This will find him wherever he is. And since we know he's fed, he may be with others in a nest by now. Promise me you won't take chances."

"I'm coming with you," Edgar said.

Alexis looked at him critically. "Are you sure?" They'd talked about him acting as her backup, but they'd agreed he needed to get into better shape before fighting regularly at her side.

"She mentions nest, I think ambush. Yeah, I'm sure. You need another set of eyes. Besides, I can handle myself with a crossbow."

She raised her eyebrows. "You can?"

He shrugged. "How hard can it be?"

"Let's see if we can't find you something a little more your speed." She wasn't about to argue against him coming—he was right; she could use the backup. But no way was she giving him an unfamiliar weapon. Fortunately, she had just the thing for a newbie vampire hunter.

While Leena waited upstairs, she and Edgar headed into her Batcave.

"Now, *this* is what I'm talking about," Edgar said, walking to the wall of weapons and taking a crossbow off its hook. He lifted it, aimed at the target on the far side of the room, and released the arrow. He missed by about eighteen inches.

"Try this," Alexis said. She handed him a Glock that had been converted to fire wooden bullets by a gunsmith she knew in Pomona. He aimed, fired, and nailed the bull's-eye. "Not as sexy," Alexis said with a wry smile. "But it has a better chance of keeping you alive."

She picked up the crossbow. It was her kind of weapon. In addition, she slipped on her leather jacket, the one that had the spring-loaded stakes in the sleeves. She slid a third stake into the cuff of her boot.

"You're really taking that thing out?" Edgar asked, eyeing the crossbow. "Not exactly inconspicuous."

She shrugged. He was right, but it was after midnight, and she'd killed her first vampire with that crossbow. Even though it had failed her in the alley, she still considered it her good-luck charm.

Armed, they headed out. They were in the driveway saying good-bye to Leena, when Edgar got paged. He glanced at the screen, frowned, and called in. A second later he clicked his phone shut and shook his head. "A homicide. I have to go in."

"Not one of mine?" Alexis asked.

"Shooting. Domestic dispute. As human as it comes, but I've got to get over there."

"I'll call you later and tell you how it went at the beach."

She saw the alarm fire in his eyes. "You're still going?"

"Um, yeah. It's not like I haven't done this by myself before."

"Yeah, but it's like Russian roulette. How many times can you spin that chamber and not end up dead? Hell, you almost lost the bet when you met those two in the alley."

"I'll be fine. You have to go because someone died, and you're going to stand for the victim. I get that. I respect it. But I'm doing the same thing."

"That's a fucked-up way of looking at it, Alexis. I'm walking into a crime scene. You could be walking into a slaughter. Wait for me. We'll go together."

"Edgar . . ."

"Just do this for me. I don't want you to end up dead."

"Fine. Okay, fine."

He looked at her as if he could read her mind. She pasted on an innocent smile. After a second, Edgar sighed and nodded. "All right. I'm out of here. I'm calling you later."

"I know."

Another nod, firmer this time, as if he was working hard to convince himself. Then he slid behind the wheel of his car, started the engine, and zipped away.

Alexis shot a quick glance at Leena, then marched down the driveway to where she'd left the Ducati.

"I thought you said you weren't going," Leena said.

"You believed me?"

Her friend scowled, but didn't protest. "Just be careful, okay? If this does turn out to be the vamp that got away, he's going to be pissed as hell when he sees you. A pissed vampire is a very bad thing."

"I know." For the briefest moment she considered staying, but there weren't that many opportunities for her to track a vampire. And how many people would die if she didn't go? Tonight, tomorrow, the next night? She had a chance to dust one right now, and she was damn well going to take it.

◆

CeeCee Jane Gantz dropped her backpack in the sand and rummaged through it as her stomach growled.

When she'd left home a week ago, she'd taken a loaf of bread and a jar of Jif peanut butter with her. Smooth, not chunky, because who wants little pieces of peanuts all jammed up into your teeth?

She'd also taken $175 and one of her stepfather's credit cards. The cash had gone fast. A bus ticket from Barstow. A jacket from Goodwill once she'd realized how cold sleeping on the beach could be. She'd always thought beaches were supposed to be balmy and sunny, but the water around Los Angeles turned her toes blue, and once the sun set, the air was so cold it made goose pimples rise on her skin.

Not that she was complaining. Goose pimples were a hell of a lot better than bruises.

She'd bought socks and tennis shoes, too, along with another pair of jeans. And all of that had cut into her savings. Then there'd been food. Early on, she'd been stupid. She'd bought food from vendors on the Santa Monica Pier, because how could she not? She was *there*. Finally there at the end of the world, without her bastard of a stepfather or her crackhead of a mother. It was paradise, and she couldn't pass up the corn dogs any more than she could walk past the carousel and not ride on it once. Even if she was the only rider over the age of six.

The cash had run out yesterday, and she'd sucked it up and used the credit card at an ATM, hoping Burt hadn't changed the PIN. He hadn't—but the account was maxed out, so she'd walked away with nothing but disappointment and a gnawing in her stomach that had nothing to do with nerves and everything to do with food.

The nerves part started later. Because when you have

no money and nothing to do and the only way to entertain yourself is to sit on the beach and watch the world go by, you have a lot of time to think. And what CeeCee thought about was movies. How in the movies the cops could always find you when you used a credit card.

Burt didn't like the cops, and Burt didn't like her.

But Burt did like Burt. And he really didn't like being screwed.

Which meant she'd probably made a big mistake trying to use that credit card.

She'd been in Santa Monica on the Third Street Promenade at the time, and as soon as she'd realized what a complete idiot she'd been she'd headed to the beach and started walking south. She'd stopped in Venice, tired and hungry, and not able to see much once the sun had gone down.

Now she was parked on a towel someone had left on the beach—a little karmic gift—pawing through her few belongings and wishing that the towel person had left a cooler of food and drinks as well.

She dumped the backpack out, and her in-depth search was rewarded. A restaurant packet of Saltine crackers. Two of them all snug inside a little plastic balloon.

It was practically a gourmet meal.

She savored it, nibbling at the corner of the cracker, eating slowly, trying not to think about the fact that tomorrow she'd have to either steal food or figure out a way to earn money. She wasn't naïve—she knew a sixteen-year-old girl had options. But Burt had taken that for free, and there was no way she was ever giving it up again.

Just thinking of him made her nervous, and she swiveled around, fearing he'd tracked the credit card. That he'd gotten in the truck and driven from Barstow. That he'd found her and was coming at her, unbuckling his belt as he walked. Pulling it from the loops. Twisting it in his hand.

No.

She was safe now. Sure, she was hungry, but the trash cans on the pier were full of half-finished morsels. And she had a towel now, and there were showers on the beach. Tomorrow she'd find a job waiting tables. Or washing cars. Or something. She didn't care what because anything she did was better than where she'd been.

The moon wasn't full, but it was still big in the sky, and the light it cast reflected off the sand, making the world seem like something out of one of those old black-and-white movies. The shadows seemed to move around her, but CeeCee just frowned and told herself she was being stupid. Tired. Seeing things on the beach the way little kids see monsters in closets.

Then the shadow moved again.

What now?

She shifted her position, getting into a squat so that she could take off running if she had to. She rolled up the towel and shoved it into her backpack. Then she hiked the pack up on her shoulder and sat there, muscles tensed, body ready.

And she felt like a complete and total idiot.

There wasn't anything out there. She was just being paranoid. Burt was a dick, that was for damn sure. But there were miles and miles of beach in Los Angeles, and why would he think to look for her on the beach anyway?

She started to relax—and that's when she saw the

flicker again. Nothing big. Just a hint of motion. But enough to make her certain that she wasn't imagining it.

And that's when she realized that she really and truly was a complete and total idiot. Burt might be the only sadistic asshole at 414 Rosedale Road, but in Los Angeles there were plenty of them. They went out at night, and they preyed on stupid teenagers who slept on the beach.

CHAPTER ELEVEN

The sea air hung wet and chilly, as if a blanket had been tossed over the previously sunbaked sand.

Alexis hurried down the Venice Beach bike path, vacant at this time of night. Charming cottages rose up to her left, illuminated only by pale moonlight and the occasional electric lamplight shining through a window. She noticed it all, but she wasn't really taking it in. All her attention was focused on finding the vampire.

Is he on the hunt right now? Has he found a new victim?

The moonlight provided some illumination, and she took in her surroundings as she walked. *Dammit, where is he?* The ball's inability to pinpoint the bastard's location frustrated her, but the warmth it generated let her know that at least she was close.

Maybe he's sated. Maybe draining Penny Martinez filled the bastard up.

On her right, sand sparkled in the moonlight, stretching out toward an infinity of ocean, the froth on the rolling waves glistening white in the moonlight.

She studied her surroundings, trying to intuit where a vampire would go. Surely not over there along that empty expanse of sand. Much more likely it was hiding in the narrow walkways and alleys that cut through the quaint beachside neighborhood. Possibly trolling through restaurant parking lots, looking behind dumpsters for new prey. The homeless. The runaways.

She thought of Tori and quickened her pace, heading toward the street. She'd do a pass up and down the alleys, listening for movement and hopefully catching a vampire instead of just a stray cat or two. A high-pitched scream cut the night. She froze, head cocked, trying to judge the direction of the sound.

Goddammit, it is *coming from the beach.*

She turned fast and started sprinting toward the lingering tones of the scream, the sound still vibrating in the thick night air. It had sounded like a girl, and Alexis hoped to hell she was okay, and at the same time she wished the girl would scream again to help Alexis locate her.

A movement across the sand caught her attention, and she raced toward it. She wasn't nervous—she'd taken down vamps before, not to mention mobsters and serial killers. But she *was* pissed, and the emotion curled inside her, warm and welcome. Fueling her muscles and ramping up her strength.

The beach was mostly flat, but there was a rise approaching a drainage ditch. She hauled ass up the incline, and saw a burly male with a ripped black T-shirt, tight jeans, and bushy eyebrows. *That's him. The one that got away. The one whose heart I missed. Penny Martinez's blood is on my hands. And now another girl struggles in his arms.*

Alexis didn't waste any time sizing up the details. She raised her crossbow and aimed at the vamp's back. *Steady. Steady.*

Zing!

The stake went flying—which did absolutely no good

whatsoever since the instant it was released, the vampire rolled over, taking the girl with him. The stake landed harmlessly in the sand. Goddammit all to hell . . .

The vampire ripped a chunk out of the girl's neck, then leaped up, his mouth dripping with blood, his eyes burning with hatred.

"You again," he snarled as the girl on the ground moaned, blood pouring out of her, staining the sand and looking like a pool of oil in the dim light of the night. "You damn little *bitch*."

Shit, she'd made it worse. For the girl, and for herself.

Maybe so, but now was hardly the time to kick herself about it. Especially since the vampire was launching himself right at her.

The brunt of his weight got her in the shoulder, and she toppled over from the force of his blow. She landed sprawled out on the sand, the vampire half on her and leaning in. His weight pinned down one arm, but the one holding a stake was free. No way could she stake his heart from the back, but she could hurt him, and she thrust the stake down hard at the awkward angle, managing to pierce his jacket and embed it in his flesh.

He reared up in agony and she snagged the moment, immediately shifting her weight to free her other arm—and the spring-loaded stake hidden in the jacket sleeve. She flexed, the motion sending the stake flying forward, and it slammed straight into his heart.

He fell backward, howling, and Alexis scrambled to her feet. Something wasn't right, but her mind wasn't telling her what. All she knew was that she had to get to the girl and get them both the hell out of there.

She plowed forward, running as fast as the sand would let her, then dropped to her knees at the girl's side. It was bad—really bad. The girl's face was gaunt, and it seemed to glow white in the moonlight.

"I'm going to get you out of here," Alexis said, and almost cried when she saw the girl's slow blink in reply. Her lips parted. A blood bubble formed at her mouth. "Hush," Alexis said. "Don't try to talk."

"Rr . . . ," the girl whispered.

"Please." Alexis blinked back tears, her mind full of this girl, of her sister. "Please, don't talk. Just hang on."

"Rr—n."

Alexis frowned . . . and then understood. *Run.* The girl was telling her to run, and Alexis didn't question it. She just bolted right over the girl, away from the vampire who had to be behind her. *He hadn't turned to dust. I should have realized! If he'd really been dead, he would have turned to dust!*

As she ran, she scrambled to get her crossbow freed up and ready. Fire the thing, nail the creature, and then get back to help the girl. She twisted around, getting the bow positioned, ready to release the trigger, then *blam*—his body impacted hers.

He ripped the crossbow out of her hands and tossed it aside, at the same time slamming her onto the ground. His palms pinned her shoulders, his large body straddled her, and his strength was unmatchable. She'd had a chance earlier when she'd had the element of surprise and the benefit of leverage. But now—now she had nothing.

I'm sorry. She wanted to scream the words. To Tori. To the girl on the beach. To every single victim who'd died as she was about to die. But she couldn't. He had a hand on her throat now and was squeezing tight, making the world grow even darker.

A roar filled her ears, and Alexis realized it was the pounding drum of her own pulse, growing faster and faster along with her terror. The vampire curled his upper lip, revealing long, white fangs. "Bitch," he whispered. "I'm gonna suck you dry."

His scent enveloped her. Blood mixed obscenely with men's cologne. She struggled, but it was no use, and she knew it. This was how Tori had died.

And Alexis was about to follow right behind.

She tried to resign herself to that horrible reality, but it wouldn't compute. She couldn't die yet. Not like this. Not without having taken down the monster that murdered her sister.

She tried to fight back. Tried to dig for that miraculous burst of adrenaline that would shoot through her and let her save herself and kill the vampire. The big Hollywood finish—except it wasn't happening. And instead of the thrill of victory, she felt the horror of fangs piercing her throat.

And then—*smash!*—reality shifted again, and suddenly the weight was lifted, the monster gone. She raised her hand to her neck, felt the gash at her throat, the blood seeping through her fingers. She tried to roll over to see what was going on, but her body wasn't responding. *Shock,* she thought.

Through sheer force of will, she managed to twist her head until she saw her attacker rolling over and over with a dark figure. A man, but he moved remarkably fast and when he slammed the vampire back against a utility pole rising beside the drainage ditch, the reverberating sound was testament to his incredible strength.

The vampire she'd come to kill howled and fought back, but the man showed no fear. He grabbed the vampire by his arms, lifted him, and tossed him like so much garbage. He landed with a *thud* above her line of sight, and even as the sound of the impact echoed, the man was rushing in that direction.

He paused for just a moment as he passed. Their eyes met, and she gasped.

It was the man from the crime scene. The one she'd noticed. The one who'd given her shivers. The mysterious man with the slate-gray eyes.

Who the hell was he?

♦

Her again. The woman. The one who'd captivated him as he stood on the roof. Who'd confused him as he'd watched the crime scene.

He supposed he shouldn't be surprised. Clearly, they were both chasing the same rogue.

For the briefest of moments, the thought that they were on the same path gave him pleasure, but he had no time to reflect on it. Instead, his thoughts were on Mitre. He'd pulled the bastard off her. He'd saved her. But inside himself, his own beast writhed with a fury fueled by hunger. Time to hunt, time to feed. *Time to kill.*

And, yes, time to save.

He launched himself at the vampire again, but this time the vamp was ready for him. He kicked up and out, catching Serge in the gut and sending him flying backward. Serge regrouped and rushed the vamp, who somersaulted away and landed on his feet, his face a mask of confusion and surprise as he caught sight of his attacker.

"Oh, shit, I know you," the vamp said, his voice filled with awe. "You're Sergius."

"And you're a fucking genius."

"You want her?" the vamp offered deferentially. "She's all yours, man."

Serge allowed a slow smile to creep across his face. "It's not her I want."

For a moment, Mitre looked confused. Then his eyes lit with understanding. He inched backward.

"Afraid?" Serge asked, knowing the answer was yes. "You should be."

He could see the rogue's eyes narrow in concentration as he started the process of transforming into mist so he could get the hell out of there.

"Not happening," Serge said, and leaped again. As expected, the rogue broke his concentration to shift to the side rather than transforming and taking Serge with him. Serge followed, then reached out and grabbed the back of Mitre's shirt. Within him, the daemon rumbled. Wanting to taunt and torture. Wanting to drag out the pain and revel in his victim's misfortune.

Serge hated that raw, dark part of himself. Hated the daemon that had to be appeased lest it become too powerful for him to fight. Most of all, he hated that deep, buried part of himself that enjoyed it, too. That got satisfaction out of knowing he had the power to make a killer suffer. That took delight in symbolically destroying what he himself used to be.

Now, though, he didn't have time for that perverse pleasure. "I'd like to play this out," he said, his voice low and dangerous. "A little cat and mouse. A little roughhousing. But I need to clean up your mess, so let's just get on with this thing."

"No. Please. I don't—"

But Serge didn't learn what the rogue didn't do. Time

was running out. He could smell the woman's pain, could sense the last vestiges of life draining from the teen. An infusion of vampire blood would heal the woman, but Serge was too low, too drained. If he didn't feed soon, the beast would burst free, and he would be no help at all to the females.

Do it. Do it now.

He reached out, intending only to hold the vamp steady. The only thing that could be considered good about his new self was that he could feed without leaving a mark, but he had to be able to latch on—a good grip, a moment to concentrate, and—

Wham, the guy lashed out and smacked him hard in the jaw. Serge stumbled back, and in that instant the vampire took a step to the side. Serge acted quickly, instinctively. He thrust out, and his fist plowed right through the vampire's sternum. "Now hold still," he snarled as he spread his fingers wide. He focused, his head tossed back by the power of the life force gushing into him.

At the end of his arm, the vampire howled in protest, but the strength had seeped out of him too fast to allow him to run, to flee, to do anything but shrivel down to a lifeless hull. A desiccated shell of a creature.

Serge yanked his arm back, his chest rising and falling as he gulped in air. Not because he needed to breathe, but because the rhythm of it was calming. It soothed the horror of what he had to do now to survive and calmed the daemon that was still itching for a fight.

The hole in the vampire's chest, though—dammit, that was going to raise some questions.

He knew that the PEC was baffled by the desiccated bodies that had turned up. The popular theory was that the mummified vampires had been infected. As far as Serge knew, there'd been no official inquiry into the possibility that they had been attacked instead.

But a hole in the gut suggested an attack. And that could raise unpleasant questions and turn a few too many eyes his way.

He shoved the worries from his head. No time for them now. He was pure vampire again, thanks to his victim's life force, and the females needed him. He hurried to the teenage girl's side. She'd lost almost all of her blood, and the scent of death clung to her, warm and sticky. Vampire blood could heal, but only if the human was not already on the verge of death. There was no saving this girl. No bringing her back from the brink, letting her grow up human and happy.

Goddammit all. First Penny Martinez and now this girl. And all because he'd fucked up and hadn't moved fast enough.

He pressed his hand against the teen's forehead, saw her eyelids flicker. "Don't . . . leave," she whispered, her voice so low and wretched that no human could have heard her.

"No," he promised. "I won't go. But I need to check on the woman. She tried to help you?"

"My fault," the girl said.

"No," Serge repeated. "His fault. And he's dead now." He cupped her cheek. "Hang on for me," he whispered, then slipped through the night toward the woman.

"You," she said, her voice low and full of pain but still strong. "I saw you."

"And I saw you. Here." He lifted his wrist to his mouth and bit deep, setting his blood to flow. "Drink."

She recoiled, her eyes going wide, her voice thick with revulsion. "You're a vampire?"

"Drink," he repeated. "My blood can heal you."

She shook her head, and Serge wasn't sure if it was in confusion or refusal. Was she really so repulsed by the idea that he was a vampire that she would let herself lie there in the dark, bleeding out? She wasn't on the verge of death, but without help it wouldn't be far off. And he'd be damned if he'd let her die. Not if he could help it.

"What's your name?"

She eyed him warily. "Alexis. Why?"

"I'm sorry, Alexis," he said, as he pressed his wrist against her mouth and held her tight. "But I'm damn well saving you. Whether you want me to or not."

♦

Alexis wanted to fight. Wanted to turn away and scream and do anything other than swallow his blood. But she had no choice. His wrist was right there, his wound at her mouth, his blood pouring into her.

More than that, she knew that this man—this vampire— was her best chance. As she was, no one would hear her scream for help. She couldn't die now—not like this.

And so she drank. Deep and long. And as she did, she realized she didn't want to stop. She could feel his strength flowing through her. His strength, and *him*.

He was inside her, filling her, warming her. She moaned as life poured back into her, as her mind conjured images of his hands upon her, touching and healing her.

She kept her mouth closed around his wrist and drank greedily, lost in a sensual haze.

"That's right," he said, his voice as smooth as melted chocolate. "You're going to be fine."

She realized he was about to pull away, and she clung tighter. She wanted more. Wanted *him*.

And then the reality of her thoughts crashed through her mind, and she called upon her restored strength to push away, suddenly itchy and uncomfortable and even a little bit afraid.

He leaned back on his heels, his eyes narrowed as he looked down at her, his brow furrowed as if he—a friggin' vampire—was looking for some sort of reassurance from her.

"The girl," she said, rolling over and intending to crawl toward the teen, but despite the strength she'd felt while drinking from him, her body was still sluggish. Apparently healing wasn't instantaneous. "Please. Don't—don't let her die." She clutched at him, desperate, her mind swirling wildly, images of Tori mixing with images of that poor girl on the beach. "I can't let— she has to be okay. Please. Please tell me she's okay."

She watched his eyes, but she saw nothing there. No compassion, no regret, no emotion at all. A horrible sob wrenched out of her, and she brought her fist to her mouth, all the horror and fear of the night bursting out with that one terrible sound.

She fought it back, because she had to know, and she couldn't ask if she couldn't find her voice. "She's dead," Alexis said. The words came out flat. Emotionless. "She's dead already."

If she hadn't been watching him, she might not have noticed the change. But she was, and so she saw it. One simple movement. A tightening of his jaw perhaps, but it made the muscle in his cheek twitch, giving him a determined expression. "She's not dead," he said, then tilted his head back and sniffed the air, as if confirming that statement. "Not yet." He stood up, and Alexis realized that she'd stopped breathing. "I'll take care of her."

She exhaled, her relief as sweet as wine. She managed a small smile. "A nice, helpful vampire?"

He gave her a hard look. "The moment you start believing that, you're dead."

A chill chased up her spine, and she watched as he hurried across the sand toward the girl. He bent to her, then picked her up, cradling her against his chest.

With the girl held tight in his arms, he looked like a protector. Like a savior.

She shuddered, two words filling her head: *Evil vampires.* That's what she'd believed since she'd learned the truth about Tori's death. It had been her mantra, her driving force. Vampires were vile. They killed. They tortured.

Hell, this vampire had practically told her she was right.

All true. All scary.

So why, then, when she looked at him, did she not believe a word of it?

CHAPTER TWELVE

Serge didn't compel Alexis to forget, but he did tell her that she ought to get someplace safe and sleep. He'd given her blood, but her body still needed time to heal.

He wasn't worried about her, though. Dawn was fast approaching, and she'd be safe enough. It was the teenager that troubled him, and he ran, the butterfly-like flutter of the girl's failing heart pushing him forward. Soon, she'd die in his arms, a young life snuffed out at the hands of a vampire. Lost, like so many others.

"I'll take care of her," Serge had promised the woman. But what did that mean?

Drain her to the brink and let her fade slowly into death?

A blessing, perhaps, that sweet eternity. But Serge was certain it wasn't what the woman expected.

Or take that same blood from her, and then open his own vein to the girl. Turn her into a vampire. A creature of the night. Subject her to the pain of the daemon, the pull of the darkness.

Was that what Alexis had hoped for her?

Serge knew it wasn't, and yet there was no other way. He couldn't bear to watch the light fade from this girl. Not when he could bring her back. He couldn't stand the thought that she would be buried in an anonymous grave somewhere. That would mean the rogue bastard that had attacked her had won.

In the end, it was pointless. The debate over what was right and what was wrong, what the girl deserved and what she would get. He knew what he was going to do.

He would save her, even if by saving her he was condemning her.

There was simply no other choice to be made.

◆

"The investigation into these human deaths is not an Alliance matter," Nostramo Bosch said. The director of the Division 6 violent crimes subdivision sat across from Luke in one of the conference rooms. Sara, a Division 6 prosecutor, sat beside Bosch, her placement suggesting that she was aligned with him.

Perhaps she was. Though Sara was Luke's wife and the love of his life, she knew her own mind, and didn't hesitate to tell Luke when she disagreed with him. So far, though, she'd said nothing of the kind.

"I'm not trying to control the investigation or usurp the agents' authority, either in Los Angeles or in any other jurisdiction. But I was recently named the governor of the Los Angeles territory, I make my home in Los Angeles, and I used to be the liaison between the Alliance and Division Six. I'm sure you understand why I'm interested in both these local human deaths and the similar attacks that have been reported across the country."

A few months ago, his concern wouldn't have been so broad. But he'd since been thrust into the role of Alliance chairman, and that made the entire shadow world his responsibility. Locally, there had been almost ten deaths in the last two months that they knew about, which unfortunately suggested that there were exponentially more that they didn't.

"I understand all of that," Bosch said. "My goal is to ensure you understand that you are not in charge of this investigation. You may make suggestions. You may make your opinions known." At this last, he looked at Sara. "But unless we learn that these murders were somehow politically motivated, the Alliance is here only as an observer. You do not give orders to the investigating agents or the prosecutorial team."

"Of course, Nostramo," Luke said, intentionally using the subdirector's first name. "I thought that was understood."

Bosch's eyes narrowed, and for a moment, the subtle scent of cinnamon filled the small room. "The same holds true for our investigation into the desiccated vampires."

Luke caught Sara's eyes and saw that her frown mirrored his own. "Investigation? I thought the desiccations were considered a medical matter."

Bosch's posture slackened, and he appeared tired and frustrated. It passed in an instant, his eyes sharpening after that brief moment of vulnerability. "The cause of death remains undetermined." His frown deepened. "We've also become aware that a number of vampires have gone missing," he said.

"Missing?" Luke repeated.

"It's possible that they simply left the Los Angeles area," Bosch said, "but the reports have come from friends who would presumably have been aware of any intention to relocate. Also, the vampires haven't resurfaced in other locations of which we're aware."

"You think they were staked," Sara said.

"I think it's a reasonable possibility."

"And you think they may be linked to the dead humans," Luke added.

Bosch shot him a sharp look. "Why do you say that?"

"Because you've raised it in this conversation."

"You're right, of course," the subdirector acknowledged. "We have no confirmation. Merely suspicions. But sometimes suspicions are enough. I raise the point now because I want to be clear: Division Six is currently dealing with several baffling matters. Your thoughts on any are appreciated. But your interference will not be tolerated." He stood. "For the record, I have no objection to your appointment to the Alliance table or to the governorship. But I will protect this division, and I won't allow it to become an investigative arm of the Alliance."

"That is not my intent," Luke said, also standing.

Bosch nodded, his expression tentative but relieved. "I'll leave you and Ms. Constantine, then. I'm sure you'll want to . . . debrief." The slightest of smiles touched his lips before he left the room, shutting the door behind him.

Luke lifted a brow as he looked at his wife. "Care to debrief, Ms. Constantine?" She was Mrs. Dragos now, but as a prosecutor, she continued to use her maiden name.

Sara smirked. "Cut him some slack. He respects you, but because you're here, it feels like the Alliance is all over division's business."

"His interests align fully with mine. I'm only interested in stopping a killer."

She rested her chin on her hand as she looked at him, her expression thoughtful. "What aren't you telling me?"

She really was too perceptive by half. "What makes you think I'm holding anything back?"

"Rogue vampires have killed humans since the beginning of time," she said. "There's nothing to suggest that the deaths are politically motivated." She looked at him, as if waiting for him to comment on that point. He stayed silent.

"You have other obligations now," she continued. "And while I love having my husband around, the other members of the Alliance are looking to you for direction. If you have any interest in keeping your position when the election comes up, you need to work on those relationships. You know that, right?"

"Of course," he said.

She nodded, as if his answer was a given. "But you're here, poking around division and these homicides. That means there's a big reason, and you haven't told me what. I want to know, Luke. I want to know what's going on with my husband."

"And I want to share with my wife," he said. "I'm not yet ready to share with Prosecutor Constantine."

For a moment, she said nothing, and Luke knew that she was weighing her options. Sara's belief in the judicial system ran deep, and it was against her nature to ignore information that might otherwise relate to a case. She'd loosened up, though, recognizing that shades of gray colored the world, particularly where shadowers were concerned. Still, Luke knew that it was a constant battle for her. He also knew that she would never betray his confidence. If she decided that she wanted to know his reasons, he knew she wouldn't use the information in the case.

"Tell me," she finally said.

"Sergius," he said. "I believe he's involved, though I'm not yet sure how."

As he'd expected, her eyes went wide, her face registering shock. "Why do you think so?"

"I caught his scent at the crime scene today."

"Are you sure?"

"That's a surprisingly difficult question to answer. I've known him all my life, both human and vampire. And though I haven't seen him for almost a year, I could never forget his scent." He frowned, remembering the subtle undertones he'd detected at the scene. "It was him—and yet it wasn't."

"I don't understand."

"Honestly, I don't either."

"Something about the curse?" Sara asked.

It was a possibility Luke hated to consider and yet couldn't ignore. Serge had willingly accepted the burden of a curse that transformed him into a monster. He'd known at the time that he would be undergoing a transformation, but he hadn't known that he would fall victim to a madman. Serge had become a monster, a slave, and when the curse was finally broken they'd all believed that he would become himself again. But what if they'd been wrong? What if that was why Serge had hidden himself away for so many months?

"Are you saying you believe he killed Penny Martinez?"

"No," Luke said, the speed of his answer underscoring his certainty. "The scent was on the air, but not on the girl. No, I don't believe he killed her—"

"But you are afraid that he's in trouble."

A wry smile touched Luke's lips. "Serge has been in trouble for a very long time."

She touched his arm softly, offering comfort. "And you've always been there to help him. This time, he's not letting you."

He pulled her close and kissed the top of her head, once again overwhelmed that he'd been lucky enough to find a woman who understood him so well.

"There is one thing you could do to help him," Sara said. "You're in a position now to pardon him."

"I've considered it," Luke admitted. "But I know him as well as I know myself, and he'd never forgive me if I did that without him agreeing first."

"We'll find him," Sara said. "And hopefully he'll let you help him."

"And if he doesn't?"

She offered Luke a small smile. "Then we'll hope that someone else does."

A knock at the conference room door interrupted them before Luke could respond, and the door opened to reveal Doyle. He'd looked wiped out when he'd left the crime scene, but he'd obviously fed since then. Exhaustion still lined his face, but he no longer seemed gaunt and weak, and when he strode into the room, a grim smile lit his bloodshot eyes.

"Been staring at a goddamn computer for the last six hours," he said to Sara. "But it was worth it." He slapped a photograph down on the table. "I found the bastard."

Much like the human world, which had passport and driver's license photos, the shadow world kept computerized images of as many shadowers as possible. Technically, every shadower was supposed to report for imaging every decade. Not all did, of course. For that matter, there were some vampires—turned by rogues and left to fend for themselves—who didn't even know the organized shadow world existed.

"Who is he?" Luke asked.

Doyle turned to face him, the contempt in his face obvious. They had a long history, and Luke kept hoping they were past it. Apparently they weren't. Not yet.

"When did you start working as a prosecutor?" Doyle asked.

"Dammit, Doyle," Sara said. "Leave your petty differences outside, okay? Now tell us. Who is he?"

"Mitre. Christopher Mitre. Turned about eighty years ago, so still a babe in the woods by vampire standards."

"Which is how he managed the attack during daylight," she said.

"Record?" Luke asked.

"Not even a blip," Doyle said, this time answering without hesitation.

"And you're sure of the ID?" Sara pressed.

"Not a doubt in my mind."

Sara nodded. "I'll get an arrest warrant right now." She stood. "Address?"

"Nothing solid yet. I've got Tucker trying to run him down," Doyle added, referring to his partner. "Most recent census shows him living in Stockholm."

"Apparently the cold didn't suit him," Luke said.

"I'll keep poking around. Learn what I can about the guy."

Sara stood up and started gathering her things. "What's the probability that Mitre's behind the other human deaths?" None of the other bodies had been found quickly enough for Doyle to ID the perp.

"No idea," Doyle said. "But I hope that's the case. If

we can lay them all on Mitre, then we're just looking at one sick fuck."

"If he's not the only one, then we may be dealing with an organized attack on humans," Sara said. She circled the conference table and squeezed Luke's hand before going to the door. She pulled it open, then let out a little gasp of surprise. Severin Tucker was on the other side of the door, his hand raised as if he was just about to knock.

"We got another dehydrated corpse," he said.

"That's a matter for Orion," Sara said, referring to the medical examiner for Division 6, Richard Erasmus Orion III. Lately, he'd been spending the bulk of his time searching for a medical cause behind the desiccations.

"This one's a matter for us," Tucker said, his eyes on Doyle. "Victim's our boy Mitre." He glanced around the room, looking at each of them, before letting his eyes rest on Luke. "And he's got a great big hole in his chest."

♦

Sara stifled a shiver as she looked down at the body. It looked like something you'd find in a museum, not on a beach. Dried out and shriveled, it gave good old King Tut a run for his money.

Tucker and Orion stood beside her. All three were watching Doyle, who had his hands on the mummified head. Luke, of course, had remained at Division 6. Unlike Sara, who'd been changed less than two years ago, he could no longer tolerate the sun.

Three uniformed agents milled about, keeping the humans away, and the forensics team sat on their equipment trunks, waiting for Doyle to finish.

Sara fought the urge to bite her nails, a habit she'd abandoned years ago. In front of her, Doyle pulled away from the body, then slowly stood. For a moment, his eyes were glassy as he came out of his trance. When they cleared, he looked at her and shook his head.

"Nothing. Mitre's thoughts are as dried out as his body."

Sara silently cursed. She'd been hoping they'd found the body in time to land a solid lead.

Beside her, Orion shifted, signaling for the forensics team to begin working the area around the body. "At least the state of the body deterred scavengers," he said. "Bugs prefer meat of the gooey, fleshy variety."

"Any thoughts?" Sara asked the doctor.

"Sure, but none that qualifies as a theory," Orion said. "We've been assuming that these desiccated bodies were the result of disease, correct?"

Sara nodded. They'd also tossed out the possibility of poisoning, but until they had toxicological evidence, the deaths weren't being investigated as homicides.

"With this body, nothing is different. Nothing, that is, except *that*," he said, pointing to the hole in Mitre's chest. "None of the other bodies showed any sign of injury. Other than being dried out, of course."

"So did Mitre have the same sickness and coincidentally piss someone off? Or did whoever punched through his rib cage infect him?"

"That's what I want to know," Orion said.

Beside them, Doyle looked thoughtful. Tucker, a human with a particularly handy knack for mind control, had slipped away and was now helping the uniformed officers convince unsuspecting humans that they had urgent business elsewhere and should forget all about what they'd seen on the beach today.

"It's the timing that interests me," Doyle said, and Sara nodded, because she'd been thinking along those lines, too.

"Penny Martinez," she said.

"Exactly." Doyle nodded toward the body. "That hole in his chest means that he was attacked. And the timing suggests the attack was in retribution for killing the Martinez girl."

Sara picked up the thread. "Looks like we may have somebody out there hunting rogues. Somebody who knows how to freeze-dry vamps."

Doyle and Orion glanced at each other, their expressions grim.

"Find me answers," Sara said. "And find me a murderer to go with them."

CHAPTER THIRTEEN

Serge paced in front of the obstructed windows, wishing it were night so that he could pull back the shutters and watch the Pacific crash against the shore. He was squatting in an abandoned beach house—if it could be called squatting when the house was worth several million dollars.

The place was owned by some celebrity who'd made a fortune on some television show that Serge had never bothered watching. The celebrity had moved to London, and had rented the place to a trust-fund kid who was going to one of the local colleges. Serge hadn't heard which one, and he didn't really care. The college kid, being a typical asshole male in his early twenties, had proceeded to trash the place. The put-upon real estate agent had kicked him and his buddies out, and the celebrity had told her not to bother relisting it. He'd return to the States at Christmas, and would move back in then.

In the meantime, the place was just sitting vacant, which was a huge waste. Which was why Serge had no guilt whatsoever about making use of it.

He'd used it twice before, and had taken the time to bypass the security system, have a key made, and otherwise arrange for all the comforts of home. He hadn't stayed long either time, though. The place was too posh, too plush. And he was feeling too damn raw. He'd chosen it only because it was a short walk down the beach from Luke's Malibu home. And though he'd never told Luke and Sara where he was squatting, their proximity made him feel like he was slowly inching back into the real world.

He'd come tonight, though, because he had the girl with him, and he didn't want her to awaken in a dank sewer or a dark basement. He'd told Alexis that he'd save her, and he wished that he knew whether he truly had. Instead, he was racked with doubts, wondering if he should have simply let her slip away.

But that hadn't been possible. He'd seen that innocent face, and he'd known that he couldn't let her go. He'd be her salvation—and he only hoped that he wasn't condemning her in the process.

Now she was lying still on the sofa. He'd drained her to the point of death, then urged her to drink deeply from him. She hadn't hesitated. Instead, she'd looked at him with wide, trusting eyes, and he'd felt like a hero. Maybe it was an illusion, but he'd liked the way it felt, especially after having been a monster for far too long.

With a soft moan, she stirred, and Serge hurried to her side. He knelt beside the couch, her hand enveloped in his.

She blinked, her eyes slowly adjusting, her face an absolute blank.

"It's okay," he said, afraid she'd scream in fear or curse him for changing her. Afraid, he realized, of what he'd done. "You're safe."

The blank expression remained, and he felt his gut twist in remorse. Then she slowly sat up and looked around. When her eyes came back to him, she smiled, and his fear fizzled away.

"You're the one," she said. "On the beach. I was dying, and you're the one who saved me."

"I am." He shifted position so he could look her straight in the eye. "Do you know how?"

"You turned me into a vampire." The words were flat. And then, to Serge's surprise and relief, the girl smiled again. "That's so freaking cool."

He laughed, feeling as though a weight had been lifted off his chest. The truth was, he wasn't entirely sure that she was a vampire. Certainly he wasn't. Not anymore. But he'd been one when he'd turned the girl—something he couldn't have accomplished if he'd been any other creature.

Hopefully that meant she was one, too.

He looked at her, noting the filthy hair she'd woven into a braid down her back, and the tiny bit of eyeliner that remained on her lids. "I'm glad you think it's cool," he said, "but there are things you need to know. Things you have to understand." She stared at him, as if waiting for him to spew forth wisdom, and the real weight of what he'd done hit him with full force. He'd changed her, a teenager. Old enough so that the change didn't violate the Covenant, but still young enough that she needed guidance.

"For one," he began, "you can't go home." Technically, she could. Since young vampires weren't sensitive to the sun, they could actually step back into their human lives, at least for a short time. They had to hide their hunger for blood, of course. And as time passed and they failed to age, it became necessary to move on, often faking death in order to gain the freedom to move fully into the shadow world. He wouldn't deny her the chance to say good-bye if she pressed the issue, but he knew from painful experience that it would be better to simply walk away.

"I don't have a home," she said flatly, and he caught the scent of both truth and strength. A runaway, he realized, and he wondered what it was that she'd been running from.

"You do," he said. "You have a home in my world."

She looked around the house. "Not bad."

"And not ours." He realized as he spoke that he would have to do something about that. He'd done this—changed her—without thinking. But he was in no position to take care of her. Hell, he was barely managing to take care of himself.

He pushed the thought away, forcing himself to focus on what she needed. "You're hungry?"

She nodded.

"That's the second thing you need to know. Feeding. We don't feed off humans." He went to the refrigerator and returned with one of the bags of blood he'd stocked there. "Not only is that just wrong, but it would also get the police looking in our direction. And trust me when I say that you want to live under the radar now."

"I get that," she said. "I've been under the radar for over a week."

She had spunk, this kid, and he smiled as he nodded. "I might as well tell you now so you don't find out from someone else, but there are some humans that it's legal to feed from. They're called licensed faunts. People who've found out we exist, and they trade their blood for either money or a taste of ours." He forced himself to speak dispassionately, keeping his tone level and steady despite the onslaught of vile memories brought on by the talk of such humans.

"We change them into vampires?" she asked.

He shook his head. The idea of one of the messed-up,

addicted faunts he'd encountered as a full-fledged vamp filled him with dread. "No. They just want a taste. It gives them a kick. Strength, healing power. That kind of thing."

She nodded, and he continued.

"But even though the faunts are willing, you don't want to go there. Drinking human blood from living flesh helps your daemon come out. And that's one part of you that you want to keep suppressed always. If you can."

"My daemon?"

She sounded genuinely clueless, and he searched her face, realizing that he'd been expecting it from the first moment he turned her. Usually the daemon hit and hit hard not long after a vampire made the transition.

"What do you mean by *'my daemon'*?"

He couldn't avoid telling her, even if it might scare her. "It lives in all humans. Dark and horrible. And it's ripped loose during the vampiric transformation."

Her mouth tightened with worry. "Ripped loose? Is mine out? How do I tell?"

"Hunger," he said, and saw the way she tossed down the bag of blood, scooting back from it as if it were poison. "No, not that kind. *Rabid* hunger. Not just for nourishment, but for pain. For other people's pain. And a wild fury that you can only control through the force of will."

"I'm strong," she said, lifting her chin with bravado. "I'm very, very strong."

"I know you are," he said, and he was being totally honest. He'd seen the strength in her. More than that, he'd tasted it. "But the daemon's much stronger than the will of most new vampires." She looked nervous, so he hurried on. "But don't worry. We've got that covered. The ancient vampires created a ritual called the Holding. And during the ritual, you call upon a spirit guide to help you battle back the daemon and keep it locked inside."

Her brows rose. "Sounds new-agey."

"Trust me. It's very old-agey."

She nodded and went back to sucking on the bag of blood, apparently unconcerned by the possibility of a growing malevolence inside her.

With luck, she would have reason to be unconcerned. Most vamps who lived in the shadow world had managed to lock their daemon deep inside. In some, like Luke, the daemon lived close to the surface, and it was a constant battle to keep it suppressed. In others, the daemon ran free, controlling the vampire instead of bending to the vampire's control. Those vampires were rogue. They killed humans. And now Serge killed them.

As for Serge, his daemon had lived close to the surface throughout all of his long years, and on more occasions than he liked to think about it had burst free, taking control, pulling Serge into a dark, hellish existence where only blood and death mattered. It had taken all of Serge's strength to battle it back, and the fact that he hadn't always succeeded tormented him, the humans who'd died at his hand haunting him.

Now his daemon cowered against the power of the beast that lived locked within him. A monster that would burst free if he didn't feed. He was paying the price for his earlier sins by hunting and killing rogues, and he calmed the beast in the process.

And Alexis and the girl? They were evidence. Tangible proof that he could do something good. That he could save instead of destroy.

He examined her face as the girl stood up, but there was no sign that her daemon might be rising. She'd emptied the blood bag neatly, not ravenously, and now she watched him, curiosity filling her features.

"Is there something wrong with me?"

"Why? Do you feel like something's wrong with you?"

She shook her head slowly. "No, but you're looking at me. Like . . . like I'm a bomb or something."

"No," he said. "There's nothing wrong with you. I'm just . . ." He trailed off, looking for the words, wondering how much of the truth to tell her. Maybe she was a vampire, and maybe she wasn't.

Yes, she might be like him, with a hunger that had to be satisfied in order to quell a ravenous beast. But if she was, there would be time to contend with that later. Right now, all that mattered was taking care of her. "I'm just very glad you're here," he said, realizing as he spoke how true his words were.

"Really?" She looked up at him, as if no one had ever been glad to be near her before. It had been a long time since Serge had felt his heart break a little, and he hadn't killed a human in a long time, either. But right then he wanted to head out into the world and drain every ounce of life from whatever humans had sucked the confidence from this girl.

"Really," he said firmly. "I'm Serge, by the way."

Her brows lifted, and she laughed. He grinned, waiting for her to stop, but the laughs just kept on coming. "Surge," she said. "Like a surge protector. And you are. A protector, I mean."

He rolled his eyes and decided he'd clarify his name later. "And who are you?"

"CeeCee," she said firmly. "It's short for Cecelia." She made a face. "My stepfather hates that nickname."

"He the one you're running from?"

She tilted her head. "How did you know I was running?"

"Lucky guess."

She hesitated, then shrugged. "Yeah. Him mostly. And my mom. But don't worry. Neither one of them's gonna come looking for me. I only just ran away, but I've been on my own for a long time."

"Well, CeeCee," he said, noting the way her eyes widened with pleasure at the name, "you're not on your own anymore."

Rough hands stroked her, skin against skin, the friction generating heat.

The heat reflected in those slate-gray eyes. Sergius. As the world had been fading around her, she'd heard someone say that his name was Sergius.

She moaned and reached for him, fingers outstretched. Seeking. Longing.

But she found only air, and the loss of him closed a fist tight around her, squeezing her heart, forcing out her breath.

"Please."

It was her own voice, but it was so full of need she barely recognized it.

She was moving then, her feet carrying her to some unknown destination. A thick mist swirled around her, and she squinted, calling out for him, her heart tripping when she saw flashes of him in the dense fog.

His hair, his eyes, a hint of tattoo, links of chain cir-

cling his bicep, flexing as he moved, the links strong enough to pull her toward him.

They were bound, she thought. Bound together.

"Please," she said again, and this time, he was there. Touching her. Stroking her.

And then, so softly she almost couldn't hear, he whispered her name.

Alexis . . .

Alexis . . .

She opened her eyes, disappointed to realize she was in her own bed and no one was whispering her name. With her head filled with fuzz, she sat up, trying to get her bearings as she pulled on a clean shirt. She remembered calling Leena and Edgar last night and telling them that everything was okay before she'd slid under the covers to sleep for a thousand hours. She hadn't told them the whole story, though she had told them that the vampire was dead. Of course, she'd neglected to mention the fact that she'd been injured, too, and that another vampire had stepped in to kill the one she was hunting. And, oh yeah, he'd made her suck his blood, too.

No, that would have been some serious over-sharing. Maybe she'd tell them both eventually. Then again, maybe she never would.

She shivered, but whether out of disgust or something far more complicated, she didn't know. The vampire had worked his way into her dreams, after all. More than that, he was in her blood.

She knew she should be disgusted by the thought. Disgusted at herself for letting such a creature into her mind, even if he'd forced his way in against her will.

Except, of course, it hadn't been entirely against her

will. He'd saved her life, and she damn well knew it. And he'd saved that poor teenager.

At least, he'd said he would. But had he? The vampire had saved her, so why would he lie about the girl?

Alexis didn't know. All she knew was that she didn't trust vamps, and this weird . . . *connection* . . . she felt for some mysterious vampire who'd shown up in the dark wasn't safe. She knew better. Vamps were hard, cold killers, and this one was probably a psychotic freak who knew how to play her to get what he wanted.

Damn.

With the curse still on her lips, she tugged on her boots, frustrated by her mind's fuzziness. She needed to check the scene. Make sure the girl was really gone. See what had become of the vampire she'd been chasing.

She hadn't been able to see the fight between him and Sergius, but she knew enough to know that if that bad vamp had been defeated, he was a pile of dust now.

Once she found the dust, she'd feel a lot better about what was going on. Not that she necessarily *would* find dust. When a vampire was staked, it left a pile of greenish gray dust—about enough to fill a shoe box. The trouble, of course, was that dust could be dispersed by the wind. And this vampire's dust might have been washed out with the tide or trampled by beachgoers. Still, she wouldn't feel right until she'd looked.

She hurried out of the house and found the motorcycle where she'd left it in the drive. She roared down San Vicente, then headed south on Ocean Avenue. Despite the weekend crowd of tourists and locals, she didn't have any trouble parking the bike near where she'd found the teenager. When she reached the scene, she wasn't terribly surprised to see that there was nothing there for her to find. No vampire dust, no crime scene tape. She grabbed a stick and poked through the beach detritus—bits of paper and plastic—but nothing caught her eye. Just damp sand and a few fast-food wrappers that had obviously been caught in the wind.

Well, damn. She'd been hoping to find something—anything—that could give her some sort of clue.

Apparently, wishing wasn't enough.

She took one last look at the scene and started back toward her bike. She'd gone about a hundred feet when she heard the pounding of footsteps behind her, accompanied by the sound of heavy breathing. She turned, and found herself face-to-face with a sweating, overweight guy in swim trunks and a Navy SEAL T-shirt. A camera hung around his neck.

"You're a cop, right?" he demanded.

"What makes you say that?"

He rolled his eyes, as if to say, *Oh, please.* "You're here about the mummy, aren't you? Come on. Just give me a quote. I've been out here all day, and I'm never an asshole to the cops like some other bloggers."

"The mummy?"

"I mean, it's my scoop, right? I was here when Homeland descended on the place, and—"

"Wait. Homeland Security? How do you know?"

"One of the dudes at the perimeter told me. Why, were they shitting me?"

"You say they were looking at a mummy?" she said. "In the drainage ditch. And you're asking *me* if they were shitting you?"

His face lost some of its confidence. "You mean—"

"I mean this is Los Angeles, my friend." She held her

hand out and smiled as broadly as she could. "Tori Jennings, production executive. Pleasure to meet you."

"Production exec?"

"Cable channel. Small but strong. And I'm afraid you stumbled onto a run-through of one of our new shows." She stretched the smile even broader. The last thing she wanted was some blogger digging around in the very mystery she was investigating. She glanced at her watch, then exaggerated her expression of extreme displeasure. "I've got to run. Drinks with Tarantino. You understand."

She left him with his mouth hanging open, then realized too late that she should have asked Mr. Blog back there if he'd gotten a name from the Homeland Security agent. Because she had a feeling that Mr. Severin Tucker's name was going to come up again. She frowned, considering how she could poke around Homeland without putting herself—and her fake FBI badge—on their radar.

To be honest, though, she wasn't in a huge hurry. Because as intriguing as the mind-bending agent had been, what she wanted most was to track down Sergius.

She approached her bike, shivering slightly from the vivid memory of her sensual dream, and told herself firmly that this wasn't why she wanted to find him. She was concerned about the girl. She wanted to make sure she was really okay. Confirm that he'd taken care of her as he said he would, and hadn't turned her into dinner once he was two blocks away.

It was all about the girl, and that was the mantra she repeated over and over as she drove from the beach back to her house. Because if she repeated it loud enough and long enough, maybe she could will it to be true.

CHAPTER FOURTEEN

"I wish I could track this Sergius for you," Leena said. "But I don't have a spell that will let me search for someone by name."

"Besides," Edgar added, "didn't you say he helped the girl?"

Alexis raised her brows. "Do you believe him? Because even though I want to, I just can't. That's why I have to find him. I have to know."

As soon as she'd returned from the beach, she'd called them both over even though she'd known that the odds of Leena being able to do anything were slim. But she'd had to try. And the truth was that she wanted to be with her friends. Sure, she'd toyed with not telling them, knowing how they'd worry since she'd been injured. But in the end, she'd shared everything. She'd come to rely on them, after all, and it felt nice knowing they were there, and that they cared.

She aimed an imploring glance at Leena. "Isn't there some way? I could bring back some sand from the beach, maybe track him that way?"

"Sure, except the sand's been overrun by kids and animals, and the tide must have come in and out at least once, so—"

"My blood!" Alexis said, interrupting. "He gave me some of his blood. Can you use that?"

Leena cocked her head, considering, then nodded

slowly. "Maybe. It's not too often that I have vampire blood in my toolbox, but I think I can pull something together. Yes, I'm sure of it."

"Excellent." Alexis leaned back, satisfied.

"But are you sure you want me to?"

"Why the hell wouldn't I?"

"It's just that he probably did save the girl. Why save you and then lie about her? So that means we'll both be spending our time trying to find a vampire that isn't part of the problem."

"What other vampire should I be hunting?" Alexis asked reasonably. "Until there's another attack against a human, I don't have any dirt for you to make a tracking ball. And now we know that the vampire who killed Tori is dead."

Dead.

That was the first time she'd let that simple reality sink in. She'd known that the killer was in that alley. She'd killed one of the vamps. Sergius had killed the other. Which meant that Tori's killer was dead. Gone. Kaput.

Holy shit.

She looked between Edgar and Leena, certain that her own expression had to be glowing. "Oh, my God, he's really dead, isn't he?"

Leena's teeth dragged across her lower lip. "Probably."

Alexis tensed. "What?"

"Come on, Al, you know how this works. I do the map, but then you have to get there. What if there were four vampires in that alley before you arrived? What if there were ten? We think it was one of the two you fought, but it might not have been. The only way to be sure is to look again."

She was right. Oh, dear God, she was right. How could Alexis have been so stupid?

"I could look for Sergius," Leena continued. "But I'd rather use my energy to search for the one who killed your sister. Assuming he's not dead, we know he's in town. There's no law that says he has to stay here, though. So which is more important to you? Finding Sergius? Or making sure the vamp that killed Tori is dead?"

Sergius. The name flooded her head, accompanied by the same erotic sensations of her dream. She shook it off, hoping that neither Leena nor Edgar had noticed the shiver of pleasure that had trailed up her spine. *No.* That was no reason to search out a vampire. Hell, that was a reason to stay away. But the girl . . . that poor teenage girl . . .

Still, Leena was right. The girl was probably safe. And even if she wasn't, there was nothing Alexis could do to help her now. But the vampire who'd killed Tori? She needed to know that he was dead and gone. That was why she was here in LA, after all. Why she'd sacrificed her job. Why she'd moved back into this house she'd once hated.

Edgar took a sip of coffee, then put it down, his eyes on Alexis. "You know, our little witch isn't the only one who can find your missing girl. Detective here," he said, pointing to himself. "And it's not like you don't have resources, too. This place is better stocked than NORAD."

"That might be a slight exaggeration."

He snorted. "Hardly. But I'm serious. We know he's a vamp. We have a name. And I know people who've been dancing around the edges of the vamp world for years. Got in deeper than I ever had the guts to, but it's worth asking. If it doesn't work out, Leena can do her mojo with your vamp-tainted blood. But if it does, then you haven't wasted her strength when you'd rather have her search for Tori's killer."

"Edgar, I could kiss you. You're absolutely right."

"Save that kiss," he said. "Because I can go you one better. We've got more to search on than just a name."

"We do?"

"We've got a picture, too. Or we will." He pushed back from the table and stood. "Come on," he said to Alexis. "There's somebody I want you to meet."

Two hours later, they were in Van Nuys watching as the police sketch artist put the finishing touches on a face that was all too familiar. That regal jaw. Those expressive eyes. The drawing was in pencil, but even so the eyes were perfect, dark and gray and piercing, as if they missed nothing at all.

"That's him," Alexis said. "That's Sergius."

They thanked the artist, and after Edgar promised to treat him to a beer soon, they headed back to Edgar's car. "I'll drop you at home," he said.

Alexis turned to him sharply. "At home? What about showing this around? Talking to your friends on the fringes?"

"Trust me, it'll go better if I meet them alone. These aren't the most trusting people on the planet. They thrive on paranoia, and if you show up with me, we may get nowhere."

"I don't know . . ."

"Don't give me that shit. I was a cop when you were still in diapers."

"A cop, yeah. But this isn't police work. This is—"

"All fucked up is what it is, and that means there aren't rules. You want to find Sergius and the girl, we need to play it the best way we can. Spook my contacts, and you're up shit creek until Leena does her thing."

He was right, but that didn't mean she had to like it. But since she had no choice, she nodded. "Fine. But be careful. And call me the second you find out anything."

"Will do." He grinned. "In the meantime, park yourself down in the Batcave and see what you can learn. Who knows? Maybe before dawn breaks we'll have a bead on your friend."

Friend.

The word seemed to roll over her. She knew Edgar wasn't serious, but it didn't matter. She had to shift away from him so he couldn't see her eyes. She spent the rest of the drive looking out the window and wondering why it was that every time she thought of Sergius, she felt warm and alive . . . and just a little bit scared.

◆

For a full day and night, Serge watched CeeCee, but there was no sign of the daemon. No sign of anything, really, except the almost insatiable hunger typical of the newly turned. That, and the insatiable need of the young to play video games.

"Seriously? You've never played anything? Not World of Warcraft? Not Doom? Not even one of the vampire games? I mean, there are a gobzillion of them out there."

"I'm sure there are," Serge said. "Trust me when I say that my life has been adventurous enough."

"Right. Vampy stuff. I totally get that." She paused,

her hand on the joystick of the current game, in which soldiers were racing around a labyrinth looking for demonic creatures. Like he'd said, too much like his real life.

"So, um, we'll go out when it gets dark, right?" She was looking at the heavily covered windows. It was only a few hours until nightfall, and he could sense her anticipation. An itchiness. A *need*.

Then again, maybe that was himself he was feeling. He'd started out calm. As cool as he'd ever been. As responsible as he knew how. He had this girl to mentor, after all. Couldn't lose his shit around her, right?

And for hours, he'd mentally patted himself on the back. Because Sergius—the same Sergius who'd sought out the dark kiss, the same Sergius who'd battled back his daemon for centuries and had failed at least as many times as he'd succeeded, the very same Sergius who'd survived a curse only to fall prey to a beast that lived inside him—that very same Sergius was managing to hold it all together.

And then it had started to unravel.

First it was just edginess. A restlessness. The sense that he had to keep moving. That if he didn't stay in motion, the pressure inside would build to exploding. Then it was a burning in his head. A tingling in his hands. An undefined need that he tried to keep ahead of.

"Serge?"

"What?" His head snapped toward her.

"I asked if we could go out. After dark, I mean."

"Out. Yeah, we can go out." He forced himself to stand still, then gripped the back of the sofa so hard he probably left dents in the wood beneath the upholstery. "Truth is, you could go out right now if you wanted to."

"Yeah? But you couldn't?"

He swallowed, forcing himself to focus on her words. To let the acts of thinking and speaking center him. He explained how vampires became more sensitive to the sun with age. He talked longer than he needed to, hoping the words would calm the beast that was beginning to roil inside.

No. He tamped it down. *Please. Not now. Not in front of the girl.*

It was coming on harder and faster than it ever had before, and he couldn't bear the thought of CeeCee seeing the beast emerge, watching as Serge lost all reason, all sense of self. He was tormented by the possibility that this girl he'd saved would watch him get sucked into the hell that was this new existence—and in watching would wonder at what she'd become, and doubt her own ability to control the vileness within.

"Oh, come on! You're, like, not even listening to me."

He forced a smile, unsettled by how strongly the beast had surged up, bringing with it a gnawing wave of hunger. He'd pushed it back, but it was still there, lingering beneath the surface. Growing and writhing, waiting to spring.

"Sorry," he said, hoping his voice sounded normal. "My mind was wandering. What?"

Her wide-eyed expression turned guarded. Gun-shy. And she seemed to shrink in on herself. As if the gregarious kid was only an act, and an overly exuberant one at that. "I'm getting on your nerves, aren't I?"

"No way." He shook his head to emphasize the point, at the same time wishing again that he could have one moment—just a single moment—with her asshole of a stepfather. "So what were you saying?"

She relaxed a little, and he gave himself a mental pat on the back. "I wanted to know how old you were."

"Old enough to fry in the sun."

Her mouth quirked into a smile, and Serge considered that a victory, though why the thought of his burning flesh was funny he really didn't know.

On the couch, she shifted again, her forehead puckering as if she was fighting a headache.

"CeeCee?" He moved closer, studying her. "Talk to me. You're not—"

She bared her teeth. "Grrrr!" she snarled, and then started laughing as he tried to tamp down the wildness in him that had surfaced along with the fear.

"I'm just messing with you. You sure you don't wanna play?"

She gestured with the control to the screen, and he caught a glimpse of blood and gore as the screensaver dissolved back to the game image.

Blood. Oh, God, the blood.

He reached to take the controller, compelled to play through, to get it off that screen, but he froze when he saw his fingers. They were elongating, and his skin was visibly hardening. Not yet noticeable to anyone but himself. But soon . . . soon, his hands would resemble claws, and thick scales would cover his body.

"I need to go," he said.

She looked up from her game. "Go? It's still light."

He looked at the clock on the wall. She was right. The sun was close to the horizon, but it hadn't yet dipped below.

He moved to the window and pulled the shade aside, being careful not to catch himself in the sun's fading rays. In the distance, he saw the steady figure of a jogger moving toward him on the beach.

The hunger grew. He could take. From the jogger. From CeeCee.

Oh, dear God, what am I thinking?

It was coming on too fast, too hard. He tried to push it down, to fight it, but all of his usual tricks weren't working.

"Serge?"

CeeCee's voice. It conjured images. Of the beach. Of the woman.

Alexis.

Instinctively, he let her image fill his mind, and while the beast didn't surrender, it seemed to back off just a little, and his resolve to fight it strengthened. He didn't know why—at that point he didn't much care—but thinking about the woman had bought him a little time. He knew it wouldn't last—he could feel the pressure rising. But he was absurdly grateful for just that extra bit of fight.

He looked hard at CeeCee. "You can't stay with me." He couldn't let her see him like this. Couldn't let her know what he was—what he'd become. What the hell had he been thinking? That he could mentor a girl? That he could play big brother and make everything right in her world? He couldn't even control his own fucking world.

Without warning, the hunger, pure and biting, crashed over him again, and he fell to his knees, moaning. He'd let the woman slip from the forefront of his mind, and the beast had taken advantage of that slip. In front of him, CeeCee screamed and climbed onto the couch.

"I'm okay," he said, sucking in air to calm himself, conjuring the image of Alexis and fighting the urge to analyze why the hell the mere thought of her helped him focus. "It's okay."

He moved to the window again. This time, he saw the jogger. Recognized her.

It was Sara, taking a jog in the setting sun, something he knew she did as often as possible, well aware that one day she'd be a true daughter of the night.

He grabbed a blanket off the couch and wrapped it around himself, then he threw the door open, careful to avoid the fading sunlight.

He called to her, then watched as she hesitated, as if she couldn't quite believe what she was hearing. Then she turned to face him, and he saw her surprised expression as she hurried toward him.

"Serge—my God." She stepped inside and closed the door behind her. "Luke said—"

"What?" His voice came out as a snarl, and he saw wariness in her eyes.

"That he'd caught your scent." Her tone was defiant. Challenging. "Near Penny Martinez's body."

He realized only then what a risk he was taking by going to Sara. He was a wanted man, and she was a prosecutor. But he trusted Luke, and by default that meant he trusted Luke's woman. "I didn't kill her."

She regarded him for a moment, her expression unreadable. When she spoke, he still wasn't certain if she believed him. "Come to the house. Luke's been . . . well, he'll want to see you."

"No." The word burst out of him. "I'm not. I can't. I have to—" He let his words snap off like a broken twig.

"There are things I still have to make right," he finally said. "Inside my head."

She reached out, then pressed her hand over his wrist. She had keen, intelligent eyes, and they were watching him, greedily searching for any details that might give her a clue as to what was going on with him.

Her hand seemed to burn him, the contact calling to him. Teasing him. Urging him to clamp down on that hand, to press hard, to pull and suck and take and *live*. Because he was at the end—the beast clamoring to get out, the pain crushing, the need growing, growing, growing.

He ripped his arm away.

She jumped, obviously shocked by his violent reaction, but she covered well, even managed a small smile. But her eyes never left his face.

He knew what she saw. She saw a man spiraling down, losing himself to something deep and malicious. She'd think it was his daemon, but she was wrong. It was something much worse.

"Serge." She said his name as if it were a command, and he lifted his eyes. "Serge, what's wrong with you? Have you done something? Did you—" Her breath hitched, and he knew she was thinking of Luke, of what she was going to have to tell him about her encounter with his crazy friend. "Tell me the truth. Did you kill?"

He turned then, and faced the living room. CeeCee was squatting on the couch. She'd taken her braid out, and her still-filthy hair hung in strands over her face. Her face was blank, but anger and fear seemed to flow from her, oozing from her pores.

"No," he said, his voice as rough as sandpaper. He was losing his grip. Had to make this right. Had to quench the hunger before he hurt the people he loved.

Had to *go*.

"No," he repeated. "I didn't kill. I saved."

CHAPTER FIFTEEN

Sometimes, life really shoots you a curveball. At least, that was the way Edgar looked at the world. He'd known for decades that there was weird shit out there. You couldn't be a homicide detective and not realize that.

He'd used psychics on cases—and found lost kids in the doing. He'd brought in mediums to consult—and had gotten leads from the dead. And he'd arrested some screwed-up fucks who swore they were possessed by demons.

Well, maybe they were.

But knowing all that shit existed was a lot different from actually getting up close and personal with a vampire. That one, Edgar had learned the hard way after Alexis had moved back to town. She'd shown up at his door, taken him to lunch, and then started asking him questions about his so-called crazy beliefs. He'd been defensive at first, but then he'd realized why she was asking. Her story about a vampire murdering her sister had gotten him like a knife in the gut. There'd been no question but that he'd help her, and he'd had her back ever since.

So, yeah, he knew all about vampires. But he'd never actually mingled with them. He'd never sought them out, even though he knew people who knew people who swore that they personally knew vampires. One fellow, Frank Court, had been a writer on *Three Sisters*, the show that had made Gilli famous. He'd come over for drinks one night and had sworn up and down that he could take Gilli and Edgar into the wilds. Show them where the vamps hung out. Let them rub shoulders with the dark immortals. He'd been drunk off his ass, and Gilli had sent him home in a taxi, but afterward Edgar had asked her if she'd been tempted. He hadn't been— that was for damn sure—but he couldn't put his finger on why.

His wife had looked at him with that wide-eyed gaze that had made her the darling of the tabloids and told him that there was no way in hell she'd set out on purpose to rub shoulders with a vampire. "Why not?" he'd asked. She'd looked at him with something that he later realized was pity. "Because they're evil," she'd said. "And you don't rub shoulders with evil and expect that some of it won't rub off on you. I know they're real. I know they're here. Someday maybe I'll fight them. Hurt them just a little. But until I'm ready to do that, I'm not going out of my way to meet them."

He'd taken her words to heart, and had never once sought them out. Frank hadn't suggested it again, and after Gilli died Edgar didn't see much of the writer.

Tonight, Edgar had called him up out of the blue, and now they sat together in Frank's car. In front of them, a ramshackle bar took up about half a block on the dark San Pedro street, the sign above it flashing a neon Z. Frank turned the ignition key to off and looked sideways at Edgar with a shit-eating grin. "I'm glad you called, man. This is going to rock your world."

Edgar believed him. He glanced again at the flashing Z and felt his stomach dip. "Maybe this isn't such a good idea."

Frank waved the words away like so much stale smoke. "I been coming here for months now, never had a moment of trouble. It's like wild dogs, ya know? You don't show fear, and they leave you alone."

"And they're all vamps? Everybody in there?"

Frank gave him a sour look. "Of course not. And it's not as if they're wearing signs. But you can tell. They got a way of looking."

"At you, you mean? Like you're dinner?"

Frank snorted. "Funny guy." He pushed open his door and got out. Edgar hesitated. Ever since Alexis had come to Los Angeles he'd felt alternatively like he had a window to more of the world than ever before—and like he was deeply useless. If he could help her find this Sergius and the teenage girl, though, he'd feel like he'd earned his keep. And he was damn sure that if Gilli was still alive, she'd put aside any fears of getting up close and personal with a vamp for the chance to help a young girl.

"Yo. You waiting for an engraved invite?"

"I'm coming," Edgar said, then slipped out of the car and fell in step beside Frank. Now there was no going back.

◆

The Z Bar was established in 1963 by Tom and Vivian Clamdale, who had moved back down to their native Los Angeles after dropping out of Berkeley to pursue what they considered a more laid-back and mind-expanding existence. They opened the bar as a co-op, serving up drinks that didn't include alcohol, but did include copious amounts of wheatgrass and other vegetarian offerings that the Clamdales assured their customers were necessary for healthy living. In the back room, they offered up some more elite options for their repeat, trusted customers.

In the process of exploring—and exploiting—all the various mind-expanding opportunities that Southern California had to offer, the Clamdales became reacquainted with Arnold Mink, an old friend from Berkeley. Mink had also dropped out, then spent the next two years "walking the earth." When he finally walked into the Z Bar, he told his old friends Tom and Vivian that he'd discovered the secret. The ultimate secret to what life should be. The thing that would make their grass and mushrooms and other mind-altering substances seem about as exciting as table sugar.

He'd offered to show them, and they'd eagerly agreed.

And that was how Tom and Vivian Clamdale became vampires.

After their transition, they made a point of inviting more of their kind to the bar. The human patrons never found out what had happened, but they soon decided that they didn't like the bar that much anymore, though they couldn't specifically say why. They started patronizing other establishments, and the vampires started using the Z Bar as a local place to congregate.

Derrick had discovered the Z Bar a few weeks after he'd transplanted himself from Chicago to Los Angeles, and he'd quickly made it his headquarters. As far as he was concerned, Tom and Vivian were fools, with too few years under their belt to truly see the beauty of what it was to be a vampire. One who embraced the vampiric lifestyle didn't usher humans out the door by supernatural influence. A true vampire fed off the humans who wandered in, and thumbed his nose at any semblance of the law—shadower or human—that might come sniffing around in the aftermath.

Even so, he quickly found that the bar was an excellent recruiting office. The trouble with most vampires today was that they were willing to live hidden lives. The vampires he met at the bar tended to want to change that, even if they didn't realize it until after a few long chats with Derrick. They wanted to be out in the world. To be in charge. To have bars and clubs and flaunt what they were: Magnificent beings. Gods to the lowly humans, capable of influencing thought and doling out life and death as it suited their whims.

Gods . . . and yet still they suffered. But by whose hand? The female that Jonathan had reported? The one who had injured Mitre?

At the thought of his lieutenant's name, Derrick stiffened and clenched his hands into fists so tight, his nails dug into his palms. He'd learned only an hour ago that Mitre had been found dead. A shriveled creature, dry and pitiful.

He didn't know if the girl in the alley'd had a hand in bringing about Mitre's demise, but Derrick didn't care. She'd killed Colin. She was the reason Mitre had been on the hunt. And it was a fair bet that she'd staked some of the other members of the League who'd gone missing. Whether she'd desiccated his soldiers, too, was irrelevant. Either way, he intended to find her. And then he intended to kill her.

After that, perhaps he'd move on to London, especially if he hadn't yet located Serge. The PEC had begun to push its nose too far into his business, and while Derrick had nothing but contempt for the organization, he was neither foolish nor suicidal. The world was a big place, and he could recruit for the League as easily in Europe as he could in the States. Besides, he had enough appreciation of drama to relish the idea of hunting humans in the famous London fog.

Tonight, though, he was seated at a darkened table in the far corner of the Z Bar. Vivian had brought him a fresh drink—human blood that she swore she'd harvested herself—and as he sipped it, the door opened and two humans walked in. One of them Derrick recognized, though only by sight. *Frank.* A dull name for a dull human. One of those humans who believed he understood the shadowers, without having even scratched the surface. Frank had caught Derrick's eye a few months ago, and despite Derrick's initial urge to make the human his dinner, he'd held back, instead persuading Tom and Vivian to let him come and go as he pleased at the Z Bar. The human claimed to know things about the shadow world, and Derrick didn't like the idea of humans peering through the looking glass into their world. If the human did know things, then Derrick wanted to know what.

He lifted a hand and signaled to Bella. She was standing in a corner talking to Raoul, a particularly promising new League member. She left the younger vampire immediately and floated over, the grace she'd once displayed on stage at the Bolshoi still apparent in the fluid way she moved across the battered concrete floor. Her sultry smile suggested activities other than the one he had planned, but he pushed thoughts of sex aside. That could come later. Right now, he had a job for the petite female.

"The humans over there. Go talk to them."

She pouted. "Talk?"

Derrick chuckled. "Just talk. I have my eye on the

plump one. I want to know why he's here. What he knows. What he wants. And why he brought a friend tonight."

"The price is a kiss," she said, and he willingly paid, feeling his body get hard as he pulled her close to him, his mouth closing over hers, his tongue finding not only hers, but the taste of blood. "You fed," he said when they broke apart.

She didn't meet his eyes. "I was angry," she said. "About Mitre. I thought the blood would soothe me."

"Did it?"

Her eyes blazed. "It only made me want more."

He nodded, pleased. "What happened to Mitre is one of the reasons I want you to talk to them. Feel them out. You're good at that. See if you get any hint that they know what's been going on."

"Can I flirt with them?"

He laughed; she looked so eager. "Of course. But you know the rules. It's not nice to play with your food."

Her brows rose. "Is that what you believe? I thought you loved a good game of cat and mouse."

He kissed her hard. "You know me too well," he said, then patted her ass to get her moving. "Go. I'll be listening."

She nodded, and glided across the room to where the humans sat on bar stools. Derrick listened halfheartedly at first; he wasn't particularly interested in Bella flirting with the humans, even if he knew it was only in sport. A few moments in, however, and she had his attention. She'd settled onto the plump one's lap—the human named Frank—but she was looking at the other one. "So what's your name, sugar?"

"Edgar," the human said. He didn't sound particularly eager to be there.

"Nice name. What brings a nice boy like you to a place like this?"

From Derrick's vantage point, he was looking at Edgar's profile. But he could still see the way the human shot a glance at his friend. "We're looking for someone," Frank said.

"Someone other than me?" Bella asked, with a purr in her voice.

"Oh, you're a right sweet find," Frank said. "But my buddy here's looking for someone in particular. We think he's the kind who might hang out in an establishment like this. If you know what I mean."

Bella tipped her head in that sexy way she had. "Why yes. I think I know exactly what you mean. So who is it you're looking for? Friend or foe?"

"Neither, actually," Edgar said. "He's . . . well, I just need to talk to him."

"Lots of folks come through these doors. Can you give me a few more details?"

The two humans exchanged a glance, then Frank nodded.

Edgar hesitated, then pulled a square of paper from his jacket pocket. Derrick leaned sideways to get a better look as Edgar unfolded it, then had to fight back a gasp when he saw the familiar face sketched on the paper.

"We're looking for this guy," Edgar said, as innocent as you please. "I think his name is Sergius."

Derrick stood. This had just taken a turn toward interesting.

He crossed to the bar and put his hand on Bella's waist, urging her off Frank's lap. He pulled her close, squeezing her up against his side as he aimed a brutal look at each of the two men. "Couldn't help but over-hear. You boys looking for someone?"

"This guy," Edgar said. Derrick could smell the fear on him, but he was impressed that the human didn't show it.

"I know him," Derrick said, taking the sketch from Edgar's hands. "Why are you looking for him?"

Edgar didn't quite meet his eyes when answering. "Got a few things I want to ask him. Nothing earth-shattering."

"That a fact?"

"That's a fact," Edgar said, and this time he did meet Derrick's eyes.

"Hey, hey," Frank said. "My buddy here, he's okay."

"That right?" Derrick asked, nodding slowly. "Well, since Frank comes here often, I'll take his word for it. All right, then. Here's the truth. If you're looking for Sergius, then I think you boys are in over your head."

"Might be," Edgar said. "But I still need to find him."

"Good luck. He's gone off the grid. And I'm still won-dering what you want with him."

"I told you. I need to talk to him."

"Might live longer if you changed your mind." He folded up the sketch and slipped it into the back pocket of his jeans. He had an old daguerreotype that he'd shown his men so that they would recognize Serge. In this sketch, however, his hair was shorter, and it was clear his old friend had changed with the times.

He aimed a hard look at Edgar. "Sergius is a son-of-a-bitch. He'd just as soon kill a human as look at one. As deadly as they come. Hell, Sergius scares me." He smiled, thin and predatory.

Edgar met Frank's eyes, and Frank nodded. "Well, thank you much. We appreciate the help."

"I'm serious," Derrick said. "You value your life, you don't want to get mixed up with him. Hell, just asking about him—well, let's hope he never hears about it."

They both nodded, then Edgar slid off his stool. "Let's get out of here."

Frank looked like he wanted to argue, but he fell in step beside his friend. The two left the Z Bar without looking back.

Derrick watched them go, then headed back to his booth and signaled for Bella to follow.

"You should have encouraged them to ask around," Bella said. "Maybe they'd draw Serge out."

"Not a bad plan," he conceded. "But I'm more interested in the fact that they've just demonstrated my old friend is still in the area."

"And they've seen him," Bella said. "Or someone they know has. If you still want to find Sergius yourself, we should find out who. And where."

"So we should."

"Will you see to it personally?"

"Actually, I thought that you could handle it."

"Me?"

He saw the delight in her eyes and chuckled. "Find out what you can. And once you've learned everything you can, drain them dry."

"I can play with them first, though, right?"

He brushed a kiss across her mouth and pulled her into his lap. "My dear, I'd be ashamed of you if you didn't."

CHAPTER SIXTEEN

"No, no! Please! I'll be good. I swear I'll be good!"

CeeCee's screams echoed in Serge's mind. She'd lost it when he'd told her he had to go—that he couldn't be the one to help her through the transition. That he had to leave her with Sara, who stood next to the girl, obviously irritated and confused that Serge was walking away when the girl needed him.

God help him, he hadn't wanted to. But what choice did he have? Tell them the truth? Not damn likely.

"It's not you," he'd told CeeCee, his voice hoarse, fading, because the beast had no voice. "I can't—I have to—" He hadn't been able to finish the sentence. He'd burst out of the house even as the sun slipped below the horizon. Already, his bones were starting to shift, the hunger starting to take over. Soon Serge would be subjugated to the beast, and he couldn't go through that again. Feed now, and at least he could keep himself at the surface. Ignore the hunger, and he'd lose his reason, his awareness, possibly even his sanity.

He couldn't explain any of that, though. And so he'd left. Confusing Sara, pissing off the kid, and making himself feel even lower than he already did.

Worst of all, he may have waited too long. It was rougher this time. Faster. His thoughts were rambling, shifting, losing coherency. It didn't make sense. He'd fed not that long ago—he'd drained Mitre, feasting on the bastard's life force. Never before had the beast risen so quickly, and he realized with a sudden shock what his problem was. *I saved the females.* He'd taken a vampire's form, and then he'd used vampiric powers to save Alexis. To save CeeCee. He'd given the energy back to them, and left himself ripe for the return of the beast.

Hurry. I have to hurry.

He stopped short and realized he'd been running, tearing fast through the darkened Malibu streets. Nothing here. Nothing at all. But there was a place in San Pedro. The Z Bar. A dark, seedy place. He'd found his last meal there—the one before Mitre—and there'd been other rogues in the place. He couldn't be certain, but it was his best lead yet. And even if no one was there now, maybe he could pick up the scent. Track one.

Maybe there would be time.

Please, please, let there be time.

He couldn't drive—that would take too long. And if he transformed to mist, he'd be using up even more vampiric energy. Possibly all of it. He might come out of the mist as the beast, his own mind lost inside, rampaging blindly through the city, taking and killing until the beast was submerged once more.

Serge would get his mind back then, but the price would be a path of death and destruction.

Either option was a risk, though, and the faster he got to San Pedro, the sooner he could feed. With fear weighing him down, he called upon the change and transformed into sentient mist. As quickly as possible, he shot through the sky, heading south to the small Los Angeles neighborhood. Even as mist, he could feel the beast rising, clawing at him, desperate to break free.

He had to hold on. Had to get there. Had to cling fast and hard to control.

The alley was dark when he shifted back into himself, but he could hear the crowd within the small bar that was so popular with the vampire crowd. He'd come to this place on several occasions, but never once had he entered. He'd become a true shadower, and he wasn't willing to be seen. Better to wait for his quarry to emerge.

Tonight was no different, and now he breathed deep, pleased to detect the scent of three vampires he knew to be rogue. But there was another scent, too. *Humans.* He frowned at that oddity, but the mystery was quickly displaced as he caught a hint of yet another scent—this one familiar but distant. Like something from a dream. From his past, perhaps . . . ?

He shifted, but memory eluded him and he pushed the scent from his mind. There was no time, not with the beast rising and his quarry out there. All that mattered was feeding.

He moved east down the sidewalk, frustrated when the scent faded. He tried the other direction, and was pleased to pick up the trail of a single rogue heading off toward the west. Serge smiled. He didn't have to figure out a way to lure one out of the bar or, worse, how to stage an attack inside the place.

All he had to do was track this one—and track him fast.

Serge was approaching when the rogue turned. He froze, eyes going wide. "Holy fuck, you're Sergius. Derrick heard you were in town."

Derrick. That was the scent he'd been unable to place. Derrick was alive. Derrick was *here.* And Derrick was looking for him.

Deep inside Serge, the daemon twisted, wanting to hunt and to play and to slide back into the old ways. To get lost in the blood. In the wild, freeing pleasure of pure, raw pain.

No, no, no.

He took a step forward, forcing his body to work properly, keeping the daemon and the beast down by will alone. He had to, because he had to know. Had to understand what was going on here.

Derrick is here. These rogues. These deaths. By the gods, this blood is on his hands . . .

"Who the hell are you?" Serge growled.

The younger vampire stood straighter. "I'm Raoul. I'm one of his—oh, hell, he's going to want to tell you. Let me take you to him."

No. He couldn't. See Derrick and the daemon would surely burst free. He had to stay focused. Had to focus and feed and *think*.

"Raoul," Serge repeated, his voice raw with effort. His hands itched as his skin shifted into something cold and reptilian. "Did you kill a woman last week? Did you make her husband watch and then kill him, too?"

Raoul's proud grin was brighter than the streetlight. "Brilliant, huh? Oh, man, did I get off on that or what? But seriously, come on back to the bar with me, because Derrick's gonna—"

The words stopped, cut off as firmly as a needle lifting from a record. The eyes went wide, too. And why not? Raoul had surely seen nothing like Serge before. The way his hands were elongating into claws. The way his skin had turned reptilian and his nose was flattening.

He cried out, but it was too late. Serge had reached

out and clamped his hand hard on the bastard's shoulder, his mind focused on draining Raoul dry.

And then it was over. For a moment, Serge just stood there, feeling the beast retreat, his muscles relax, his skin returning to normal. He'd been halfway through the transformation, and there was a joy in coming back to himself that completely overshadowed what he'd done to achieve it.

He'd killed, yes. But he'd done it to survive.

Unlike Derrick, who killed for the pleasure of the blood. For the thrill of seeing it spill from a human. For the taste of pain, so seductive.

Stop it . . . goddammit, stop it.

He knew he should dispose of the body—how much longer could he evade the PEC? But he had to get away. Had to move. Had to *go*. The beast was calm now, true, but his daemon had awakened and was sniffing greedily, longing for a past that Serge didn't want to return to and a man that Serge didn't want to be. Couldn't be—not again. Not anymore.

And yet still the hunger plagued him.

Alexis. He pulled her to the forefront of his mind, imagining she was in his arms and he was breathing in her scent. He wanted the feel of her skin against his. The taste of her lips, the softness of her hair. She was a storm of sensuality, and he wanted to get lost in it, certain that if he could lose himself with her, he could lose the daemon as well.

It made no sense, but just having her in his thoughts calmed him. Made it easier to fight. Easier to push the darkness down. It was strength, and right then, that's what he needed.

But why? It had to be because of what she'd seen in him, the way she'd looked when he'd promised to save the girl. Like he was a goddamn hero. It wasn't true, of course, but he clung to the image anyway, using it to draw strength as he headed back to the beach. Back to CeeCee. His ward. His responsibility. He'd talk to her now. Explain why he'd needed to go. But when he finally reached Luke and Sara's house, his keen ears picked up CeeCee's sweet trill of laughter and the warm tones of Sara's voice.

He cringed and veered away, something low and dark pushing inside him, telling him he was a fool to think that CeeCee would even want to see him. He'd walked the line between reality and the slide into the abyss that was the daemon for so long; why the hell would she want to step away from the relative normalcy of a life with Sara and Luke for the likes of him? Why, for that matter, was he even trying?

From the moment the beast had settled inside him, he'd shunned society. But that wasn't the first time he'd gone off the grid. For what felt like a dozen lifetimes, Serge had avoided the world, sleeping in abandoned basements and closed subway lines, taking care not to be seen, and only hunting when the clawing, writhing pain inside him refused to be ignored and he had no choice but to feed. He'd hoped it would get better. Had fought and battled and tried to quash that part of him down until it was nothing more than a hard knot of pain inside of him. But he'd never managed, and now he had both the daemon and the beast tugging at him.

He cast another glance toward Luke's house and the young girl inside. No, he had no business going in there.

He'd given her a new life, yes, but he damn sure wasn't the one who could show her how to navigate it. Not with the beast always so close to the surface. Not with the daemon writhing within him, still hungry. Still demanding.

Just give in. Feed. You've fought so hard to remain in a vampire's form, why not just be *a vampire?*

He was sated with the life force he'd taken, but he still craved blood. *Blood.* The center. The focal point of all things both human and vampire.

You know you want it. Want to lose yourself in it. Drink its sweetness. Wallow in its power. Take, Sergius. Take, and be.

♦

Leena groaned and rolled over, then cried out when she hit her head on something hard. She opened her eyes and sat up, her head fuzzy, but no longer feeling like it was about to explode. She blinked and tried to get her bearings. This was her house, and she was on the floor. She'd been curled up in a ball, but she didn't remember arriving at the house at all.

The last thing she remembered was leaving Alexis and Edgar. Then—

Then what?

Then she was going to go home. She'd planned to work the map spell and see if the vampire that had killed Tori was on the hunt. With luck, the answer would be no because the killer vamp was dead. But she had a feeling that Alexis wasn't going to be that lucky.

After that, she was going to do some poking around in

her books to figure out a way to find the vampire that had given his blood to Alexis. *Sergius*.

Something about that name made her shiver. There was no reason for it at all, but she wanted to run from it. Wanted to tell Alexis to run. Wanted to take her friend by the shoulders and shake her and tell her to stay far away, because if she got close everything would change, and not in a good way. No, not good at all.

Portents and predictions . . .

Over the years, Leena had learned to trust her visions, but this wasn't a vision. It was simply a bad feeling. Not even so much *bad* as *odd*. She didn't understand it, and she wasn't going to share it with Alexis. Not yet, anyway. Especially when she knew that Alexis wouldn't listen. No way her friend would back off until she found out what had happened to the girl. And Leena could only hope that this Sergius had saved her as he'd promised, because otherwise Alexis would never forgive herself for failing the kid on the beach.

Wincing, she climbed to her feet. A hundred fingers clenched her head, their nails digging into her tender scalp. The headaches were getting worse, but what really made Leena nervous were the blackouts. She'd actually gotten in a car and gone from Brentwood to West Hollywood, and she didn't remember a bit of it.

She thought about telling Alexis, but what would be the point? She had enough on her mind without worrying that Leena was going to slide off into pain and suffering and be absolutely no use to the team.

Enough on her mind . . .

Finding the girl. Finding Sergius. Finding the vamp who'd killed her sister.

All things Leena could help with—all things she *would* help with, and right now. *Come on, girl. Get your ass moving.*

Except the headache had started up again. Slow to build, but there, pounding in the background, like some persistent knocking at a door. A visitor who couldn't be turned away.

She'd long ago stopped hoping that the headaches would disappear. She knew better. Her mother had suffered from them, and so had her grandmother. But it wasn't the headaches that worried her. These blackouts were new, and they scared her. For years, her mother had beaten her, called her stupid and useless and made Leena feel about an inch tall. But those moments of horror had been interspersed with hugs and kisses and what seemed like genuine adoration.

Leena had been ten when she'd realized that her mother's vileness always followed a headache, and that her mother never seemed to remember what she'd done afterward. For years, Leena had thought she was lying, hiding behind a false curtain of memory loss. Now, though, she had to wonder if her mother had been telling her the truth.

The possibility turned her blood cold, and she forced the thought from her mind. She could never do that—could never beat her children. Shout horrible things at them. She wasn't that person, couldn't ever be that person.

She thought of Alexis, the first close friend she'd had in a life filled with acquaintances. She knew that friends were supposed to share hopes and dreams and fears and all that stuff. Hell, she'd been out for drinks with Alexis and Brianna in New York before the move to LA, and she'd watched the way the actress overshared, giving the other two women blow-by-blow descriptions of her dates with actors, of her encounters with lascivious producers, of her drunken nights at Hollywood parties. Just the thought of revealing herself that much to someone made Leena want to go hide under a bed. But at the same time, some small part of her wanted to share her fears. Wanted the reassurance from Alexis that she was totally okay.

Maybe they could find time to grab a drink, and maybe Leena would get up the nerve. Her mouth curved into an ironic smile, because *maybe* was as much of a crutch as the cane she'd been using since her first—and last—year hunting vampires. She'd had a stake; he'd had a knife. After that, Leena had done her fighting with herbs and spells, letting other people act as her eyes and ears and legs and arms.

So, yeah. *Maybe* she'd talk to Alexis. But maybe first she ought to keep her head in the game. This wasn't about her headaches or her insecurities or any of her stupid shit. This was about finding the vampire that had killed Alexis's sister. This was about continuing the Dumont legacy in the only way she could.

She touched her fingertips to her temples, but this time it was only out of habit. No sign of the headache lingered. She felt awake. Refreshed. And with renewed determination she went to the black lacquered cabinet that had belonged to her mother and her grandmother before her. She opened the door and pulled out the roll of crushed black velvet. It smelled of lavender and anise and soot, and when she spread it on the table, the odors washed over her like memories.

Mostly, though, it smelled like power. Because this was magic . . . and with it, she'd find a killer.

♦

Alexis was getting nowhere.

She'd been holed up in the cellar for hours trying to track down a vampire she only knew was named Sergius using that amazing computer equipment that Edgar so raved about. Needless to say, she'd managed to find exactly nothing. Searching in the human world was easy. Searching for a vampire? Not so much.

Now light streamed in through the small window that was actually at ground level. It flashed and snapped as it bounced off the water in the pool, a kind of mystical Morse code, telling Alexis that night had passed. It was a brand-new day, and she'd managed to accomplish nothing.

A new day?

With a start, she realized that she'd worked through the night, and wasn't tired at all. She reached for her coffee cup, but it had gone cold hours ago. She'd been running on adrenaline, not caffeine.

Not adrenaline. *Him.* His blood.

It flowed in her, and she sat stiffly at her desk, waiting for a wave of disgust that she was certain would come. But it didn't. Instead, there was something oddly comforting about knowing that his strength surged through her. It warmed her.

She told herself that made sense. He'd helped her, after all. And he'd promised to help the girl.

She told herself that . . . but it wasn't true.

No, that curling warmth she felt inside her wasn't because of trust or gratitude, it was pure, hedonistic pleasure. A decadent sensuality that she couldn't share with anyone else, certainly not with Leena, who'd taught her everything she knew about vampires. And not with Edgar, who looked at her as a daughter, and whose eyes would surely fill with disappointment if he knew the direction of her dreams.

She hadn't invited Serge in, but she hadn't pushed him out, either. She'd awakened with the memory of Sergius's hands stroking her, of his lips caressing her. A dream, a fantasy, and yet it had lingered.

It lingered still.

She knew it was the blood. *His blood,* now flowing in her veins. That was the excuse, the reason.

And yet the hard truth was that if she could slice her vein and let that blood flow out of her, she wouldn't do it.

All she feared now was that she was searching for him for the wrong reasons. Was it truly about finding the girl? Or was his blood playing sweet tricks on her?

No. He was a vampire, plain and simple. If he'd helped the teen, she'd give him a pass. But blood or no blood, if it turned out that he'd harmed the girl, he'd soon feel the pain of one of her stakes through his heart, dreams and fantasies be damned.

Enough. Time to get back to work. For that matter, time to focus on something other than Sergius, and she was damn well going to learn what she could about Homeland Security, and what that particular agency had to do with vampires.

She pushed herself up out of her chair and crossed the room to the coffeemaker. Maybe his blood had kept her awake throughout the night, but now she wanted more conventional indulgences. She filled her cup, then poured in about a gallon of cream to cool it off. She chugged down half the mug on her way back to her desk, then downed the rest as she dialed. The phone was answered by an efficient operator, but when Alexis asked to be put through to the agent handling either the Penny Martinez murder or the discovery of the mummified corpse on Venice Beach, she might as well have heard crickets chirping in response. "I'm sorry, ma'am, I don't have that information. Is there a particular party to whom I can direct your call?"

"Sure. Why don't you transfer me to Agent Severin Tucker." She held her breath, expecting the operator to pause, and then tell her that no such agent existed. To her surprise, the line clicked and after a few seconds of hold music, another voice came on.

"Division Six."

Alexis stalled. Division 6? "I'm trying to reach Severin Tucker."

"I'm sorry, but Agent Tucker isn't available. If you'd like to leave your number—"

Alexis hung up, pondering how to proceed. What she wanted was an actual meeting with the elusive Mr. Tucker. In person and in public. And, of course, well armed. She wasn't entirely sure how she'd manage that, though, particularly since Agent Tucker presumed he'd wiped her memory. Not to mention the little fact that since she wasn't really with the FBI, she could hardly call to suggest an interagency meeting.

She may not have a way through Agent Tucker's door yet, but in the meantime she would learn everything she could about him—and about Division 6.

"What is it?" she asked Marcus James, the one person

she knew who actually worked at Homeland. They'd met in college at one of Brianna's famous parties. They'd gone to a couple of movies and shared a few dinners, but Alexis had cut it off after Brianna had commented on how perfect they were for each other and how Marcus was falling for her. Alexis hadn't been the least bit interested in dating. All she'd wanted was to finish college with a degree and a GPA that would impress the FBI recruiters. Personal distractions would only take her away from that goal.

"Great to hear from you, too," Marcus said. "I'm well. Life's been busy."

"Sorry. I'm sorry. I'm just—"

"Working a case? Busy? Don't worry, I get it."

"So?" She tried to hide her exasperation. She needed answers, not small talk.

"Honestly, I've worked here for years, and I'm still not entirely sure. It's elite, that much I know. Division Six is where the secret stuff goes to hide."

That was intriguing—vampires certainly counted as *"secret stuff"*—and Alexis filed the information away. But she still didn't have any concrete information about Division 6 or Severin Tucker. Or about Sergius or the teenage girl. All she had was more questions. Which meant that after hours of working, all she was really doing was moving backward.

Well, damn.

She tapped a key on her computer, determined to try a different approach. Sergius had run away with the girl in his arms. Maybe she could track both of them. She logged into a website to which she had no legal access, the password for which she'd paid a very steep price. It took a moment for the image on her screen to resolve, and then she found herself looking through the various cameras set up along Venice Beach. Private webcams and security cams, public surveillance videos, ATM vids. Whatever footage from last night that she could get streamed to her computer. She was hoping for a glimpse of the attacking vampire, but so far she'd seen nothing. As far as she could tell, the whole episode had taken place in a section of beach that was completely lacking in surveillance.

Maybe a satellite had been over the area at the time . . . ?

Her hand tapped idly on the phone as she tried to think of someone she knew who could access the satellite coverage logs. She was just about to snatch it up and dial—a long shot, but her roommate at Quantico might have a contact—when its sharp ring made her jump. She snatched up the handset then smiled when she heard Edgar's voice.

Her smile quickly faded.

"Don't you dare go after him by yourself," he said. "We go together. Do you promise me?"

Alarm slithered inside her, tightening her chest until she had to work to breathe. "What happened? You found him?"

"Found some people who know him. He's dangerous. A monster. Shit, Alexis, I'm sorry about the girl, but—"

"No." The word came out barely a whisper.

"I know," Edgar said. "I'm so sorry."

"But he saved me. Why would he do that if—"

"He was playing with you," Edgar said. "Don't you get it? It's like my Gilli always said—they're devious. Vile. Inhuman. And they sure as hell don't think like us."

She was shaking her head, wanting to scream out in

protest. To shout that she could feel him inside her and she didn't believe it. But she did—dammit, she knew better than anyone what a vampire was capable of. How the beasts could snuff the life from an innocent. Hire a girl to sell her blood, then turn the tables on her and take her life.

"Promise me," Edgar said.

"I promise." Her voice sounded dull. Far away.

"Do you want me to come over?"

"No. No, I'm okay."

"I think I should come over."

"No, really. I won't do anything stupid. Besides, it's daylight. I'll call Leena, though, and tell her I want her to track the bastard sooner rather than later."

"But you won't go on the hunt without me? Not for this one? You swear? Swear it, dammit, Alexis. I mean it."

"Fine. I swear." She forced herself to relax. "I'm sorry. I shouldn't have snapped. It's just—"

"Shooting the messenger. Yeah, I get it."

"I do appreciate it," she said, and she meant it. He may have brought terrible news, but there was no doubt that Edgar had her back.

"I know you do, kid. Now get some rest."

As soon as he hung up, she realized that the energy she'd felt earlier really had drained out of her, presumably flushed out by the strength of her fury. She began to pace, wanting that energy back. Needing to feel the burn. Wanting to find Sergius in her blood again and hoping against hope that when she felt his heat, she'd also feel the falsity of Edgar's words.

But she didn't believe it—couldn't believe it. He was a killer, and she knew it. She'd rushed to Venice Beach to save someone from one vampire only to consign her into the arms of another.

That teenage girl's blood was on her hands as much as it was on Sergius's and the vampire he'd killed.

Goddammit all to hell.

She knew she should sleep, but also knew she couldn't. For that matter, working was out of the question. No way could she focus on a computer screen.

Instead, she climbed the stairs back to the main level, then moved through the house to the front door. What she needed was a ride along Mulholland on her bike. Taking the curves fast over Los Angeles—that, maybe, would get her head back in the right place.

She yanked open the door, prepared to take off into the rising sun, then stopped as her cell phone rang in her pocket. She checked the readout and saw it was Leena.

"The bad news is the vampire from the beach wasn't the one who killed your sister," Leena said. "But the good news is I've found him."

"Where? It's daylight."

"In the subway. I took a picture of the map. I texted it to you," she added, even as a trill on Alexis's phone announced the incoming text.

"So he's on the hunt," Alexis said, feeling a weariness settle over her. The map wouldn't find the killer any other way. Which meant that Alexis was always a hundred steps behind—and most of the time that meant that the human quarry died.

CHAPTER SEVENTEEN

The subway service tunnels beneath Los Angeles echoed with the noise of passing trains, but Serge didn't notice. All he knew was the daemon. All he felt was the hunger and the darkness. That all-consuming black that had lifted up to cover him like a veil, winning against his will and burying him deep.

Now he saw through the eyes of evil. And inside him, hunger roared.

He stalked through the dark tunnels, his mind no longer fully his own. He felt need—to hunt, to kill—and a passion to rend and rip. To wallow in blood. To bathe in it. To become it.

Once upon a time he'd walked through the streets of London this way. London, Rome, Berlin. How many times had Derrick been by his side? How many times had they proven their magnificence in those wretched hives of humanity? And now, once again, his friend was in town.

Ah, yes, the possibilities were endless.

He threw his head back, his arms out, and reveled in the power that was *him*.

Like night, he moved through the tunnels, a dark force. A shadow. He searched the corners. The areas heated with Sterno cans. The hovels carved from blankets and old grocery carts.

Hollow-eyed humans looked up at him as he passed,

their expressions dull. He kept moving. He wanted to feel the fear. He wanted to draw it out and consume it and let it fill him up.

Wanted and wanted and would take and take.

Except . . .

Except part of him wanted none of that.

The weak part. The part that tried to be in control. The part that never managed, truly, to keep the power that was Sergius down.

Now he stalked, keeping that whining, crying, remorseful part of himself squashed deep and firm. Blood would push him down even more. Blood, torture. Pain. All those things killed that part inside of himself that felt regret and remorse. That part that felt so fucking human. Time to try to shut it down completely. Lately, it had been too damn strong, managing to fight both the magnificent power of the daemon and the wildness of the beast. But the true Sergius had a toehold now, and that meant the daemon was riding high. He'd crush the weakness. Bury it forever.

He just needed to find fresh blood.

He rounded a corner and saw an area in the tunnel where a pile of stones suggested there'd been a collapse. He remembered when the tunnel under Hollywood Boulevard had done that very thing, and he eased forward, intrigued by what the destruction had left behind. What he saw was a treasure trove. A group of teens sitting around a fire. Their faces fresh, their eyes dancing. They weren't homeless, they were playing. They'd come down here to get high and drink and fuck. And to die.

For a moment, he merely watched them, letting anticipation build. He picked a pretty female with blond curls and a doll-like face, so round and white she already didn't look human. He was going to approach, invite her to take a walk with him, command her to come. But he didn't have to. She stood, whispered something to her friend, and began walking unsteadily toward the dark shadows that shielded him from view.

He stifled a grin. Truly, there were no challenges left in the world.

Around them, the ground seemed to vibrate as the trains shook the earth. The girl stumbled, and as she did, a figure emerged from the dark to help her. A male. A vampire.

The other vampire took the girl's elbow and smiled wide and thin. "Careful, beautiful. Be a shame if you hurt yourself."

Serge froze, hidden in the shadows, watching this interloper interfere with the female he'd marked for his own. He felt a growl rise in his throat and forced it down. Quiet . . . quiet . . .

"Come with me," the vampire said, holding out his hand for the girl.

She lifted a cocky brow. "Why should I do that?"

"I'll show you the best time you've ever had."

That seemed to impress her, and she took his hand. "Come on," she said, huskily. "I know a place."

Serge followed, bloodlust building—both for the girl and for the rogue who'd claimed her. The girl led them both through twisting tunnels forged from broken rebar and rock, stopping at a makeshift bedroom with moldy mattresses covering the floor. A scrawny teen lay passed out on one.

"Clever girl," the rogue said. The female smiled in reply, sultry and full of promise. He grabbed her arm and pulled her roughly toward him.

Serge stiffened, as if feeling the impact of the woman himself. He watched as her fingertip trailed down the rogue's chest, then over the waist of his jeans to his cock. The vampire bent his head, opening his mouth to drink deep of the female, and as he did, the darkness that had consumed Serge roared—tightening and wanting and thrumming from the mere thought of blood. *Now. Time to take now.*

He burst from the shadows, full of fire and fury, the pleasure ratcheting up higher when he saw the vampire's eyes widen in terror—and the girl's in confusion. In one quick motion he was at the rogue's side. He slammed the younger vampire back against a wall, only to have him bounce back, snarling.

"You're in my territory, fucker."

Serge didn't bother with a clever retort. He grabbed a rough piece of rebar and called upon the strength of both the beast and the daemon to rip it out of the concrete pillar from which it protruded. The metal emerged from the concrete with stunning velocity—more than enough to slice through the rogue's neck and decapitate the bastard where he stood.

"*Shit!*" the girl yelled. "Holy fucking shit!"

He grabbed her by the shoulders and yanked her around to look at him. Deep within, the weak creature that was Serge cried out in protest. But there was no stopping now. Now was the time for taking. For claiming. For *becoming.*

He slammed her back against a wall, and her eyes went wide. He knew what she saw—his fangs, bared and ready to rip her down to the bone.

She screamed, but the whole area was shaking then;

another train was passing. And fuck it, what did he care if humans came? That was just more to dine on.

He moved in, faster than the girl could comprehend, and heard her whimper. "Don't worry," he said. "Dying doesn't hurt at all."

And then he yanked down on her hair, tugging her head to the side, exposing the same neck that the rogue had coveted. He bent his head down, pressed his fangs to her throat—and yet he couldn't bite down.

No.

The word ripped through his consciousness.

No, goddammit, no!

He fell to his knees, his palms gripping his skull. He was Serge now, dammit. *Serge.*

His will.

His control.

His mind, and he fought back, pummeling the daemon, making it release its claim so that the daemon was no longer *him,* but was simply *it.*

Almost there. Almost sane.

Another blow—another lash in the battle—and the daemon was pushed farther down. Again, and again, and again.

Bent over, exhausted, Serge breathed in deep, his body raw. His thoughts in a jumble.

In front of him, the girl cowered, apparently not having the sense to run. "Go," he growled. Then louder when she didn't move. *"Dammit, go!"*

The daemon was deep now, but still fighting him, fighting hard, and he stood up, hands clutched to his head as he wrestled for control.

Finally, the girl went. She tore out of there, even as Serge slammed his fist against the wall of crumpled stone. Over and over and over, using the pain of his own ripped flesh to focus, to pull himself out, to battle down the daemon and stomp the shit out of it. Because if he didn't, everything could be lost. He'd drown inside the daemon, and Serge would be no more.

Then again, perhaps that would be best. Not to let the daemon win, but to conquer both daemon and beast at the same time. To save the world by destroying himself. A stake, positioned just so. The proverbial falling upon one's sword, taken for a more literal spin.

But he couldn't do it, and right then he hated that weakness in himself that would cling to this bastardized half-life even while risking the humans that he sought to protect. He had failed at so many things—had caused so much harm. It was his legacy, his yoke.

He feared that this moment was an offer of redemption, but he was too much the coward and the fool to take it. That the moment would never come again, and that when he inevitably faced Derrick, the lure of the dark would be overwhelming and he'd be drawn once again into the abyss, and he would not emerge unscathed.

◆

Alexis poked her way through the subway service tunnels beneath Hollywood Boulevard. She wasn't cursing, but the temptation was there; so far she'd seen nothing but trash and the homeless, and she desperately wished that Leena's skills had GPS precision.

She heard a moan and hurried forward, only to find herself facing a mini porn show: two junkies going at it on a mattress that had to have seen more rats than humans. Cringing, she turned away and noticed a break in the cement wall. She climbed through it, careful not to snag her clothes on the rough edges of the rebar. Dim yellow light from the work lamps mounted along the walls fought the dark to illuminate the space, mostly failing and leaving sprawling shadows that seemed to writhe and move in the corners. Gamely, Alexis eased forward, feeling like that girl in every horror movie, the one who went into the dark, scary place even though everyone in the audience was yelling for her to go back, go back, go back.

But she couldn't go back. Because she wasn't the virginal heroine or even the slutty best friend. She was the monster hunter, and this was what she did.

A faint rustling in the distance caught her attention, and she hurried that way, picking her way over rubble. After a moment, she came to another break and saw motion ahead of her. She eased behind a pillar and peered around, then sucked in air as she saw the scene in front of her. *It was him.* Sergius. He looked out of place in neat jeans and a button-down shirt. More like a businessman than a vampire. As she watched, though, the image was destroyed. He took a piece of rebar and quickly decapitated a vampire while a strung-out female gaped nearby.

She clapped her hand over her mouth to stifle a gasp, but her eyes never left him. He was a hunter, just like her, except he hunted his own kind.

The realization had barely fired in her mind when he lunged and was at the girl's side so quickly that Alexis hadn't even been able to follow his movements. Her mind screamed in protest—*no, no, not him*—even as she raised the gun to fire one of her wooden bullets.

But then he'd pushed the girl away, his body bent over as if in pain, his fangs bared, and he'd growled at her to go, to leave, to get the hell out of there.

The girl went, but not Alexis. She remained, gun raised, watching the vampire named Sergius with dread mixed with fascination. Had he done the same with the teen from the beach? Come close to feeding off her and then let her go? Or had he succumbed, drawing in her blood and letting her languish in his arms?

She stayed that way for an eternity—watching him, her finger on the trigger, unmoving, but ready to fire. His face was subtly illuminated by the dim light. And he looked so overwhelmed with sadness, it made her heart twist and she had to fight the inexplicable urge to go to him. To hold him and comfort him.

No. What the hell was she thinking? He was a *vampire.* According to Edgar, he was damn dangerous. And even if he had let the girl go—even if he had saved the teenager—she had no business pitying him. Resolved, she gripped the gun more firmly, as if it were the physical manifestation of her determination.

"Do it, then." His voice, rough and anguished, filled the space between them. To her horror, she realized that she'd moved out from behind the pillar, and that she stood directly in his line of sight. "Go ahead," he repeated, pushing himself to his feet and spreading his arms wide, baring his chest like a target. "Dammit, Alexis, *do it.*"

She dropped her gun arm. For a moment, he only stared at her. Then his lip curled into a sneer that didn't quite meet those warm, gray eyes. "You're a fool," he said, then turned his back to her.

Her heart was pounding so hard in her chest she was

certain he could hear it. But despite her fear, she wasn't about to let this be over. She took a step toward him, then another. She paused about five feet away, knowing damn well he could close the distance between them in the blink of an eye. "I probably am," she admitted.

"You call yourself a hunter? A noble human who takes out the vampires who scurry in the dark?" He turned to face her, and what she saw in his eyes this time scared her. But it wasn't fear for herself, it was for him, and once again she found herself fighting the urge to reach out to him. "Well, I'm a vampire. I've killed. I've destroyed. I've walked the earth for longer than you can imagine, and I've left my dark mark upon it. I am death," he said, taking a step toward her. "I am Legion. And I am your enemy."

He grabbed her hand and the gun, forcing a gasp from her as he pressed the muzzle against his chest, directly over his heart. "Do it," he demanded as the air seemed to shimmer between them. "You're a hunter, damn you, *hunt.*"

For what seemed like an eternity, they stood like that. Her holding the gun, him demanding with his eyes that she fire. Then she took a step backward, yanking the gun away and aiming its muzzle toward the ground.

"I'm a killer," he said, but there was defeat in his voice.

"Prove it, and I'll take you out in a heartbeat. But you pushed that girl away just now—did you think I didn't see? You saved me. And you promised you were going to save the girl on the beach."

"CeeCee," he said, and she smiled at the name. She hadn't gotten a good look at the teen, but somehow, the name suited her.

"Then it's true? You didn't harm her?"

The sound he made was full of contempt. "What is harm?"

She lifted the gun again. "Tell me where she is."

"Is that supposed to frighten me into cooperation?"

"Please, Sergius—that's your name, right? Please, I have to know."

"It's Serge," he said. "Not Sergius, not that. Not from you."

"From me?"

But he didn't explain. Instead, all he said was, "She's safe," but there was such regret in his voice that she immediately went on alert.

"Where?"

"Safe," he repeated.

"Show me."

"What?"

She gestured with her gun, indicating the way out. "I said, show me."

"Now?"

"Hell yes." She met his eyes. "Move."

She'd spoken firmly, and she held the gun. There could be no doubt that she was serious. And yet all he did was laugh.

"What the hell is so funny?"

"I'll go with you if that's what you really want, but it won't do you any good. The second I hit the street, I'll be dust. And good luck finding CeeCee then."

Well, shit. She'd forgotten what time it was.

"Come back tonight," he said. "I'll take you to her then."

"Tonight," she repeated. "You expect me to believe that you'll just be here waiting for me? I don't think so."

"You have an alternative proposition?"

"We wait," she said.

"It's not yet noon."

"You have an appointment?"

"I don't," he said. "I'm completely unencumbered." He glanced around, then brushed some dust off a pile of rocks. He sat gingerly and looked at her with eyes lit with mirth. "So," he said, "what do you want to talk about?"

CHAPTER EIGHTEEN

Edgar got his key in and out of his back door as fast as possible, then ushered Frank into the kitchen, grateful that Frank had driven; right then, Edgar didn't want to be alone.

The sun had been up for hours now—it had been a bitch fighting traffic all the way from San Pedro to his house in the Valley, and even the breakfast they'd grabbed at Du-par's hadn't soothed his mood. He was edgy. Anxious. Hell, why beat around the bush? He was fucking scared.

Once inside, he closed the door and locked it tight. The North Hollywood house was small, and although that sometimes bothered him, today it was a comfort. The walls didn't feel claustrophobic, they felt reassuring. This was his place, and no matter what bad stuff was outside, he could always find sanctuary here.

He tapped in the alarm code, then drew in a deep breath. Frank, he saw, was eyeing him warily.

"What?" Edgar demanded.

"You look freaked."

"I am. This vampire—this Sergius—sounds like he's a serious badass. And I know damn well that Alexis isn't going to back off just because of that. She's going to go even more balls-to-the-wall. I shouldn't have called her. *Shit.* I should have waited until I could talk to her in person."

"Calm down, Ed. The girl used to be FBI, right? I think she probably knows how to handle herself. She's not going to go rushing into a vampire's lair, right? I mean, you said the girl was smart."

"She is." But Edgar knew she was also impulsive. Still, he felt somewhat better. Alexis was eager, but she wasn't rash. And it wasn't as if she knew where to find the vamp during the day, anyway. For that matter, she didn't know where to find him at night.

"So, you okay?"

"Sure," Edgar said, although it wasn't entirely the truth. He'd hunted vampires, true. But strolling into a bar filled with them—talking to that one behemoth of a vampire—well, it had been a heady, terrifying experience.

"All right then. We'll talk tomorrow." Frank's broad grin split his face. "Un-freaking-believable, isn't it? What did I tell you? They're right there, knee-to-knee with us humans, and most of us don't even know it."

"Damn straight," Edgar said, shooting for bravado. Truth was, he figured he'd be just as happy without that knowledge.

He keyed off the alarm and let Frank out the door they'd come in, the one that opened onto the driveway at the back of the house. He closed the door again, then pressed his forehead against the cool wood and told himself not to call Alexis again. They'd talked. She'd said she wouldn't go out. That was enough. He wasn't going to hover like he was her father or some such shit.

Still . . .

It wasn't that long a drive to Brentwood. He could pick up some bagels on the way. Tell her he figured she might want a friendly ear. Not like he was checking in on her at all.

Resolved, he grabbed his keys off the kitchen counter where he'd tossed them and pulled open the door. The gasp escaped his mouth before his mind even processed what he was seeing. The female vampire from the bar, holding Frank in her arms. Frank's head lolled to the side, his body limp, his neck ripped open.

For a moment, they just stood there, her smiling at him, and him wondering how the hell she could be outside during the day. Wasn't she a vampire? Didn't they eschew the sun?

Then she dropped Frank on Edgar's front porch and started to push her way inside.

"I don't invite you in!" he yelled, but she just laughed and kept on coming.

"Now, is that any way to treat a guest?"

He turned and bolted toward the bedroom, moving faster than he had since his days in uniform. Didn't matter. In what appeared to be a blink of the eye, she was right there in front of him.

"Sweet," she said. "I always like to play with my food."

Involuntarily, his eyes darted toward the door.

"Oh, him? He was just an appetizer." She poked him in the stomach. "You're the main dish."

Think. He had to act. Had to do something.

His Glock was on the bar separating the kitchen from the living room. He hadn't taken it to the bar—Frank had suggested that would be a bad idea. And the truth was he knew damn well a bullet wouldn't hurt a vampire. But the door was wood—could he break it and get a stake?

Or maybe a chair.

With speed born of fear, he practically dove under her outstretched arm and into his bedroom. A simple wooden chair sat in front of a card table where Edgar kept his bills and checkbook. He grabbed the chair up and swung it at the wall, ending up with a broken leg in one hand. A makeshift stake with a nice sharp point.

The vampire pouted. "And here I thought we were getting along so well."

He lunged at her, the stake out, but all she did was grab him by the wrist and twist his arm around behind him so that he cried out in pain—then screamed in anguish when the bone actually snapped.

"That's what happens when little boys don't play nice," she said. "And this," she added, sinking her fangs deep into Edgar's neck, "is how little boys get dead."

◆

Alexis.

Serge sat and watched her. The way she held her chin up. The way her eyes fired with determination. The scent of her filled the tunnel, overcoming the putrid air, heavy with decay and despair.

She was hope, this woman. Hope and life, and though he'd meant it when he told her to go, he couldn't dismiss the simple truth that he was glad she'd stayed.

He'd almost lost the battle today—almost killed a human and destroyed that tiny part of himself that didn't fill him with disgust. He'd seen the chance for freedom when she'd pointed that gun at him. Could imagine the moment of impact when her wooden bullet lodged within his heart. Had he truly wanted that? For a moment, yes, but the moment had been fleeting because when he'd looked into her eyes he'd seen something reflected back at him that he hadn't seen in a long, long time.

Hope, and the possibility of redemption.

God, I'm a sentimental fool.

Maybe, but that didn't change the fact that something about this woman centered him. More than that, she gave him strength to fight the beast and the daemon. She was like a pinpoint of light cutting through the darkness of his soul.

She'd sunk to the floor, her back to a concrete pillar, her gun propped on her knees, held loosely but still at the ready. Silence hung between them, but Serge didn't find it awkward. On the contrary, he was grateful for the chance to look at her, to memorize the small details that made her *her*. The slight bump on her nose. The fullness of her lips. The intelligence that lit those pale blue eyes.

Her hair was pulled back in a practical ponytail, and she wore threadbare jeans and a ratty T-shirt under the same serviceable jacket she'd worn when he'd first seen her. She looked like a warrior, but there was an air of easiness about her that made him think she'd look just as natural in a ball gown, and equally at ease in nothing at all.

He fought to keep the image out of his head; that was a place he had no business going, no matter how enticing the thought might be. Sex was one thing—the fast release of need, the quick dance into pleasure. But there was no future in it, not for someone like him. And this woman deserved more than a fast fuck. Her body was meant for more than base pleasure and then abandonment. And while Serge had no illusions about the depths of evil that dwelled within him, he would not defile her simply to satisfy his own base needs.

"What are you thinking about?" she asked, the question making him smile. "What?" A dimple formed in her cheek. "I didn't realize I was making a joke."

"Just meandering thoughts. Forgive me for being a truly inadequate host."

"A formal one, though. Talking like that, it sounds like we're at a tea party in Jolly Olde England."

"I've done that," he said. "I much prefer this atmosphere."

She cocked her head, her eyes narrowing as she examined him. "Bullshit."

"You don't believe me?"

"What are you punishing yourself for?" she asked.

He shifted uncomfortably, realizing that whatever thread of control he'd held had been tugged from his grasp. "I'm a vampire, aren't I? You're the hunter. Why the hell didn't you kill me?"

"Honestly, I'm not sure. You're a vampire, and yet both times that I've seen you, you've saved someone, including me."

"Don't be naïve."

"You're saying you didn't save me? CeeCee? That girl who just ran the hell out of here?"

"I'm saying that you're assuming you know my motives."

She looked hard at him, then slowly nodded. "Fair enough. So why don't you tell me?"

A whisper of a smile touched his lips. "I don't think so."

Another silence. "Actually, it's been three times."

"What?"

"I've seen you three times," she clarified. "At the crime scene you didn't save anyone, but you were watching. And you were pissed off. Because Penny Martinez was dead?"

"Yes."

She nodded. "Me, too." Her shoulders rose and fell. "I know it's really that vampire's fault, but I can't help but blame myself for that poor girl's death."

"His name was Mitre," Serge said, "and he was a son-of-a-bitch. He killed the girl, make no mistake. But if anyone else is to blame, that falls on my shoulders."

"Is that your cross to bear?" she asked. "Carrying the weight of the world?"

"I bear only what's mine. I was there that night, too. And I wasn't injured. I could have caught him, but I hesitated and moved too slowly. He got away, and the girl died."

"You were there? In the alley when I fought those two?"

"I was."

"I don't understand. Why did you hesitate?"

Because I couldn't leave your side. But he couldn't tell her that. Couldn't reveal that part of himself any more than he could risk adding more weight to the already heavy burden of her guilt. "How did you track him?"

Her brow rose. "Shifting the subject?"

"A subtle, but effective maneuver. And I truly want to know. You went after him on the beach that night. How did you find him?"

"Honestly, I didn't know it was him. I heard about the attack on Penny Martinez—"

"You're a cop."

She shook her head. "Past tense."

"I saw you flash a badge. You're saying it's a fake?"

"An extremely expensive, highly professional forgery, thank you very much."

"I'm impressed."

"I was an agent once. When I quit, I didn't want to lose access." An it-is-what-it-is shrug tugged at her shoulders. "This way works for me."

"You quit to hunt vampires."

"Yes."

"Why?"

"You wanted to know how I tracked the vampire. What was his name? Mitre?"

"I do. I'm extremely interested." He also wanted to know the answer to his question, but that could wait. There were still hours until the sun went down, and he was enjoying her company far too much to press this early in the game.

"The truth is I didn't know if Mitre had killed her or not. I suspected, but I was really just there to hunt whoever had killed her."

"You still haven't answered my question."

"How, you mean?" She grinned, wide and slightly flirtatious. He knew she was playing, but that smile tugged at him. Why this woman? Why now, when he was as ghastly as he'd ever been. When there was no future for him, much less for him and anybody else? "A girl has to keep some secrets."

"The dirt," he said, remembering the oddity of her collecting the sample. "Somehow you used the dirt to track him."

"Aren't you the clever vampire?"

"You're a witch."

"Now you're not so clever. No, I'm not. In fact, a few years ago if you'd told me that witches and vampires existed, I would have said you were a loon."

"And now?"

"Now I know that there's a hell of a lot more out there that I don't understand, and honestly I'm not sure I want to."

"What do you want?"

"Isn't it obvious? I want them dead."

"Vampires."

Her brow furrowed, then she lifted her face so that she was looking directly at him. "It's been my focus for a long time now."

"And you've never wavered." He made it a statement, not a question.

She drew in a breath, then stood. In four long strides she crossed the small area to him. "Why were you on the beach that night? Why were you at the crime scene?"

"The same reason as you."

"To kill the vampires?" Incredulity laced her voice.

"The ones that attack humans, yes."

"I see. Then there are nice, helpful vampires. You told me not to believe that."

"I told you not to believe it about me."

"And if I do believe it?"

He said nothing.

"Why did you help me? Why did you help CeeCee? You did help her, right?"

"I did."

"Well? Why?" She looked steadily at him, waiting for

him to allay her fears about the girl. Waiting to hear that he'd saved CeeCee as he'd saved Alexis.

But he couldn't tell her that. He'd saved, yes. But he'd also condemned, and so he told her the only answer he could. The only one that was true, even if he didn't fully understand it himself. "Because you asked me to."

♦

"Oh." She took a step back, his simple statement knocking her a bit off-balance.

No, that wasn't true. She'd been off-balance since the moment she'd seen him. And not just down here in the subway, either. Since the first moment she'd met his eyes at Penny Martinez's crime scene.

It wasn't a trick, wasn't some funky vampire voodoo. There was just something about him that got under her skin. That made her feel itchy and shy and garrulous all at the same time. It was a sensation she needed to fight— she knew that. As Edgar had said, he had a reputation for being dangerous. But here, now, that was hard to believe. Perhaps she was as naïve as he had said, but she saw something inside him. Something she trusted.

"We still have a lot of hours left before the sun goes down," Serge said. "Do you want to fill it with small talk? How do you like living in Los Angeles? Do you prefer the beach or the mountains? Have you seen any good movies lately?"

"I'm not sure I'm a small-talk kind of girl."

"I'm glad to hear it."

"I want to talk about you," she said. Why not? She was feeling bold. Might as well lay all the cards out on the table. "I was told not to look for you. I was told you were dangerous."

"More dangerous than most vampires, you mean?"

"Obviously."

"And yet here you are. You came because you wanted to find CeeCee?"

She shook her head. "I didn't come down here to find you. I'm hunting the vampire who killed my sister." She saw his gaze flick up at her as she revealed that fact. She hadn't meant to tell him, but now that it was out, she didn't regret it. He might as well understand the depth of her enmity.

"And you believed he or she was in the tunnels?"

"That's right."

"Why?"

In response, she only shook her head.

He laughed. "A girl has to keep some secrets?"

"Exactly."

"Fair enough. In that case, tell me this: Who told you I was dangerous?"

"Do you deny it?"

"No," he said, with a firmness that made her want to stand up and leave that place. She forced herself not to move. They were playing a game, and if she showed weakness she would undoubtedly lose.

"I had someone make inquiries."

"Did you? That was very resourceful." Humor laced his voice. "Of whom?"

"I don't know. He went to a bar. Apparently the patrons are mostly vampires."

The mirth faded from his face. "Do you know what bar?"

"No, but he's fine. He called me after he left. Wanted to make sure I knew what a danger you are."

"I'm not the only dangerous vampire in town."

"No," she agreed. "You're not the one going around killing innocents."

"You believe that?" His gray eyes examined her, as if trying to look past the words and find a deeper meaning.

She considered responding glibly, but the question seemed too important. "I do," she said. "I saw the fury on your face when you looked at Penny Martinez's body. Perhaps you are dangerous—I don't know. You're a vampire, so I'm damn sure willing to believe it. But I don't believe you're the one behind all these deaths."

"Behind them? You believe the deaths are organized?"

"Don't you?"

"I'm certain of it," he said. "Someone is inciting the rogues to hunt. And I am dangerous, Alexis. I'm dangerous to them."

"Rogues?" She shook her head. "I don't know what that means."

"They're vampires, but they don't abide by the code. They kill. Viciously. Painfully. And with absolutely no qualms about treating humans as nothing more than a source of amusement."

She felt sick. It had been a rogue who had killed Tori, she was certain of it. How long had he played with her? How long had he drawn out the pain. Oh, God . . .

"Are you okay?"

She jumped, surprised to find that Serge was right beside her, his hand on her arm, his eyes looking deep into hers. "I—yes." She stepped back, breaking contact. "I was just thinking about—"

"Your sister. I'm sorry. I didn't mean to bring back dark memories."

"You didn't bring them back. They never leave me."

"It consumes you, then?"

"Oh, yes."

"And it is that vampire you seek? What will you do once you find him? Go back to the FBI?"

"For a while, I thought so. But now . . ." She trailed off, not certain she wanted to voice what had been growing inside her.

He said nothing, simply watched her, and somehow that quiet certainty that she'd speak when ready prompted her to share what she'd kept in her heart.

"I loved Tori—nothing will ever change that. And I'll dance in his dust once I stake the bastard that killed her. But I can't forget the other victims. And there aren't that many people who know what I know. Who can do what I do." She looked at him. "What *we* do."

"Don't delude yourself into thinking I'm like you."

"I wouldn't," she said, though she was afraid that she'd put at least one foot on that path already. Because despite what Edgar had said, she didn't fear this man. This vampire. *Vampire.* She needed to remember that. She cleared her throat. "So. How long have you been a vampire?"

"Are we doing the getting-to-know-you dance?"

"We are," she said firmly.

"All right, then. I was turned a long time ago. Longer than you'd probably believe."

"I've become remarkably open-minded lately."

"I was turned just shy of two thousand years ago."

"Oh." Maybe she should reevaluate that whole open-minded thing. "Seriously?"

"Cross my nonbeating heart."

"You were around for the fall of Rome. For the Renaissance. The French Revolution. Hell, you were around when silent movies were invented."

"Actually, I spent some time with Thomas Edison and Nikola Tesla. I've a particular interest in science and inventing, and they were both fascinating to me. Edison was an ass, of course, but geniuses often are."

She could only shake her head. And, oddly, she found herself slightly jealous. Not of the whole living-as-a-bloodsucking-monster thing, but about the immortality. About seeing all of that. "What's in your head—it's astounding."

His smile seemed strangely ironic. "I've had my moments."

"So what happened? You were walking through the woods one night in—where did you live, anyway?"

"Not too far outside of Londinium," he said.

"Right. So, were you attacked?" She thought of Tori. Would Alexis be happier if instead of killing her sister, a vampire had changed her? She wanted to say no—that was perverse, unnatural. But there was that gut-level allure.

"I wasn't attacked," he said, his expression darkening. "I sought it out."

She nodded slowly. "I can understand that. I was just thinking that there's an appeal to being able to watch history pass by."

"An appeal, perhaps. But it comes at a price. Everything that's not within the natural order does."

"But you sought it out anyway?"

His smile lacked humor. "I did."

"Why?"

"Because I was young and vain." He shrugged, the gesture nonchalant, but she could tell that he felt anything but casual about the story. "I thought I could handle it."

"You couldn't?"

"It was . . . difficult."

She wasn't sure she wanted to ask, but she couldn't hold back the question.

"What was the price?"

"Evil. Inside me."

Suddenly her heartbeat seemed very loud. "Like the rogues?"

"Exactly like that."

She swallowed. "But you controlled it, right?"

He looked at her, and for a moment, she wasn't entirely sure how he was going to answer. She clutched her hand around her gun and forced herself to breathe and relax.

Finally, he offered her a small smile. "I saved you and CeeCee, didn't I?"

The relief was like a ray of warm sun after a long swim in a cold pool. She didn't like thinking of him as vile—as if he could do the things that she'd seen, as if he could rip out the throats of humans like these rogues did. "So you think they have a leader? The rogues, I mean. Do you know who?"

"I have an idea."

She waited for him to say more, but only silence hung between them. "Is Homeland Security involved somehow?"

If she'd intended to surprise him, she'd succeeded in spades. He tilted his head back and laughed and laughed.

"Do you want to tell me what's so funny?"

"For centuries—hell, for millennia—we've tried to keep our existence secret. The way we operate. How we live. And we've blithely believed that we've succeeded. And then you come along and prove that no matter how careful we are, someone is going to find us out. There's no hiding, there's no hiding at all."

CHAPTER NINETEEN

Derrick watched Bella twirl into his apartment, her face glowing. "You fed well, my dear."

"It was exquisite. The fear. The struggle." She trembled, as if words couldn't describe the extent of her rapture. "Foolish little worms to think that they could come into our world and make demands. Ask about one of our kind. There's a price to pay for hubris, you know."

"And you saw that they paid dearly."

"Of course." She slid against him and twined her arms around his neck. "And now I'm in the mood to celebrate."

He kissed her—hard and lingering. "And what else do we have to celebrate? He told you who was looking for our Sergius?"

"He didn't say a word, not even after I drained him almost to death. Not even when I threatened to pull out his heart and crush it in my hand. He protected her to the end."

"Her?"

Bella's smile widened. "He died with his secret, but he took me for a fool. I found notes. Messages on his answering machine. I took them, of course. When the police investigate this murder there won't be anything in the house to suggest that we exist. We'll stay in the shadows, my love, until you deem it time for us to emerge."

"Soon," he promised. "But you intrigue me. A woman, you say?"

"Her name is Alexis. Apparently she fancies herself a vampire hunter. So did Edgar, of course, but he's dead now."

"Interesting."

"Is it?" Bella's beautiful brow curved up. "Why?"

"Because Mitre told Jonathan he was injured by a woman."

"The same one?"

"It's certainly possible." He frowned, considering his options, then looked once again at his beautiful Bella. "I charge you with investigating, my dear. Take her, torture her. Find out the truth. And if she is the one who's been killing my men, then you leave her for me. I'll kill her slowly, to make sure she truly understands the nature of pain."

♦

Only minutes after darkness fell, they emerged from the tunnels. Alexis had brought her motorcycle, and since Serge had no car, they rode together. He'd insisted on operating the bike, but she'd turned him down flat, and now he found himself seated behind her, his arms around her waist as they raced down Wilshire toward the Pacific Coast Highway.

She whipped in and out of traffic with such ease and skill that Serge couldn't help but enjoy the ride. He'd owned a variety of vehicles at various points in his life, and he'd always gone for speed.

There was no denying that the sensation was glorious. The power of the bike beneath them. The rush of wind through his hair. And, yes, the soft warmth of the woman in his arms. She'd filled his mind in unexpected ways. Primed his blood and gave him strength. He didn't understand it, and under other circumstances he would have run from it. But at least for the moment, he was tied to her. On this bike. On this mission. She deserved to know the truth—he'd saved CeeCee, but not in the way she'd expected.

Once Alexis knew, it would be hate that he'd see in her eyes, and he would welcome it. The Alexis in his arms was a woman who inspired fantasies. A calming of the daemon. A taming of the beast. A future without pain and death.

Foolish thoughts. Better to have her hate him, slap him down, drive a stake through his heart, either real or metaphorical. He didn't care. All he knew was that if he was going to keep his sanity he had to be rid of her, because having her near him without truly having her was the way into madness.

Already he'd shared more with her than with any woman he could remember. She'd asked more about his past and how he'd learned about vampires, and he'd told her about growing up in Londinium. About the rumors of the Dark Lady whose kiss could bring immortality.

He hadn't fully explained the daemon. About the writhing, craving need that had risen inside him, and how he'd fought it so futilely for so long. He hadn't told her about the curse or the beast. But he'd told her a bit about the good times. About dancing at court with ladies-in-waiting. About seeing plays at the Globe Theatre. About drinking ale with Leonardo da Vinci, the two of them huddled over a sketch, trying to design a machine that could actually fly.

She'd listened with wide eyes, making soft noises of delight and amazement that had soothed his soul and urged him on.

When he'd felt spent, he'd asked about her life, and she'd seemingly obliged, but he couldn't help but notice that she'd skipped over her childhood, failing entirely to mention her parents and saying little about the sister she'd lost. Only when she'd talked about the FBI had she been truly animated. It had started out as a quest and had turned into a passion.

"Do you miss it?" he'd asked.

"No, but I think that's because I'm still basically doing the same thing."

"Chasing bad guys, you mean."

"Yeah, exactly." She'd leaned forward, then, her elbow on her knee and her chin resting on her fist. "I want to know who's organizing the rogues."

"I know you do."

"But you won't tell me?"

"I'm not inclined to wish you dead."

"I can handle myself. And one way or another, I will find out. Or do you have some other reason for not telling me?"

He'd laughed. "You mean am I protecting someone? No. Quite the opposite."

Her eyes had narrowed. "You want to kill him yourself."

She'd been right, of course, but he hadn't admitted it, and she was smart enough to know when to change the subject. He was smart enough to know that wouldn't be the end of it. But for now at least he was keeping Derrick's name out of it. Not because he didn't trust her, but because Derrick belonged to him. The lure of their past had almost made him lose control. *Almost.* Serge had pulled it back, but could he do it again, and again after that?

No, he'd be the one to take Derrick down. And in doing so, he would amputate one more thing that triggered the beast.

Now, though, Derrick and the rogues were long forgotten, pushed aside by the roar of the wind through their hair.

"Here?" Alexis shouted over the engine.

"The next left," Serge replied, letting go of her waist for long enough to point.

She took the turn fast, expertly handling the bike, and when she eased off the accelerator at the main gate of the community, Serge had to admit that he took a great deal of pleasure in simply being along for the ride. It was unexpectedly freeing.

"Gate code?" she asked.

He gave it to her, and she punched it in. The gate swung open, and they rolled down the hill toward the houses that lined the beach on the exclusive, private drive.

"Here," he said, pointing to a parking area. She killed the engine, and they both got off. He led her down a walking path that meandered between two well-manicured properties. He was leading her to the shore, then they would walk north in the surf until they reached Luke and Sara's house. He could have had her park closer, but he'd wanted to prolong the moment.

"Are we close?" she asked after they'd passed two houses, including the one Serge had been squatting in.

"There," he said, pointing to Luke's wooden deck.

"Great. Let's go." She curved in, away from the water and toward the dry sand.

"No," he said, firmly grasping her elbow. "The girl's had a hell of a time. We'll find a place to look in, to watch. It's still early, so we'll probably see her. If not, then too bad. We're not knocking on the door. We're not announcing ourselves. You're not undoing whatever good Luke and Sara have done for that poor kid by smacking her in the face with memories when she sees either you or me."

Her nod was both serious and contrite. "You're right. Of course." A brief hesitation, and then she cocked her head, looking at him with new curiosity. "Luke and Sara?"

"Her family," he said firmly.

"Family? So this is her home?"

There was hope in her eyes when she asked that, as if returning her home would have made him a true hero. "It is," he said, and he knew he was speaking the truth. Her biological family had never given her a home, and they were no longer hers anyway. She'd been born into the shadow world, and she'd find new parents in Luke and Sara. The kind of mentors she deserved.

He ignored the voice in his head that pointed out that *he* should be CeeCee's mentor. He was the one who'd made her. The one she wanted. And possibly the only one who could truly explain what she now was. He'd made his decision when he'd put her into Sara's care. When the beast had been about to burst free. Since then, he'd wanted to come to this very house and talk to her. Or at least talk to Sara. But he hadn't. He didn't want to face CeeCee's pleas or Sara's recriminations.

"I want to see her."

He nodded, then led her around the side of the house. With luck, the girl would be in the den—and she wouldn't be fighting her daemon or sucking on a bag of blood. With even more luck, no one would notice Serge and Alexis lurking about.

For once, fate smiled on Serge. Their view through the window was unobstructed, and they could easily see Sara sitting next to CeeCee on a small couch.

Alexis rose up onto her tiptoes, and Serge closed his hands around her waist, steadying her as she looked inside.

"It's a puzzle," she said. "They're working a jigsaw puzzle."

She eased back, regaining her footing, but he didn't remove his hands. He liked the feel of her, the warmth that flowed through him merely from the simple act of touching her. It didn't last long. She turned, and he had no choice but to release her, though he mourned the loss of contact. She moved away from the window, clearly wanting to ask him something.

"This way," he said, taking her hand and tugging her toward the beach. If Sara or Luke were paying attention, they'd undoubtedly hear them. But with any luck, the roar of the ocean would cloak the sound.

"You healed her the way you healed me. And then you brought her home to her family?"

He hesitated, his eyes searching hers, then slowly nodded. "I brought her home," he said, and saw her shoulders sag with relief. "But it's not what you think."

A crease formed between her brows. "What do you mean?"

"I mean there was nothing I could do for her."

"But—with me. I drank, and now I'm—"

"You're fine. But you weren't anywhere near as far gone as CeeCee."

"So you *changed* her? You made her like . . . like you?"

"I did," he said, and the weight of his words seemed to hang between them. She was shaking her head, and though he knew he should let her hate him—should encourage her to walk away—he couldn't keep his own counsel. "You would rather she was dead? Rotting in the ground? Everything that she was meant to experience ripped from her? No chance to even find out who she really is?"

"Who she *is*? She's a vampire."

He thrust his arm out toward the window. "And what does that mean, exactly? She can walk down a beach on a summer night. She has a warm bed and people to look after her. Yes, she's a vampire, but she's still in the world. Some say that's a curse. Others, that it's a gift. But if you're so certain that she's nothing more than a monster, then kill me now and go after her next."

"Damn you," she said, but it was a whisper and not a scream. Even so, she punctuated her words with a blow. He caught her fist and pulled her roughly toward him, a move she countered with a swift kick to his shin that sent them both tumbling backward.

She ended up sprawled on top of him, her body straddling his, her chest heaving against his. Her lips parted, her eyes wide with shock.

He didn't think, didn't analyze. He simply acted—and took her mouth with his. With one hand he clutched at her hair, urging her closer, tasting and consuming, and then groaning in pure, animal pleasure when she melted in his arms and the kiss wasn't merely him taking but them joining. A single moment of heaven that was all too fleeting, because a heartbeat later she broke free of his embrace and climbed to her feet.

"I didn't—that was a mistake."

"Was it?" he asked.

"Don't," she said. "I can't do this."

He rose as well. "Alexis, it's okay. It was only a kiss." That was a lie, of course. It was so much more.

"Is that what it was? Not a bribe? Not an enticement to forget the fact that you turned the poor kid into a vampire?"

"Is that what you think? Do you really believe I had a choice?"

"I don't know! How can I know when—dammit!" Her phone was chirping, and she yanked it out of the pocket of her jeans and glanced at the display. He saw her frown, curse, and then answer the call. And then he saw the blood drain from her face, and he caught the ripe, cloying scent of fear and horror draw tight around her.

"What is it?" he asked as soon as she hung up.

"My friend Edgar," she said. "He's dead."

CHAPTER TWENTY

Serge offered to come with her to Edgar's house, but Alexis refused, though she had to admit to herself that she was tempted by the idea of having him around. It was that temptation that scared her. That, and her own reaction to what he'd done to CeeCee. She'd been furious, disappointed, scared, and a dozen other horrible emotions that she was more than happy to show him. But what she hadn't shown him was the tiny bit of traitorous relief. Because, dammit, she believed him. Had he not turned her, the girl would be dead. Instead she was alive and working jigsaw puzzles in Malibu with a woman who truly seemed to adore her. Sure as hell beat her own childhood.

But that was all white noise now anyway. Edgar filled her thoughts, and instead of Serge, it was guilt that rode with her on her motorcycle. She should never have told him Sergius's name, should never have agreed to let him investigate. And she sure as hell shouldn't have agreed to that police sketch.

Goddamn her! She'd been playing at this like it was a real investigation. Like she could somehow protect them all because she knew the truth. Some child's version of good winning over evil. But it never did, did it? That's why Tori died, and now Edgar was dead, too.

Her vision blurred, and she blinked rapidly at a red

light, forcing herself not to cry. She had a job to do now, and tears would only get in the way.

At Edgar's house, she parked her bike, then drew in a deep breath, making sure she at least appeared calm even if she was screaming on the inside. She pulled out her badge, then hurried up the driveway, moving around to the back of the house. Lieutenant Sanders was there, and she approached him first. "Thank you for calling me."

He nodded, looking like he'd aged a hundred years since the last time she'd seen him, back when she was still with the FBI.

"I know you two were close. I thought you should know. But you shouldn't have come. I've got a crime scene to work here, and it's a nasty one."

"You said the wounds were primarily around the neck. That makes it my crime scene, too." She flashed the badge, then slid it back in her pocket. "This is clearly a task force matter."

His brow furrowed. "I agree. And I've already called it in. But I didn't think you were on the task force anymore. Didn't I hear that you quit a while back?"

"Quit? Don't be ridiculous." She pointed toward one of the bodies, lying in a heap outside the back door. "If you'll excuse me." She hurried quickly away, her heart pounding. *Shit*. Someone from the task force was already on their way, and that meant that she needed to get the dust and get out of there fast. She paused by the body of a man who'd undoubtedly been Edgar's friend, then bent down. He'd fallen half on and half off the sidewalk, and she scooped some of the dirt from the yard into her hand, then shoved it into her pocket, not caring if anyone noticed.

She had it, and she knew she should leave. But she couldn't—not yet. Not without seeing what was inside that house.

Not without seeing Edgar.

She stepped inside, using her badge to forestall any questions. What she saw made her stop dead in her tracks. *Blood*. So much blood. He'd been tortured, and brutally. This wasn't about the kill, this was about the pain. And all because she'd pulled him in, asked for his help, and shown him that all those crazy things he believed were absolutely true.

Her stomach twisted and bile rose in her throat. For so long, she'd held the mission to find Tori's killer close, until it felt like a part of her rather than a distinct goal. Not this. This was new and fresh, and it flashed like a beacon in the dark.

She'd find Edgar's killer. She'd find the bastard tonight.

And her only regret would be that you could only kill a vampire once.

◆

"Yo," Doyle said, elbowing Tucker in the ribs. "You recognize her?" They were at a crime scene in North Hollywood. An LAPD cop and a civilian, both with their necks ripped out. The woman he was pointing to was hurrying away from the house that Doyle and Tucker were heading into. She'd been at the Mitre crime scene, and Doyle couldn't help but wonder what she was doing there.

"Told me she was FBI," Tucker said.

"Well, shit," Doyle said. "I was hoping the feds weren't involved. Lot more complicated when we have to clear out multiple agencies."

"Your call. We can take a pass on this one."

Doyle considered, then shook his head. The kill was recent, and he needed to get into the victims' heads. He'd been hearing too many rumors that the attacks on humans were organized, planned and directed by some kingpin-type vamp. So far, he didn't have a bead on who that ringleader might be, and he wasn't inclined to pass up a chance to find out.

"Clear 'em out," he said, then headed toward the first body while Tucker went off to do his thing, messing with the officers' minds while the other PEC agents arrived and helped him clear the scene.

Doyle, however, was interested only in the vics. The first one was outside, lying in a heap. It took no time for Doyle to get into his head, and the truth was there wasn't much in there. A layer of euphoria—he'd been mingling with vampires and the foolish fuck had thought that was cool—and then nothing. Just the red flash of pain and then the black static of death.

Whoever had killed him had attacked him from behind.

Well, shit.

Frustrated, he moved inside the house, ignoring the looks from the human officers who hadn't yet encountered Tucker and his mind fuck. He found the body and bit back a wave of disgust. Goddamn vampires, they were fucking animals.

He brushed aside the human cop who tried to stop him, then bent and laid his hands on the body's forehead. Edgar Garvey was the vic, and he sure as hell hadn't deserved to die like this.

A wave of loathing washed over Doyle for the vampire who had murdered these two men, for the dark twisted world he lived in, and even for himself, half human and half daemon and not really belonging to either world. But he had his gift, and though he cursed the toll it took, at least he could do this. At least he could look into the mind of the dead and maybe, just maybe, help balance the scales.

◆

Tears streamed down Leena's face. "I can't believe it. I can't believe he's gone."

Alexis's stomach clenched, and she reached out to grab Leena's hand. "I know. Dear God, I know." She felt hollow, lost. It was like losing a parent. Only this time it felt more real, because Edgar really had been family in a way that her parents never had. "Oh, Leena." She squeezed her friend's hand and felt the returning pressure.

"Can you concentrate? Can you find who did this?"

Leena brushed the back of her hand under her eyes and looked at the dirt on the table, along with the bowls and herbs. "For Edgar, yes. Absolutely yes." As if to punctuate the point, she focused on the table, taking the dirt in hand. "If you're ready to hunt, I'm ready to do my part."

"I'm ready," Alexis said. "I just hope our killer's on the hunt himself." It was a perverse wish, but she'd long ago come to terms with the fact that in order to find a vampire, that vampire actually had to be on the prowl.

As she watched, Leena went through the motions of tracking the vampire's aura. Of pulling it into the ball. Of turning the ball into a map. She was working hard, faster than usual, calling her powers out with more force than Alexis had seen her do in the past.

Beads of sweat formed on her forehead and upper lip, and her fair skin splotched red from concentration. After what seemed an interminable length of time, Leena finally looked up with an exhausted smile. "Look," she said. "Our vamp's on the move."

Sure enough, that pinpoint of light had appeared on the etched surface of the ball. Alexis took it and peered closely, trying to discern the location.

"I'll get the street map," Leena said, but Alexis only shook her head.

"No," she croaked, realizing her throat was thick with fear. "I recognize it." She met Leena's eyes. "Oh, God, Leena. He's *here*." She lunged sideways, going for the gun she'd left sitting by the kitchen sink. She didn't make it.

"*She's here,* you mean." The voice was cold and feminine, and before Alexis made it to her weapon, a dark figure was at her side, mouth at her neck, and Alexis knew that this was the end. This vampire had found her, and she was going to kill her, and damn Alexis all to hell, but it wasn't Tori she was thinking about, but Serge.

"No!" Leena's scream cut the silence as she rushed forward, shoving the end of her cane toward the vampire. But the female only grabbed the cane and pulled Leena close, then pressed a palm against her chest and shoved her so hard she slammed into the far wall.

"Don't worry," the female said, turning her attention

back to Alexis. "I'm not going to kill you straightaway. You and I are going to have so much fun together."

"Can't I play, too?" *Serge's voice.* Alexis blinked, certain that she was dreaming. That the female had already bit her, drained her, and she was hallucinating as death approached.

"Sergius!" The female's cry was delighted. "Derrick will be so thrilled!"

On the ground, Leena screamed, her hands clutching at her temples as she writhed in pain, and Alexis could only stand there, fearing for her own life and listening to her friend suffer.

"We haven't been properly introduced," Sergius said, his attention only on the female.

"I'm Bella. And you are nothing short of a legend." She shook Alexis, who stiffened and tried not to be afraid. "Would you like the honor of the kill?"

His eyes were cold, hard, like nothing that Alexis had seen before. And as he walked toward her, she knew this was the end. Oh God, oh God, how could she have been so stupid? How could she have trusted a vampire? How could she—

And then it was over. With speed too fast to be seen, Serge whipped out a stake and drove it hard into the female's chest. The woman's mouth formed a surprised O, but that was all. Then she was dust, gone, and with nothing to hold Alexis up anymore, her knees went limp and she started to fall.

Serge's strong arms caught her, pulling her back up, pressing her to him. A swell of relief passed through her—she'd doubted him. She'd doubted him, and yet he'd saved her anyway.

"Alexis," he murmured, his lips touching her hair. "God, Alexis, if I'd been even a little bit later."

"I'm okay. I'm okay."

But the world was still tilting, because through the haze of relief, she saw Leena stand. Saw her grab Alexis's gun from where she'd left it on by the sink. Saw her aim it at Serge.

"Leena, no!"

"It's Sergius," her friend said, her eyes wilder than Alexis had ever seen them. "It's Sergius, and he has to die."

◆

He's right there. The vampire. One of the pair she'd been searching for.

His chest opened to her. A gun in her hand. A wooden bullet, and a clear shot to satisfaction and revenge.

Eva didn't take it.

Not because he deserved a second chance, but because she could use him. It was all so clear now. Alexis had led her to Sergius, just as Eva had seen in that very first vision. A blinding flash of prescient knowledge the first time that Leena had taken the girl's hand. A spark that let her know in no uncertain terms that somehow, someway, Alexis was the key to finding Sergius and Derrick. That somehow Los Angeles played into it.

And then, when Leena had learned that the vampire Alexis sought was in Los Angeles, the pieces fell into place. They moved here, and the hunt began.

Now she'd found Sergius, just as the vision had predicted. And if she let him live a little bit longer, Sergius could lead her to Derrick.

It was hard to think—her head still throbbed. But she fought through the pain, and knew what she had to do. It wouldn't be hard.

She'd been patient for so long . . . she just had to wait a little bit longer.

Wait . . . and keep the little bitch down.

Not that Leena wasn't without her uses, just like all the others before her had been. And there'd been so many before her, starting with her own daughter.

The men had arrived unexpectedly, surprising Derrick, who held Tomas in his arms. The other one, Sergius, had already grabbed her, had ripped open her vein and was drawing in her blood. She'd been fading, losing her grip upon life, his actions proving that it wasn't her help that he'd truly wanted, but her blood. He wasn't worthy of what she could offer, of the way she could bind his daemon. How could he be, a filthy vampire? A bastardization of nature?

Death might be coming for her, but he'd die there in the cookhouse, too, she was certain of it. The Dumont men were fools; not one of them truly understood what she was, what power she wielded. But they were not weak, and they knew well how to defeat vampires. Derrick and Sergius would see no more of the world. Their reign would end tonight.

Except it didn't.

The men took Derrick away, but she later learned that they didn't kill him, choosing instead to torture him for eternity, locked deep within a crypt with no blood to nourish him.

They'd planned the same fate for Sergius, and they'd rushed him, not the least bit mindful of her limp body when he tossed it aside, a barrier between him and the raging men. Still, there'd been no escape for the vampire, and of that she'd been glad.

But she hadn't anticipated her own daughter. The foolish child had made a noise, and the vampire had heard it. He'd grabbed the girl from the cupboard in which she hid, and he'd used her as a shield. It had bought him time and distance, for the child's father wasn't Tomas, but the eldest Dumont male. And thus Sergius had escaped, tossing the child back into the cookhouse at the last possible minute and buying himself a few precious seconds.

Evangeline, however, continued to lay dying, bleeding on the floor as the men rushed out, searching for a vampire they would never catch.

She'd called the child over, and the little girl had come, tears streaming down her face, her small voice whispering, "Maman! Maman!"

Evangeline had hardened her heart, clutched the child, and uttered the words she'd been warned by her own mother never to use. An abomination, even for one who delved into the darkness as she did. But it was either that, or die.

And Evangeline chose to live—her body gone, but her spirit alive inside the body of her daughter. Cramped down, buried deep, able to rise only through the force of extreme will that left the girl clutching her head and fearing that her skull would explode from the pressure.

The girl never knew what lived inside her. And when she grew and aged, Evangeline moved to the next one. A granddaughter. Then a great-granddaughter. And on and on until she'd settled in Leena. And with each generation, Eva had to fight her way out again, able to claim only snippets of time, using those moments to search for the vampires who'd destroyed her world.

Now that she'd found them, she'd fight brutally to keep control of this body. To keep Leena down. She needed it now. Because she had a plan.

Because Sergius could lead her to Derrick, and she'd finally be done with the both of them.

"Leena!" Alexis's voice cut through the haze of memories. "Leena, put the gun down. Edgar was wrong. He's not dangerous. He's helping. I swear, he's helping."

Slowly, she lowered the gun. Slowly, she managed a smile.

Inside, she could feel the girl twisting, trying to regain control.

But Eva wasn't having that.

Leena might never have known that Eva lived inside her, but Eva had witnessed every moment of her life. She knew how to be the simpering little gimpy Leena, and she'd play the part until the end.

Then—when she finally plunged the stake into Sergius's and Derrick's murderous hearts—she'd tell them the truth: that it was Evangeline who took their lives, just as they'd taken everything from her.

CHAPTER TWENTY-ONE

Serge clung to Alexis, barely able to comprehend the horror of what would have happened if he'd arrived even a moment later.

He'd almost talked himself out of coming, but the memory of how her face had looked when she'd found out about Edgar had haunted him. He hadn't known her long, but he understood the core of her—he'd seen it and had recognized it in himself. She wasn't the type to sit back and wait for justice. She was going to go on the hunt.

She might not want him at her side, but he didn't care. She was in his blood now, and he wasn't going to see her destroyed.

And yet she'd come so close.

He pulled her closer, holding her, then pushed her away and searched her eyes. "Damn little fool! You were going to go out? By yourself?"

"Fool?" Unexpectedly, she laughed. "In case you didn't notice, she didn't attack me on the hunt. She came to me." Her brow furrowed. "Why was she here?"

"You've been hunting rogues," he said. "You can't expect to stay under the radar."

She nodded, then stepped back from him and ran her fingers through the thick waves of her hair, now loose around her shoulders. She flashed him a quick smile. "I don't know why you came here, but thank you."

"Yes," Leena said stiffly. "You arrived in the nick of time."

"Are you okay?" Alexis was looking at her friend with concern. "Your head?"

Leena raised a hand to her temple. "It's better now. Just a dull ache."

"Do you want to crash here?"

For a moment, the girl seemed to consider it, her eyes never leaving Serge. They were old eyes, and he found himself hoping that she'd leave, but whether that was because he wanted to be alone with Alexis or because the girl made him uncomfortable, he didn't know.

"No," she finally said. "Thanks, but I think I want to go home." She nodded at the pile of dust. "We found the vampire that killed Edgar, but we're still looking for the one that killed Tori. Maybe I can work on that tonight."

"Don't even try," Alexis said. "You'll get a migraine, and it's not worth it. Not tonight. Just rest, okay? Promise me?"

The younger girl nodded, and Alexis went to her side, then pulled her into a hug that Leena stiffly returned. They broke apart, and Alexis handed her the fallen cane, then walked her outside to her car. Serge followed at a discreet distance. Foolish, perhaps, but he wanted to stay close enough to protect Alexis.

When she returned, her smile was timid. "So. Thank you." Another ghost of a smile, then she eased past him into the kitchen. "I want a glass of wine. Do you? I mean—do you drink?"

"I do, and thank you." He grinned, hoping to lighten the mood. "A snack would be good, too. The kind that doesn't coagulate." It was a ridiculous attempt at levity, but it seemed to work. She rolled her eyes and nodded.

"Right," she said. "Have a seat and I'll see what I can find."

She ended up bringing two glasses and a bottle of Malbec to the table along with a plate of cheese and fruit. "I'm not really hungry," she said as she nibbled on a slice of cheese. "I eat when I'm nervous."

"Who can blame you for being nervous? You almost got killed."

Her smile was tremulous, and she didn't quite meet his eyes. "I'm not sure that's why I'm nervous."

Oh. He hid his own smile behind a sip of wine. "So why did Leena want to go home? She's looking for the vampire that killed your sister?"

Alexis nodded, apparently grateful for the change in subject. "She's the one who came up with the spell that lets me use the dirt to track the rogues."

"And your sister's killer? How is she tracking him?"

"That was trickier. It took her a while to figure it out—just recently, actually. That night in the alley when Mitre got away was the first time she'd tried it. It uses blood—mine, since I shared blood with Tori—and some of her hair from an old hairbrush I found packed away."

"Blood is a powerful thing."

"I know." Her throat moved as she swallowed. "I've felt yours. Your blood, I mean." Her voice was low. Sultry. And it stroked his senses in dangerous and appealing ways.

"Did you?"

"Are you surprised?"

"That depends. How so?"

"Nothing terribly overt. I felt stronger. More alert, I guess."

"That's not unusual," he said. "Anything else?"

"I had a dream about you."

"Oh?" Without thinking, he reached out and took her hand. Her eyes met his, but she didn't pull away. "And was it a good dream?"

The heat from her hand was spreading through his body like hot oil that stroked and filled him, and he had to physically fight the urge to lean over and kiss her. "Alexis? Tell me about the dream."

"It was good," she said simply, but there was a world of heat in her eyes. "Very good."

"Tell me about it." He wanted her voice to surround him, her words to seduce him.

"It was after you saved us. It was like you were there. And we were touching."

"Like this?" he asked, trailing a fingertip down her arm.

She swallowed. "A bit."

"Just a bit? Maybe like this?" He lifted her hand, then kissed the tip of each of her fingers. He could tell that she was trying to fight it, but a small moan of pleasure escaped anyway, and that was all the encouragement he needed. He drew her forefinger into his mouth, his tongue sliding over her skin, making his body throb with heat and longing.

"Not exactly," she whispered. "But you were there, and you were touching me, and I was touching you, too. Your back. Your arm. I still remember the pattern of your tattoo."

He stiffened. "My tattoo?"

She frowned. "You don't have one? It was in my dream. A chain that went around your bicep." She leaned toward him, brushing the white shirt that covered his arm. "Right here."

He caught her hand, keeping it pressed against him. "Wait," he said, then released her hand, while slowly leaning back. Even more slowly, he unbuttoned his shirt, then slipped out of it, his eyes never leaving Alexis.

◆

Dear God, he's getting undressed!

Alexis sat transfixed, staring at this perfect specimen of a man. A chest with only the slightest smattering of hair and defined abs, but not so much so that he looked like he should be posing on the beach following an Ironman competition.

She was so enthralled, in fact, that he had to call her attention away from his body with a quick clearing of his throat. She jumped a little, turning her focus to his arm. And to the tattoo that she'd seen so clearly in her dream.

"Is this the tattoo you saw?"

"Yeah. And that arm. And that chest." She smiled, unsure why his tone had suddenly turned serious. "Is that a problem?"

"No. But it is unusual." He pushed back from the table into a standing position. He held out his hand, beckoning to her, and she found herself standing without hesitation and taking his hand. He led her out of the kitchen to the back door, then through the sliding glass and onto the flagstone patio. They walked toward the pool, which had a Jacuzzi built into the side. Overflow cascaded down a wall of rocks to the main pool, warming the water below. Serge sat on the edge of the whirl-pool and ran his fingers through the water.

"Serge?"

"You have an unusual mind," he said.

"Do I?" She kicked off her shoes and sat on the edge with him, then rolled up her jeans and stuck her feet into the hot water. It felt like heaven, and she didn't even care that it was soaking the cuffs of her pants.

"Usually a human can't feel the blood connection."

"The blood connection?"

"When a vampire gives his blood to a human, he can track that human. Feel their emotions." He glanced at Alexis as he said that, and she felt her cheeks warm. "It only lasts as long as the blood is in the human's system, but vampire blood lingers for quite a while."

"But the human doesn't usually feel it?"

"No."

She closed her eyes and concentrated, then shook her head. "I think I must be normal. I know you're sitting right there, but I don't *feel* it."

He laughed, then edged closer, his eyes on her face. Slowly, he cupped her cheek in his palm. A small sound escaped her lips. "Trust me," he said. "You're exceptional."

And then he was kissing her, his lips warm and consuming and so very tender. She eased away, and the pressure of his kiss seemed to linger on her flesh. She told herself she didn't want to feel it, but that was a lie. She *did* want it. Everything inside her head told her she should pull away, but why? Why should she? Edgar was dead. She'd almost been killed by a vampire bitch. Everything was horrible and frightening, and somehow, magically, she'd met this man—this vampire—who stood like an oasis in the midst of it all.

"What is it you want?" His fingers traced a path down her neck, then along her collarbone, then farther down until his fingertips seemed to be dancing upon the swell of her breast.

"You." The word was an admission, and while she hated her weakness, she couldn't deny the truth. She felt safe with him. His touch made her feel alive. The desire that coursed through her was unlike anything she'd ever felt before, and yet she trusted it. It felt right somehow, all the way down to her toes. She didn't want to fight it. For so long, it had felt like she was fighting everything. Right now, she just wanted to *feel*.

Boldly, she leaned forward and pressed her hands to his chest, her palms against his skin, his flesh as strong and hard as she'd imagined. She should have known it would be like this—this visceral longing, this compulsion to touch and be touched. She'd had that dream, after all. And he'd been hovering in her thoughts since the first moment she'd seen him.

"Were you always fit, or did this come after you became a vampire?"

"I was a soldier when I was human. It was in my best interest to stay stronger than my enemy."

"So does that mean the stories are true? That a vampire remains as he was when he was turned?"

"The same age, yes. The rest, no." A slight grin played at his mouth. "When I took the dark kiss, my hair brushed my shoulders."

"Really?" She tried to imagine him with longer hair. Now it was so short that it was almost military. Just long enough for her to plow her fingers through. It defined his angular face and strong jaw. Long hair would soften his features, though she doubted it would weaken them. She couldn't imagine Serge ever seeming weak.

She stroked her palms over his chest, taking pleasure in his soft moans, then even more pleasure in his touch. Slowly, he drew his fingers down to the hem of her shirt. As if he was performing a sacred ritual, he slowly tugged it over her head, then tossed it aside, leaving her in her bra. He gave her a teasing grin, then eased his fingers around to her back, expertly unhooking the clasp.

"Not bad," she said. "You must have had a lot of practice."

"Actually, no," he said. The grin had faded and his eyes were serious. "You could say I'm quite out of practice."

"Oh." A little frisson of delight shot up her spine at the idea that in his eyes, there was something special about her.

And then, before she could talk herself out of it, she leaned in and brushed his lips with her own. He caught her in his arms, holding her firmly and kissing her deeply. She surrendered herself to him, to the power of his kiss. Already shirtless, he needed only moments to slide out of his jeans and into the hot tub. She followed suit, tentative about the heat of the water, but he laughed and scooped her up. He settled her on his lap and the hard length of his erection pressed against her, teasing both of them, and stealing her thoughts so that she could barely concentrate on the words she wanted to say to him.

"Tell me I won't regret this in the morning."

"I know that I won't," he said.

"This shouldn't be happening. It shouldn't be real."

His hand brushed her cheek. His lips caressed her ear. And his fingers slipped between her thighs and stroked her silky wetness. "It's real," he said. "I'm not sure it gets much realer than this."

"It does," she said, because she couldn't stand it any longer. Any pretense of reason was washed away by his touch, and all she wanted was him. To be with him, joined. To feel him tremble in her arms and know that she'd brought a man like him to the brink and over it.

With a low moan, she pressed her lips to his, her tongue demanding entrance even as she lifted her hips. She felt his hands slide around her waist, and she reached down between them, stroking him, wanting to feel how ready he was for her.

She writhed a bit, teasing herself with the tip of his cock, but not for too long. She didn't want foreplay. Not tonight. Not now.

All she wanted was him. And so she took what she wanted, lowering herself onto him with one bold, quick stroke. Impaling herself. Taking him in, claiming him, consuming him.

His moan was low and guttural and filled with pleasure, and she felt her muscles contract in response.

He pulled his mouth away from hers only long enough to whisper her name, and then he kissed her hard, their teeth meeting and their tongues dancing.

She pulled back, gasping for air, then arched her back as he grabbed her hips, holding tight to her as they pistoned together.

"Alexis," he whispered again, and then his body seemed to explode in her arms. She'd been on the brink herself, and he pulled her over the edge with him. She clung to him, breathing hard, feeling him soften inside her, but not wanting the connection to break. Wishing they could stay like this forever.

Not possible.

A small voice of reason reminded her of more than the impracticality of living a life in a hot tub. The sun was going to rise in an hour or so. A fact that she murmured into his ear, along with a whispered invitation to come check out her bed.

"We'll have to properly break in the mattress," he said. "Unless you're too tired?"

"I'm pretty sure I'll never be tired again," she said as he scooped her up and carried her inside. They dripped all the way to the bedroom, but he stopped by the attached bath for towels. When they ended up under the covers she was warm and content—and very ready for a repeat performance.

Fortunately, he was happy to oblige.

This time they took it slow and easy, using all of the bed to stretch out, to explore and touch until she was certain he knew every inch of her body, and she was confident that she knew every bit of his.

She lay on her back as he slid into her, his hands on either side of her, his arms strong enough to hold her all night if she'd wanted. It was tempting. She watched his face as he moved rhythmically inside her, the way his mouth curved with pleasure. The way his eyes crinkled at the corners and burned with a sensual heat.

Slowly, almost painfully, the sweet pressure built. Her mouth opened and she drew in long gulping breaths as the climax rose inside her. Still, she held his gaze, almost to the very end, when the world was hanging by a thread and all she wanted to do was fly off into the void.

"Let go," he whispered, and she closed her eyes and

let the explosion take her, while he held her close, the wild shudders from her orgasm rocketing through both of them.

After, they lay together quietly, and she just watched him, awed by the night. By him.

He brushed a loose strand of hair from her face, then traced the curve of her lips with his fingers, the feel of it sending shivers through her. "You're incredible," he said. "Soothing and sweet."

"Am I? Soothing suggests snuggling under the covers and sliding off into sleep." She pressed her palm against his chest. "Is that what you want?"

"Not even remotely. But it's almost dawn. And you're human. Don't you think sleep would be a good idea?"

"As a theoretical concept, I'm all about sleep. But right now? I couldn't sleep for anything."

CHAPTER TWENTY-TWO

The scream of dying zombies filled the living room of Luke and Sara's Malibu house, and it wasn't any less noisy in the hallway. Luke gave his friend Nicholas Montague a helpless shrug as he stepped over the threshold into his wood-paneled office. "The girl was thrilled when she learned we owned an Xbox, and after what she's been through I could hardly deny her. If course, I didn't expect her to be at it quite so much," he added with a wry grin.

"You don't fool me," Nick said. "You're enjoying having her around."

"I am," Luke admitted. "Though I wish the circumstances were different."

When Sara had told him about CeeCee, Luke had been afraid that coming home and seeing her would hurt. Despite the centuries that had passed, the loss of his own daughter still ached. And recently he'd lost his ward, a vampire who, like CeeCee, had been turned in her teens. It was strange having a young woman in the house again, but all in all it was easier than Luke had expected.

Nick followed Luke into the office and shut the door behind him. Nick was Luke's friend and advocate, and Luke had asked him over to discuss his growing suspicions about Serge. He'd told Sara the truth when he said that he didn't believe that Serge was involved in the death of Penny Martinez. Now, though . . . now he was beginning to fear that his friend might have had a hand in the death of the poor girl's killer.

"The girl's doing okay, though?" Nick asked.

"All things considered, she's doing amazing. A remarkable kid, actually. Sara's already in love with her. Of course, she has her moments. She's pissed as hell at Serge, and she's let it rip a couple of times." The temper Luke had been able to handle. The tears had just about melted him. "For the most part, though, she's happy to hang with Sara or play video games. We took a walk on the beach as the moon was rising. She loved how well she could see in the dark." He grinned. "Remember those days? When everything about being what we are was shiny and new."

"I do," Nicholas said. "Then the daemon hit."

"Indeed." Luke nodded, then sighed. "We keep waiting. Watching. So far nothing."

Nick settled into a chair as Luke took the one opposite. "Interesting," Nick said. "Serge has been through a lot. Maybe the fact that he made her has affected her? Kept her daemon suppressed? Possibly even nonexistent?"

"We can hope for it. The girl's an innocent. If she can be spared the horror of facing her own inner evil . . ." Luke trailed off with a shudder. Unlike Nick, who'd had a relatively easy time controlling his daemon, Luke fought a constant battle with his.

"So about Serge," Nick began. "You said he just told Sara to take her? How did he look?"

"Ripped, she said. Horrible. She said it was like his daemon was coming out, but somehow different, too. And he was in a hurry. That much was very clear."

"How did he end up turning the girl?"

"He told Sara that the girl was attacked by a rogue. He fought it—killed it. But not in time to save her."

"Let her die, or turn her," Nick said.

"Exactly."

"Is this what you wanted to see me about? Or is there more?"

"That's part of it," Luke said. "The truth is, I'm concerned he might be in trouble. Worse, I'm concerned he might be involved in the recent attacks."

"The humans?"

"No. The desiccated vampires."

Nick dropped into one of Luke's chairs and put his feet up. "You've mentioned this to Sara?"

"The prosecutor? No, I haven't. We did speak about Serge—I caught his scent at the Penny Martinez crime scene and told her as much."

"But you don't believe he attacked her?"

"The scent was near the scene, but not the body. He was there for some other purpose, but I didn't know what. That was what I told Sara, and it was true at the time."

"But something's changed."

"Penny Martinez's killer was desiccated."

"Mitre," Nick said, then nodded. "And you're thinking that maybe Serge visited the scene in order to catch Mitre's scent and track him."

"It's a possibility I have to consider. Especially since CeeCee was camped out on Venice Beach, and Mitre just happened to be killed there."

Nick nodded slowly. "The pieces fit together, except for one thing. How is he supposedly drying out the rogues?"

"He was able to consume a shadower's life force while he was cursed," Luke said.

"True. But he didn't leave them desiccated. More than that, the curse was lifted—Petra's certain of that," he added, referring to his wife, who also happened to be the witch who'd cursed Serge in the first place. Though she'd placed the curse, it had been controlled by someone else—a madman whose death had freed Serge from the torment.

"Does she still have a connection to him?" While the curse had been in effect, Petra had often found herself inside Serge's head. It wasn't a place she had liked to be.

"A very vague one. But even though the curse has been lifted, we can't avoid the simple fact that he's like no one else. There is no creature that has lived to see that curse removed. We have no idea what the ramifications are. And considering how vile Serge's daemon has always been, the ramifications could be horrible."

"I know," Luke admitted. "That's at the heart of my concern, especially since Sara said that he looked so wretched. And damn him for not coming to me for help. He's been like a brother to me, and yet he stays away now?"

"If he is behind the deaths, can you blame him? With your position, he might think your loyalty would be skewed."

"He would be wrong," Luke said firmly. "If it takes a formal pardon to prove that to him, then so be it."

Nick whistled through his teeth. "What does Orion say about the desiccations?"

"He's at a loss. Doyle and Tucker have managed to chase down a few leads, though. They found solid connections between two of the dead humans and two of our mummified vamps. Security camera footage putting them at the same locations within the same time frame."

"That supports your theory," Nick said, frowning. "That Serge was at the crime scene waiting to catch the scent of a rogue."

"I know," Luke said.

"But a rogue hunter? I wouldn't have guessed that of Serge."

"No?" Luke frowned. "I'm not so sure. I know the very idea of a rogue disgusts him. He sees too much of his own torment there."

"Destroying his own sins by proxy."

"Something like that," Luke agreed.

There was a soft tap at the door, and then Sara opened it and stuck her head in. "It's Doyle."

"Must be important," Nick said, and Luke understood the deeper meaning. Luke and Doyle weren't exactly buddies. If Doyle was stopping by Luke's house, there was definitely a reason.

"Have him come in," Luke told Sara. "You might want to stay, too."

"Oh, I will," she said, then disappeared, only to reappear a moment later with Doyle in tow.

"What happened?" Luke asked.

"I'm coming here first as a courtesy," Doyle said. "Because I know he's your friend."

Luke caught Nick's eye, saw his own trepidation reflected there. "Who?"

"Sergius."

"What about him?" Luke asked.

"I've seen him," Doyle said, then tapped his skull. "In here."

"A victim," Luke said, his blood running cold. Doyle

wasn't getting any images from the desiccated vamps. If he'd seen Serge, it was in the head of one of the dead humans. *Shit*.

That complicated things. Luke was now in a position to help Serge, who was technically a wanted man for the murders he'd committed while cursed. Luke had no qualms about pardoning those crimes since Serge had not been himself.

Nor did he have an issue with pardoning the desiccation of the rogues if it had indeed been done by his friend. The rogues killed humans, which was an offense punishable by death under the Fifth International Covenant. Why should Luke care if that punishment came after trial or by Serge's hand?

But if Serge was the one killing the humans . . .

It wasn't something Luke liked to think about, and he hoped to hell Doyle was wrong, even though he feared Doyle was right.

"What did you see?" Luke asked.

"A cop was killed today," Doyle said. "Vampire attack. I got called to the scene, and the death was recent enough that I was able to get in. Got a good image, too."

"He was killed today? And you suspect Serge?" Only young vampires could maneuver through the sun. There were ways to travel, of course—cars with specially treated glass, for example. But it was still a point worth raising.

"Not in this death, no," Doyle said.

"Then what the hell are you talking about? You just told me you saw him."

"I saw a woman. I haven't been able to identify her yet, but she's the one that took out the cop."

"And Serge?"

"He was all over the guy's thoughts. That Serge was dangerous. That he had to warn *'her'*—I don't know who. But his impression was that Serge was a killer."

"And yet Serge didn't kill the cop."

"No," Doyle agreed, "he didn't. But Tucker and I have been working this for a while, and other than the deaths, the one consistent thing we're hearing is that the rogues are organized. That they have a leader."

"You're thinking it's Serge."

"And I'm thinking this cop somehow found out. So Serge sent one of his soldiers to kill him. Now, what I want to know is what you're going to do," Doyle demanded. "You two used to be attached at the hip. You gonna help us track him down, or are you going to sit back and watch the show unfold, hoping like hell your friend gets away with murder?"

Luke kept his face casually blank, though his thoughts were raging. "I'll do what I have to do, Ryan. Just as I always have."

◊

Serge found Alexis sitting at the bar in her kitchen, a cup of coffee forgotten in her hand. He went to her, wanting to touch her, and pressed his hand gently onto her shoulder. He'd awakened to find her gone, and an unreasonable sense of dread had rocketed through him. Now, touching her, he felt calm, and that feeling only intensified when she tilted her head back and gave him a watery smile.

"Couldn't sleep?" he asked.

"I keep thinking about Edgar. He was so innocent before he met me."

She'd told him a bit about the detective last night, and now Serge knelt in front of her and took her hands. "He knew about the shadow world. You told me that he knew about it long before you even had an inkling."

"Knowledge and action are two different things."

"You can't blame yourself."

"Oh, believe me, I can. I'm doing a remarkably good job of it." She managed a smile. He reached out to brush a lock of hair off her cheek, wishing that he could offer her real comfort, not just words. "It's almost light," she said.

He glanced at the door and the gray sky that would soon burst into orange and purple. "I should go," he said, hoping that she would beg him not to.

"Right," she said. She pushed her chair back and stood. "Before you can't. And I need to get in touch with Leena. The busy life of a guilt-ridden vampire hunter."

He took her hand. "Don't."

She closed her eyes, and he could sense her gathering herself, strengthening her resolve. "Sorry. My head knows I shouldn't feel guilty. My heart will catch up soon. In the meantime . . ." She shrugged. "I guess I really should keep busy. It'll keep my mind off it." She leaned forward and pressed an awkward kiss to his cheek. "I—well, last night—thank you. It was hard, learning about Edgar. Then that vampire. Everything. You made it—well, thank you."

He swallowed, hoping his disappointment didn't show. She'd needed comfort, and he'd given it. He was a fool to think that anything more would grow out of it. To think he could have anything more than that. He was what he was, and Alexis deserved more than a monster in a man's body. Considering the way she was pulling away from him now, she'd figured that much out as well.

"The sun," he said, as regret weighed on him like lead. "I must go." And he did, moving faster than she could see to her door, then out to the pool, where he transformed into mist and rose into the fast-brightening sky.

CHAPTER TWENTY-THREE

Jonathan Marcus Worthington III met his first vampire when he was fifteen. Or so he thought. Turned out the chick was just some overgrown goth girl who liked his money.

He'd let her suck him off, then headed back to his dorm room at Dayton Prep, the New England boarding school where his parents had dumped him.

For years afterward, he hadn't thought about vampires. He'd been too busy scoring coke and exam answers to pursue that little hobby. But when he got kicked out of Yale after his first semester, he'd moved to New York and had started trolling the goth subculture again, asking questions, searching for answers. It had taken him a long time, not to mention moves to Philly, San Francisco, and finally Los Angeles, but at last he'd found a real, live vampire. Well, a real undead one. He'd played it cool, of course, doing whatever she wanted—sex, blood, anyway and anyhow. Her name was Hanna, and she was sexy as hell and dark as sin. She used to talk smack about something called the Covenant and the PEC, some sort of police department for vampires. All bullshit, she'd say. Humans were cattle. Humans were food.

And then she'd look at him with that thin-lipped smile of hers, and he'd realized that he was a human, too, and that he'd be lucky to get out of her room alive.

He hadn't, of course. Hadn't gotten out alive, that is.

Instead, he'd been dead when he'd walked out of her room. Undead, with his undead lover at his side.

And for the first time in Jonathan's existence, he'd been happy. He'd been in charge. He'd been master of his own fucking domain without concern for rules or codes of honor or parents or nosy-ass friends telling him he was losing his shit, man.

He was a god. A goddamn, fucking god, and he had a beautiful goddess at his side.

And then some human with a wooden stake took her from him.

Some low-life *insect* with a superiority complex actually had the gall to think that he knew the way the world should be. That humans were superior and vamps should be iced. Fucking loser, and Jonathan had spent the next six months tormenting the bastard. Going after his family. His kids. Feeding off them. Draining them. Taking them to the point of death but not killing them. Not until the human—a supercilious bastard named Maury—was about out of his mind with rage and worry.

Then Jonathan had picked them off one by one. He saved Maury for the last, of course. And he didn't even drain that asshole's blood. Because he didn't want it inside him. Didn't want the foul stench of the idiot human lingering in his veins.

He'd cut the man's throat and left him to die.

Two days later, he'd awakened to a pounding at the metal door of the abandoned storage shed he was squatting in. No back door, so running wasn't even an option. He readied himself, prepared to fight the humans to the death. But when the door finally burst open, it wasn't a human. It was a vampire.

And he was smiling.

Derrick. And he'd welcomed Jonathan into the League.

Derrick had become Jonathan's friend, his mentor, his leader.

Now it was Derrick he needed to talk to. And the older vampire was going to be pissed.

Jonathan stared at the phone in his hand, not quite able to believe the call he'd just received from Warren, one of his friends in the PEC, a friend he'd converted over to Derrick's way of thinking. And flipping a PEC employee—even one who only worked at a computer— was a big fucking deal to Derrick. It had earned Jonathan major brownie points.

Now, though, it meant that Jonathan had to be the one to deliver bad news.

Bella was dead.

Beautiful, sexy Bella, now nothing more than ash.

At least that was the only conclusion Jonathan could draw, because after Bella's mission to get information out of the humans who'd infiltrated the Z Bar, she'd disappeared off the map. She'd been scheduled to check in with Warren to find out what the PEC knew about the human deaths. But he never got her call.

And Bella wasn't sloppy. As far as Jonathan was concerned, that meant Bella was dead.

The League members were dropping like flies. And even though Derrick had it under control—because Derrick always had everything under control—Jonathan couldn't shake the cold whisper in the back of his head that said he was an idiot to stay in town, and that the one thing he should do if he didn't want to meet the sharp end of a stake was get the hell out of Los Angeles.

◊

Alexis stayed at the kitchen table watching her coffee turn cold and wondering about the regret she'd seen on Serge's face, not to mention how quickly he'd left.

And why not? It's not like she thought her attraction to him was one-sided—he'd clearly wanted her last night as much as she'd wanted him. But that didn't change the fact that their passion had been driven by all that had happened between them.

She told herself it was for the best; she hardly needed to start something with a vampire.

And she told herself that she didn't truly care that he'd run so fast from her, because she didn't feel anything real for him—just lust. Simple male–female attraction mixed in with the compelling pull of his blood.

She told herself all of that, and yet she didn't believe it. So she sat holding an ice-cold cup of coffee and staring at a quickly brightening sky and wondering what she could have done differently that would have made him stay. Because the hard, simple truth was that the house felt empty without him. And, dammit, she felt empty, too.

"Enough."

Just saying the word aloud spurred her to action, and she shoved back from the table and marched to the sink. She dumped her coffee, splashed water on her face, and told herself sternly that the time for acting like a mooning teenager was over. She had a job to do, and with Edgar's death it had become that much harder—and that much more important. A vampire had killed him, and she intended to inflict some serious payback on the rogues.

She threw on the clothes she found on her bedroom floor, shoved her hair into a baseball cap, then headed over to Leena's. Only after ringing the doorbell did she remember that it was still incredibly early, but Leena answered the door so quickly that Alexis wondered if she'd been expecting her.

"I thought you might come," she said. "Now that Edgar's dead, you've lost one of your major sources for tracking the toothy bastards. You're going to need another mole in the task force."

The words were harsh and Alexis gaped at her friend, then reached out to touch her arm. "Are you okay?"

Her eyes softened and a soft smile touched her mouth. "I'm sorry. Yes. I'm fine. I'm just so—I don't know. I can't believe he's dead. I think I'm processing anger right now. Grief will come." She stepped away from the door, shifting her attention away from Alexis and toward the floor. "Come in."

"I'm alternating between grief and anger," Alexis admitted.

"I just wish I'd already figured out how to do a capture spell," Leena said. "We could have used it on that bitch of a vampire last night, and you could have staked her." Leena had recently come up with the idea of devising a spell that would hold a vampire in a mystical prison at least long enough for the hunter to move in and stake him. "Instead, you had to rely on Sergius. And if he hadn't been there, we'd probably both be dead."

"But he was there," Alexis said firmly. "And there's no point kicking yourself over what-ifs. You'll get it eventually. Are you any closer?"

"I am, actually." Leena's smile was cold, and Alexis was once again struck by how much Edgar's death had impacted her friend. She seemed harder now, and while Alexis had come over hoping for comfort, right then she felt removed from Leena, as if they were business associates rather than friends. She cleared her throat and managed a smile. "That's great."

"It is," Leena agreed. "I've got a new perspective on things," she added with a laugh. "A new lease on my magic." She smiled as if at a private joke, then shook it off and aimed a real grin at Alexis. "It's not perfect yet, but I'm getting very, very close. Of course, the biggest problem is that I don't yet have a way for you to operate the spell, so I'd have to go with you on the hunt." She tapped her leg. "Obviously that's not happening. But I'll work it out. I've had a long time to think about just what to do."

"Did you try to track Tori's killer?"

"I did. No luck. Either he's dead or he's not on the prowl."

"Too bad. I could use a hunt right now. I'm at loose ends. Edgar's death was like a stake through *my* heart, you know? And at the same time, part of me is mourning the fact that I've lost my connection to the LAPD. I know I'm not really being a heartless bitch, but I still feel like a shit for thinking about how much I've been inconvenienced when it's Edgar who's dead." She blinked, and the tears that had been welling in her eyes ran down her cheeks.

"Well, it's not like you don't have another way. Now that you're cozy with that vampire, he can help, right? Isn't that supposedly his whole raison d'être? To kill other vampires?"

Alexis brushed the tears away, the motion hiding her

frown. Leena's business-like approach was disconcerting, but she was also right. Except that Serge was gone.

"Gone?" Leena said when Alexis told her as much. "You can't let Sergius go. He told you he knows who's organizing these rogues. Make him take you to their leader. Use him. You've made this your mission—you can't back out because you made the mistake of spreading your legs for him."

Alexis winced a bit from Leena's vulgarity, but at least that explained the coldness. Leena was no fool; of course she'd figured out that Alexis had slept with Serge. And considering how much she despised vamps, it only made sense that she'd be a bit edgy. And the truth of it was, Alexis probably deserved the reality check. Serge *was* a vampire, after all. *A vampire*. One of the creatures that Alexis had dedicated her life to hunting.

Except that what she thought she knew about vamps didn't fit with what she'd learned about Serge. More important, it didn't fit with what she felt for him.

In the end, she didn't even stay an hour at Leena's. She told her friend that she was going to go home so that Leena could continue working on the capture spell and Alexis could think about alternative ways for tracking the rogues. She promised she'd also think about how to contact Serge again, but Alexis wasn't sure that was going to happen; he'd wanted to leave, and she wasn't inclined to beg him to come back.

She ended up spending the day at loose ends, filling in the time with a lot of naps, which made sense considering how little she'd slept the night before. But the naps weren't entirely restorative. She ended up dreaming of Serge, and she woke up at dusk feeling edgy and needy and bitterly alone. All the more so when reality struck her once again, and she remembered that Edgar was truly gone.

Even the hours she spent working out didn't take the edge off, and when she was well and truly frustrated with herself she went down to the Batcave, among all the expensive equipment that her parents' money had bought. She sat in front of the $12.99 police band radio and settled in to listen. It wasn't ideal, but it was mindless, and with luck maybe she'd hear a call in which the dispatcher said more about the injury than she actually should.

Amazingly enough, after two hours of mind-numbing, static-filled chatter, that's exactly what happened. A woman had been attacked in an alley and the paramedics were called in. A neck wound. The victim died en route to the hospital, but detectives were needed at the scene.

Bingo.

She'd hit the scene, snag some dust, and get Leena to do her thing. With luck, she'd find something to kill tonight. At the very least, she'd be in motion, and her mind would be on something other than Serge and how quickly he'd rushed away from her after what she'd considered a night of uncommon bliss.

◊

"We should leave Los Angeles," Jonathan said. He was fidgeting in front of Derrick's desk, his usually meticulous hair sticking out in all directions.

Derrick fought the urge to slap the younger vamp down. He was scared; Derrick got that. But at the moment, Derrick wasn't interested in mollycoddling his men. No, he was interested in revenge.

"Bella's dead," he said flatly. Jonathan was right; no other conclusion could be drawn. "Do you think I cared nothing for her? That I would leave this place without seeing her avenged?"

The younger vamp ducked his head. "I'm sorry. It's just that everything seems to be going so wrong lately. Maybe we should just leave until things cool down."

"Are you scared?"

Jonathan shook his head.

"Don't lie. It doesn't suit you. Here." He lifted his wrist to his mouth and bit down hard, setting the blood to flow. "Drink, and be restored."

Jonathan genuflected, then came around Derrick's desk, knelt in front of the elder vampire, and drank.

The power. Such glory, such delicious exultation simply from knowing that his strength was being drawn into these disciples. He let his head fall back, closed his eyes, and simply gave himself to Jonathan.

After a moment, the younger vampire released his wrist, then stood, bowed, and moved back around the desk. He seemed to glow with power now, and Derrick could feel the strength and courage rising in the boy.

"Has your fear faded?"

"It has," Jonathan said. "And my mind is clear. So please understand that it is not out of fear that I speak, but from intellect."

Derrick frowned, irritated that the boy hadn't fallen into step, but he waved at him to continue anyway.

"There are League members in Europe, Derrick. Your teachings may not be widely known there, but those who follow you are loyal. We can go now, then return to Los Angeles when the timing is better suited for success."

"The timing is excellent now. Trust me. I have reason to stay here."

"You don't even know for sure that Sergius is in town."

"I believe that he is," Derrick said.

"Because of the sketch?" Derrick had shown it to all of his lieutenants. "Even if he was here, there's no guarantee that he's stayed. Not only that, but have you considered that it might be Sergius who's killing us?"

"The cause of the desiccations, you mean?"

"Exactly. What if he's targeting the League?"

Derrick couldn't help the laugh that escaped his lips. "Why the hell would he? You've never met him. Serge is a wild thing, a man after my own heart. You wouldn't believe the things that I've watched him do. He's a killer, my young friend. Serge's only friends are pain and death."

"*Our* pain? *Our* death?"

But Derrick wasn't going to listen to such nonsense. Jonathan didn't know Sergius, whereas Derrick's fondest memories were of the two of them traveling together. Killing together.

"You needn't waste any more thought on him. It's the girl I'm concerned with. The girl who's been hunting us. The girl who took my Bella from us."

Jonathan bowed his head. "I'll happily destroy her, with your permission."

"No. I wish to do it myself. Bella didn't tell me where the girl lives, but she found papers. Go to her apartment. Find out who the woman is. When you have the information in hand, we'll go pay her a visit together. But fair warning, Jonathan. This kill belongs to me."

♦

CeeCee wasn't as interested in the Xbox as she pretended to be, although it did feel good to sit on the couch and mindlessly shoot monsters. That was the trouble—*monsters*. Because now she was a monster, wasn't she? A vampire.

Maybe even worse.

She'd eavesdropped last night when Luke went into his office to talk with his friend Nick and then later with that PEC agent, Doyle.

They were worried about Serge. About the fact that he might be killing humans. And that he might be doing some really weird shit to some other vampires.

Not that she cared, she told herself. She was still mad at him. And she was going to stay that way for a long, long time.

But if they were worried about him, then that must mean they were worried about her, too.

She closed her eyes, dropped her remote hand to her lap, and just let it lie there. She was tired and antsy. She'd slept for a few hours that afternoon, but not long enough. She would have liked to sleep for a couple more hours, but that had been impossible. Too many thoughts in her head.

She felt the couch shift, and she opened her eyes to see Sara sitting next to her, smiling that smile. CeeCee liked Sara. She reminded her of Mrs. Dawson, her fifth-grade teacher. The one who told her how smart she was and used to invite her to the school on weekends to make posters for the classroom. CeeCee knew that the room had more posters than it needed because of all the weekends they spent together, but she was so grateful to be out of the house—away from her mom and Burt—that she never said anything. She was afraid that if she did Mrs. Dawson would quit inviting her.

"You doing okay?" Sara asked. CeeCee shrugged. She was still pissed at Serge, of course. But she had to admit that it was okay here. They let her go down to the beach—day or night, since she wasn't light-sensitive yet like Luke. And they'd fixed up a room for her.

Sara set a plate of cookies down on the table. "You need the blood to survive, but I still haven't lost my taste for food. I've even found that it helps keep the daemon down. Memories of pre-daemon times, maybe." She glanced sideways at CeeCee. "Still no stirrings?"

"Nothing," CeeCee said. It was weird talking about the daemon. Her stepfather had always said that she was an evil girl. That she'd been born bad. If that was true, her daemon should be ripping her apart. "I mean, I'm hungry," she added, "but that's normal, right? When you're new?"

Sara squeezed her hand. "That's normal."

"Serge is supposed to be the one telling me these things, isn't he?" She wanted to sound all cool and matter-of-fact, but she couldn't keep the anger out of her voice.

"You don't like it here?"

"No, I do. You and Luke are great." She managed a self-deprecating snort. "Nicest place I've ever been, that's for sure. But . . ." She trailed off with a shrug.

"Serge will be back," Sara said.

"He shouldn't have left." CeeCee hated how whiny she sounded. How needy.

"No," Sara said, "he probably shouldn't have."

CeeCee looked at her more closely, surprised that Sara was telling her the truth. Talking to her like she mattered. Like she deserved to know what was really going on.

"Would it be selfish of me to say that even if he shouldn't have, I'm glad he did?"

"Really?" Her voice sounded needy, and she hated that. She wanted to be all cool and adult.

"Really," Sara said. "I can't have kids now that I'm a vampire, and, well, I'm not saying you're a kid, but I will say that it's nice to have you here. I like hanging out with you. So does Luke. He had a daughter once, you know. And even after all this time, he still misses her. Maybe it sounds a little presumptuous, but having you here fills a gap for both of us."

CeeCee's chest felt tight and she nodded, hoping she wouldn't do something embarrassing like cry. "I'm glad. I like it here, too."

"But it doesn't make the hurt go away, does it?"

CeeCee looked up at Sara, relieved that she understood. "Is it because he's the one that made me? Is that why it matters so much?"

"Partly. That and he saved you from something horrible. But at the same time he pushed you into this completely unfamiliar world, where you don't even know your own body anymore. He should have stayed around. Made sure you understood what was happening to you."

"Then why didn't he?"

"I don't know exactly. But Serge has walked this earth for a very long time, and when you're that old, sometimes things get bottled up. He probably needs to work through stuff. But I promise, it doesn't have anything to do with you."

CeeCee nodded, because she could tell that Sara really believed that. But if Serge was the monster that Nick and Luke thought he was, then it had everything to do with her. And she wanted to talk to him. Wanted to know the truth. About what he'd done. And about what she was.

Heck, she wanted to so bad it almost felt like he was right there with her. Like he was watching over her. Some vampire version of a guardian angel.

But he couldn't be, could he?

She shot a glance toward the window and realized that night had fallen once again. The ocean that had glowed a brilliant orange the last time she'd looked was now black with frothy gray waves.

He couldn't really be out there, could he?

She told herself it was wishful thinking, and she'd seen enough crap over her sixteen years to know that wishful thinking was nothing short of stupid.

Still, there was that feeling. That burning in her veins. Like something was coming. Something was near.

Serge.

She stood up, pulling her hand away from Sara.

"CeeCee? Are you okay?"

"Yeah. I'm just . . . I don't know. Antsy."

"Is it—"

"My daemon?" CeeCee answered. "No."

"You're sure?"

CeeCee nodded. "Totally. I just want to take a walk. I'm still all pissed off at Serge. I guess I just feel like walking it off. Is that okay? Can I go outside? I like the ocean."

"Of course you can," Sara said, her expression making CeeCee wonder if Sara saw through the lie. Except how could she, because CeeCee wasn't really lying. She *was* antsy, and she *did* love the ocean.

So what if she also wanted to see Serge? Because she had to see him. She had to know what he was—and she needed to know what that made her.

CHAPTER TWENTY-FOUR

Serge stood across the street from Luke and Sara's Malibu house, his hands clenched at his sides as he fought down the rising daemon and the writhing, spitting beast.

He'd felt their gnawing power ever since he'd left Alexis. With her, they'd been calm, controlled, and he'd been the stronger for it. But away from her the darkness returned, and he'd locked himself underground, taking refuge in the first abandoned building he'd found after he'd fled.

Alone, he battled it back down. But he wasn't truly alone. She was in his thoughts—Alexis. That door was closed, but the memory of her remained, and though it sent melancholy coursing through his veins to think of her, he did it anyway, reveling in the recollection of her scent, her touch, the sweet caress of her hair against his skin. And most of all the way she'd looked at him, like she saw something good inside. Something that he could cling to and cherish and try to believe.

How he'd fought and fought with his darkness until the sun finally set and he'd crawled out into the night, letting his mind go and his body take him until it led him here. To CeeCee. To the girl who'd made him a hero in Alexis's eyes. Maybe by seeing her again he could see himself that way, too. Because if he didn't, he was certain that without Alexis at his side, he'd eventually lose himself to the lure of the dark—no matter how valiantly he fought.

"Spying on me?"

He whipped around to face CeeCee.

"You shouldn't be here," he said, his voice almost a snarl. He didn't want her to see him like this, to catch the scent of his self-pity. "Luke and Sara will wonder where you are."

"Sara knows I'm outside." She plunked down onto the ground next to him, looking calm and happy and perfectly well adjusted.

"She doesn't know you're with me. I don't think she'd approve."

"Because you went all *grrr* on us the other day?"

His smile came uninvited, and some of the tightness in his chest melted. "Something like that, yeah."

"Is that why you're here? To make sure I don't go all wonky, too?"

"Wonky? You mean your daemon? I think Sara and Luke are capable of helping you through that."

She crossed her arms over her chest and cocked her head, her expression telling him clearly and concisely that he was an idiot and she wasn't buying any of his crap. "I mean like you. It's not normal, right? What you do? Turning the vamps into mummies."

A frisson of anxiety shot up his back. "Who says I do that?" She couldn't have seen him kill Mitre. She'd been yards away on the sand, and unconscious, too.

She shrugged. "I'm not stupid. I can piece things together."

He got it, then. Of course Luke must be looking into the desiccated corpses, and naturally he'd discuss the case at home. With Sara for sure, and maybe even with Nick.

"You didn't answer me," she said. "That's not normal, right?"

"No," he agreed. "It's not normal."

She met and held his eyes for a moment, then pulled her knees up to her chest and hugged them. Suddenly she didn't seem so well adjusted. Suddenly she seemed vulnerable as hell.

"So that's why you're here, right? You're afraid I'm going to lose it and suck the life out of your vamp friends."

The harshness of her tone made him recoil as much as the words themselves. "What? CeeCee, *no*."

"Yeah? Then tell me. Why are you here? Why did you leave me with them and then come back? Why aren't you gone?"

He closed his eyes and clenched his hands into fists. The questions were so simple. Words requiring words in response. But how to find the right ones? How indeed, except to dig for the deepest, most basic truth.

And what is that, Serge?

Did he even recognize truth anymore?

She didn't press, but she didn't stop looking at him. He stared blankly across the street at the glowing lights inside Luke and Sara's house. Beyond, he could hear the ocean crashing against the shore. He couldn't see it—the house blocked his view—but he could picture it clearly in his mind. The moonlight on the froth, the water and sand painted in black and white and gray.

"I just wanted to see you," he finally said, because it didn't get more basic than that. "And I want . . . to help you."

She seemed to take that in. After a moment, she nodded. "Sara's worried. Because my daemon hasn't come out. I guess that's pretty unusual."

"It is," Serge said. "But I wasn't really a vampire when I turned you. I was—I don't know, I guess I was masquerading as one."

"So what does that make me?"

"Honestly, I'm not sure. I was transformed by a curse. You, from my blood. What that means to you, though, I don't entirely know. Maybe it means you're the first daemon-free vampire. But maybe it means the beast is inside you, too, but it's going to take a while to show up."

He watched her face, looking for signs of anger or disgust. But all he saw was calm acceptance, and it felt as though the weight of the world had lifted from his shoulders.

"I guess I can handle it. Whatever it is. I mean, you're handling it, right?"

"Yes," he said firmly, because that's what she needed to hear. And because it was true, especially when he kept Alexis in his mind. "Yeah, I'm handling it."

"Okay, then. So how does it work? How do you turn vamps into dried-out mummy things?"

"Something else I don't really know."

She cocked her head to one side. "What's that mean? You aim your super-secret mummifying laser at them and they just dry up?"

He had to laugh. "Not exactly." And then, because she was right and one day she might need to know, he told her. "I have to touch them. And then I just have to concentrate. It's a bit like drawing liquid through a straw, but very fast. One minute they're right there. The next, they're nothing but a shell."

She snorted. "Considering what that asshole did to me, I have to say I think that's pretty cool." He grinned without thinking. Honestly, he liked her attitude.

They both looked up as they heard the back door click. And though neither of them could see Sara, her voice soon rang out, calling out to CeeCee, urging her to come back inside.

"I should go." CeeCee stood and wiped the rear of her jeans. "I like her, and I think she'd worry."

Serge nodded.

"Will you—will you come back? To see me more, I mean."

"You don't want me as a mentor," he said. "Luke, Sara . . . they're the ones who can help you."

Her chin lifted a bit and he saw hard determination on her face. "Who said shit about you being a mentor? Maybe I just think you're cool."

He stood as well. "Maybe you bumped your head against a rock on that beach."

"Ha ha," she said. She looked like there was more she wanted to say, but then Sara called again, and CeeCee only waved and scurried through the brush to the dark road.

Serge watched her go, knowing that he'd be back. He told himself it was because he had to keep an eye on her. Had to see how she changed as the hunger grew. If it developed into a ravenous need that couldn't be satisfied by blood. If her eyes became reptilian. If—

He shook his head, because that wasn't the real reason at all. No, he'd return because CeeCee was his. Even if

Luke and Sara kept her in their family until the end of time, she always would be. The responsibility of that awed him, even as he found himself smiling and looking forward to seeing her again.

And that, he thought, was a small slice of amazing.

♦

As soon as CeeCee was gone, Serge felt at loose ends. Inside him, the beast curled, its hunger taunting him. He pushed it down, holding on to the pleasure he'd felt during his talk with the teen. But it wasn't enough. The beast had seen a chink in Serge's armor, and it was cunning enough to push and prod and fight for release.

But Serge was a fighter, too. Too bad for him his best defense against the monsters inside him was a woman who didn't want him. He could still see her, though. Could reach out through the blood connection and hold a tiny bit of her close to his heart.

It wasn't perfect, but right then he needed it. Needed to keep the beast down. Needed Alexis.

He stood there, eyes closed, reaching out to her, blood to blood, searching for some hint of her inside him. Something warm. Something perfect and strong and beautiful.

Something determined. Something angry. Something on the hunt.

His eyes flew open as a cloying fear cloaked him. Goddammit all, she was after a rogue.

He knew he shouldn't be worried. She was well trained, after all. And she'd killed many a rogue. But that was before Derrick had caught on to her. Before he'd sent Bella in to assassinate her. This could be a trap. She was smart enough to know that, and yet fool-hardy enough to go anyway. Dammit, dammit, *dammit*.

No way was he letting her go alone. Yet he was all the way in Malibu, and from the images and thoughts he was pulling from the blood connection, she was in West Hollywood, wandering down dark alleys, searching for her prey. A long distance to cover, and if he went by car he would never make it.

Without even consciously making the choice, he trans-formed into sentient mist, rising up and whipping over the darkened California coastline before going inland to the West side, his mind locked on her, using her essence to pull him closer, closer, until he transformed back into himself on the roof of a darkened convenience store.

She was below him in the alley, moving with long, purposeful strides. She wore the familiar leather jacket, which was undoubtedly loaded with stakes and her dart pistol. Her face was hard, and she held a small orb in one hand and a stake in the other, most of it hidden from view by the way she had it palmed.

When she'd gone another few yards, a scream ripped the air, and Alexis broke into a full-on run. Serge dropped all pretense of staying out of sight and raced forward, only to come to a halt when he saw Alexis neatly stake a rogue, even as she urged his shaken victim—an elderly homeless man—to get the hell out of there.

As dust from the rogue collected at her feet, she slid her palms together, as if telling herself that was that. She was still grinning in smug satisfaction when the howl rang out—*"Biiiiiiittttttccccccchhhhh"*—and a new vam-pire leaped from a rooftop across the alleyway, knock-ing her to the ground and sending the stake she still held in her hand skittering across the asphalt.

Serge was already racing into the fray when another vampire landed next to the first. "Kill the bitch," the new one said, before flying across the alley to land hard against the brick wall of one of the local businesses.

"Shit!" The one crouching over Alexis looked up to see Serge—and when he did, Alexis thrust up, nailing him through the heart and causing a storm of dust to rain down on her.

His friend pushed away from the wall and started to follow. But that wasn't happening. Fear for Alexis and the brutal pull of his rising hunger fueled his actions, and before he could talk himself out of it—before he even really realized he was doing it—he grabbed the bastard, held him down, and pulled every bit of life from his worthless shell.

The desiccated remains fell to the ground, and he backed away, calmer now, but realizing that he'd probably just made a terrible mistake.

Slowly, he turned to look at Alexis, who was on the ground gaping at him. "That's not . . . normal, is it?"

He couldn't help his ironic smile. "No. It's not normal at all."

CHAPTER TWENTY-FIVE

Alexis sprawled on the ground, astounded by what she'd just witnessed. The vampire who'd been about to attack her was now a dried-out shell. The man she'd recently made love to—the man she'd thought didn't want her—was standing above her, his hand reaching out for her, his face a warrior's countenance.

She hesitated a second, acknowledging how desperately she wanted his touch, then let him tug her to her feet. There were things to talk about. Lots of things. But first she wanted to know what had just happened. She opened her mouth, planning to ask just that, and found herself saying instead, "Why are you here? You left me without even looking back."

He winced, and though it was petty, she was glad. She didn't want to be the only one suffering.

"I made a mistake," he said. He held her hand tightly, and she had the feeling that if she tried to tug free he wouldn't let her go. She didn't try. "Not even vampires are infallible."

She glanced at the desiccated body. "But you're not, are you? Not a vampire, I mean."

His expression hardened, and he looked away. "No. Not exactly."

"Is that why you left? You were afraid I couldn't handle the truth?"

"Can you?"

"Serge." She stepped closer to him, gratified when his arms encircled her. "I already know that you suck blood to live. And that you saved me and CeeCee. The fact that you live off . . . whatever it is you live off isn't going to substantially change the equation."

He shifted, refusing to meet her gaze. "We should go."

Immediately, she was on alert. "Are there other vampires around?"

As she watched, he tilted his head back, tested the air. "No."

"Then we're staying. And you're not avoiding this conversation."

The corner of his mouth twitched, but didn't quite end up in a smile. After a moment, though, he did look at her, and she considered that a victory. "You talk about how I saved the two of you, but I'm no hero. There are things I've done, Alexis. Things I can never tell you."

"I believe you, and I don't want to know. But it was *this* man," she said, pressing a hand to his chest. "This man who I invited into my bed. This man who gave me the best night of my life. Believe me when I say that the only awful thing you've done to me is walk out."

"I thought you wanted me to."

She looked at him with astonishment.

"There was the scent of regret all over you."

A small laugh escaped her. "I'm not surprised. I was full of it. I should never have let Edgar do something so foolish. I was swimming in grief, but you were like a buoy. And then you left."

"I'm so sorry. And I'm also relieved."

She lifted up onto her tiptoes and brushed a soft kiss over his lips.

"Best night of your life?"

"I mean it, you know. Not a figure of speech, not placating. Best night ever."

"Would you believe me if I said I felt the same? That never in two thousand years have I felt the way I do in your arms? That when I'm with you all I want to do is look at you and touch you? That I hate the bad things I've done even more when I'm around you? That just knowing you're beside me soothes me and helps keep the daemon down, the beast at bay? Makes me a little more human?"

She swallowed. "I really make you feel that way?"

"From the moment I saw you. Honestly, I don't know that I would have tried to save CeeCee if it hadn't been for you. She meant something to you, and so she meant something to me." He shrugged. "Now she really does mean something to me, but that night on the beach I was only interested in feeding."

"You said something about a daemon. Is that what you are? Instead of a vampire, I mean."

"No," he said. "The daemon's inside me. And what I am now . . . well, that's a more complicated question."

"I'd like to understand."

He hesitated for a moment, then nodded. "It's not a pretty story."

"I've come to realize that very little in your world is."

"All right. I already told you some of this. How I went looking to be made into a vampire?"

"You called it the dark kiss."

"I did. Of course I didn't know what it was called. Not then. Luke and I had heard rumors about immortality."

"The vampire who's taking care of CeeCee? Along with the woman. Um, Sara?"

"That's him. He's closer to me than a brother. Even back then we were almost inseparable. And one day, I heard a rumor about a dark lady whose kiss granted eternal life. We both wanted it, and we both paid a heavy price." She saw the pain of memory flash across his face. "Luke lost his family in the grab for immortality. He had the sweetest little girl . . ."

"I'm so sorry. And you?"

"Me? I didn't lose much. Just my sanity."

She licked her lips, certain she didn't want to hear, but at the same time knowing that she did. "What do you mean?"

"That's the daemon," he explained. "It's impossible to explain the horror of it without actually experiencing it. But I'll try. It's like, well, it's evil, pure and simple. A deep, pain-loving malevolence that lives deep within every human."

"Every human?"

He nodded. "For the most part it's buried, though if you look at some of your more vile sociopaths, I think it's safe to say their daemons have wiggled their way free. There's something about the mortal coil that traps it."

"But vampires aren't mortal."

He gave her the kind of smile a teacher bestows on a prize pupil. "Exactly. And the daemon rises up. It takes control. It pushes you to do things you wouldn't do, and yet it's still *you*. It thrives on pain. On degradation." He shut his eyes, and she saw a tremor run through his body. She reached for him and clutched his hand.

"It was bad for you."

"Worse than bad. There's a ritual—it's called the Holding. Vampires use it to control the daemon. To push it back down when it first emerges. Some are successful. They walk the earth feeling almost human. Sara's like that. With others, the daemon is battled down, but it still fights to get free. It's a constant battle, but with enough willpower, the vampire can stay in control. Luke is like that, and every year that passes it's become easier for him. Sara's helped a lot. She soothes the daemon in him as you do for me."

The words were like warm cotton inside her, and she squeezed his fingers. "I'm glad. So, you can control it? Like Luke?"

His jaw twitched, and he shook his head. "Not like Luke. Sometimes I could control it. But most of the time, no. For most of the last two millennia it's been the daemon running the show, not me. Although to be honest, after a while it was hard sometimes to tell where I stopped and the daemon began." He looked at her, as if gauging her reaction. She nodded, hoping she looked encouraging. In truth, she was trying very hard not to be scared. "Vampires like that—the ones that can't control the daemon—they're rogues. When the daemon's out, that's when humans get killed. It's rogues you've been hunting, Alexis."

She nodded her understanding, and thought about what Leena had said about all vampires being evil. Now she understood better. They all had the potential to be evil, but some fought it like the devil. Like Serge, and damned if she didn't admire and respect his determination. "So that makes you a rogue?"

"I was a rogue," he said. "I have been." He stepped away from her, then walked back, and she could see the tension in his body. "Some just give in to it, but I've been fighting it for thousands of years. It's exhausted me, ripped me up from the inside. In some ways, I've won. In some ways, it's better. But it's also so much worse."

"I don't understand."

He ran a hand through his short hair. "There came a point at which I couldn't take it anymore. Where I was having moments of lucidity mixed up with the horror of the daemon taking over. It was hell. No, it was worse than hell. Then I was cursed."

"Cursed?"

"There was a time when my friends were in trouble. I thought that by taking on this curse, I could save them. I thought I could fight against the power of the monster that would rise within me."

"That's one hell of a risk."

"At the time, it seemed like nothing. I was exhausted from fighting the daemon."

"Did it work?" she asked. "Did you save them?"

"It worked," he said. "But there was no way to lift the curse. At least, none that we knew of."

"But there must have been a cure," she said. "You're okay now. Aren't you?"

He nodded. "I am. But for a while, I truly was a monster. And worse than that, I was controlled by a madman. He used me to kill and to maim, kind of like a remote-controlled robot. I did what he wanted because my mind was no longer my own. I wasn't a vampire. I wasn't the daemon. I wasn't anything that had ever been seen on this earth before." His voice was harsh, and she could hear the pain in it. She felt chilled just listening to him, as if the horror of what he'd experienced was seeping into her bones. And though she wouldn't say it out loud for anything, she'd be lying if she didn't at least admit to herself that some of what she felt was fear.

"So what happened?"

"A battle," he said with a half smile. "From my experience most dramatic changes in this world come about as the result of battles. The madman died. The curse was lifted. And my friends thought I was back to being Serge. My daemon high, perhaps, but a vampire once more."

"Considering what I saw, I'm guessing your friends were wrong."

"They were. And they still don't entirely know the truth. You and CeeCee are the only ones who know for sure."

"I don't know. Not really. I saw, but I don't understand what I saw."

"Neither do I. Not fully. The truth is that my friends are partly right. The daemon torments me still. But I'm learning to battle it down."

She took his hand. "I'm glad I help."

"But that's not the only bit of darkness living within me now."

"What do you mean?"

"The monster from the curse is gone, that much I know. But something was left behind. Something new, born in me. A beast. A raging beast, like something out of a storybook. Scales and talons and a wicked hunger."

She realized she was staring at him, completely confused. "Scales and talons? I didn't see anything like that."

"Because I fed off that vampire. I drew out his life force. That's what I survive on now instead of blood."

"So feeding keeps you from changing into a horrible, scaly monster?"

"It does. And there's more."

She nodded, not sure how much more she could process.

"Feeding determines my form. Or, more accurately, my nature."

"I don't understand."

"I fed on a vampire, so now I'm a vampire. If I'd taken the life force of a werewolf, I would be weren. A jinn, I'd be a jinn."

She licked her lips. "And if you don't feed?"

"If I don't feed, then I become the beast. Mindless once again. Raging. Killing. Until its hunger is satiated and I transform into whatever creature I fed upon during my wild rampage."

"That's unbelievable," she breathed.

"It's horrible," he said. "And it's why I do what I do."

"What you do?"

"I find rogue vampires, and I take their life force. I take from them that I can stay a vampire."

"You fight the bad ones. You take them out just like I do. You shouldn't feel guilty if you benefit from that. Believe me, I get a huge happy buzz when I dust one of them."

"Once upon a time, I *was* one of them." His voice was gentle, but firm.

"I'm sorry," she said. "I know." She managed a weak smile as she looked at him. Him. *Serge*. The vampire—no, the man—who'd saved her. Who'd made love to her. "I understand what you're saying, but you're not that guy anymore. From everything you've told me, you've survived a dozen kinds of hell. I didn't know anyone could be that strong, but you have been. You've kept fighting. Even now. And instead of rolling over with self-pity or walking the streets and draining everyone who comes along, you're doing a little bit of good for the world when you feed."

He shook his head.

"What?"

"You're looking at me through rose-colored glasses."

"No," she said firmly. "But I am looking at you." She went to him and pressed her hands to his face, her eyes drinking him in. She leaned in and brushed her lips over his, then pulled away slowly. "And I see you. I really do."

CHAPTER TWENTY-SIX

She still wanted him. *Him.*

Such a simple thing, and yet it changed the world.

He clutched her tight, his fingers stroking her hair as her forehead rested on his chest. Her breathing came soft and even, but her pulse had kicked up high. He caught the scent of desire, and it shot through him, stoking his already burning need.

She was so real in his arms, but she was ephemeral, too. The whisper of a promise. The chance to be a better man. To feel like Serge, and not the monsters within.

He pressed a soft kiss to the top of her head, then asked plainly and simply, "Are you sure?"

She tilted her head back to look at him. "I thought you could sense my feelings through the blood connection. Don't you know that I've never been more sure?"

"Thank God," he said simply.

She laughed, then moved back into his arms, drenching him with the scent of pleasure, of *need*. Her mouth was desperate against his, and he returned her passion, pulling away only when it struck him that they were still in an alley. "Not here," he said. "Do you trust me?"

"I do."

"Then hold on," he said, shifting into sentient mist, Alexis dissolving into his arms, their essence mixing and twining as he traveled from the alley to the pool deck in front of her back door.

"Wow," she said, reaching for him as she steadied herself. "That was . . . weird."

"Just one of my many entertaining parlor tricks."

"Yeah? Well come into my parlor and entertain me some more." She took his hand and tugged him to the door, quickly unlocking it and pulling him inside and into her arms. "Can I ask you a question?"

"Anything."

"That couple, Luke and Sara? You said they were your friends. And you're trusting them with CeeCee."

"Yes?"

"Why don't you tell them? About the beast, I mean."

"It's complicated," he said.

"Is it? How?"

"Because Luke's a big deal now. He's the chairman of the Alliance—I guess you could say that's like the United Nations for shadowers—and he's also the governor of the Los Angeles territory."

"So? How is that a problem?"

"The deaths are baffling the local shadow police."

"Division Six," she said.

"That's right," he said. "I forgot you already knew some of this."

"But not all. I know about Homeland, and that Division Six is part of it. But what it does . . ." She trailed off with a shrug.

"Division Six is the Los Angeles branch of the PEC. That's the Preternatural Enforcement Coalition. Had you heard of that one?"

"No, and it's a mouthful."

"It's housed in the criminal justice building and it's hidden within Homeland."

"I'm still not understanding how all that is a problem with Luke."

"I tell Luke the truth and he'll either arrest me or pardon me. Arrest me, and I'm executed. Pardon me, and he's destroyed politically."

"Killing vampires who kill humans is a bad thing?"

"It's a crime. They're supposed to be tried. What the rogues do is a crime, but so is killing a rogue. Just like in your world, there are courts and juries and judges. Not to mention prison and death row and very unpleasant punishments."

"All right. I understand that getting arrested wouldn't be at the top of your list. But haven't you considered that maybe there's a third option? Maybe he won't do anything except be your friend?"

"I couldn't expect him to do that."

"Why not? You told me yourself that you took on a curse to save your friends. You don't think your best friend would keep his mouth shut to protect you?"

"He's done more than that on several occasions," Serge said, thinking of all the secrets Luke and Nick had kept for him over the years.

"So why wouldn't he continue to?"

He didn't answer. What was there to say?

She reached over to take his hand. "You're the same man you were before."

He shuddered at the thought. "I hope not."

"Your core, Serge," she said. "A man who battled his daemon for centuries instead of just saying fuck it and going all-out rogue. A guy who let himself be turned into a monster of all things in order to save his friends. And now you're hunting rogues, staying alive the hard way instead of just stealing the life out of whoever comes along."

"Is that what you see?"

"I see what you are. I'm sorry if you can't. Or won't."

He kissed her hard, letting her words soothe him. Wanting to believe them. Hell, he wanted to wallow in them. And with Alexis at his side, maybe—just maybe—he finally could.

◊

She lost herself in his kiss, her fingers twined in his hair, her tongue lost in his mouth. Right then, he was her entire world; there was nothing else she needed. Not food, not drink. Just this man. Just his touch, his soft words, his sweet caresses.

His hands gripped her rear, urging her toward him. The length of his erection pressed against her, and she heard his moan of pleasure and felt her body respond, warm and needy. Desperate, she clutched at his shirt, her fingers boldly flicking his buttons open, her hands stroking his chest. She wanted to claim him and be claimed, and then she wanted to beg for more.

After a moment he broke their kiss, smiling down at her with eyes that reflected the depths of her own desire. "Alexis." He spoke her name as if it was a benediction, a request, a plea. She nodded, answering yes, yes to it all.

"My bed." She forced the words out, then tugged him upstairs.

The room was dark, illuminated only by wavering light from the pool that came in through the open drapes, making sensual shadows move across the wall.

"I want to touch every inch of you. I want to claim you," he said. "You're mine, Alexis. Don't ever doubt it."

"I won't," she said, trying to speak above the rapid beat of her heart.

His hands stroked her, fingers clutching at her shirt and tugging it off. "I've craved this. Craved you. The feel of you. The heat of you." And she was hot. Her skin felt bathed in sunlight, tingly and aware and in desperate need of the quenching, soothing satisfaction of his touch.

"Please," she begged, pressing his palm to her breast. "Don't wait."

He groaned with desire, his hand stroking her nipple, then caressing her so gently she thought she would go insane with need. Methodically, his hands slid down, sliding under the waist of the sweatpants she'd pulled on. She drew in a breath, her mind in a haze, and before she knew it she was naked beside him.

"You're amazing," he whispered as he caressed her hip, his touch causing sparks of desire to rocket through her, priming her body, making her desperate, itchy, and oh so ready.

He stripped as she watched, enjoying the view and taking pleasure in the knowledge that this magnificent man wanted her. That he was hers—because the truth was she didn't doubt that. They fit together, and despite everything that should be pushing them apart, she knew with a certainty as basic as the need to breathe that what was between them was real and solid and special.

"Now," she said when he was back beside her. She took his hand and pressed it against her sex.

His finger slid inside her and she arched up.

"More," she begged, as he shifted, his body covering and claiming her, heat ricocheting through her as his mouth closed over her nipple, sucking and teasing and taking her so close that her entire being seemed to teeter on the edge of a magnificent precipice.

She reached down, lifting her hips and guiding him to her. With a low growl of pleasure, he thrust inside as she rose to meet him, her body so ready for him, so hungry and desperate that she clung to him like a wild thing, her fingernails digging into his shoulders as her hips pistoned in rhythm with his thrusts until finally, sweetly, her orgasm exploded through her, a cacophony of light and sparks and undiluted pleasure. He clung to her, his own climax following hers, drawing it out, making the pleasure so intense it was almost unbearable.

"Alexis," he said, saying her name with all the reverence of a prayer.

She curled up against him, sated and satisfied. She never wanted to leave his arms. "We make a good team," she said, twisting a bit so she could see him.

"We do indeed." His eyes crinkled as he inspected her, then he sat up and held out his hand to tug her up, too. "I have an idea. Come on."

"Come on? I'm naked. Where are we going?"

"You have weapons? A place where you work and train?"

She'd slid out of bad and was pulling on her T-shirt and underwear. "Yeah. Why?"

"You'll see. Come on."

She led him downstairs, feeling a sense of smug satisfaction when he released a low whistle. "I'm impressed."

"Thanks. I've worked hard."

"Show me your weapons. Particularly that spring-loaded device you have hidden in your jacket."

She had no idea what he was thinking about, but she

did as he asked. He looked at the device—which was really a contraption she attached to her arms and then concealed with the jacket. "Nice," he said. "Want to make it better?"

"Better how?"

"Responsiveness for one. Aim and power for the rest. Especially power. Get it to deploy faster and harder and you won't have the problem you had with Mitre. He was in position when you moved to release, but by the time the device triggered he'd shifted. Shave a second off that, and you would have nailed him."

She tilted her head as she looked at him. "And you can do that?"

His grin was defiantly arrogant and completely sexy. "And a whole lot more."

"All right. Show me."

He did, and after less than thirty minutes of tweaking, tightening, and shifting various components of the device, he'd done exactly what he promised.

"Not bad," she said. "You might be handy enough to keep around."

"I think I can earn my keep. What else have you got?"

She eased closer and hooked her arms around his waist. "Honestly? I can think of about a dozen things. But would you think less of me if I told you that killing vampires isn't actually at the forefront of my mind right now?"

"No? What are you thinking about?"

She didn't bother to answer. Instead she lifted herself up on her toes, pressed her mouth against his, and showed him.

◆

They made love again, this time faster. Rougher. As if it had been years since they'd touched and not minutes.

Serge didn't believe in soul mates—at least he never had before. But with Alexis in his arms, he had to admit that he was beginning to understand. Maybe the fact that he'd been hunting rogues really had earned him redemption. Hell, maybe the woman in his arms was his reward.

"You're quiet," she said, raising herself up on her elbow so that she could look more directly at him. "Is that your subtle way of telling me that you want to go to sleep?"

He let her words wash over him. He'd never believed that he'd find heaven. How miraculous that he'd found it in a woman. "Absolutely not."

"Good, because I was prepared to take drastic measures to keep you awake."

"Were you?"

"I had an entire devious plan worked out," she said.

"In that case, I'm exhausted. I've got to get some sleep."

"You just want to know my devious plan," she said.

"Caught."

"You definitely are," she said, reaching down and circling his cock with her hand. "The plan started something like this," she said, then stroked him in long, slow movements designed to make him more than a little crazy. Step two was designed to take him from crazy to insane, and she accompanied the slow movements with soft kisses.

Step three took him to the edge.

Her mouth closed over him, stroking and teasing, drawing him out, pulling him closer and closer, until he had no choice but to let go, twine his fingers into her hair, and surrender to ecstasy.

He held her after, and then they both laughed when her stomach growled. "You make me forget to eat," she said, pushing herself up to a sitting position.

"I'll get it," he said. "What do you want?"

"I think there's a bowl of fruit in the refrigerator."

"Stay right there." He headed toward the door, but paused after only a few steps, his attention drawn to the line of family photos on her dresser, particularly the one in the middle. A waif of a girl with large eyes and a wide smile on her face. She looked about sixteen and was wearing a cheerleader outfit. There was something so strangely familiar about her . . .

"Serge? Are you still here?"

"Sorry. I noticed your pictures. Who's the cheer-leader?"

"Cheerleader? Oh! That's Tori. That's my sister." He heard the pain in her voice. "That was Halloween, about two months before she ran away."

"Your sister?" His voice sounded flat, because he realized why the girl in the photograph looked familiar.

She had fuchsia hair that had been coated with so much gel it stood out from her head like railroad spikes, and most likely with as much strength. Her skin was so pale her freckles appeared to float in front of her, as if leading the way. Dark shadows rimmed her eyes, accentuated by the thick line of kohl. She wore a white tank top with no bra, through which he could see quarter-sized brown nipples on breasts that would have been more appropriate on a thirteen-year-old. Hip-hugger-

*style jeans shifted on her body as she moved, as if trying
to find some actual hip to in fact hug.*

"You into suck or puncture?" she asked. "Oh, and I
guess John-O told you my rates, right? And I don't do
more than two pints. Makes me too damn woozy, you
know?"

Considering he doubted she had two pints of blood in
her entire tiny body, he certainly did imagine.

"I make my living selling this," she said, gesturing to
her body. "Pretty much any way you want it. I don't do
drugs, and if you want a fuck, you gotta put some jam-
mies on your hammie. But that's about as safe as I get,
you know? I mean, hell, if I wanted to play it safe, I
coulda got a job waiting tables. Let some wanker grab
your tits, and he'll double the tip, too."

He'd been lost then, the daemon tormenting him,
gathering strength, and though he had no memory of
the actual act, he was certain that he'd been the one
who'd killed her.

He'd killed Alexis's sister.

Finding Alexis wasn't a gift—it was a goddamn punishment. Bringing him so close to a woman who made
his heart swell for the first time in centuries, only to find
out that the vampire she was hunting—the one she'd
rearranged her entire life to find and to kill—was *him*.

CHAPTER TWENTY-SEVEN

"Serge?" Alexis sat up, alarmed. He was just standing there, his back to her, his body frozen. "Serge, are you okay?"

After a moment, he turned and looked at her with haunted eyes.

"What is it?" She got out of bed and went to him. "Is it your daemon? The beast?"

He laughed, hard and bitter. "The daemon? Yeah, you could say that."

She didn't understand what was going on, and she cast about her room, trying to figure out what had happened as cold fingers of fear clutched at her. Everything had been fine until he'd gotten out of bed and then asked about Tori's picture—

Tori.

Her stomach twisted as trepidation rose. Surely not . . .

But it made sense. Oh, dear God, it all made sense. She'd gone after Tori's killer in that alley and Serge had been there, too, hidden above her.

The world seemed to turn to red and then gray. Her knees gave out and she started to fall. He was there, then, moving to her side in a flash, holding her up.

"No!" She jerked free, falling, then half crawled and half ran to the bedside table. She ripped open the drawer and snatched the gun she kept there—the one loaded with wooden bullets. "Goddamn you! You killed her!

Oh, my God, please, please, tell me you didn't kill her. Tell me you didn't kill Tori!"

She was crying, but even through her tear-blurred vision she could see his face, and the pain on it was clear. He didn't need to speak. She knew the answer.

"I'm so sorry," he said. "I'm so damn sorry."

She held the gun out, and it trembled in her hand. But she couldn't fire. Couldn't do anything but collapse to her knees and weep.

"You shouldn't have to bear this," he said. His voice was raw, gravelly with pain, but still firm and deep. "I wasn't here, Alexis. We never met. You won't remember me or the pain. I know you can't forgive me, but at least I can give you this."

Her mind. He was trying to mess with her mind.

"No." The word wrenched out of her, and she realized she'd raised the gun again. "Don't you take this from me. Don't you try to make me forget."

She saw the shock register on his face and she held tight to the gun. This was the vampire she'd been hunting. The one she'd sworn to kill. A murderer. A monster.

Serge.

Again, she dropped the gun. "Get out," she whispered.

"Do it," he said. "Do it now. Fire the damn thing. Dammit, Alexis, you know what I did."

She couldn't. Not him. Not Serge.

She tossed the gun aside. "I can't. Not you. Not ever."

"Alexis . . ." His voice was heavy with pain.

"It wasn't you. Something inside you, yes, but you've fought it. You're not a monster."

"The hell I'm not."

"You think I don't know evil? I've looked it in the eyes. I grew up with it." She thought of her parents. So cold to her. So vile to Tori. "That isn't you. You fight it. You don't embrace it." She drew in a breath, her lungs feeling like cubes of ice. "No, Serge, you're not a monster. But I don't think I can look at you, either. I don't think I can—" She swallowed. "I can't be with you. Please. Please go."

"I have a hundred regrets, Alexis. But all of them pale in comparison with this."

She couldn't look at him. Couldn't bear to see her own regret reflected in those eyes she'd come to love. Instead, she crawled into bed, buried her face in the pillow, and stayed there long after she'd heard his departing footsteps and knew that she was once again alone.

◆

"Turn here," Jonathan said from his seat beside Derrick. They'd forgone traveling as mist so that they could communicate, and now they were in Derrick's Jaguar—he'd acquired a taste for fine cars once he'd learned to operate the things—and were heading to the woman's house. Their little female problem. The bitch that Derrick intended to kill.

Jonathan had done well. He'd returned from Bella's with a name—Alexis Martin—and an address.

"That's it," Jonathan said. "The third one on the left."

It was a stately home. Two stories, manicured lawn, pleasing architecture. Who would have thought that the bitch vampire hunter would live right here in the heart of suburbia?

He smiled, thinking of the gossip her brutal death would bring to this quiet street. Who said Derrick never did anything for humans? He was about to provide them with a grand spectacle.

Another car approached from the opposite side, then pulled into the drive and parked.

"Dammit."

"Should we go in anyway?" Jonathan asked. "Just two guys," he added as two men in suits stepped out. "How much trouble can they be?"

"If they're aligned with our girl, possibly too much. Don't discount the situation. She's killed enough members of the League to be taken as a serious threat. If her visitors know how to wield a stake, we'd be foolish to go in now."

"So we wait?"

"We wait."

♦

Alexis moved through the house numb. *Serge.* All this time, the vampire she'd been hunting was the man she loved.

And God help her, she did love him. She wanted to hate him—she really did. Wanted to beat on him and batter him with all the horrible, hateful emotions she'd built up inside her. He'd killed her sister, after all.

Except he really hadn't. He'd been a different person back then; the Serge that she'd come to know had been buried deep within a tortured soul. He was a man who'd paid a dozen times over for the crimes he'd committed. A man who'd never stopped trying to become better, not even after thousands of years. It was awe-inspiring, and she had to wonder if she would have had that kind of strength, or if she would have simply let madness take her, let herself slide into the black, sloughing off torment and living only to exist. To kill.

She shivered, because that wasn't Serge. He may have fallen into darkness, but he'd managed to climb out of it.

No, she thought. Serge hadn't survived the encounter with Tori any more than Tori had. The Serge who'd killed her sister didn't exist anymore. And the Serge who existed now was the man she loved.

Love, however, wasn't always enough, and she'd spoken the truth when she told Serge that she wasn't sure she could look at him again. Would she see Tori every time she looked into his eyes? Could she stand being that close to a reminder of the family she'd lost?

She hugged herself, pulling the sleeves of the ratty, comfortable sweatshirt she'd tugged on tight around her. It was late, well after two in the morning now, but she still eyed the phone. Leena wouldn't mind if she called so late, but she hated to wake her friend. Especially since Leena seemed so touchy and out of sorts lately.

Alexis frowned, undecided, then jumped when her doorbell rang.

Serge?

No. She didn't want it to be Serge. She needed distance. Time to think. Time to heal.

Maybe it was Leena. Maybe she'd caught a vibe and had come over to comfort Alexis.

"Who is it?" she called as she approached the door. Then she peered through the peephole right as her old boss, Tony Gutierrez, looked straight into it.

Surprised, she opened the door. "Tony, I—"

"Alexis Martin, you're under arrest for impersonating a federal officer." He exhaled loudly. "Shit, Martin, I flew in today so that I could do this instead of some agent you've never met. You gonna invite me in, or do I have to plow through the bullshit on your front porch?"

In shock, she stepped aside, ushering him in, along with the unknown agent who accompanied him. She felt nothing, she realized. Was she still numb from Serge's revelation, or from this horrible new reality? She'd known the possibility of getting caught existed, of course. But she'd never really believed it would happen.

"How?" she managed to croak out the word.

"You showed up at Edgar Garvey's house flashing that fake badge. Dammit, Martin, what the fuck have you been up to—no, shut up and let me Mirandize you."

He rambled off the familiar words, then asked her if she understood. She heard her voice saying that she did and that she wanted a lawyer. But the words were hollow. She didn't really want anything except Serge's arms around her telling her that somehow, someway, it would all turn out all right.

CHAPTER TWENTY-EIGHT

From the roof of the neighboring house, Serge watched and listened. *Arrest. Counterfeit badge.*

Goddammit, this wasn't good. And once again it was his fault. Edgar had caught Derrick's attention when he went out flashing a police sketch of Serge, after all. Somehow, everything he did circled back to stab Alexis through the heart.

No more.

He couldn't give Alexis her sister back, but he could negotiate her freedom.

The price would be steep, of course. But for Alexis, Serge would do what he had to do, even if it meant selling his soul.

Serge stood outside Luke's house, the surf pounding behind him, the windows brightly lit in front of him. He breathed in the salty air and told himself he was a fool for hesitating. This was Luke, after all. A man who was closer to him than any brother could be.

And yet that was part of what fueled his hesitancy. Because deep in his gut, Serge knew that he should have come to his friend before. Should have told him what was happening, listened to his advice, and taken whatever help he could offer.

He hadn't been able to see that path, though. Not then, when all he could see was the beast within him. Alexis had changed that—she'd shifted the lens through which he looked at himself—and for that, he owed her the world. More than that, he loved her.

Alexis.

She wouldn't be scared—she was too strong for that. But she would be frustrated. He stood still, reaching out, seeking her through the blood connection. It was starting to fade, but he could sense her just enough to revel in the connection and to confirm that his suspicions were right. Not fear—irritation. At the system, at herself, and worry that she'd screwed up and that her mission to take out the rogues had been permanently compromised.

Not if I have anything to say about it.

Determined, he strode to the back door. It opened just as he was about to knock, and he found himself face-to-face with Luke, who looked at him with flat, emotionless eyes.

"You are a goddamn fool."

Serge grinned. "Good to see you, too, brother."

"Dammit," Luke muttered, then pulled Serge into an embrace. Fast and quick, but the emotion was real, and when he pushed away, Luke kept his hands on Serge's shoulders, his eyes on him. "For months, I was afraid you were dead."

"There were days when I wished I was."

"You spoke to my wife. You entrusted me with CeeCee. And yet this is the first time I've laid eyes on you in over a year."

"You know why."

"I have my suspicions," Luke confirmed.

"I'll tell you everything, but there's something I need first."

"Tell me one thing. Have you harmed any of the humans?"

Serge almost sighed in relief. He could handle anything, he thought, except for Luke to play the fool. To pretend he wasn't suspicious of his friend, when he knew damn well what Sergius had once been. "I have not."

Luke nodded slowly. "All right. Tell me what you need."

"There's a woman," Serge said, though words were inadequate to describe Alexis. "She needs help."

"I see."

"See what exactly?"

"In your eyes. I see the way I feel when I look at Sara. Or am I wrong?"

"No," Serge admitted without hesitation. "You're not wrong. You told me once that Sara eases your daemon. Alexis does the same for me."

"And is that the only attraction?"

He couldn't help it; Serge laughed. "No. Most definitely not."

Luke's grin matched his. "Glad to hear it." He paused only slightly. "It's complicated, though. With a human."

Serge thought of Tori. Of the chasm that had opened between him and Alexis. "More complicated than you know."

"It usually is." Luke looked at him, his gaze missing nothing. "So tell me how I can help Alexis."

Serge did, explaining how she'd been arrested. And then—a sign of faith in his friend—he told him the rest. "She's the one who's been killing the rogues. Well, the rogues who've been staked, anyway."

"A vampire hunter? You're right. It is complicated."

"She hunts rogues because one killed her sister. The girl was found in New York," Serge continued, forcing the words out. "Near an abandoned subway station that had been expertly converted by some sort of mechanically inclined squatter." He'd worked his ass off to make that old station a home. It had taken him a full week just to do the floors.

Luke gaped at him, obviously having grasped the bigger issue. "Does she understand our nature? Does she know how the daemon once consumed you? How you fought? How much you've won?"

"I've told her, yes. Does she understand? She says she does, but also that she can't be around me. There's too much pain. I can't blame her, and I also can't stop loving her, and I certainly can't stop protecting her. I want you to get her out, but be warned—hunting rogues has become a mission with her. She won't stop simply because it's a vampire who frees her."

"The PEC has no jurisdiction over humans who kill rogue vampires. You can rest assured that she won't end up in a PEC cell."

"Good."

He looked hard at Serge. "You say she's responsible for the vampires that have been staked. Tell me about the ones that have been desiccated."

Serge hesitated. "What is it you think you know?"

"I think I know quite a bit. That you're behind those deaths. That you're hunting rogues."

"You always were too perceptive by half."

"What I want to know is why."

"I have to feed, Luke, and I will not feed off the innocent."

"Feed," Luke repeated. "And yet you don't take the blood. Orion says it remains intact, albeit powdered."

"I take their life force."

"I saw you do that once before. During the curse."

"I'm happy to say I have very little memory of what I did during that time."

"So explain to me. How is this happening? I thought the curse was lifted."

"It was," Serge began, then told Luke what he'd told Alexis the night before.

"I wish you'd come to me before."

"What could you have done?"

Luke's brow furrowed in confusion. "Done? I don't know. If nothing else I would have helped you carry the burden."

"I should have," Serge agreed. "But now I come to you with a new problem, and I'm not asking for something intangible like support. I need to know: Will you help her?"

"It's not the PEC that's arrested her, Serge. Last I checked, I wasn't employed by the FBI."

"You're the Alliance chairman, Luke, don't play naïve with me. Get on the phone. Call the FBI director. Hell, call the president. They know the truth. You can have her pardoned. You can have her transferred to Alliance jurisdiction. You can get her out of jail."

"You're right, of course," Luke said. "And I might be persuaded to do just that."

"You'd demand a price from a friend?"

"If it's in that friend's best interest, absolutely. Especially if it benefits me as well."

"You really have become a politician."

"The mantle's uncomfortable, but I'm getting used to

the burden." He stepped off the deck and into the sand. "Let's walk."

They walked in silence until Serge couldn't take it anymore. "What do you want me to do?"

"For one thing, I want to pardon you."

"Don't."

Luke eyed him warily. "Why shouldn't I?"

"It would be a politically foolish move."

"Apparently I'm not the keen politician you think I am, because it seems perfectly reasonable to me."

"Luke . . ."

"Hear me out. I'm not making a grand gesture. I want something in return."

"What?"

"You," Luke said.

Serge stopped, oblivious to the surf rolling in around his ankles. "What?"

"I want you working for PEC."

Whatever he was expecting, that wasn't it. "Say again?"

"It makes perfect sense. You're in a unique position to work any undercover job we need."

Slowly, Serge took his head. "To do that, I'd have to kill."

"That's what death row is for," Luke said reasonably. "Let those creatures pay the price for their crimes by fueling our best warrior. It's the perfect solution. Say we need to get an agent to go undercover, but all of our operatives are known. Say we need a werewolf or a jinn. You become our executioner. Take the life from a death row inmate, become that creature, and slide into the undercover position."

"I don't change my appearance, just my nature."

Luke waved the comment away. "You're known more

by reputation than by looks. Obviously we couldn't use you for every assignment, but you could fill a very large need." He smiled. "I'm going to have to tell Doyle that you're not responsible for killing the rogues—and I'm going to have to tell him the truth about the desiccations. He'll assume I knew all along, of course, which should make for an uncomfortable conversation. It'll be worth putting up with his flak, though, if you come on-board."

The possibility of being useful was undeniably tempting, but it couldn't work. "I can't, Luke. I take the form and features of whatever life force I've drawn in, but I can't control the daemon when I'm in another form. Hell, I can barely control it as a vampire."

"I thought Alexis helped with that."

"What are you saying?"

Luke smiled. "I'm saying I have an idea. And I think you'll like it."

♦

Five paces by six paces was the size of Alexis's world. At least she didn't have to share it. The tiny space was all hers. For now. Undoubtedly once she was tried and convicted, she'd be shipped off to a minimum-security prison and stuck with a roommate who snored. Or worse.

Shit. She wanted out of there, but the bail hearing wasn't until the following afternoon. In the meantime, she'd used her one phone call to talk to Leena, who sounded absolutely determined to get her free. She'd taken it upon herself to find Alexis the best attorney her substantial bank account could hire. Unfortunately, Leena didn't seem to have any magical solutions for the uncomfortable quarters. Alexis was just going to have to wait it out.

She paced the five, then turned and paced the six. On the return trip, the door opened and a huge man walked in. He had a scar across his right cheek, and although it took her a second, Alexis finally recognized him as one of the men from the Penny Martinez crime scene. If she recalled correctly, he'd acted like he was in charge.

"Let me guess. Now I'm in trouble with Homeland Security, too. Or is it Division Six?"

"The latter," the man said. "And you're not in trouble."

She glanced around the cell. "Great. Let me out."

"All right," he said.

"Really?"

"At the very least we should discuss the possibility." He gestured to the tiny cot. "Can we sit?"

"Um, sure."

She perched on one end, and he sat on the other. "I'm Lucius Dragos, by the way."

"Serge's friend?"

"The same."

"Oh." She shifted, trying to find her center. He seemed like a perfectly nice guy and he was Serge's best friend, but to Alexis he was a powerful vampire, potentially dangerous, and apparently at the top of a preternatural infrastructure. The whole situation was a bit like sitting down to chat with your boyfriend's relative, who just happened to be the president of the United States. Awkward, no matter how much you wished it wouldn't be. "So why exactly are you here?"

"I understand you've been hunting rogues."

She flinched; he might as well have tossed ice water all over her.

"Don't worry. The PEC doesn't have any jurisdiction over humans who kill rogue vampires. But we do have jurisdiction over rogues. We catch them. And we punish them."

She nodded, wondering what this had to do with her.

"Would you be interested in helping us do that?"

"Helping you? Are you offering me a job?" This was the oddest conversation.

"Actually, yes."

"Oh." She tried to wrap her mind around this shift in reality. "So, what exactly would this job entail?"

"Doing what you're trained to do. Investigating. We don't have many humans on staff, but sometimes a human perspective can be helpful on a case. And it will help that you're already trained as an investigator. Essentially you would be doing exactly what you've been doing, but it would be sanctioned." He glanced around the cell. "Which would help you avoid future insults like this."

"I'd still be hunting rogues?"

"Among other things, yes."

The idea was mind-boggling. It was a chance to return—more or less—to her life as an FBI agent and still pursue the path she'd set out on after Tori's death.

"I'm pleased to see that you're seriously considering the idea," Luke said. He was studying her face. "There is one other bit of information you should have before you answer. I've asked Serge to come work for the PEC."

"Really? That's great."

"You think so?"

"I do. There's a lot he feels guilty about—I'm sure you

know. That's a way to work through it. To feel like he's being productive. Hell, to actually *be* productive."

"I agree completely. Unfortunately, Serge hasn't yet agreed. In fact, he's made it clear that he'll refuse unless his condition is met."

She almost hesitated to ask. "What condition?"

"He'll only do it with you as his partner."

Her pulse increased, thrumming so loud in her own ears that she was sure Luke must have heard it, too. "Why?" she asked, working to keep her voice nonchalant.

"Don't you know?"

"Because I calm him. I keep the daemon from coming out."

"Yes," Luke said. "But it's more than that."

She searched his eyes and was surprised at what she saw. Serge had told his friend about the truth, and she was so relieved that he'd finally shared the burden that she couldn't hide her smile. "I'm glad he told you."

"So am I," Luke said. "Without you, he's not willing to take on other forms. But that wasn't entirely what I meant. You would be an asset to the team, yes. But he also simply wants you by his side."

Her heart twisted. "He told you that?"

"No."

"Then—"

"I know Serge almost as well as I know myself."

She felt the tears rise and cursed herself. This was a negotiation, not relationship counseling. "Did he tell you? About my sister?"

"Yes, and I'm sorry."

"I don't know if I can do it. Work with him. See him every day." But that wasn't true. What she was afraid of was that she *could,* and that she'd hate herself for it, because she owed Tori more than that.

But what did she owe all of the other men and women, dead because of rogue vampires? How many could she hunt down with Serge by her side? Most of all, without Serge, how long would it take them to find the one rogue who was the kingpin, urging all the others to kill. She didn't believe that Serge would simply let the leader continue to rally his troops—no, he'd take care of the leader himself, and then disappear back into the dark.

The thought filled her with an overwhelming sense of loss, and she knew then that even if she couldn't have him, she also couldn't bear the thought of completely losing him. And she damn sure couldn't let him take down the ringleader without her.

She looked at Luke, her mind made up. "I'm not saying I forgive him, but I'll do it. At least for now."

CHAPTER TWENTY-NINE

"I'm glad you agreed," Serge said. "The thought of you in a cell ripped me up inside."

"It wasn't my idea of a good time, either." They were standing next to each other, and Alexis reached out automatically to take his hand. She caught herself and shoved her hands in the pockets of her jeans. *Not going there.*

The truth was, she was glad to be free. Glad to be partnered with Serge and to have a purpose again. A real job. But from the first moment she'd seen him after she'd followed Luke into his Malibu house, Alexis had realized just how hard this was going to be. She needed to keep her distance—needed to protect her heart and keep Tori, her family, at the forefront. Yet the attraction was still there. That longing. That need. And it was all she could do not to tell Serge to ignore everything she'd said and to pull him into her arms.

They stood only inches apart, and yet the space between them seemed as wide as a chasm, filled with unspoken words and a thousand regrets. It weighed down the air until Alexis couldn't stand it anymore. "I'm so glad you've told Luke and Sara, and that you're using the beast to fight rogues instead of letting it control you."

"I couldn't do it without you. I need you at my side if I'm going to control it."

"I know, and I'm glad I can do it. Glad that I can help

you like that. And I appreciate more than I can say that you worked this out. Got me this job, I mean, so that I can work out in the open instead of from my dark little cave." She grinned. "Leena's going to freak when I tell her. Hell, she'll probably want to sign up, too." She drew in a breath. "But what I really want to say is that I'm sorry. I'm sorry that it can't be more. That I can't give you more than just partnership. I know it's not enough, but—"

"You're everything to me," Serge said. "But I would never demand more than you can give. Want, yes. But I understand. And under the circumstances, I think you're giving me more than I deserve."

She shook her head. "We've already talked about that, and no. You deserve everything good in the world, I'm just not the one who can give it to you."

They stood in silence for a moment; then he shifted. "I'm going to go take CeeCee up on that rematch on the Xbox. When you feel like coming in, I think Luke and Sara want to talk about how we're going to approach our first assignment." His fingers brushed her shoulder in a gesture of good-bye. The contact was simple, yet shocking at the same time. It sent a buzz of electricity coursing through her, warming her. Her body seemed to beg for more, but that was a demand she wasn't willing to succumb to. Instead, she tightened her grip on the deck railing and looked out over the ocean, its roiling waves mimicking her own jumbled emotions.

After a few moments, she walked back inside, expecting to find Serge with CeeCee. But the living room was empty, and she found the girl in the kitchen with Sara.

"Hey," Sara said, flashing the same welcoming smile that she'd greeted Alexis with when she'd arrived. "Luke and Serge went into his office. CeeCee and I are working on dinner. She's taking a break from zombies. Grab a stool, and help yourself to some wine."

"Thanks." Alexis poured herself a glass and settled in at the counter to watch. "It's a good thing I saw the Xbox. Otherwise considering the world I've stumbled into, I might've thought you meant literal zombies."

CeeCee snorted and rolled her eyes.

"It's a lot to take in, isn't it?" Sara asked as she worked some pastry dough in a bowl. "I was right where you are not that long ago. Knowing this whole world exists takes some getting used to."

She turned to the sink to wash her hands, and Alexis couldn't help but notice that the sink fronted a huge window with a view of the ocean. There were no curtains or blinds that Alexis could see.

"What about the sun?" Alexis asked.

"I'm still new enough that it doesn't bother me," Sara said. "But we have electronic shutters on those windows that haven't been replaced yet."

"Replaced?"

"Serge invented a type of glass that keeps the sun out. Makes living in a house feel almost normal."

"Serge did?" She'd seen his inventor's heart in action, but still she clung to this new detail. A pearl that rounded out the picture of the man who'd come to mean so much to her . . . even if he wasn't a man she could have.

"He's really pretty cool," CeeCee said loyally, and Alexis was happy to see that she seemed to have forgotten any anger she might have had with Serge for leaving her with Sara and Luke.

"From what I understand, we have you to thank for CeeCee," Sara said.

"I think Serge had more to do with it than I did."

Sara laughed. "He definitely added a certain something to the equation. Do you like baked Brie?"

"I'm sorry?" Alexis blinked at the shift in topic.

"The cheese," Sara said. "Some people don't like it."

"No, I think it's great."

CeeCee took a long sip from the mug she'd been holding. "This is what I think is great lately." She wrinkled her nose. "Who woulda thought blood would taste so good?"

"She can still enjoy food," Sara said. "But in the early stages vampires crave a great deal of blood."

"Don't worry," CeeCee added. "No humans were injured in the making of my dinner."

"And I swear the Brie contains no hemoglobin," Sara added, making Alexis laugh. "Oh, hell," Sara said, scowling at the pastry she'd rolled out in front of her. "Are you any good in the kitchen?"

"Not at all," Alexis confessed.

"That's better than me. Want to help? We have to wrap this around the Brie, but I'm thinking it may be easier to chuck it all and order a pizza."

"Hang on." Alexis came around the counter, and between the two of them they finished wrapping the pastry around the cheese and got it in the oven.

"You're an angel," Sara said.

"I'm happy to help. I have to confess that this isn't—"

"What you expected?"

"Not at all."

"I hope it's for the better."

Alexis laughed. "Definitely."

Sara's phone rang and she grabbed it up with a frown.

"The office. I hate to ask, but would you mind watching the oven?"

"Not a problem." As Sara went off to take her call, Alexis took a seat on one of the bar stools next to CeeCee.

"Want some?" she asked, pushing the travel mug toward Alexis with a grin.

"You're a laugh riot."

"Sorry. Sara says I'm coping well. I'll have to take her word for it."

"I'm betting that's a pretty big understatement."

"Yeah, no kidding. So you used to work for the FBI? That's pretty cool. Although I think the PEC is cooler, so you're moving up in the world."

"I think so, too."

"Of course, the coolest thing about the PEC is that they're super-secret." CeeCee grinned. "And that's always fun. I keep telling Luke and Sara that they should let me work there, too. Luke said he'd think about it, but I'm not sure if he really meant it or if he was blowing me off."

Alexis laughed. Apparently teenage angst lingered even in vampires.

"Smells good," Luke said as he and Serge entered the kitchen. Sara followed soon after, and they all settled around the table, just like normal folks hanging out with friends.

"So how are we going to approach this thing?" Luke asked. "Alexis says you know who's organizing the rogues?"

"You know?" Sara said, frowning at Serge. "And you didn't say something before?"

"He's saying it now," Alexis said, feeling compelled to stick up for him.

"No," Serge said. "Sara's right. I should have said something as soon as I suspected. And I'm still not one hundred percent sure. The truth is that I intended to investigate on my own." He looked at Luke. "It's Derrick."

"I see," Luke said. He turned to Sara. "Perhaps he should have come forward sooner. But with Derrick at the helm, I understand why he didn't."

"Someone from your past?" Sara asked Serge.

"From my darkest days, yes. I need to confront him," he added, and Alexis understood what he meant. By confronting Derrick, he'd be confronting the monsters inside himself, too.

Alexis looked around the table at all of them. "No matter what should or shouldn't have been done in the past, we're doing the right thing now. We just need to work out the plan."

"Simple," Serge said. "I'll make contact. Get in with him. Go out on hunts with his men. Of course, I'll pull a few fast ones before any humans get hurt—and in the process we'll take some of Derrick's men out. That's where you come in," he added, nodding at Alexis.

She looked between Luke and Serge. "I thought you were going to use the beast? That you were going undercover in different forms?"

"Eventually," Luke said. "Right now, these human deaths are our focus."

"Fair enough," she agreed. "But why not just kill him straightaway? If you can get in close to Derrick, just put your whammy on him and turn him into a mummy. End of problem."

"We considered it," Serge said. "But we need to find out who his lieutenants are, especially in other states, possibly other countries."

"Of course," Alexis said. "We need to shut the whole thing down."

"Exactly."

They talked a bit more about timing and planning and getting Alexis familiar with Division 6. When the oven timer rang, the conversation shifted from work to food and the beach and video games and other normal stuff. It was nice. It was normal. And it underscored Alexis's belief that she'd made the right choice.

Serge offered to drive her home, since Luke had brought her from the holding cell, and while she said good-bye to Luke and Sara, he wandered into the living room to talk with CeeCee.

Alexis headed in their direction when she was ready to go, but she stopped when she heard their voices, not wanting to interrupt their conversation.

"I'm glad you're settling in," Serge told the girl.

"I totally am. And you don't have to feel bad about bringing me here. I get what happened to you. And the truth is, you did save me." She rose up on tiptoes to kiss his cheek, then flashed him a grin and bounced back to the kitchen, giving Alexis a wave as she passed.

"Didn't I say you were a hero?" Alexis asked Serge, and this time she did squeeze his hand.

"When I'm around you, I feel like one. And CeeCee? Right now I feel pretty good about that, too."

◆

Serge pulled the car into her driveway and killed the engine.

"Thanks," she said. "For the ride."

"You realize that I'm coming in with you, right?"

"It's not necessary. No one knows I've been released, remember?"

She was right. Luke had arranged things so that she was transferred from FBI to Homeland jurisdiction. As far as anyone knew, she was still incarcerated, and they intended to keep it that way until Derrick was no longer a threat.

"Even so," he said. "I feel better playing it safe. Okay?"

She didn't protest, and for that Serge was grateful. He wanted as much time with her as possible, even if it was just sitting together sharing the same air.

"Maybe we could watch a movie. Or something."

"I'd like that," he said. "But I can think of something I'd rather do than the movie."

"Serge . . ." Pain and regret fueled her voice, but the scent of desire filled the car. Perversely, he was glad of it, even though he knew that the desire only brought her pain.

"No," he said quickly. "Not that. I want you to train. You're excellent in the field, but you can be better."

"I'll never be as good as you. I don't have the 'vampire' advantage."

"No, and that worries me. I want you to be as strong as possible."

"Well, I have a weight room. I work out."

"There's another way to make you stronger. My blood, Alexis."

He saw the color rise in her cheeks and her throat move as she swallowed. "Right. But I already have that."

"A bit, but it's fading. I used the connection to track

you to the alley the other night, and it was already a very thin thread. Am I wrong? Can't you feel that the strength I gave you is starting to wane?"

"Yes. A bit."

"Then let me do this for you. Let me make you stronger. You're walking into this world, Alexis. Let me give you the tools you'll need to survive."

"I don't know."

"Alexis, please. What if you're taken? What if I need to find you?" He reached for her hand, gratified when she let him take it, and losing himself in the heat that was always there between them. "The blood connection isn't foolproof—certain herbs and metals can block the effect—but it's better than nothing. And the thought of losing you is more torturous than all of my battles with the daemon and the beast."

"I—all right."

The relief that washed over him was palpable. It wasn't a cure-all, of course, but it would help. And it had the added, selfish benefit of being a tangible connection to her, something he still desperately craved, but knew that he could only have in tiny, stolen quantities.

And then, before she could change his mind, he lifted his wrist to his mouth, bit down to break the skin, and extended it to her. "Drink," he said.

Her eyes flickered up to him, and he saw both longing and determination in her expression. Then she bent her head and drank deep, her mouth hot on his flesh, their bodies melding as the blood connection grew.

He could feel his blood inside her, could smell her desire. She wanted him, there was no denying it now. And the deeper she drank, the more intense her craving became. A bittersweet need that she refused to fulfill. And so he kept the blood flowing, let her drink her fill, because right then, it was all they could have of each other, even though Serge knew that for him it would never, ever be enough.

CHAPTER THIRTY

The woman, Alexis, was out of their hair and as far as Jonathan was concerned, that was a very good thing. He may have suggested to Derrick that they leave Los Angeles, but he really didn't want to. With the bitch gone, though, things were getting back to business as usual, and the message of the League was spreading.

Even though he knew damn well that she was locked up, he still kept an eye on her house. Not every day. Not like a stakeout. But often enough. Just in case.

It was dull work, and he tried to mix it up. Some days he just drove by and sniffed the air to search for a hint of life within. Other days he watched the house, afraid to trust his nose in a neighborhood where so many human scents commingled.

Sometimes he came at night, watching the house from the car or the roof of a neighboring home. Tonight, he'd been bored enough to shift into bird form and perch in a tree in the girl's front yard.

And it was a good thing, too.

Because tonight he saw her. And not just her, but a male, tall and muscled, with a hard, familiar face and eyes that looked like they'd seen everything. Jonathan couldn't catch the male's scent while he was in bird form, and he couldn't transform without being seen. Just from looking, he couldn't tell if the male was human or vampire or something else. Since the woman was human, he assumed the man was, too. But there was something so familiar about him, and he couldn't imagine why a human would affect him in that way. Unless he was feeding, he really had no more use for the creatures.

That face.

That jawline.

Those piercing gray eyes.

Shit. The sketch. That was the face from the sketch.

Which meant that he was looking at Sergius, and the vampire—the badass, kill-everyone-around, Derrick-sees-him-as-an-equal vampire—was hanging out in a car with a human female.

Jonathan watched for a minute longer, because maybe Sergius was playing a game?

But no. Because as Jonathan watched, the woman's mouth closed over Serge's wrist. Serge tilted his head back, and Jonathan frowned, intrigued. Because Jonathan knew real passion when he saw it. And what he saw right then was pretty damn interesting.

♦

"Higher," Serge said, as she leaned to the side and thrust her leg up and out, slamming him hard in the gut. "Excellent," he said. "You're feeling it already."

"I could fight a thousand vampires," she said, truthfully. She'd hesitated when he'd offered his blood, not because she didn't want the extra strength, but because she knew how hard it would be to have Serge in her head. And it was hard. But as long as she focused on the training, she could forget how much she wanted him. How deeply her blood burned with desire.

"We should take a break. We've been going at it for five hours straight."

"I can go longer."

He laughed. "I'm sure you can." He grabbed a towel from a basket and hung it around his neck. "But we've been working all night, and you need sleep. For that matter, I could use some, too."

"Oh. Right. So, I guess you can take the guest room. It has blackout shades so you don't have to worry about the sun."

He looked at her for a moment, his expression suggesting that he had something to say. He didn't, though. Just said a quick good night and left her holding her own towel and fighting the urge to run after him.

It's the blood talking. That's all. The blood.

But she knew that wasn't it at all. Instead, it was the man.

She considered calling Leena, but she hadn't talked to her since she'd made her one phone call after her arrest. After that, things had moved too quickly. Luke had come, she'd agreed to work for the PEC, she'd been released from the FBI and processed as a prisoner at Division 6, just to keep up appearances. After that, she'd gone with Luke to his house, and now she was home with Serge. It would be exhausting to cover that much ground in one call. Maybe they could get together tomorrow. Today, Alexis was fighting her own demons by herself.

The house was quiet, but she could tell she wasn't alone. Serge's presence seemed to fill the place up so much that there was no escape. Everywhere she went was him. Everything she saw was him.

And the truth was, it felt right that he was in the

house. That realization scared her, but there was no escaping it. He was her partner now, but that word meant so many things. Her colleague. Her mate. Her love.

Yes, my love.

"Tori, what have I done?"

She'd been clinging so desperately to her lost family that she'd been blind to the fact that a new one was springing up around her. Leena, Edgar, even CeeCee and Luke and Sara.

And Serge. Most of all Serge.

She loved him, and staying away from him was only hurting them both.

She pressed her hand against the wall and closed her eyes. She'd made a mistake. A huge one.

Now she had to decide exactly what she was going to do about it.

◆

Serge tried to sleep, but thoughts of Alexis kept intruding. They'd trained hard, working closely, their bodies sweating, touching. He'd wanted more, and it had taken all of his willpower not to throw her down on the mat. Not to run his hands over her soft curves and trail kisses up her neck.

Even now, it required superhuman strength for him to stay in this room when all he wanted to do was to step into the hall and search for her and hold her close.

He couldn't, though. Because even though he could feel her desire for him in the blood that connected them, she'd made her choice, and now they both had to live with the hell of it. He could shoulder that burden, but it pained him that Alexis would suffer for his mistake, too.

And that knowledge made the weight of his regret that much heavier.

He shifted in the bed, imagining she was there. That her soft scent was filling the room. That her sweet voice was whispering to him.

There was no voice, of course, but after a moment of blissful imagination, he realized that the scent was real. She was nearby, and even as he turned his head toward the door, he saw the knob turn and Alexis step inside. She paused in the doorway, silhouetted in the ambient light.

His whole body went tense with an electric combination of hope and fear. "Why are you here?" It came out a whisper, and he held his breath as he waited for the kick in the gut that would surely come in response.

In the silence that followed, he could hear the beating of her heart, followed by her soft, almost whispered reply: "Because I love you."

Those four simple words hit him harder than any blow in a fight. "Alexis." It was the only word he could manage, and it came out ragged.

She moved to him, sliding onto the bed beside him. Somehow, he forced his body to function, to wrap his arms around her and pull her close. She clung to him, her lips on his neck, his cheek, then closing over his mouth and claiming him. "I missed you," she said, when she finally pulled away.

"I'm sorry," he said. "I'm so, so, sorry."

Her smile was a little sad, but her eyes held no reproach. "That's all in the past." She cupped his cheek with her hand. "And I'm the one who's sorry. I was trying so hard to protect the memory of the sister I loved that I almost lost the man I love."

"You could never lose me."

"I swear I won't ever try again."

He buried his face in her hair, breathing in her scent if only to assure himself that she was real.

"Kiss me, Serge," she begged. "Kiss me hard. We can go slow later. Right now, I just have to have you. I have to know that this is real."

"It's real," he promised, more than happy to satisfy her demand. With their need taking precedence, they tore at each other's clothes without a thought about rips and buttons or any of that nonsense. Their mouths met, hers hot and furious and demanding. "Do you know what you do to me?"

Her smile was mischievous. "I have some idea."

"I need you, Alexis. I've always needed you, and I didn't even know it."

"Serge." She pulled herself up, pressing her mouth to his. Then she rolled over, forcing him onto his back, her fingers twined into his hair as she held his head in place. Her mouth crushed his, claiming him, her tongue hot and her taste sweet.

He was hard, so damn hard, and when she shifted her hips and lowered herself onto him it was a miracle he didn't explode right then. They moved together, lights on and eyes open, never breaking their gaze, never losing that connection. He felt her climax approaching at the same time as he saw it reflected on her face. A glassiness in her eyes, a parting of her lips. The muscles around his cock tightened, teasing him, bringing him over the edge with her, until they both burst open with an exultant cry and she collapsed upon him, her body so soft, her scent so very sweet.

He pulled her close, the possibility of breaking contact

unthinkable. Then he rolled her onto her back and proceeded to make love to her again, this time slow, so
slow, until he thought the both of them would die from
the agony of anticipation.

Afterward, she fell asleep in his arms, and he spent the
next few hours watching her, thinking that somewhere
along the way he really must have paid the price for his
crimes. How else could he deserve something so precious as Alexis?

◆

Alexis woke up feeling wonderful, except for the fuzzy
head and sharp pain that seemed to get her right behind
the eyes.

"Hey," Serge said, brushing a kiss over her lips.
"Good morning."

"Is it morning?"

"For me it is. The sun's been down for about two
hours now. I thought we could get in one more training
day. Tomorrow night I'll see if I can't track down Derrick. I think the Z Bar is the place to start." He slid his
palm up her bare thigh. "Then again, I can think of
ways to get a workout that don't involve training."

She curled her arms around his neck and smiled up at
him. "Sounds wonderful," she said, but she couldn't
help wincing as he moved, shifting their position on the
pillow.

Immediately, he pulled back, concern in his eyes.
"What's wrong?"

She pushed herself up into a sitting position. "I'm sure
it's nothing. I've just got a headache." She pressed her
fingers to the bridge of her nose. "A nasty one."

"What can I get you?"

"A couple of aspirin, maybe."

He had them for her in under a minute. "Anything else?" He reached for her and she took his hand and squeezed.

"You have a good bedside manner, Dr. Serge." The image of Serge as a doctor amused her, and she laughed, which was a mistake, as it brought the headache back in full force. "I don't think this is anywhere near as bad as Leena's migraines," she said. "Suddenly, I'm boatloads more sympathetic. I'm sorry," she added, lying back against the pillows and closing her eyes. "I'm going to be useless to you for a while."

"Just rest. We can train tomorrow. And there's no reason we can't bump the schedule up. I'll go see Derrick today."

Alarmed, she opened her eyes. "Do you think that's a good idea?"

"Might as well go sooner rather than later, and it's not as if we're missing out on anything. You weren't going to go with me anyway, remember? But I do think I should take you to Luke's before I go."

"Luke's? You mean because of Derrick?" She shook her head. "You're being paranoid. Even if he has spies at the PEC, all the paperwork says I'm locked up tight. And you're going to be gone what? Maybe two hours, max? You're just going to talk to him, right? Reconnect?"

He nodded, but she could tell he didn't like it.

"I'll be fine," she said. "Seriously." She reached for her phone. "I'll even call Leena and see if she can come over."

"Do that," he said.

She rolled her eyes but dialed, then left a message for Leena to call her when she got her friend's voice mail. "She'll call back, and I'll invite her over. But she won't even need to come, because you'll be back." She looked hard at him. "You're not really worried, are you?"

After a moment, he shook his head. "I think I'll always worry about you. But like you said, you don't even exist right now outside a jail cell."

"See? There you go."

"One hour," he said.

"Good. I'll nap. And I'll be refreshed when you come back." She wasn't sure she would. Her head was starting to pound even more.

"I love you," he said, and the words curled around her, warm and soft like a blanket.

"That's exactly what I wanted to hear. Now go fight the bad guys. And by the way," she added as he stepped toward the door. "I love you, too."

As soon as he was gone, she settled back against the pillows again. She couldn't help her smile even though the tug of muscles on her face was making her head feel worse. She hoped she was right and that it would pass by the time he got back, but she was afraid she'd been sorely mistaken. Now her stomach had jumped on the illness bandwagon, but her head was pounding so hard she didn't want to get up to go track down some antacids. Instead, she curled up in a ball, staying that way even when she heard Serge's footsteps in the hall.

"Did you forget something?"

He didn't answer, but a second later she heard the door open. She shifted, tilting her head back to look at him and reassure him that she was still doing okay.

Except it wasn't Serge who was staring down at her.

She rolled off the bed, going for the gun she kept on her bedside table, but he was beside her in a flash holding down her arm. She fought, but her pounding head was a disadvantage, and in no time he'd overpowered her.

"Hello, Alexis. I'm Jonathan. And I have a friend who's dying to meet you."

She only had time to scream Serge's name once, but she knew it would do no good. He wasn't in the house, and Jonathan was moving too fast. Her scream was still hanging in the air when the vampire grabbed her in his arms, transformed into mist, and the world dissolved around Alexis.

CHAPTER THIRTY-ONE

Heads turned and whispers filled the room when Serge walked into the Z Bar. He glanced around, his gaze finally landing on the woman behind the bar. She had pudgy cheeks and a tiny nose, giving her a face that resembled a hamster. "I'm looking for Derrick," he said. "I'm Sergius."

Her eyes widened almost imperceptibly, then she stuck out her hand. He ignored it, and after a moment, she withdrew her fingers, then wiped them on her apron. "I'm Vivian Clamdale," she said. "This is my place."

"Derrick," he repeated. He wasn't interested in this woman or in her customers. More than that, though, the Sergius that Derrick used to know wouldn't be interested in them, either. Sergius had always had his own agenda; had always been the biggest badass in the room. If he wanted to reestablish himself with Derrick, he had to be that vampire again.

Looking at Vivian and her customers—some of whom were rogues he recognized—Serge thought that it wouldn't be too hard.

"Now," he added, because the woman still hadn't answered. "Or I'll just start looking for him myself."

"In the back," she said, her eyes darting toward a door off to his left. "I'll take you."

"I'll find it," he said, then headed that way. As he did,

he saw her pick up a phone and send a text. Undoubtedly telling Derrick that Serge was on his way. Good.

He pushed through the doorway and found himself in a long, dark hall. On alert, he took a step forward, testing the air, searching for anyone who might be hiding in the shadows. *Nothing.*

The door at the end of the hall flew open and Derrick stood there, his arms outstretched. "Sergius! My God, I feared those bastard Dumonts had destroyed you as they almost destroyed me."

"And yet we're still here, and the Dumont men now rot in the earth," Serge said.

Derrick threw his head back and laughed. "Ah, Sergius! You are the same, after all. I'd feared you'd changed."

"Did you?"

"The Sergius I remembered would not remain hidden for so long. I was certain you were here in Los Angeles, and yet you were a chimera, a shadow, nothing more than a rumor."

"You assume that I was forced under by the PEC agents sniffing around. I assure you that wasn't the case." He kept his eyes on Derrick's face, well aware of all that was riding on this conversation. He had to convince his old friend that he hadn't changed. That the darkness still thrived within him. "I've been pursuing a purpose of my own. That's one of the reasons I came tonight. We had a uniquely beneficial relationship in the past. I hoped we could resume it. That, and I missed the company of my old friend."

"And I you. Come in, come in." He stepped back so that Serge could enter the small room in the back. It was set up as an office, and Serge raised a brow in question.

"Tom and Vivian appreciate the customers I bring into their establishment, and they've done an excellent job spreading my message."

"I've seen the results of your work—I assume I'm correct? You've been sharing your philosophy with the younger generation? They've been putting it into practice?"

"You've been very observant."

"I find it amusing to watch the PEC chasing its tail. The rogues have them baffled."

Derrick frowned. "Them, perhaps. But someone has been playing a game of cat and mouse, and I'm afraid that my men are the mice."

"I'd heard rumors that rogues were disappearing. I've heard rumors of worse things, as well."

"It's horrible," Derrick said. "So many of my men have been found completely desiccated."

"And you have no inkling of how they came to be that way?"

"None. It's baffling." He waved a hand as if pushing away these disturbing thoughts. "But enough of this. We'll have plenty of time to discuss political philosophy. What I want now is to hear about you. I wonder, for example, who replaced me as your companion. We had good times together, didn't we?"

"Very." Serge fought the rising memories of his time with Derrick, memories that disgusted him but made the beast and the daemon curl with pleasure. *Alexis*, he thought, reaching out through the blood connection, seeking her strength to calm him.

He couldn't find her, though, and that failure sparked a tiny flicker of worry.

"Was I tossed aside and replaced?" Derrick asked. "Let me guess. By Lucius?"

"Luke?" Serge said, adding a note of scorn to his voice. "Haven't you heard? He's the new Alliance chairman. Far too tame for me."

"Indeed. Then perhaps a woman?"

There was nothing strange about Derrick's voice, but Serge stiffened anyway.

"A woman?"

"Just a guess, of course. I can imagine you with a woman at your side. Fiery of spirit. A hunter."

On guard now, Serge shifted position, his muscles tensed and ready. Derrick had said nothing volatile. And yet still Serge felt his trepidation building.

"Of course, I would never have imagined you with a woman who hunted our own kind."

Alexis. Dear God, Alexis.

"What have you done, Derrick?"

"You're a fool, Sergius, to think that you could walk into my territory and play games with me. The world truly has changed over the last century. Because you never were a fool before."

Behind them, a door opened, and four vampires filed in, all wielding stakes. Serge ignored them as he rushed Derrick, fueled by a fierce need to destroy this threat to Alexis. This bastard who would surely kill her at the first chance, if only to antagonize Serge.

When he was only inches away, he stumbled under the unexpected weight of a metal mesh that fell from the roof. *Hematite.*

"It's been a pleasure talking with you, my old friend. I'm sorry to say we won't be working together. But you see, I don't need you. After all, I already have your woman."

And with that, Derrick dissolved to mist. Serge tossed the mesh aside—hematite no longer affected him—and immediately spun around, ready to defend himself against the four vampires. But they were gone, too.

Derrick hadn't even tried to kill him, and Serge damn well knew why. Hadn't he done the same thing far too many times in the past? Why torture your enemy when you can torture the person your enemy loves most?

Alexis. Again he reached out, searching for her. Again, he found nothing. Derrick was too smart to have his plans foiled by something as simple as the blood connection. Now Serge had to be smarter. He had to find her, and if he couldn't track Alexis, then maybe he could track Derrick.

And he knew just the person to help him.

◊

Serge pounded on Leena's door, waited about two seconds, then broke the thing in. She stood there, crossbow raised, ready to release the arrow.

"He's taken Alexis."

"Who?" Her expression didn't change, and she still held the crossbow.

"His name is Derrick. He's been organizing the rogues. Alexis and I had a plan to infiltrate his organization, but he must have gotten wind of it."

"Derrick," she repeated, her voice low.

"Dammit, Leena, I need your help to track her."

"The blood connection?"

"He's blocked it."

"I have no way of tracking her, either." The crossbow came down, and Serge stepped farther inside.

"You have her blood. She told me you used it." *Used it to track Tori's killer. To track me.*

"And that blood has served its purpose. It can't be used again."

"Goddammit!" He lashed out, his fist putting a hole through her wall.

"We'll find her. What about the men under him? Would they know where he took her?"

It was possible. "Let's find out." He took another step toward her. "I can get us there faster," he added, and without waiting for her reply he transformed into mist, becoming corporeal once again only after they'd reached the Z Bar.

"Out," he said as he burst through the door. The place was mostly empty now, and the few vampires who were left looked at him and rushed out, obviously not wanting to die that night.

Vivian Clamdale was still behind the bar, and Serge vaulted it with one clean leap. She backed away, obviously about to transform, but Serge grabbed her.

And in that moment of contact, the beast rushed up. Desperate. Hungry. *Demanding.*

It reached out, ready to take from this woman, this vampire, this fucking bitch. Ready to draw the life from—

No.

With a violent shove, Serge pushed her back, sending her tumbling against the bar.

Beside him, Leena gaped, but he ignored her, all of his focus aimed at controlling the beast, on keeping it down.

Alexis. He couldn't feel her. But he could remember her. Could conjure her. Could tap into his love for her.

Alexis, Alexis, darling Alexis.

"Stop!" Leena's voice rang out, and Serge whipped sideways, his eyes going wide as he saw Vivian held in what looked like the kind of heat shimmer that would rise from a hot street in the summer. "I can't hold it for long."

"You could never hold me for long enough," Vivian spat back, fighting against the spell that contained her. "I have his strength within me, and I cannot be defeated."

"His strength?" Serge looked at Leena. "His blood. Can you—?"

"I can," she said, and before Vivian had time to figure out what they were talking about, Serge leaped forward. Leena dropped the force field so that he could get through. He practically flew at the vampire, knocking her backward onto the ground. And then, before she could anticipate his next move, he used a bar knife to slice her arm, then bled her until she'd filled a shot glass from the bar.

And then, because he just didn't like the bitch, he used the stake that Leena tossed him and slammed it through her heart.

"You're sure this will work?"

"I can do it," Leena said, using her finger to draw an intricate pattern on the oak bar in blood. "I've actually been working out a spell for tracking a vampire through its blood. Alexis originally wanted to use her blood to track you—that was when she was trying to find the teenage girl and all she knew was your name. Even after she found you, I kept on working on it. I thought it might come in handy."

"You were right."

"It will weaken me, but for Alexis I can manage."

"How is it that you know witchcraft?"

She eyed him sideways, her lip curving into the slightest of smiles. "You could say that it's in my blood. My mother was a sorceress, and hers before that, all the way back into our dark, distant past."

An odd sense of déjà vu washed over him. "What's your surname?"

"Dumont," she said.

A chill chased up Serge's spine. "I knew a witch once. She was a slave at the Dumont plantation outside New Orleans. I asked her for help."

"And did she agree?"

"The evening went awry. It didn't end well for anyone."

"Then I was fortunate to be born in a different generation. Let's hope tonight goes better." She nodded at the pattern on the bar. "It's ready."

As he watched, she pressed her hands against the wood and tilted her head back, her mouth open and her eyes closed. She muttered something in a language he didn't know. At first, nothing happened. Then the blood on the bar began to shimmer and glow. As if it were quicksilver, the blood pooled up and eased over her hands. No, not over, *into* her hands. Until the pattern that was on the wood seemed etched under her skin. The pattern quivered and glowed, and then a tiny dot of red appeared.

Leena opened her eyes and turned her head. Her teeth glowed white in the dim light of the bar, giving her a lean, dangerous look. "Got it," she said. "Let's go."

CHAPTER THIRTY-TWO

A dozen ice picks rammed into Alexis's skull. And that horror had been joined by wave after wave of nausea and bloating and stomach cramps so horrible she wanted nothing more than to double over, clutch her knees to her chest, and moan.

She couldn't, though, because she was strapped to a post—hands tied behind her back, legs strapped at the ankles, head held stable by duct tape across her forehead.

Twice she'd almost vomited, and her mouth was now swollen and dry. She felt miserable. Wretched. Positively vile.

But that was nothing compared with the horrific knowledge that the only reason she was being tormented was to entrap Serge.

"You're going to die first," she told Jonathan. "He won't even think twice. You're like some little bug he has to swat out of the way." She grimaced as a wave of pain hit her. But she fought through it and shifted her attention to the vampire who'd introduced himself as Derrick. "He'll take more time with you, though. He'll want to watch you suffer."

"I don't doubt it for a moment," Derrick said. "Sergius has always thrived on the suffering of others. He was the master of pain and of death. My mentor, my friend. Certainly my equal in that regard." He took a casual step toward her. "Did he tell you? When he had you in bed and his cock was deep inside you, did he whisper sweet nothings? Did he share with you how he'd drained young women purely for the joy of watching them die? Did he make you come by telling you of the still-beating hearts he'd ripped out, for no reason other than to hear his victims scream?"

Nausea overwhelmed her, but she refused to turn away. She met his eyes defiantly. "Is that why you're luring him here? Because he's not that person anymore and you can't stand that he's decent and you're still vile?"

Faster than she could see, his hand lashed out, slapping her hard against the cheek, the pain increased exponentially since she couldn't move her head to absorb the blow. "It would serve you well to watch how you speak to me."

"Why? I'm dead already."

He chuckled. "True. But there's still the question of the pain, isn't there, Alexis, darling? I owe you a great deal of pain. How many of my men did you kill?"

"Not nearly enough," she said.

"No, your death won't be easy. Not easy at all. But until then let's be friends, shall we? Come on, darling. Give us a kiss." And then his mouth was on hers, and she squeezed her eyes shut as she tried to jerk away, but was foiled by the binds that held her. He forced his tongue in and she gagged. He pulled away, laughing, his fangs scraping her lower lip.

"I suggest you get your hands off my woman." *Serge!* She opened her eyes, afraid her mind was playing tricks, but he was there, the door behind him hanging open on one hinge. Jonathan was crumpled, headless, at his feet. And beside him, Leena stood, a crossbow tight in her hands.

Alexis wanted to cheer, but her joy at seeing him was stolen by the knife Derrick pressed against her throat. "Bravo, Sergius. It took you a bit longer than I anticipated, but at last you've made it to the party." Serge took a step forward. "Ah, ah. Careful my friend. I can cut off her head with one stroke. And that's a death even you cannot defeat."

Hesitation filled Serge's eyes, and she watched his face as he calculated what to do. Beside him, Leena hadn't moved, though she appeared to be talking to herself, muttering low, unintelligible words.

A fresh wave of nausea crashed over Alexis and her stomach and chest convulsed, her body wanting to bend over and fight the pain, but unable to do so. Simultaneously, she felt the flick of the knife as Derrick tightened his grip.

Serge's cry of *"No!"* mingled with Leena's, and Alexis squeezed her eyes shut, afraid that this was the end.

But then the press of steel was gone and she opened her eyes and saw Derrick frozen in front of her, only inches away, a heat-like shimmer surrounding him. A second later, an arrow pierced the shimmering air, landing dead-center in Derrick's heart. The vampire's mouth opened in a gape of surprise, and then there was nothing. Just dust cascading to the floor.

The shimmer disappeared, and Leena dropped her crossbow and sagged against her cane.

"Dead," she said. "And about time."

In an instant Serge was at Alexis's side. He ripped

through her bindings, and she collapsed, shivering, into his arms. It was getting worse. She felt hot and cold and she was certain that any moment her head was going to explode.

"She's ill," Serge said. "Alexis, what's wrong?"

But she could only shake her head.

Leena approached, then stood over them, frowning down. "Tell him," she said. "Tell him what's wrong with you."

Her friend's voice sounded harsh. "Leena?"

Leena laughed, but there was no humor. "I said to tell him. Tell the vampire who killed your sister why you're dying."

More nausea rose inside her as the truth washed over her. *Dying.* Oh, dear God, Leena was right—she was going to die right here in Serge's arms.

"Dying?" Serge repeated, his voice frantic. "What the fuck are you talking about?"

"The spell," Alexis whispered, forcing the words out past the pain. "When I gave my blood for the map. The scar on my wrist. I pledged vengeance. I pledged death. Either I killed the vampire I was hunting or the magic would have my life."

"No." His voice was firm, unbelieving. "No, that isn't possible." He turned to Leena. "You're a witch. Can't you do something?"

"It's a vengeance spell. She made the pact of her own free will."

"But things have changed. And you have power to alter the spell."

"I have power? You're asking me to use my power? Funny how things never change, isn't it?"

The words flowed over Alexis, and she tried to understand what was going on. But the conversation wasn't making sense.

"Never change?" Serge repeated, his voice full of disbelief. "No. No, it can't be true."

"You and your friend took everything from me," Leena said. "You took what I loved. Now you can watch as I take what you love. Cure her? Not possible. And now you suffer. And the irony is that she chose that, too. And of her own free will."

◆

Trapped.

Inside her own body, Leena watched what was going on. Watched as someone who looked like her and talked like her but *so* wasn't her tormented her friend. Threatened death.

And Leena knew the threat wasn't idle.

She tried to lash out. Tried to break free. Tried to find a way to slam at this prison with all of her consciousness and fight the creature that had pushed her down.

Tried to make the tiniest of chinks.

She'd come close a few times—so close that she could almost feel her limbs. Could almost grab control.

But it was never enough. And each time she thought she was close, she was crushed once again by the weight of a much more powerful sorceress.

◆

"Evangeline?" Serge gaped at the girl, trying to reconcile the fact that this young woman who'd been Alexis's friend was really Evangeline.

"Mostly," she said, her smile thin and tight.

"I took nothing from you," Serge said. "Don't do this. Don't destroy Alexis. She's innocent."

"You took my life."

"And yet here you stand."

She snorted. "I had to destroy my daughter to do so, and her daughter after that."

"Had to?" he repeated, finally understanding what she'd done. The vile depths of the magic she'd used. "Or chose to?"

"It's your fault Tomas is dead." Her eyes flashed wild. He forced himself to keep his voice calm.

"Derrick killed Tomas. Not me. Not Alexis. Take me, and let her live." Beside him, Alexis murmured a protest, but it was weak. Her skin was gray and clammy. Time was running out. He forced himself to be calm, to think.

"Fool! I killed Derrick because there was no other way to torment him. You? You really seem to love her. What better way to pay you back than to make you watch her die?"

"Please."

Her body convulsed, and for a moment he clung tight to hope. Then she gathered herself. "Please?" she repeated. "As if you have a right to beg. You're vile, and you know it. You think she deserves you? That she'd want you?"

"You're right. I was vile. And no, I didn't used to think that I deserved her. I do now. She gave me the gift of making me believe it."

"She was wrong," Eva said. But her eyes . . . there was something about her eyes. "And why place blame? Soon you'll both be dead and it won't matter."

He latched on to those eyes. It was Leena, he was certain of it. The girl was inside. Fighting, but weak, and time was running out.

"She's your friend," he said, hoping to give her something to grasp. Something to help her rally and fight. "How can you watch her suffer like this?"

Another convulsion, and Serge told himself not to hope. Not yet.

"Everything she's done for you. All the time you've worked with her."

"I haven't worked with her," Eva snarled. "I've worked only for myself."

"Bullshit. You hate vampires? She's hunted them for you. You were a team. She's your friend. You're destroying someone close to you. Hurting you as much as you hurt me."

"No!" shouted Eva.

"*Yes!*" shouted Leena. Her eyes flew open, wide and full of pain—but clear. For now at least, they were clear.

"I can't undo the spell," Leena said. Her voice was raw, every word ripped from her throat. "But I can take it from her." She nodded toward Alexis.

"No . . ." Alexis's voice was weak. "No, you can't. You'll die."

"I will anyway," Leena said. "She's stronger than me." She winced, doubling over as if someone had kicked her in the gut. "I don't have much time." She focused on Serge, ignoring Alexis's weak protests. "I'll take the spell from her, and then you take the life from me." She reached out and grabbed his hand. "I remember now—we're mixed up enough that I have some of her memories. Take the life force . . . and then you can save yourself the way you once asked her to do." Another convulsion. He squeezed her hand.

"Hang on," he said. "You have to hang on for long enough."

"I know. I can." No more time to waste. She reached out and grabbed Alexis's wrist. A cry wrenched its way from both of their bodies, and then Serge saw a diamond-shaped scar rise on Leena's wrist.

"Now!" Leena said. "She's fighting! Oh, God, she's coming!"

Serge didn't hesitate. He reached out, grabbed her arm, and drew her essence in. "Thank you," he said, before her consciousness faded. "Thank you for saving Alexis."

And then the girl lay dead on the floor, her body desiccated, the sorceress dead.

In his arms, Alexis clung to him, her face pressed against his chest.

He stroked her hair. "I'm sorry. I'm so, so sorry."

"You had to," she said, her voice stronger already. "I know you had to."

He rocked her gently, letting her cry, wishing he could erase the grief, but knowing only time could do that.

After an eternity, she lifted her head. "What did she mean about saving yourself?"

He closed his eyes and reached deep inside his new soul, now filled with the bubbling, vibrant power of magic.

Slowly, he stood, not quite able to believe that he could see the way. That he could, finally, suppress the darkness.

"She meant that she gave me the two things I wanted

most in this world. You. And the power to keep the darkness locked deep inside myself."

"How?"

"For the price of a kiss, I'll tell you."

"That," she said, her lips brushing his, "is a price I'm very willing to pay."

CHAPTER THIRTY-THREE

"Get it!" Alexis screamed. "Stake it! Stake it or it's going to get me!"

"Well, don't run toward me!" Serge hollered back at her. "Dammit," he said as the daemon raced straight toward her. "Alexis, *no*!"

"Oh, man!" CeeCee turned to Serge with a pained expression. "Why didn't you stake it? Now Alexis is dead!" She flopped back on the couch. "Jeez, Serge. Sometimes you're so lame."

He shrugged and glanced sideways at Alexis, who was holding back a laugh. "I don't know," he said, pulling her onto his lap. "She's pretty spry for a corpse."

"You guys are both lame," CeeCee said. She looked toward the opposite couch where Luke and Sara sat talking. "At least you're better than Luke. He can't even get past the first level without the zombies eating his brain."

"Thanks," Luke said, aiming a wry grin at her.

"Want to play another one?"

Serge laughed. "I don't think we have time. Alexis and I should be getting the call any minute now."

As if on cue, the phone rang, and Serge lifted his hand, calling on the power of the air to bring the handset to him. He'd gone to the detention block that morning to feed. No longer did the beast say when, though. When Serge had been infused with Leena's and Eva's essences, he'd been able to work their magic. As Leena had suggested, he'd used that magic to subdue the beast and the daemon so that he was no longer ruled by the hunger. Could, in fact, keep both the beast and the daemon locked deep inside forever. Or pull them out and use them. Either way, he was the one in control now.

He'd wielded that control recently, using the power of the beast to take the life force of a jinn who'd killed not only his entire family, but half a dozen humans as well. Serge had spent the morning getting used to the raw power that flowed through him. Every jinn had a proclivity for a certain element, and Serge's ability now centered on the air, giving him the ability to open wormholes in much the same manner that paradaemons could. More important than that, though, a jinn had the capacity to alter his appearance. To take on the form of another, even if only as an illusion. And since it was Serge's mission to step into the shoes of a jinn who believed he was a target for assassination, that was the most important skill of all.

"Hello?" he said into the phone.

"We have the location," the Israeli PEC agent they'd been working with told him. "You're going to a formal ball in Cairo."

"Hang on. You can give the location to my coordinator." He handed the phone to CeeCee, who scribbled notes on the back of a take-out menu. She was happily ensconced in Luke and Sara's home now, but she'd wanted a role within the PEC. And while she was too young and too inexperienced for anything heavy-duty, Serge had suggested that the girl act as a sort of intern, stepping in as an assistant when Serge and Alexis were in the field. It had been a suggestion that CeeCee had jumped on, and it had the added benefit of scoring major brownie points for "Uncle Serge." Her daemon still hadn't surfaced, but neither had the beast. And while both Serge and Luke were keeping a close eye on the girl, CeeCee herself repeatedly said that she was content, and that she'd deal with whatever came along. Serge was confident she would deal just fine.

Now CeeCee read the information back to the agent, then hung up and nodded at Serge and Alexis. "Okay. You're ready to rock-and-roll."

Beside him, Alexis lifted her bag of weapons and surveillance equipment. On this mission, she'd work with him by remote, feeding him the information he needed about the people he came in contact with while he played the roll of the target jinn. With any luck, they'd have an assassin behind bars by sunrise.

"Be careful," Sara said as Serge reached out, drawing on the jinn's power to open a wormhole behind him.

"You'll call me when you want to come back, right?" CeeCee asked.

"We will," Alexis said. "But don't expect us for a day or two."

CeeCee went to Luke and Sara, squeezing in between them on the sofa. "It's going to take you that long?"

"Hopefully it won't take any time at all," Serge said. "But I thought we'd stay for a while." He kissed Alexis's temple. "Maybe take a cruise down the Nile?"

She hooked her arms around his neck, molded her body to his, and brushed her lips over his ear.

"I think that sounds like heaven," she said, and then she kissed him, so hard and so deep that he barely even noticed when the wormhole closed around them.

And he certainly didn't notice the sound of CeeCee's voice trailing after them as the vortex sucked them away. *"They get to have all the fun . . ."*

Can't get enough of J. K. Beck's sexy
Shadow Keepers? Get ready to sink your
teeth into *When Temptation Burns,* coming soon
from Bantam Books.

WHEN TEMPTATION BURNS

On sale 7/31/2012

Turn the page to take a peek inside. . . .

CHAPTER ONE

"Your turn, Kevin!" Stu yelled, rubbing his fist, his knuckles red from having just pounded the shit out of Jordan Lowe's nose and jaw. "Go for the nose. Come on, Kev, nail the fucker!"

Kevin Whalton cringed; Stu's shouts were making him even more nervous than he already was. He glanced around the darkened alley, half-hoping there'd be someone else in the shadows behind the locked-up Laundromat. Nobody.

"Fucking hell, Kevin. *Now.*"

He jumped, scared as a rabbit, but he did what his friend demanded. He tightened his fingers into a fist, lashed out, and watched as his knuckles smashed into their victim's nose.

No—not a victim. He had to remember that. Had to remember who was the dangerous one here. Because if everything Wes and Stu had told him was true, Jordan Lowe could never be a victim.

Jordan's head slammed back, making a sick crunching sound as it impacted the brick wall. He howled—literally howled. A low, pained keening that bounced off the wall and filled the dark space around them.

Kevin glanced back at Stu, who was miming punching movements and shouting, "Hell, yeah! That's the way! Get in another—come on, man, show the freak what you've got."

Wes stood a couple of yards from Jordan, his mouth pulled into a tight smile. "You fucked with the wrong people, puppy dog. We know what you are, and we are so going to take you down." He swiveled his head to look at Kevin. "Another. Get in another."

Kevin hesitated, a little sick to his stomach. Less than an hour before, they'd all been having drinks at a bar a few blocks down. Everything had seemed perfectly normal then. Hell, Wes and Stu actually knew Jordan pretty well; they'd been hanging with him for weeks. But tonight they'd pulled Kevin aside to tell him that they didn't trust Jordan. That they were certain he was a mole. And that Kevin was going to want to see the shit that went down.

Then they'd put something in the guy's drink. And when Kevin had asked Stu why, Stu had just grinned and said that if they didn't dose his drink, Jordan would be able to rip all their fucking heads off.

At the time, Kevin had believed it, because why the hell would Stu lie about what Jordan was? About what he could do?

Now, though . . .

Well, now Jordan looked whipped. Like he couldn't beat up a six-year-old girl, much less three college sophomores.

"Goddammit, Kevin. Are you a fucking pussy or what? Hit the mongrel bastard! Hit him!"

"Do it!" Wes added, and their voices bolstered him. Made his muscles tighten and his pulse quicken. "Goddammit, do it now—do it and I swear to God the unholy fuckwad will show you that everything we've told you is true!"

That did it. Kevin lashed out, his right fist connecting hard with Jordan's temple even as his left jabbed into the kid's gut. Jordan went down, doubling over as he clutched at his stomach. Then he looked up, and Kevin stumbled backward.

Holy fuck—Jordan's eyes were yellow.

Yellow and wild and full of hate and anger.

Kevin shivered, not sure what he was seeing. Not sure what to believe. He'd gotten in with Wes and Stu and the rest of them because they'd told him what was out there—and that they needed his help to stop it. To stop *them*. But until tonight it had all been theory and conjecture and folks making speeches about what they knew and what they believed. Until tonight Kevin had never actually seen one of them. Hell, he hadn't even been sure if he believed in monsters or if he just wanted to get on Wes and Stu's good side.

But he believed now. Fuck, yeah, he did.

"Don't fight it, pup," Wes said, giving Jordan a kick. "We wanna see. Don't we Stu? Don't we Kevin?"

"Shit, yeah," Stu said, bouncing like a boxer itching for a fight. He pulled out a knife, the blade glinting in the dim light from the alley's streetlamps. "Scared, fucker? It's pure silver. That's gonna hurt." He lunged forward, the blade aimed at Jordan's stomach, but at the last second, Jordan thrust his arm up, moving fast considering how battered he was, and knocked the knife to the ground.

Quicker than Kevin could see, Jordan had Stu pinned on the ground. "Think you're clever?" he rasped, his body bent over Stu's. "How clever will you be when I rip your head off with my goddamned teeth?"

Jordan's skin started to ripple, and Kevin could see his bones shifting beneath his skin. A loud roaring filled Kevin's head, and his knees started to give out—fuckin' A, he was about to faint.

"Kev! Kevin!"

Wes's voice pulled him back, and he blinked, groggy.

"Get Stu's knife, man! Now!" As Wes spoke, he was lunging toward Jordan with his own knife. Kevin couldn't move; he couldn't do anything but stare at the creature in front of him. Holy shit; they'd told him what would happen, what the kid was. But telling and seeing were two different things. And seeing was fucking terrifying.

"Now, goddammit, or Stu's dead!"

Jordan was clutching Stu's head in his hand, and he slammed it against the asphalt with a sickening thud. The noise spurred Kevin to action, and he darted sideways for Stu's lost knife, then rushed forward, leading with the point of the blade. He felt the resistance as the tip hit Jordan's skin, then the give as it slid into the muscle, the full force of Kevin's weight pushing it right to the hilt, right to the bone.

On the other side of the creature, Wes was jabbing, too, his mouth moving, his words a mishmash of unintelligible curses with only a few words like *silver* and *fucking* and *werewolf* coming out clear.

Another roar echoed—only this one wasn't inside of Kevin's head. It was coming from Jordan, who'd reared back, arms flailing as he knocked aside their knives and climbed to his feet. Kevin braced himself, certain he would need to do battle with this, this *thing*. But then Jordan turned and loped off down the alley, leaving Stu curled up in a ball and moaning on the pavement.

"Catch him!" Wes cried, pulling out a gun and firing it so close to Kevin's head that for a moment he thought he was deaf. He wasn't, though, and Wes's shouts pushed through the cotton that now seemed to fill his ears.

"Goddammit, I missed the fucker! Catch him! Run! Shit, we have to catch him. If he gets away, we're dead. We're totally fucking dead."

He was dead.

No other possible outcome.

He'd been stupid. Lazy and reckless, and somehow they'd found him out.

And now he was dead, or he would be soon enough.

Except he couldn't die—not like this. Not without letting someone know how bad it was. How close *they* were. And how dangerous.

His legs pumped as he moved down the alley, the weakness unfamiliar after so many years of pure, glorious strength. He'd known about the dangers of silver, of course. What werewolf didn't? But he'd been arrogant and foolish enough to believe they'd never get him with it. To believe they'd never find out about him. That he'd be smart. That he'd be safe.

He'd been an idiot, and soon he'd be a dead one.

Not once in his wildest dreams had he imagined that they would lace his drink with colloidal silver. But they had, and he'd drunk it down, and it had ripped his advantage away from him right then and there, weakening his muscles and making his mind fuzzy and confused.

Once he figured out what they had done to him, he managed to get away, pushing through the thick Friday night crowd to the kitchen, then out the back door through the alley. He'd run aimlessly in the dark, just wanting to put distance between him and his tormentors. He'd thought he'd lost them, had even leaned against a Dumpster to take a deep, self-satisfied breath.

And then they'd arrived with their taunts and their jeers and, most dangerous of all, their knives forged of silver.

He'd fought, but he'd been weak. Extraordinarily weak. That he'd managed to get away at all was a miracle. That they were following was a curse.

Right now he had only one thing to be thankful for— that Wes's silver bullet had only nicked his heart. If it had pierced it, he'd already be dead, and all his warnings would be lost.

They still might be if he didn't hurry. But he was weak. So damn weak.

The footsteps pounding behind him were a warning he'd slowed his pace. *Go.* He had to get somewhere safe. Had to find a shadower.

For three months, he'd been deep undercover, trying to find out what the humans were up to. About four weeks ago, he'd managed to wrangle an introduction to Wes, and that had gotten him closer, because the frat boy human was poised to go far within the organization.

Jordan had spent this last month watching and learning and trying to get closer. Close enough to gain trust, to learn what *they* were up to. The humans who wanted him—and all the shadowers—dead and gone. If he couldn't tell someone, then all that time would be for nothing, and he *couldn't* let it be for nothing. Because then . . . because then . . .

His head was fuzzy, his thoughts crashing into each other. *The silver.*

Had to hurry. Had to move.

With concentration like he'd never known before, Jordan forced his heart to beat harder, his blood to surge stronger. Forced his legs to *go.*

Something fast whipped by him, brushing his sleeve, and when he realized that one of his tormentors had thrown a knife, a new burst of fear fueled his speed. He didn't know why they hadn't used the gun—wait, yes he did. *There were people, and a gunshot would draw attention.*

He peered around him and realized that although he was still racing down the alley that ran parallel to Northridge Street, there were people up ahead. They were mingling at the intersection of the alley and the sidewalk of a perpendicular street. The sound of laughter coupled with the scent of alcohol wafted toward him, and Jordan almost cried out in joy. Without even trying, he'd stumbled upon another bar, upon people. *Dear God, he needed people.*

To his left, a door burst open, a yawing metal mouth against a pockmarked face of brick. The stench of fried food and flowing alcohol wafted out. He'd found the back door to the bar where all the people were gathered.

His forehead creased in concentration as he tried to figure out what to do. Thinking was so hard; and his thoughts were all jumbled. *Go in. Go in and get lost in the crowd.* Yes. Yes, that was what he should do.

He shifted, then stumbled toward the door, pushing inside past a couple who were emerging, a tangle of arms and legs and lips. He sniffed—*human.* He pushed off the wave of disappointment. The odds that he'd randomly find a shadower bar had been thin. But this would do. He just needed bodies. Just needed to hide.

Hallway. Dark. Flooded with the scent of sweat and lust. To his left and right were restrooms. Ahead, flashing lights and pounding music. He headed into the light, his hand steadying him against the wall. Other humans passed him, coming from the direction he was heading. Their eyes cut to him, then cut away, their faces twisted with fear and repulsion.

He was changing.

His own pain, his own fear—it was pushing the change even as the silver kept the wolf from fully bursting free. His bones were bulging, his face deforming. The humans would be no help to him—he could tell that much from the terror on their faces.

He needed to *think,* dammit, but his head was too full of cotton. He had to find a shadower soon.

They were coming. Of that he was certain. They'd find him, and they'd kill him.

He'd always thought that despair would be a cold, frenetic thing, but now he knew that it was warm and languid. A quiet acceptance. A slow descent into the thick sludge of acquiescence.

Just before the hallway opened onto the main dance floor, another hall intersected, veering off to the left. He turned, ignoring the sign that said the area was for employees only. It was quieter here, and he realized he could think better now that he wasn't walking straight into those damned pulsing lights. Ahead, he heard voices. If he could get to them, just get to them, then maybe—

His knees buckled, and he grabbed at the wall for balance. But the walls were spinning, the silver in his blood working its way into his brain. He closed his eyes and sagged to the ground, hoping to stop the horrible, gut-wrenching rocking.

Bile rose in his throat, and he sucked in air through his nose, but the nausea kept building.

"Hey—hey, mister? You okay?"

Slowly, he peeled open his eyes and looked up at the three women staring down at him. No, not three. Just one, but she was blurry around the edges, coming in and out of focus. He sniffed. Another human.

"I'm—" He didn't finish the sentence. For that matter, he wasn't sure the words had even left his lips. But the girl had knelt down, her face full of concern. And when she did, he saw the mark on the wall behind her. An elaborate *S* painted in gold and bisected by a silver arrow.

They were here!

"I'm going to call nine-one-one," the girl said, pulling out a cell phone.

"No." He croaked out the word, then thrust out his hand to grab hers. "Don't."

Her eyes went wide, and he followed her gaze. The bones of his hand were elongating, pushing against his skin. And thick tufts of fur were sprouting. *The change.* But slow. Foreshortened by the silver. And instead of making him stronger, the strain on his body was exhausting him, draining him dry and taking him to the very edge of death.

"What are—?"

"Go," he snarled. "Get the hell out of here."

She didn't argue, just took a step back, then turned

and ran down the hall, back toward the noise and the lights.

He threw himself against the wall, fingers scraping for the notch that had to be there. *Please, please let it be there.* He had to get in—had to get safe—before his human tormentors found him. Surely they were in the club now. Surely they were tracking him. Surely they'd meet the woman and she'd point, horrified, down the hallway. And then they'd come with their guns and their knives and they'd—

There.

His fingernails found the crevice between the wall panels. A subtle click, and then one of the panels swung open. He fell into the dark space, kicking the hidden doorway shut behind him.

But he could go no farther. He'd reached safety, and in doing so had sapped his meager supply of strength.

In front of him, a beautiful pale face loomed. *Vampire.* He could smell the blood along with the revulsion. There was no love between the weren and the vamps, but they would unite against their human enemies. They had to, Jordan thought. Because if they didn't they would all surely die.

With effort, he opened his mouth, lips parting just enough to make a sound. He saw the vampire's eyes narrow, long lashes dark against ivory cheekbones.

Help.

He tried to force the word out, but it wouldn't come. How could it when there could be no help now?

"You shouldn't be here. This isn't a place for you."

He tried again to form words, but he was too far gone, his life slipping away. *No. No, no, no.*

Conjuring strength he didn't know he possessed, he

struggled to force out three little words. Three words that he hoped would save them all.

"Get," he said, then sucked in a breath and tried again. "Get the percipient."

And then, with a gasp, Jordan Lowe laid back his head, and died.